I0730605

BY HIS PLAY

CALLAHAN BILLIONAIRES

TRACY LORRAINE

Copyright © 2025 by Tracy Lorraine

All rights reserved.

No part of this book may be reproduced in any form or by any electronic or mechanical means, including information storage and retrieval systems, without written permission from the author, except for the use of brief quotations in a book review.

Model - Shaun Collins

Photographer - Michelle Lancaster

Development Editing by Pinpoint Editing

Content Editing by Rebecca at Fairest Reviews Editing Services

Proofreading by Lisa Staples

ABOUT BY HIS PLAY

An all-new steamy and angsty billionaire fake engagement romance from the USA Today & Wall Street Journal bestselling author, Tracy Lorraine

Kieran Callahan is every woman's fantasy—charming billionaire, star running back, and heartbreakingly handsome.

He's also my best friend.

When my grandmother's final wish puts me in an impossible situation, I tell the biggest lie of my life:

Kieran and I are engaged.

I planned to tell him the truth—really, I did.

But before I can come clean, a nosy nurse and a sleazy tabloid blow up my little secret.

Now, the media's in a frenzy, and instead of setting the record straight, my best friend turned fake fiancé agrees to play along. All for Grams.

But spending so much time together blurs the lines we swore we'd never cross. And I'm seeing him in a whole new light.

Suddenly, Kieran isn't just my best friend. He's the man who makes my heart race. The one I can't imagine my life without.

We only have a few days before everything goes back to the way it was...

But what if I don't want it to?

Dear Reader,

By His Play is a standalone fake engagement, friends to lovers romance set in the Callahan Billionaires world.

You can live your whole life not realising that what you're looking for is right in front of you
- David Nicholls

ALSO BY TRACY LORRAINE

Harrow Creek Hawks Series

Callahan Billionaires

By His Vow #1

By His Rule #2

By His Play #3

Seattle Saints

Broken Saint #1

Never Forget Series

Never Forget Him #1

Never Forget Us #2

Everywhere & Nowhere #3

Chasing Series

Chasing Logan

Standalones

Naughty & Nice

WOULD YOU LIKE A FREE BOOK?

Get your free copy of The Mistakes You Make, the prequel to my dark college romance series, Maddison Kings University. Subscribe to my newsletter for your free copy!

PROLOGUE

Effie

"You've got this, K. Get out there and smash them. I'll be watching, I promise."

"I know. I just hate you not being here." I vividly picture the pout that'll be playing on his lips. Sure, he might be displaying his drama queen tendencies, but with everything going on, I'll give him a free pass today.

He's playing in the conference championship. The final step to the Super Bowl. It's been his dream for as long as I've known him. And that's a pretty long time.

A bitter laugh threatens to escape. I'll never understand what he sees in me that has kept us connected all these years. Honestly, I've mostly given up thinking about it.

Kieran Callahan is an enigma that even I, his best friend, can't figure out.

"You don't need me there," I assure him. "And anyway, I'll be screaming so loudly at the TV you'll probably hear me from there."

"Maybe if we were at home. But out here..." He trails off.

His voice cracks, showing his nerves, and it makes my own anxiety spike.

He's not going into this game pumped for the win like he usually does. He's stressed and feeling the pressure. All I want to do is fix it.

"Enough of the negativity, Callahan. Get your head out of your ass and go out there fighting. You're going to be the best goddamn running back on that field. Now get out there and make sure every motherfucker watching knows it."

I cringe at my own pep talk. But sometimes, I've just got to swallow my pride and tell my best friend how it is.

He's the best football player I've ever known. Okay, so until recently, he may be the only professional football player I've ever known, but he doesn't need to know that right now.

"I've got this," he says, a little hesitantly.

"It's just another game," I assure him. "I'm watching, your brothers are watching. And we'll all be there with you for the next one."

He's silent for a moment. My nerves grow as I wait for what he's going to say next.

"We're gonna do it, Luck," he says shortening my lucky charm nickname he gave me all those years ago. "We're gonna fucking do it."

"Hell yeah, you are."

"You got it. I'll see you on the other side."

"I'm with you all the way," I promise.

We both pause for a beat before we simultaneously chant, "Three. Two. One. Win."

And then just like always, Kieran cuts the call.

I blow out a breath as I lower my cell to my chest and close my eyes, praying that he can get into the right headspace.

I give myself ten seconds before looking down, and when I do, my eyes immediately lock on the ring on my finger.

My stomach knots.

It's okay, I tell myself.

He'll never know.

I'm just doing what I have to do.

Blowing out a long, slow stream of air, I tuck my cell into my pocket and reenter the room I stepped out of only minutes ago.

The TV shows the build-up to the game and a mix of excitement and nerves flutters in my stomach as I think of Kieran in the locker room going through the rest of his pre-game ritual. I became a part of it junior year of high school. It was the last game of the season, and he wanted to make a killer impression on their coach before embarking on his final year. They dominated that game, and he put it down to me. He has called me without fail before every single game he's played since that day. And no matter where I am or what I'm doing—I'm almost always either sitting in the stadium or in front of a TV, ready to watch—I take the call.

I'm sure it's a habit that many would say I should have broken a long time ago. But I can't. It means too much to Kieran, and I love that I'm able to help him and be a part of his success.

I've enjoyed every second of watching his career grow. He deserves it. He's an incredible player and a wonderful person.

"Everything okay?" Grams asks as I lower into the chair beside her.

I look over, relieved to see the sparkle in her eyes that I love so much. It's becoming less and less every day now.

Sadness tugs at my chest. Apart from Kieran, Grams has been the one constant in my life. The thought of losing her, of living a life without her, terrifies me. But there isn't much I can do about it. Not only is her mind giving up, but her body is too. Every single second that passes is one less I get to spend with her.

It's why I'm not in San Francisco at the game right now, supporting Kieran in person.

I hate that I'm not, but I couldn't leave her.

I fight the pained sigh that threatens. It's like my heart is being ripped in two with the need to be in both places at once.

But Grams needs me more right now. Kieran will have more games, and anyway, I'm watching, I'm supporting him, just...from a distance.

"Yeah, everything is great. Kieran is a little nervous."

"Well, that's to be expected. He'll want his fiancée by his side for big days like this," she says so confidently that I'd question her diagnosis if I didn't know better.

My stomach knots and my eyes drop to my ring again.

"Yeah," I muse.

"I just can't believe it...after all these years. I mean, I knew. That boy has loved you from the moment you met. But I never thought I'd see the day when he figured it out. I just wish I could be there on the big day."

A giant ball of emotion crawls up my throat. My nose itches and my eyes burn.

"You're going to make the most beautiful bride, Effie."

Pain shoots up my arms as I curl my fists, digging my nails into my palms in an attempt to distract myself.

"You'll be there," I choke out. "You're too stubborn not to be."

It's a lie.

She's not going to make it. And not just because of her declining health.

It's because all of this is fake.

Kieran friend-zoned me a long time ago.

But what are you meant to do when your only grandmother's dying wish is for you to get engaged and marry the man of your dreams?

You give her exactly what she wants.

1

KIERAN

I walk down the quiet hallway with my arms full of gifts.

I may not have been here before, but after listening to Effie talk about it so much over the past few months, everything feels very familiar.

She even managed to describe the scent pretty accurately.

It's not a hospital. But also...it kinda is.

A nurse darts across the hallway ahead of me, but she doesn't look up.

Continuing forward, I take note of each door number, my heart rate increasing with each one.

I haven't told her that I'm coming.

Sure, I said that I'd see her after the season ended, but I never gave dates. Hell, I'm glad I didn't.

The past couple of months have been hard.

It doesn't matter how many times my teammates, my friends, my brothers, tell me that my performance wasn't what lost the playoff game, I still feel the weight of that crushing loss on my shoulders as if it happened just yesterday.

I wasn't at my best. And as much as I hate to lay the reason for that at my best friend's feet, I am. I feel guilty as fuck for it, but I can't help it.

She wasn't there.

My lucky charm wasn't there when I needed her the most.

She was right not to be. She needed to be here with Grams. But fuck...I needed her.

When I called before the game, she answered. She was there with me in spirit. I knew she was watching the game, cheering me on. But not being able to look up and see her in the stands...it knocked me off-kilter.

It's stupid. Really fucking stupid. But I can't help it.

I need her.

I always have, and something tells me that I always will, too.

I come to a stop outside Gram's room.

I haven't seen her for too long. Far too fucking long. And I can't lie...I'm terrified of what I'm going to find.

Growing up, she was there for me almost as much as she was for Effie. Seeing her decline—or more so, hearing about it more recently—has been hard. Not as hard as being here, though...

Guilt slams into me with the force of an eighteen-wheeler, causing me to suck in a sharp breath.

What I've been going through is nothing compared to what my best friend has been dealing with.

I hate that I haven't been able to get out of my head sooner and be the friend she needs me to be.

Being the reason we lost that game is going to live with me for quite some time, but nowhere near as long as if I'm not here for Effie.

For almost as long as I can remember, she's been my lucky charm, my biggest supporter, and the best friend I could ever ask for. She deserves for me to try to be even a fraction of the friend she is.

Forcing down my guilt and regrets, I shuffle the things in my arms and reach for the door handle.

There's no time like the present.

Nothing but the sound of an old gameshow on the TV greets me. Not immediately hearing her voice makes me realize how much I've missed her.

It's been too long. Far too fucking long.

Moving into the room, I find the two of them sitting in matching floral armchairs.

"Time for tea," Grams says lightly.

Hearing her sound like herself makes my heart sing, but I'm not naive enough to think that's how it always is these days. I know better than that.

"I've got quite a few things here, but tea isn't one of them," I confess.

There's a beat of silence before Effie squeals and launches herself from the armchair.

"Oh fuck," I grunt, dropping everything in my arms just in time to catch her as she flies at me.

"You're here," she sings, wrapping her arms around my shoulders, clinging to me as if she hasn't seen me in a decade, not a couple of months.

"Aw, look at you two," Grams says, watching us closely.

Effie tenses in my arms, but she doesn't let me go.

"Hi, Grams," I say as Effie continues to cling to me. "Looking as beautiful as ever."

Proving to me that she's still the same woman I've always loved, her cheeks burn scarlet at my compliment.

She might play the innocent, but she's told us enough stories from her past that would prove otherwise.

Finally, Effie releases me, and after rescuing the bouquet of flowers that hit the floor not so long ago, I walk over to greet Grams.

Her eyes are glassy when I crouch down in front of her.

"It's so good to see you in person. I thought I was only ever going to see you on a screen again," she confesses, making my chest ache.

"It's been a busy few months," I explain.

"So I hear," Grams says coyly.

"I'm going to go and get a vase for these," Effie says before rushing out of the room as if she's being chased.

Concern fills my veins.

Sure, she was excited to see me, but something isn't quite right.

Even more guilt floods me. While I've been drowning in my own bullshit, I haven't been there for her in the way I usually would.

"She's missed you so much," Grams says as I perch my ass on the edge of the coffee table before her.

I hang my head in shame for a moment.

"I've missed her too. And you. How are you doing?" I ask, unsure of how she's going to respond.

She seems lucid, like her old self right now, but I know from talking to Effie that it can change all too quickly.

It's selfish, but I can't help but hope I can get more time with her.

"I'm fantastic. This place? It's great. The food is outstanding. Better than Effie's cooking, that's for sure. Don't tell her that," she adds quickly, making me laugh.

I wink. "It can be our secret." Although, really, it's no secret. Even Effie knows she's a terrible cook.

"Are the nurses nice?"

"Everyone is so lovely. And they take good care of our girl."

I smile.

For as long as I can remember, Grams has been trying to get us together. She doesn't even try to cover up the fact that she dreams of watching Effie walk down the aisle toward... well, me.

I swallow thickly.

It's not that I don't want to settle down one day. I'm sure it'll be...lovely.

King and Kian are sure doing a good job of making a long-term relationship look kinda fun.

But I see enough of my teammates trying to juggle football and family life to know that I don't want to deal with that anytime soon.

My focus needs to be football. I don't want the distraction of a woman for more than a few hours at a time.

The ones I spend time with now know exactly what I'm willing to offer, and it's never more than a fun night before I send them on their way.

Other than my mom and sisters, Effie has been the only woman who's had a permanent place in my life, and I'm more than happy for that to continue.

"I'm glad you both had people looking out for you," I say, my heart aching, knowing that it should have been me.

"Don't give me that, young man," Grams teases, making my brows pinch together.

"Here we go," Effie announces, reappearing with a vase that's almost bigger than her. Her blonde hair is pulled back into a tight ponytail and she's wearing her thick-rimmed glasses. One look at her and I'm taken straight back to school.

Effie and I were—and still are—the most unlikely of friends. I was the bad boy player and she was the nerdy good girl.

I guess some things never change.

"Grams, I hope you're behaving yourself," she warns lightly, but there is a tightness to her expression I don't like.

Grams lets out a full belly laugh. The sound of it lights me up inside, although not as much as hearing Effie laugh will.

She's struggling. I don't need to see the dark circles under her eyes and the worry lines etching her face to know that. I could hear it in her voice during our calls, sense it in her messages.

Picking up the flowers, I take them over and help her unwrap and arrange them.

I have no fucking clue what I'm doing, but I try to make myself useful by cutting stems and handing them over.

"They're so beautiful," Grams sighs when we place them on the dresser beside the television for her to enjoy. "Just like my Effie."

"Grams," Effie warns.

"What? It's true. Isn't it, Kieran? Our Effie is the most beautiful girl in the world."

"Okay, that's enough," Effie states.

I glance over at my best friend to find her cheeks blazing pink as she stares down at her feet. She never has been very good with compliments, even if they are from her sweet grandmother.

"She's right and you know it," I say, returning to my seat on the coffee table so Effie can take the armchair.

"Sit here," she argues, happily changing the subject.

I give her a hard glare, silently letting her know that her argument is futile. After a few seconds, she lowers herself to the chair.

I watch her for a moment longer, taking in the way she chews her nail, her body continuously moving.

She's nervous.

"Eff, what's—"

"So, what have you been up to recently? You've been very quiet," she blurts, unwilling to hear my question.

Grams watches us closely with a slight frown on her brow.

"Not much, really. It's been pretty quiet." It's not a lie. Sure, there has been plenty going on, but I've excused myself from pretty much everything in favor of locking myself in my apartment.

10

My brothers and my teammates have tried to pull me out of it and force me back into real life, but I've been too happy in my own miserable company.

Okay, "happy" might be the wrong word.

"I don't believe that for a moment," Effie laughs.

"He's been busy, dear," Grams pipes up. "Just look at all the gifts he brought you. He's missed you as much as you've missed him."

Effie's eyes widen and her cheeks burn brightly all over again.

"Ah, Eff. You missing me?" I tease.

I know she has been; the words didn't need saying. I've missed her too. But something feels off with Gram's comment, add that to the shifty way that Effie is acting and my curiosity is piqued.

Silence hangs in the air between us. There's noise from the corridor, but no one pops their head into our room, and the TV continues to play behind me.

"I love those flowers so much," Grams finally says. "And those sunflowers. I really do think you should have a sunflower bouquet at the wedding, Effie. They're your flowers. Don't you think, Kieran?"

"U-uh," I stutter, unsure what to say to that.

Effie, on the other hand, hops out of her chair like her ass is on fire.

"We should probably get going, let you have your afternoon nap."

Grams' face drops, but she quickly covers it.

"I guess you two don't want to be spending your afternoon with me when you could be getting reacquainted."

Grams wiggles her brows, her smile getting wider.

I frown. I know we haven't seen each other as much as we usually would, but we're not exactly long, lost friends.

When I glance back at Effie, I find her shaking her head at me, silently asking me just to go along with it all.

"I'll see you tomorrow," Effie says to Grams before leaning down to kiss her cheek.

"Okay, sweetie. Enjoy him, and don't do anything I wouldn't do."

What the—

Before I have a chance to question Grams, Effie grabs my hand and attempts to drag me out of the room.

Seeing as she's barely five foot and I'm six-four and well over two hundred pounds, she doesn't stand a chance. That doesn't stop her from trying, though.

"Rock her world, Kieran. She needs it," Grams calls, despite the fact we're now in the hallway.

"What the hell was that?"

"Nothing," Effie says tightly, her little legs taking on a life of their own as she practically races for the exit.

"Eff, wait," I demand, eating up the space between us in just a handful of easy strides, although I don't stop her until we're out of the building.

It's a gorgeous, sunny day in St. Louis. The warmth of the sun wraps around me, but it doesn't relax me in the way it usually would.

Finding her wrist, I pull her to a stop and step in front of her.

"What's going on?"

Effie's eyes fill with tears, and she looks away, trying to hide them.

"I'm so glad you're here," she blurts, her voice cracked with emotion. "It's been...It's been really hard," she confesses before falling into my arms.

2

EFFIE

"Are you nearly ready?" Kieran calls. "Our reservation is in twenty minutes."

My stomach sloshes, acid burning up my throat.

You should have told him.

Everything I should have done taunts me, but it's too late now.

I never meant to lie to Grams. It's just...she deserves for all of her dreams to come true.

And I could actually help with this one.

Even if it's fake. Just one little white lie—and a cheap engagement ring—to make a dying woman very happy.

"Yeah," I call back, dragging my eyes from the piece of jewelry that I'm currently wearing on the other hand.

It was such a relief to see Kieran standing there in Grams' room earlier. I've missed him more than I could ever explain. But as soon as reality hit, I hated myself, because his arrival meant that everything was going to get harder. And it's already really freaking hard.

A ball of emotion crawls up my throat, my eyes threatening to fill with tears.

I don't know how I have any left at this point. Every single time I leave that care home, they're uncontrollable. The prospect of each visit potentially being the last time I'll get to see her is too much.

"Eff?" Kieran calls again.

I blow out a long, slow breath.

"Y-yeah," I half say, half sob as I stand tall, wipe beneath my eyes, and smooth my hair down.

I've been craving my best friend's presence for weeks—months—now. I refuse to let one small white lie to make a dying woman happy ruin that for me.

You've got this, Effie. Hold your head high and enjoy spending time with your bestie.

With one last look at myself in the mirror, I blow out a long, slow breath and take a step toward the door.

I'll never look good enough to be on his arm.

I'm not a jersey chaser, and I never will be.

I'm okay with that.

I'm okay with the fact that Kieran will never look at me and want me like he does them.

I have to be.

Kieran friend-zoned me a long time ago.

It's been years.

I should have come to terms with it by now.

I mean, I have. He's my best friend. I would do anything to keep him in my life in some way or another. Every now and then though, when I'm feeling vulnerable and fucked over by life, I can't help but wonder what it would be like to be his girl, not just his bestie.

I banish those thoughts as quickly as I pull the door open and find the man in question waiting for me. He's leaning against the opposite wall with his hands in his jeans pockets, wearing a navy t-shirt that fits him so snugly it should be illegal. His hair is perfectly messy, as he stares down at his cell.

The second he notices me, he looks up, wearing his signature smirk.

"What?" I ask as I step out into the hallway.

The scent of his aftershave hits me, and I swallow thickly.

I love my best friend dearly—he's one of the best people I've ever met—but is it really fair that he not only gets the personality but the looks as well?

His smirk grows as his eyes drop down the short length of my body. His attention makes my blood heat, but I try to play it off.

"You look good," he says innocently, pushing from the wall.

"Thanks," I whisper, following him down the hallway with my maxi skirt grazing over my legs.

"When was the last time you got laid?" he suddenly asks, making me almost trip over my feet.

"W-what?" I stutter.

He spins around once we're in the kitchen, picks up my purse from the counter, and turns to me, holding it out.

"Simple question," he says as if he truly believes the words.

But then, I guess it is when you've got willing women throwing themselves at you every day of the week. Some of us don't get the chance to be so selective.

His eyes hold mine as if he's trying to drag the answer to the question out of them.

He quirks a brow when I stand there, silent.

It's not because I don't want to tell him. We've always been open about almost everything in our friendship. The problem is...I can't remember.

"A while ago."

His chin drops. I don't know why he's shocked, but he is.

Did he really think I was spending my days hanging out

TRACY LORRAINE

with Grams and then going out hunting for a hookup come nightfall?

Men—or more specifically, their penises—have been about the furthest thing from my mind. To be honest, even when I was in Chicago and living my normal life, they weren't exactly high up on my priority list.

Sure, I have dated. I've even had a few unmemorable boyfriends, if you can call getting past a handful of dates before discovering the guy is an epic douche canoe a relationship.

I came to the realization many years ago that there is only one man on this Earth I can rely on. And he's currently staring at me as if I have told him I'm really an alien.

"Eff," he sighs.

"Don't 'Eff' me. It's sex, Kieran. I've got other things to worry about."

His mouth opens and closes, but no words come out for a few seconds.

"Yeah, I know that. But...you're stressed and—"

"I'm fine," I say in a rush, cutting off whatever he was going to say next. "Can we please just go out for dinner?"

"I'm worried about you," he confesses quietly behind me after I've tugged my purse from his hand and walked away.

My heart squeezes, making me feel like a dick for shunning his concern.

Pausing at the door of my grams' modest home, I spin back around to face him.

"I know, and I really appreciate it. I'm so glad you're here. But my underused female parts are not something you need to lose any sleep over."

His eyes drop momentarily to my previously mentioned parts, and my cheeks heat.

"I just want you to be happy," he says, surging forward.

"I know. But right now, I'm living here in my grams' house

16

and supporting her in her f-final... however long," I choke out. "My focus is her. There will be time for me later."

Without hanging around to hear him dispute my words, I rip the door open and race through it.

Ignoring my car, I march toward his, knowing that he'll want to take charge.

"We're going to our place, right?" I ask once he's backed out of the driveway.

When he told me earlier that he'd made a reservation, I just assumed.

Now, though, I can't imagine going anywhere but our favorite place in the city.

"Do you know me at all?" Kieran asks with a laugh, instantly making me relax. "I sorted it out before leaving Chicago."

His words remind me of the long day he's had.

When he first showed up, I expected him to tell me that he'd flown. But no sooner do we emerge from the care home and I see his car parked up, I discover that wasn't the case.

Kieran had jumped in his car first thing this morning and driven almost five hours to me. Even now, hours later, a smile pulls at my lips.

It's not the first time, and I'm sure it won't be the last, but he made the journey to see me. Not anyone else in the world. Me.

Thousands of people—women—across the country clamor for my best friend's attention, and yet he drives for miles to spend time with me.

"Thank you," I whisper, my voice cracking.

"I'm sorry it took me so long to get here. Things have been..."

Reaching over, I squeeze the hand resting on his thigh in support.

"It's okay. Whenever you're ready."

He blows out a long, slow breath, letting me know that I'm not the only one struggling with the things life has thrown at us recently.

The ding of my cell phone cuts through the heavy silence in the car and I pull it from my purse, frowning at the message from Jasmine, my assistant who has been keeping my job and our team functioning in my absence.

"Everything okay?" Kieran asks, glancing over.

I tap out a quick response to her query and shove my cell back into my purse.

"Yep, just work stuff."

"You're on sabbatical, you don't need to be involved."

Guilt twists up my insides. I hate that I'm letting my team and the Foundation down. But I can't be in two places at once.

"It's fine. I like still being involved, even if it is from a distance. "Shall we go eat?" I ask, changing the subject, my eyes landing on our favorite little hidden gem in the city.

It's a stylish bistro that's concealed in the backstreets. We found it by accident when we were visiting Grams a few years ago, and it very quickly turned into our number one place.

Pushing the door open, I take a moment to appreciate the warmth of spring before Kieran wraps his thick arm around my shoulder and guides me toward the front door.

The owner, Melanie, is there waiting for us with a beaming smile on her face.

"I've missed you guys," she cries enthusiastically before giving us both a hug as if we're long-lost friends. "Sorry about how your season ended," she says to Kieran, making his body lock up.

"It is what it is," he lies, his deep, raspy voice giving away how he really feels about their final game of the season.

Melanie doesn't have much to say about my life. As is to be expected. Unlike Kieran, my day-to-day movements aren't plastered all over social media for everyone to know about.

I might have accounts, but I barely ever post anything personal about me. Unless you really know me, you'd have no idea that I'm currently on a sabbatical from work so I can spend my days here in St. Louis with Grams.

Melanie shows us to our favorite table, right at the very back of the restaurant, where we can remain hidden from prying eyes should anyone recognize Kieran, and after talking our ears off for a good ten minutes, she finally leaves us alone.

As per our tradition, a few minutes later four glasses—two whiskey and two prosecco—are placed on our table. I groan at the sight of the amber liquid.

"You know you love it really," Kieran teases as he lifts the glass of his favorite from the table.

He won't drink more than a sip of either, but the gesture brings a wide smile to my lips.

It's a tradition we started many, many years ago, and as much as I hate the whiskey part of it, I love that he keeps it going.

"To Grams," he says simply as he waits for me to clink my glass against his.

His eyes hold mine, and I have no doubt that he can see the emotion pooling in them.

"To Grams," I say weakly before lifting the glass to my lips and taking a sip of the disgusting liquid.

There once was a time when I thought I might get used to it. But it's yet to happen. Just like Kieran's hatred of the bubbly stuff.

The strong alcohol burns down my throat, but unlike usual, I welcome it and swallow another mouthful.

I can't remember the last time I had a drink, and suddenly, the freedom a couple of glasses could offer seems very appealing.

Kieran watches me with pride on his face as I take my third sip.

"Don't tell me that you've finally developed a taste for the finer things in life," he teases.

Sucking in a deep breath, I place my glass back down as the whiskey warms my belly.

It might taste foul, but it sure has its benefits.

"There's never been an issue with my taste," I argue with a smirk.

"I mean, the fact that I'm your best friend would attest to that."

Shaking my head, I reach for my preferred drink and hold it up.

"To my best friend and his massive ego," I say, almost managing to keep a straight face.

He narrows his eyes but doesn't argue as he clinks his glass to mine.

"To my best friend who puts up with my giant ego and always keeps me grounded."

I stick out my tongue at him like a child before swallowing down two big mouthfuls of delicious bubbles.

"Come here," he says after opening his phone camera ready to take a selfie.

"Really?" I complain, although do as I'm told and shift closer.

"Yep. Brax wants to know if I got here safe."

I smile, and to my relief, it actually looks genuine. It's amazing what the presence of your best friend can do.

"We look hot," he muses before sending it to his teammate and close friend.

3

KIERAN

"Whoa," I say, reaching for Effie's arm when she trips over her own feet as we leave the restaurant. "Lightweight as ever, I see," I tease.

"Shurup," she slurs.

"Eff, you've had two glasses of prosecco and three sips of whiskey. How are you this wasted?" I ask, as I lead her toward my car.

Sure, she's never been a big drinker. It's hardly a surprise because she's tiny. But she can usually handle more than two glasses.

"S'been a while."

"You don't say."

"I missed you, Kieran."

A genuine smile pulls at my lips, one that I haven't felt for what feels like years.

I knew I needed to get out of Chicago and break the cycle I'd found myself in after the playoffs, but I didn't appreciate just how much better I'd feel the moment I laid eyes on Effie.

She's always been my safe place.

From the very first time we met, she didn't care who I was, what sport I played, or who I was friends with.

In fact, she was completely indifferent to everything about me.

In return, I was beyond intrigued by the quiet pocket rocket I'd been paired with in chemistry all those years ago.

All my life, people wanted to be friends with me for bullshit, superficial reasons.

And then there was Effie.

While everyone else let me get away with almost anything, she refused to take any shit.

She kept her cards close to her chest, and it took a very long time to get her to open up. But when she did, I felt closer to her than I had anyone. Ever.

And the best bit about our friendship? Unlike everyone else, she didn't want anything from me.

She wasn't searching for a way up the social ladder or to fund some lavish lifestyle. She was just her.

Just Effie.

"You good?" I ask as she slumps in the passenger seat.

Her eyelids are heavy and she's got a lazy smile playing on her lips. I can't help but laugh at her.

"Yeah, I'm good. Take me home?"

"You got it."

After strapping her in, I climb into the driver's seat and start the engine.

"Thank you for coming," she whispers as we take off down the street.

My breath catches as she reaches for my hand and entwines our fingers.

She squeezes, and I can't help but do the same.

I knew things were hard here, but I didn't appreciate just how much she's been struggling.

Guilt knots up my insides as I think about what a selfish asshole I've been recently.

I lost a football game. So fucking what? Effie is losing something so much more important than that.

Seeing Grams today really helped to put things into perspective.

Yeah, losing fucking sucked. Especially knowing that my performance was one of the reasons. But no one died.

I'll get a chance to try again and redeem myself next year.

Effie isn't going to get any more time with her grandmother.

A heavy sigh passes my lips, and I try to let go of some of the tension pulling at my muscles.

"There isn't anywhere I'd rather be," I say honestly as her breathing gets heavier.

Brushing my thumb over her knuckles, I continue driving in silence, lost in my own thoughts.

I don't remember my grandparents. Not really.

They were hardly ever around, and when they died, I was too young to understand.

But that's not the case with Effie and Grams.

For all intents and purposes, Grams was Effie's mom.

She sure did a hell of a lot more for her than either of her parents did.

My parents might be far from perfect. But at least they've always been there for us.

Effie's parents put her into boarding school and then...left.

Their careers and lavish lifestyle were both more important than their only daughter.

Sadly, it was the same for several kids at our school. But unlike many of them, Effie was lucky enough to have Grams.

She did all the things parents would do. And as our friendship blossomed, she became the grandmother I never had.

After a while, she wouldn't just turn up to support Effie, but me as well. She'd come to my games when she could. She was there at prom and graduation, clapping just as loudly for me as her own granddaughter.

Pulling up to her house, I kill the engine and sink lower in the seat.

I've been here more times than I can count. It feels more like home to me than anywhere I lived with my mom or dad.

It's the only home I've ever known where I feel welcome and relaxed from the second I walk in the front door.

It always smelled of cinnamon, thanks to her almost constant baking. The decorations were soft and cozy, unlike any place I ever lived.

It was like a home you see on the TV with the "perfect" American family.

It was "normal."

Something that my life never has been.

I was born into wealth. Something I'm very appreciative of.

If it weren't for the Callahan money, I may not have had the start in life, or the career I have now.

But it's not always easy. Money doesn't buy happiness.

It doesn't buy the kind of contentment and warmth that being inside Grams' home always gave me.

"Penny for your thoughts," Effie suddenly whispers, making me jump.

"I love it here," I confess. "Feels like home."

"It's not the same without her."

"No," I muse.

I'd be lying if I said I didn't sense the gaping hole when I walked into the house earlier.

Gram's presence was always so warm and inviting. Sure, the house still feels like home, but something is missing.

Someone.

"Some days after I've visited her, I just sit here in my car. It shouldn't be like this. She deserves better," Effie says, her voice cracking.

My lips part to respond, but what is there to say to that?

"Come on. We should head in," I eventually say reluctantly.

As much as it might hurt to be in there without her, we can't spend the night in the car.

Effie sighs.

With my heart in my throat, I push my door open and climb out.

By the time I get around to her side of the car, she's already on her feet.

"You good?" I ask, remembering all too well how wobbly she was when we left the restaurant.

Her eyes meet mine, and it's all the answer I need.

She collides with my chest at the same time her sob rips through the air.

With my arms wrapped around her, I rest my chin on the top of her head and let her cry.

I have no idea how long we stand there with nothing but the cool evening air blowing around us, but eventually, Effie's sobs subside, leaving us in silence.

Without saying a word, I lead her toward the front door and wait for her to dig the key out.

Together, we walk into Gram's house with heavy hearts.

Although faint, the scent of cinnamon is still there, but much like the woman herself, it's fading away.

"Go get ready for bed. I'll make you a drink," I say, turning toward the kitchen as Effie makes her way to her bedroom.

I work on autopilot as I warm the milk and reach into the cupboard for the hot chocolate powder. Everything is exactly where it's always been.

With two fully loaded mugs, I take them to her bedroom

and place one on her nightstand before lowering myself to the chair in front of her vanity.

Her room looks exactly as it did the first time I came here. It's girly and full of memories of her childhood. There are photos of her and Grams showcasing almost every year of her life. There are pictures of the two of us on field trips, at my games, or just hanging out.

Each one of them brings a smile to my lips as the sound of running water comes from the bathroom next door.

By the time she emerges dressed in a pair of pink plaid shorts and a white tank, my hot chocolate is cool enough to drink.

Her face is now clear of makeup and her eyes red and puffy from crying. It makes my chest ache. I wish I could do something to fix it. Her hair is piled on top of her head, ready for sleep, and she's abandoned the contacts she wore tonight in favor of her trusty thick-rimmed glasses. She looks cute as hell.

She watches me sip my drink for a moment before her eyes move to mine.

The cream and marshmallows are melting; it looks nowhere near as good as it did when I brought it in, but that doesn't matter to her. She's always been able to see what's beneath the surface. It's just one of the many things I love about her.

"Thank you," she breathes before pulling her covers back, propping her pillows against the headboard, and climbing in.

No sooner she's settled, than she reaches for her mug. She wraps her tiny hands around it and lifts it to her nose, inhaling a deep breath.

"So good," she muses before taking her first sip.

Her eyes close as she savors the sweetness, and I'm hit with a strong jolt of nostalgia.

There were many times that I'd sneak into her room after practice, and we'd sit on her bed laughing our asses off about

BY HIS PLAY

something that happened that day at school while I warmed up with one of her hot chocolates.

I always liked school, but everything about it got better once we became friends. For the first time in my life—and other than my family—I knew that someone loved me for me. It meant everything after already suffering through the discovery that kids I'd previously called friends were only using me. That was a bitter pill to swallow, but only a few weeks into our friendship I just knew that Effie was genuine.

"What are you doing?" she asks when she lowers her mug and opens her eyes.

"Uh..."

"You're too far away," she says, throwing the covers back for me to join her.

I glance down at myself, and then at the empty side of the bed.

I'm still dressed in jeans and a shirt from dinner.

"Wait," I say after abandoning my mug and stalking across the room.

I pull my t-shirt off as soon as I step into the hallway, and I'm down to my boxers as I walk into the guest room.

Sorry, Grams. I chuckle to myself as I try to imagine what her reaction to me walking around in my underwear would be.

I pull a t-shirt and pair of sweats from my duffle bag and quickly return to Effie.

She's sitting exactly where I left her, and she watches me closely as I round her bed and climb in.

"I hate being here alone. Feels so much better with company," Effie confesses as she sinks lower, snuggling into her pillow.

"Is that in the house generally, or your bed?" I tease, knowing full well which one she means.

"No man has ever slept in this bed with me."

"I'm more than happy to be your first," I quip as I mimic her position and lie so that we're face to face.

Her eyes bounce between mine before she begins to study my face.

"Penny for your thoughts," I whisper.

"I bet women would pay thousands to be me right now."

"Thousands? No, no chance." Her lips part to argue, but I quickly follow it up with, "I'm worth way more than that. It's gotta be at least a million or I'm not interested."

She laughs, but it's not as real or as deep as I'd like.

"You're something else, Kieran Callahan."

"Maybe so, but you wouldn't have me any other way."

4

EFFIE

I wake with my stomach growling and my mouth watering.

For a blissful few minutes, I'm a teenager again on break from school and spending long, relaxing days with Grams.

I stretch my legs out and groan, happy to lose myself in the illusion that everything in my life is as it should be.

But all too soon, the fantasy I'm happy to lose myself in begins to fade and reality slips back in.

Although it's painful to know that Grams isn't the one baking up a storm in the kitchen, amusement rolls through me at the thought of who is.

I almost don't believe it, but the scent of sugar and cinnamon is too much to deny. That isn't a shop-bought scent. That's real.

Curiosity has me throwing the covers back and climbing out of bed.

Finding one of Kieran's old hoodies in one of my drawers, I drag it over my head and slip into the bathroom to freshen up.

It's no surprise that he's awake before me. Years of being up at sunrise to train has become a habit that he's unable to break in the off-season.

I cringe as I come to stand in front of the mirror in the bathroom to wash my hands and brush my teeth. My eyes are red and puffy, showcasing both the effects of the alcohol and my emotional outburst last night.

Drinking was only going to end one way. There may have been times in the past when I've been a fun drunk, but now isn't it. And I'm sure Kieran has the makeup smears on his shirt to prove it.

Splashing some cold water on my face in the hope of rectifying the situation, I keep my eyes downcast as I grab my toothbrush.

My stomach continues to rumble as the scent of cinnamon only increases through the house. It's as if I haven't eaten in a week, despite the incredible meal we shared last night.

By the time I've finished, my patience to see what he's up to is at an all-time high.

Quiet music floats from the direction of the kitchen as I silently pad toward it and as I get close, I realize that Kieran is singing along.

A smile twitches at my lips as I try to predict what I'm about to walk into.

I discover not twenty seconds later that that was impossible.

I come to a stop and rest my shoulder against the doorframe as he pulls the oven open and slides out a tray full of cinnamon buns.

My stomach growls as I watch him turn and place the tray onto one of Gram's counter protectors.

He stands and studies his creations for a few moments before reaching for a cooling rack and embarking on transferring his buns.

I stand there with a smirk on my face, feeling happier than I have in a long time.

He looks larger than life, standing in the middle of Grams' modest kitchen. But then I guess that should be expected when he's a six-foot giant. I'm used to Grams pottering around in here, and she's even shorter than I am.

"Ow, fuck," he complains when a bun burns his finger.

Unable to hold it in, I snigger, alerting him to my presence.

He spins around with wide eyes and his pointer finger in his mouth as he tries to soothe the burn.

"The cinnamon butter is hot," he mumbles around the digit, making me laugh even harder. And it only gets worse when my eyes drop to his chest, and I take in the mess on his t-shirt.

"Oh my god," I blurt.

"Baking is hard," he complains after letting his hand fall to his side.

"Anyone would think Grams hadn't taught you well," I tease.

Both of us have spent more hours than I can count in here with her over the years, making all kinds of things.

I'm not a natural cook. Kieran always found it easier than me. Considering he's grown up without having to do anything for himself, I expected him to be clueless. But we quickly learned that wasn't the case. All my hours spent in this kitchen making memories with Grams didn't turn me into a natural chef.

There's a lot about our childhoods that align, but while I was learning how to cook, sew, and a whole host of other things with my grandmother, Kieran and his brothers were looked after by nannies. From what he's said, they were all wonderful and good at their job, but none of them were a replacement for a parent or grandparent.

I always felt sorry for him because I knew he was missing

31

out. Or at least, he was until Grams took him under her wing as if he was her own.

"Haven't baked a single thing in years," he confesses. "I might kill us both with these."

Moving closer, I take a better look at his treats.

They look incredible. The dough is golden and soft looking, the cinnamon butter sticky and sweet.

It's been far too long since I've had a fresh, home-cooked cinnamon bun for breakfast.

Tears burn my eyes as memories of times gone by flicker through my head like a movie.

"Shit. It was meant to make you smile," Kieran whispers, clearly chastising himself over my reaction.

Ripping my eyes from his goodies, I turn to look at the man himself.

A laugh tumbles from my lips at the sight of flour on his cheek and in the scruff on his chin.

His hair is still a mess from sleep, and despite his concern over my reaction, he's relaxed and happy.

"You're cute," I say, reaching up to wipe the flour from his skin.

"Not usually what I hear from women, but I'll take it."

"Ah, sorry," I tease before clearing my throat and putting on my best sultry voice. "Oh, Kieran, you're so hot and sexy." I trail my finger down his arm, over his bicep, and let out a sigh. "I can barely hold myself back."

"You're trouble," he laughs, staring down at me with amused eyes.

I shrug one shoulder, feeling completely at ease in his company.

"Just how you like me," I say, mimicking his words from before I fell asleep last night.

He gives me his full panty-melting, megawatt smile, and I can't help but take a step back.

I may have been teasing him before, but my best friend really is hot as hell.

"So...would you like to have a go on my buns?"

He manages to keep a serious face for all of ten seconds before the grin returns and his laughter fills the air.

"No need to look so horrified."

"You're an idiot."

"A cute one though, right?"

Shaking my head, I make my way to the dining table when he gently pushes me in that direction.

"So, what's the plan today?" I ask, ignoring his need for me to stroke his ego.

"Whatever you want," he says as the coffee machine comes to life, adding the rich scent of beans to the sweetness already in the air.

"My time here isn't about what I want," I confess.

He doesn't say anything for the longest time, making me regret saying those words out loud. Not that they were necessary in the first place. Kieran already knows.

"You need to do something for yourself," he concludes as he lowers a plate and mug of coffee before me.

"No. I need to be here for Grams."

"You are, Eff. You've been here for her every day for months. Trust me, there will be no question in her mind that you love her. That you're here for her."

I can't help but shake my head. "Some days she might. But others, she doesn't even know my name, let alone that I'm here for her." The words cause physical pain in my chest. Every time I walk through her door and she's got that blank look in her eyes, a little bit of me dies. I'm not sure how much longer I can keep up the brave face that's required of me.

"We'll go and see her later. But before then, I'm taking you out for a little Effie time."

"Kieran," I warn.

His eyes hold mine, refusing to release them until I concede.

"Your job might be to look after Grams right now. But mine...mine is to look after you. So eat, then shower, and then I'm taking you out."

"Kieran," I try again, but this time I get nothing but his hard glare. "Fine," I sigh, lifting my cinnamon bun to my lips.

I take a bite and instantly groan in delight.

"Oh my god, this is so good."

His eyes sparkle with my praise.

"Women always love my buns."

"What is this place?" I ask as Kieran drives up to a huge building on the outskirts of town I've never seen before.

It's new, that much is obvious, but it's also fancy as hell.

"The Cove?" I mutter as we pass the sign that gives nothing away.

This is clearly a place for celebrities to come and hide out.

It suits Kieran. Me, not so much.

"Don't complain," Kieran mutters as he pulls the car up directly outside the entrance. The valet immediately moves toward us.

"Kieran," I warn.

"You deserve this. Just...embrace it."

Before I have a chance to argue, my door is opened, and I have little choice but to get out.

"Thank you," I murmur as I step past him.

Kieran is a little more confident as he shakes the man's hand, no doubt slipping him a tip and coming to stand beside me.

"Do you trust me?" he asks ominously.

I stare up at the huge, immaculate white building before me.

"Sadly, I do. Do your worst."

With his arm draped around my shoulder, he guides me inside.

I expect to see people, but much to my surprise, other than one lady sitting behind a reception desk, the place is deserted.

"Is this place open?" I whisper, terrified of making too much noise.

"No."

"N-no?" I stutter, looking up at him.

"It doesn't open for another week."

"Then how—"

"Effie," he laughs.

"Oh. It's a Callahan place, isn't it?"

"Kingston's latest pet project. There isn't a single inch of this place that isn't five stars, and I don't know anyone more deserving of trying it out than you.

"We have the entire place to ourselves. The spa, the restaurant, the rooms. Whatever you want to do, all you have to do is say."

I stand there in silence, gazing up at the ornately painted ceiling above me.

This is the kind of place my parents love. They thrive on being photographed in exclusive resorts like this. Showing a side of their lives that is nothing but fake.

All I've ever tried to be is the opposite of that.

"This is too much," I say weakly.

"For my best friend, nothing is ever too much," Kieran says with the most genuine of smiles. "Now, I don't know about you, but I could really make use of the sauna."

"I didn't bring a suit," I confess as he leads me toward the back of the vast entrance hall.

"Ah, no need to worry about that."

"I'm not going anywhere naked," I argue.

"Why not? It's only my eyes that'll be on you."

He's teasing, I know he is. But it doesn't stop heat from rushing through my veins. It's closely followed by a huge onslaught of fear.

Kieran has seen more than his fair share of beautiful women. I'd hate to even imagine what he'd think of my body compared to theirs.

I'm not a tall, slim supermodel.

I'm short with more curves than any of those women would accept.

"I'm joking, Eff," he assures me when I come to a grinding halt a few feet before the sign directing us to the spa. "Everything you need for today is waiting for you in the locker room."

"You've thought of everything, haven't you?"

"Not a chance. All I know is that you deserve to be treated like the queen you are."

I stare up at him, all my earlier concerns falling away as the sudden urge to just let go of it all gets the better of me.

"Thank you."

"Anytime, Luck. Anytime."

5

KIERAN

I sink into the warm, bubbly water of the jacuzzi and wait.

The place is deserted.

It's perfect.

Heaven.

I didn't think King would go for it when I asked for a little preview of his latest project that's set to open in only a few days' time, but to my surprise, my big brother was unusually accommodating.

It was probably Tate. He's softened a lot since her, and then Prince, came into his life.

A smirk pulls at my lips as I think about the changes in my big brother.

I never thought I'd see the day where he willingly changed a diaper, but apparently hell has frozen over, because he is the most incredible father.

Soft music plays around me, mixing with the sound of running water. There are people running around everywhere behind the scenes getting this place ready, but you wouldn't know from in here.

I lose myself in the tranquility of the moment and rest my head back.

Minutes tick by, and I'm not joined by anyone.

I wasn't lying when I told Effie that everything she needed was in the locker room. I ordered it first thing this morning and gave the spa manager strict instructions to leave it out for her.

She should be ready by now.

Gazing around, I decide to take matters into my own hands.

Pushing from the water, I climb out, quickly rub myself down with a towel, and head toward the door for the ladies' locker room.

Cracking it open, I shout, "Effie?"

"I'm coming," my best friend calls back.

I don't know what it is, but there is something in her voice that gives me pause, and without thinking, I push the door open and walk in.

"What's wrong?" I ask when I find her standing in the middle of the room in her white fluffy robe with her arms wrapped protectively around her middle and tears in her eyes.

Her bottom lip trembles as she watches me approach. "I shouldn't be here. I should be with Grams."

"Effie," I sigh, taking her face in my hands and holding her eyes. "It's okay to look after yourself."

She feels guilty for taking some time out. I get it.

"As soon as we're done here, we'll be at her side. And I promise you, you'll feel better because of it."

She nods once, but she doesn't look like she really agrees.

"I promise, Eff. Now," I say, changing tact, "let's see this swimsuit. It looked hot when I chose it."

"Kieran," she complains, her grip on the robe tightening as her cheeks heat.

"What? It had your name written all over it."

"I never would have chosen this."

"Exactly why I did. Come on. Show me."

She lets out a pained sigh before huffing, "Fine," and pulling the front of her robe apart.

"Holy fuck," I breathe, my eyes widening.

My breathing picks up as heat races through my body.

I know she's got a banging body; I'm not blind. But shit.

My lips part to say something, but it's like words suddenly don't exist as filthy images I should not be having about my best friend flicker through my mind.

That scrap of red fabric would be perfect to bind her hands before her back while I...

Effie quirks a brow at me and I remember where, and who, I am again.

"T-that...that was a good choice."

"You're not supposed to look at me like that," Effie snaps, quickly pulling the sides of her robe closed again, covering up the insanity hiding beneath.

"What? I'm still a man, and you look—"

"Stop," she demands, having reached up on her tiptoes and slapped her hand across my mouth.

"Sorry," I mumble against her palm.

I give her my best puppy dog eyes in the hope she'll drop her hand.

But she doesn't immediately, and like a child, I stick my tongue out and lick her palm.

The second her hand falls away, I burst out laughing at the look of disgust on her face.

"Ew, you're so gross," she predictably complains before rubbing her hand down her robe.

"Can we go out there and relax now? It was boring on my own."

She stares up at me for a beat, a smile emerging. Her face is clear of makeup, letting me see the smattering of freckles she has on her nose and cheeks. Her hair is tied up and she's wearing her glasses. Team that with the robe and she looks adorable as hell.

"Fine. Just...don't look at me like that again."

Without waiting for a response, she takes off toward the door I came in through a few minutes ago.

"I'm allowed to think my bestie is hot, you know."

She shakes her head, letting me know that she heard me, but she doesn't comment.

"Wow," she breathes as she steps out into the pool area. "This is beautiful."

It's not the first time that she's been to a place like this. She's been to the spa at The Broadway more times than I can count. But this place has that beat. The decoration and interior design are insane. The full wall of the waterfall opposite us sure helps with that wow factor as well.

"King didn't do too bad, huh?"

"He should be impressed," she muses as she walks the length of the pool, making a beeline for the jacuzzi just like I knew she would.

"I know you're watching."

"How? You've got your back to me," I say, doing exactly what she's accusing me of.

"I know you, Kieran Callahan. I know how your mind works."

"And yet you're still my friend. That's impressive."

"It can change," she warns as she shrugs off her robe, throwing it onto the closest lounger before quickly climbing into the water.

I want to comment on just how good her ass looks in the suit, but I refrain.

Any other woman I've ever met would want to hear just how hot she looks. But not my best friend. She'd rather I tell her she looks ugly and unattractive—which I'd never do, because she's not. Both inside and out, she's the most beautiful woman I've ever met. It's why we're still as close as ever despite the many differences in our lives.

"Good, right?" I ask, joining her and sitting on the opposite side so I can observe her.

She lets out a long breath before her eyes find mine.

"You might have been right," she reluctantly admits.

"I'm sorry, I think I got a bubble in my ear. What was that?" I tease, a smug grin wide across my face.

"You were right. I needed this," she says again in a rush despite the fact she knows I heard her loud and clear.

"I know," I state proudly. "I know exactly what you need."

She shakes her head again, and I can't help but laugh at the small smile playing on her lips.

"Just think how happy Grams is going to be later when you tell her about how well I've treated you."

I expect her to laugh, or maybe agree, so I'm shocked when she tenses.

"What?" I ask, a frown pulling at my lips.

"N-nothing," she stutters, making me even more curious about her reaction.

Lifting her hand from the water, she fidgets her ring around her finger.

It's not an unusual move for her, but she usually only does it when she's nervous.

I remember watching her at school when we were getting ready to sit a test. Whether it be a ring, or necklace, or even a pen, she'd be constantly fidgeting with it.

"That's pretty," I say, nodding toward the diamond ring she's twiddling.

She gasps again, and her hand sinks beneath the water.

"It's nothing special," she says in a rush.

"What's going on?" I ask, my voice taking on a more serious note.

Effie studies the bubbling water for long seconds, and I quickly conclude that she's not going to respond.

Scooting closer, my thigh bumps against hers beneath the water.

"Effie?" I whisper, reaching out to tuck a loose lock of hair behind her ear. "Whatever it is, you can tell me. I'm here for you. Whatever you need."

She nods, letting me know that she's hearing me, but she still doesn't respond.

Resting my arm across the back of the jacuzzi, my fingers brush her shoulder, and shock forces her to turn and look at me.

Her eyes bounce between mine as she fights some kind of internal battle over whether to tell me what she's thinking about.

"I mean it, Effie. Anything you need, anything you want, all you've got to do is tell me. I'd raise hell for you if necessary, and you know it."

Her mouth opens and closes. She's right on the cusp of saying something when a soft voice rings around us.

"Good morning. Are you two ready for your treatments?"

We both turn sharply toward the woman talking to us. I don't know what Effie's reaction is, but I glare at her in the hope it'll scare her off so we can finish this weird conversation we're having. Sadly, it doesn't work, and the woman moves closer.

"I have you down for full body massages and then facials to start," she explains, focusing on Effie.

I sense my best friend glance at me curiously. While a massage might be a pretty regular thing in my life these days, a facial...not so much. But hey, when in Rome and all that.

"Sounds great," Effie says, surging from the jacuzzi and climbing back out as if she's got the hounds of Hell snapping at her heels.

She has her robe on and is following the therapist toward the door in the blink of an eye.

In a rush, I jump out and fold my own robe over my arm.

"Hey," I say, quickly catching up to her. "Are you okay?"

She looks up at me with a wide, fake smile on her face.

"Yeah. Everything is great. I'm so excited about this."

I don't get a chance to question her. Not that I want to with an audience. Instead, I'm guided to a room and greet my masseuse while Effie is led next door.

It's no big deal. We can talk later. Maybe she'll have figured out the words she needs to say by then.

I tell the masseuse not to go easy on me, but holy hell, for a relatively small woman, she really knows what she's doing. She gives our sports therapist at the facility a run for her money.

By the time I walk out of that room, I feel alive in a way I haven't for quite a few weeks. Oh, and my face is nice and soft too. Shame I'm the only one who's going to get to feel it.

Sure, I could go out and hook up here. Without sounding too arrogant, it would be pretty easy. But I'm not here for my dick. I'm here for my best friend, and the last thing she needs is a night out as my wingwoman.

She isn't back from her treatment when I return to the pool. I'm not surprised; I booked her in for the full works.

I make the most of both the sauna and steam room before retreating back to the jacuzzi with my cell.

Just like earlier in the day, it's boring alone, but at least I know Effie is being treated like a queen.

After ignoring numerous emails from both my agent and our team publicist, I reply to a few messages from the guys and my brothers, and assure my mom that I've arrived safely, and that Effie is okay.

Effie emerges a while later with a shiny face, red eyebrows from where they've been waxed, and freshly painted nails on her hands and feet.

"How do you feel?" I ask.

"Depends on which bit of me you're referring to. My brows are naked, but my muscles are loose."

I chuckle. "I mean, shit could be worse."

She rolls her eyes at me.

"I know you want to make the most of this. But...can we go?" she asks.

I frown, not expecting that request to come so soon. But I understand.

"Of course. Meet me out the front in thirty?"

"Twenty," she states, letting me know just how desperate she is to go and see Grams.

"You got it, Luck."

I leave her at the entrance to the ladies' dressing room before making my way to the men's.

I'm ready in ten and waiting for her on a couch in reception. She isn't far behind me, and as soon as she emerges, she makes a beeline for the exit.

I fall into step beside her, and silently we make our way to the car.

She says a few words, but nothing about the conversation we started in the jacuzzi, and once I hit the freeway and decide to bring it up, I notice that she's fallen asleep.

At least I achieved my goal; she's a little more relaxed.

All I need now is to find Grams awake and alert, and the three of us can have a good afternoon.

Sadly, just under an hour later, it's clear that isn't how we're going to spend the rest of our day.

6

EFFIE

The instant I saw the grim expression on one of the nurse's faces as we walked through the care home, I knew.

So, when we slipped into Grams' room, at least it wasn't a surprise when she turned and looked straight through me.

She didn't say a word. It's all I can do to suck in my next breath as pain radiates through me.

The second Kieran saw it, he reached for my hand and squeezed in support to let me know that he was there.

It helped—of course it did. His presence over the past few hours has meant everything to me. But it's never going to be quite enough, because he can't fix this.

No one can.

I have no other option but to sit around here and wait for this hideous disease to steal the most important person in my life.

But despite feeling like I'm dying inside, I don't let it show.

If experience has taught me anything, it's that things can flip on a dime, and any second she could find herself again. When—if—that happens, she won't see me sad and miserable.

She deserves better than that. So instead, I attempt to swallow down the giant lump of emotion in my throat and hold my head high as I walk to her bedside.

Kieran watches the entire thing. His concerned stare burns into me as I greet Grams and kiss her on her cool cheek, but he doesn't say a word. Not until I make it obvious that it's his turn to talk to her.

Watching him lift her tiny hand to his lips so he can kiss her knuckles makes the ball of emotion clogging my throat grow even larger, but I just about hold myself together.

"I took Effie to a fancy new spa this morning," he starts as he lowers his ass to the farthest chair from her, knowing full well that I'll want to take the closest. "You've been treated like a queen, isn't that right, Effie?"

I smile at him, loving how he so easily falls into this. I know it's awkward and uncomfortable talking to someone who clearly has no idea who you are. I'm sure he's got a million other things he could be doing right now. But he isn't. He's here with us.

His words from earlier in the jacuzzi come back to me, and guilt floods through my veins.

"I mean it, Effie. Anything you need, anything you want, all you've got to do is tell me. I'd raise hell for you if necessary, and you know it."

He would, too. Which is why I feel so awful for keeping my mouth shut about what I've done.

I've never lied to Kieran. Hell, I've never lied to Grams before either, and yet here we are.

I tell myself like I have done a million times over the past few weeks, that it's a means to an end.

My fingers drop to my ring, and I twist it around, hoping that it'll calm my nerves and banish my guilt. But it doesn't. It makes me feel worse, because with Grams lost in her own mind, it means I don't need to shift the ring to the other hand and keep up this facade.

Pushing all that aside, I reach for her hand and continue what Kieran started, telling her all about the spa this morning.

She stares at me as if she's listening intently to what I have to say, but I know she's not. I doubt she even hears my words.

The only noise she makes is to cough, and each time she does, it's like someone pulls another strip of my heart away.

Back in the day, she was a smoker, and it's left her lungs wrecked. Every time she gets even a cold, it goes straight to her chest.

She's been battling a cough for years, but recently, it's changed. It's deeper, rattlier.

I'm busy telling Grams about my mani-pedi and all the colors I had to choose from and how impossible it was without her help when one of her nurses joins us.

"Good afternoon," she says, smiling brightly at me before turning to Grams. "How are you feeling, Nora?" Predictably, she doesn't get a response, but that doesn't stop her. Laura chats away as if they're in a full-blown conversation as she does her checks. It's impressive, but then, I guess it is her job.

"And this young man that Effie has brought with her?" Laura starts, making me cringe. "Phew, if only I was thirty years younger. She's found herself a good one there."

My heart launches into my throat, and my eyes jump to Kieran's. Thankfully, his expression instantly settles me. He's got a soft smile playing on his lips and a twinkle in his eye. He's loving this. I really shouldn't be surprised.

Pushing from his seat, he moves a little closer and holds his hand out.

"I'm Kieran," he says, introducing himself.

"Oh, sweetie," Laura says, blushing. "I know exactly who you are."

"Right," Kieran mutters, shooting me a look.

"These two here never stop talking about you."

"Oh god," I complain. "Don't listen to her; it's all lies."

"Grams loves me," he says with a nonchalant shrug before dropping back into his seat.

"How is she doing?" I ask, turning the conversation away from Kieran's ego.

Laura's sigh is all the answer I need.

"She's struggling with this cough. I'm afraid it's turned into an infection. We've given her antibiotics, and we're hoping we've caught it early enough."

But what if you haven't?

I swallow down that question. It doesn't need asking. We're all achingly aware of the outcome here.

"Has she been like this all day?"

"On and off. She was better this morning. We had a chat about the weather and the birdsong outside."

It's like she wraps a band around my chest and squeezes tightly.

I wasn't here.

Glancing at Kieran, I see guilt etched in his features.

It's not his fault, though. He was trying to do something nice for me.

He did. And it was amazing.

I just...I should have been here.

I have time to do amazing things once I'm no longer needed.

My priority now has to be Grams.

"That's good," I force out.

"I'm sorry I don't have more positive news," Laura says before finishing up and leaving us alone once again.

"I'm sorry," Kieran whispers after long, silent seconds.

Shaking my head, I look up at him through my lashes. "Not your fault. None of this is your fault."

He smiles sadly.

"Are you hungry?"

I think for a moment. I should be—it's been hours since our breakfast—but I'm not. "No."

"Effie," he warns.

"I know, I know. It's just..." I look at Grams, and my stomach tumbles again.

How can I sit here and eat like everything is okay?

"You can go and get something," I offer.

He scoots forward in his chair, his eyes holding mine.

"I will, if you promise to eat something."

Just the thought of food makes me feel sick, but he's right, so I nod anyway.

"Any requests?" he asks as he stands.

"No, whatever you want is great. Can you get me an—"

"Iced coffee?" he finishes for me. He knows me too well.

"Yeah."

"You got it. Be good while I'm gone."

He leaves the room, the sound of his heavy footsteps drifting away, and everything instantly gets harder.

I don't think I really appreciated just how lonely and heartbreaking this entire situation is. His support and friendship since he got here has made it all so much easier.

He'll be back, I tell myself.

But it does little to lessen the pain.

Ripping my eyes from the door, I focus on Grams once again. Her eyes are closed, her face soft and peaceful as her chest rises and falls gently. Her breathing is rattly; I can hear it from here, reminding me that all is not well.

I sink lower in the chair and just watch her, silently praying for a different outcome but knowing it's impossible.

Soon, I'm going to have to return to normal life. To Chicago, my job, my apartment.

But as much as I might miss normality, I'm nowhere near

ready to deal with everything that needs to happen to get me there.

Aware that I need to let my father know what's happening, I pull my cell from my purse and wake it up.

I scan my emails. There are five from Jasmine that I need to read and deal with, but they can wait. I also have a message from Brax, Kieran's teammate, checking in to make sure I'm okay. I appreciate the hell out of his friendship and concern but I ignore it for now and pull up my chat thread with my father.

A bitter laugh tumbles from my lips as I take in the stream of one-way messages.

I add another to the long list, letting him know that she's declining.

I've been updating him every week on Grams' condition. He never replies. And on the rare occasion he does, I know it's his assistant who's sent it.

I'm not sure what pisses me off more—the fact he doesn't reply, or when he has someone else pretend that he cares.

I should stop messaging really. But I can't help hoping that one day he might just realize what he's about to lose. It's a lost cause, I know it is, but I can't let it go.

I let out a pained sigh and slump lower in the chair.

I've got a million things that I want to say to Grams, but no words pass my lips. I should confess my sins, but the thought of her learning that her one wish for me has been based on lies ensures the words stay firmly locked inside.

Slipping the ring from the right hand, I push it onto my ring finger and study it.

It's where it's lived for the last month or so while I've happily lived in fantasy land.

Seeing the happiness on Grams' face made the lie so easy.

I told myself that I was going to tell Kieran. It was inevitable that he was going to turn up at some point. But there was never a good time. He was so focused on the playoffs, and then his disappointment when it didn't go their way. I didn't want to stress him out further.

I figured that I could tell him when he got here. But facing him, the weight of my lie was too much and I chickened out.

I had the perfect opportunity to tell him earlier in the jacuzzi. And again, I choked.

He'll understand. I know he will.

Hell, he literally told me he'd do anything to make me happy.

He'd agree to keep up this charade to make Grams happy. He'd probably delight in making it look even more realistic.

I just...

What if he gets completely freaked out and runs?

It might be unlikely, but the fear is still there. He's spent his entire life telling me that he doesn't want to have a serious relationship or get married and do the whole two-point-five kids thing. His career is his life, and he doesn't want a distraction. The last thing I want to do is tell him what I've done and scare him off.

I sit there in silence, toying with my "engagement" ring and talking myself into a tailspin.

I'm not usually this much of a mess. I've never second-guessed myself so much in my life. I put it down to the grief and stress I'm currently experiencing.

I have no idea how much time passes; all I do know is that nothing changes around me until the door is pushed open and the scent of food wafts through the room.

"I got your favorite," Kieran announces, wincing when he notices that Grams is sleeping. "Sorry."

He passes a takeout bag over, and despite my nose confirming that it is indeed my favorite, my stomach turns over in protest.

"Please, Effie. Try. For me."

7

KIERAN

Watching Grams deteriorate more and more every day is devastating. But watching Effie fall apart in front of my eyes is even worse.

With Grams, sadly, there is nothing we can do. She is in the best place, with the best care possible. Effie did her research and chose the highest-rated—and most expensive—facility she could find. It was pure luck that it happened to be in driving distance from Grams' home. It wouldn't have mattered if it were miles away, though, Effie would have made it happen.

But Effie...all I want to do is make it better. I want to wrap her up in bubbles and protect her from all the pain she's feeling.

If only it would help.

I feel completely useless.

Sure, my presence helps. Or at least, I think it does.

She tells me it does, and I have to hope she's telling the truth, because other than supplying her with copious amounts of iced coffee and attempting to feed her, I'm at a loss for what else to do.

As Grams gets worse, she refuses to leave her side. It takes everything I have to get her to come home at night.

I fear that if I weren't here, she'd be living in the chair next to Grams' bed, and that isn't good for anyone.

For Effie to be here properly for Grams, she needs to look after herself first.

If only she'd listen...

Grams was awake last night, and although she was struggling, she was lucid. Effie wanted to make the most of it.

Since I've arrived, there have been very few times that she's looked at us both and known who we are. I understand Effie wanting to savor the moment while she could.

But while she might have been lucid, she wasn't entirely making sense, rambling about how we've made all her dreams come true.

As nice as that all was to hear, it was nicer still to see her and Effie interacting. Or at least, it was, until she slipped back to sleep and Effie fought her tears.

She's trying to stay strong while we're in Grams' room, but it's getting harder and harder as Grams slips away from her.

Every night, she's been crying herself to sleep.

I feel like I'm losing a little more of my best friend despite the fact she's right there in my arms, sobbing into my chest.

As always, I'm up with the sun. As quietly and as gently as I can, I roll out of bed and pad across Effie's room.

When I came here, I didn't have any intention of sleeping in my best friend's bed. But every night, she's been so sad I haven't been able to leave her.

Even now, knowing that she could wake up alone pains me.

I just can't stay lying there, staring up at the ceiling.

I have to move. My body and my mind crave it.

It can probably be said for most professional athletes—or at least it is for those that I know. Exercise is our therapy.

Everything feels wrong if I don't get up and instantly start moving. Get my blood pumping and empty my mind.

After freshening up, I pull on a fresh t-shirt, some shorts, and my sneakers before popping my earbuds in. Leaving a note for Effie in case she wakes—not that I don't expect her to know where I am; she's not in the best frame of mind right now—I slip out of the house.

The morning air is fresh, but I welcome the chill on my skin as I take off down the street.

The sun is rising over the horizon, casting this town in a soft orange glow. It's pretty, and I can totally understand why Grams made this place her home.

She had the means to move anywhere in the world. Effie's parents might be selfish assholes, but they show they care with money. It's the easiest option and a less risky way of showing affection when you're rich beyond your wildest dreams, I guess.

But she never moved. Something tells me she never spent the money, either. I think in the coming weeks, Effie will probably discover that Grams is sitting on a fortune. Not that Effie has any interest in her parents' wealth either. Much like me, she'd rather earn her own money and live her own life than be tied to them and their unrealistic expectations for her.

There is a job and life ready for her should she decide to pick up the phone and offer up her services. Not her services as a daughter; however, they've made it more than clear over the years that they're not interested in that.

My feet hit the asphalt harder as I push myself to max speed. Anyone watching would probably think I'm running from something.

I guess I am.

Expectations.

All my life, Dad expected me to follow the path he wanted for me. Just like Effie's parents did for her. It worked with my older brothers, Kingston and Kian. They toed the line and are now CEO and CFO of Callahan Enterprises.

Good for them. They both deserve it. They've worked their asses off to get where they have, and they're kickass at their jobs.

That life, though...from a very early age, I just knew it wasn't for me.

Sitting in an office all day, board meetings, managing people and money and projects, and whatever else they spend their time doing...it sounds awful.

From the first moment I picked up a football, there was only one thing I could picture myself doing.

And it wasn't just a want. It was a need.

I need to play. I need to push myself physically.

It took a long time for Dad to come around to the idea.

He had my place at Callahan Enterprises mapped out. He noticed from day one that I was the creative one of his three sons, and he was pushing me toward marketing. But it was never going to happen. No matter how hard he pushed, I pushed back more until he had little choice but to let me do my own thing.

He is proud of what I've achieved, sure. He comes to a lot of games every season and supports me. I'm grateful for it, because I know how easily he could have turned his back on me for not falling into line.

Of course, it helped when I started my foundation. Dad saw that as me putting one step into the corporate world and backed me all the way with Callahan Enterprises being one of the KC Foundation's biggest sponsors.

Football will always have my heart. It'll always be my life. But the Foundation allows me to give back. It helps me to support those who aren't as fortunate in life and give them a chance to play professionally.

I've lost count now of the number of players we've helped

to secure a future. It's incredibly rewarding, and I can't wait to see some of those names filter into the NFL in the years to come.

I know Effie feels the same. It's why she stood right by my side when I started the foundation. She's my wingwoman and will be forever.

We miss her at the office. The place isn't the same without her smiling face. But it's only temporary. She'll be back; there are just more important places for her to be right now. And when she does return, I have no doubt that the KC family will pull her in with open arms and make her feel like she's returned to a safe and loving place.

I keep running until my legs and lungs are screaming, but I welcome the pain.

Despite the cool morning air, sweat covers my skin, my shirt sticking to my body.

I pass a few people, mostly other runners, but no one pays me any attention and I'm thankfully able to lose myself without interruption.

Before long, I turn back on a loop that I used to do as a teenager when I stayed here with Effie and make my journey back to the house.

When I'm only a few minutes away, I slow to a stop as I approach one of Effie's favorite coffee shops.

I wipe my sweaty face with my arm, hoping that it makes me look a little more acceptable, before pulling the door open and walking inside.

There are a few people sitting around, but thankfully, there isn't a line, and I walk right up to the counter, ordering two of Effie's favorite and a box full of pastries.

I've woken her up with the scent of cinnamon buns a couple of times this week. I love seeing her smiling face when she comes to find me—and the buns. But as much as I need something to keep my hands and brain active, I don't need to be baking every single morning. And I'm not sure croissants are in my repertoire yet.

I rest my ass against one of the stools at the counter as I wait for my order and pull my cell from the safety of the zip pocket on my shorts.

I find a stream of notifications from several apps, but it's the message notification from my brother that I open.

King, Kian, and I are pretty close. As close as we can be when our lives are dominated by our careers.

> Kian: About fucking time, Bro. Kinda wish you'd told me instead of letting me find out online.

"The fuck?" I whisper before clicking the link that follows his message.

The website opens and my stomach lurches into my throat at the words that are staring back at me.

Chiefs star, Kieran Callahan, to marry his childhood best friend in a small, romantic ceremony.
Effie Campbell's grandmother is delighted about the union that she's been dreaming of since the two of them met at school.
"It's been so wonderful seeing Nora so excited for her granddaughter. Effie is a regular at our care home, and we're all thrilled for her," Laura, Nora's nurse, explains. "Her happiness is infectious, and her ring is beautiful."

8

EFFIE

Waking up alone is normal. Even with Kieran spending the night with me, I never expect him to still be here.

I wish he was, though.

I've never felt lonelier than I do in the mornings here.

I was so used to waking to the sounds and smells of Grams. The emptiness, the silence. It's painful. I feel it right in the pit of my soul.

Having Kieran here has been such a relief. But I can't help needing more.

With a sigh, I throw the covers back, pull on one of Kieran's old college hoodies, and pad to the bathroom.

I put off looking in the mirror for as long as possible, but I can't help but look up when I'm brushing my teeth.

I'm a mess. My eyes are bloodshot and sore, the circles beneath them dark and haunting. My skin is pale, and I've had a breakout.

Everything is falling apart.

Grams is...Grams is bad. I don't need to be sitting beside

her for hours to know. The grim looks on the nurses' faces every time I see them...the truth is clear as day in their eyes.

Two days ago, they explained how the antibiotics they gave her for a chest infection haven't helped, and it's progressed to pneumonia.

I blow out a long, pained breath as I lower my toothbrush to the sink.

I'm going to lose her any day now.

Pain explodes in my chest. It's like something being wrapped around my heart, making each breath harder and harder to take.

I'm numb as I make my way to the kitchen.

Kieran's absence is strikingly obvious. I don't need his note to tell me that he's not here. I can sense it.

The little life that had come back to this place with his arrival has drained out.

I start the coffee machine on autopilot. I probably won't drink it—I'm not sure my stomach can take it—but it's better to be doing something than it is to think.

Thinking is heartbreaking.

I need the distraction of something else.

If it weren't for Kieran, I'd already be in my car and heading for Grams, but he'll tell me off if I don't wait for him. And while I can take it, I don't have the energy to deal with it.

Instead, I grab my cell, ignoring every notification and call the care home to see how her night was.

It's another twenty minutes before the sound of the front door slamming echoes through the house.

Startled, I jump to my feet and twist toward the door just as a harassed-looking Kieran bursts through.

He lowers a box from my favorite bakery to the counter, along with two take-out coffees, but he doesn't say anything.

My heart jumps into my throat, my stomach twisting.

"Kieran?" I whisper, not liking the energy that's radiating from him one bit.

He stills with his eyes focused on the other side of the room as his chest heaves and his fists clench at his sides.

"What's going on?" I ask, but deep down, I know exactly what it is.

He knows.

Somehow, he's found out about what I've done.

It takes another second for him to turn my way, and the moment his eyes lock on mine, I suck in a deep breath.

He hates you.

"Kian sends his congratulations," he says, his voice hard and flat, void of any emotions despite the warring ones I can see in his eyes.

Confusion. Anger. Disbelief.

"Kieran," I say again in place of anything that might be more useful in this situation.

His nostrils flare and his lips press into a thin line. "That isn't going to help, Effie. How about you explain why my brother is sending me a link to our engagement announcement instead?"

Having my suspicions confirmed makes my knees go weak, and I crash onto the chair I was previously in.

Dropping my head into my hands, I beg for it to stop spinning.

"I'm sorry," I whimper.

"You're sorry? It's all over the fucking internet, Eff. Apparently, we're having a small and intimate ceremony."

A sob rips free.

"Look," he barks, forcing me to lift my head and focus on the screen he's thrust in my direction.

His cell is going crazy. Every second, a new notification pops up.

When it starts ringing with a call from Kat, the team's publicist, he pulls it back and immediately cancels it.

"Why?" he demands. "And why didn't you tell me?"

"I...I didn't think...I was going to. And then you showed up and—"

"And you had every chance to tell me what you'd done, but you decided not to?" he asks, hurt clear in his voice. "This isn't how we work, Effie. We don't keep fucking secrets. No matter how hard shit is, we talk."

The tears I've been desperately trying to keep in finally spill over my lashes. He watches me with his brow wrinkled and hurt in his eyes.

This isn't what I wanted. This is the last thing I wanted.

Ripping my eyes away, I look down at my right hand and pull the ring from my finger.

With Grams mostly sleeping or unaware of her surroundings, I haven't had to put it on my ring finger. It made the lie so much easier to keep up with.

"Th-that's an engagement ring?" Kieran balks.

After sucking in a deep breath, I lift my head and hold his eyes.

"I didn't do any of this to hurt you. G-Grams—" I choke, struggling to force the words out. "Her dream was to see us... you know..."

He remains silent, his eyes boring into mine.

"I never should have done it. But it seemed simple enough, and the way she smiled when I told her. She was so happy. All she could talk about was how she could go happy because she knew that you'd always look after me and treat me right.

"It gave her something to focus on. We'd spend hours planning, and she'd lose herself in the excitement of it all."

My words dry up as I think about the time I spent with Grams while living this lie.

It was wrong. So wrong. But also, I don't regret it. I can't.

In her final weeks, I gave her hope. I gave her happiness, and I relieved her worries about leaving me.

"I'm sorry I lied. I should have talked to you about it first. But you were so focused on the playoffs and—"

"Don't turn this on me. Nothing is ever more important to me than you. Ever."

"I know," I mumble, ashamed over how this has gone. "It was never meant to get out. It was supposed to be mine and Grams' little secret."

"And you really believed that? Fucking hell, Effie." He groans, dragging his sweaty hair back from his head and pulling until it has to hurt.

"I wasn't thinking."

"No, you weren't," he agrees.

We stand staring at each other in a stalemate. I have so much more to say, and so does he. But neither of us let the words free.

Finally, he lets out a heavy sigh before announcing, "I got your favorite and pastries. Eat. I'm going to shower."

My lips part to respond, but I'm too slow. He's already gone.

"Fuck," I breathe, dropping my head onto my folded arms on the table.

Could I have fucked this up any more?

K ieran never takes long showers. He's usually in and out in under ten minutes. But this morning, he's gone for over thirty.

I have one sip of coffee before pushing it away.

I can't stomach it. It tastes like acid.

Instead, I stay exactly where I am and wallow in self-pity.

"Get dressed," Kieran barks the second he emerges,

dressed and looking devastatingly good. If I didn't already feel like a mess, then I would looking at him. He's every inch the football god that everyone makes him out to be.

Was it naive of me to think that I could tell Grams we were engaged and expect the news not to leave the care home? Yep, apparently it was.

I didn't expect it to be leaked. Hell, I didn't really expect it to be taken seriously. If Grams was of sound mind, she would never have believed me. But she wanted it so badly, it was easy to skip the bits that didn't make much sense. Like the fact that Kieran had apparently proposed, but I hadn't seen him in months.

There were so many red flags that I'd convinced myself it would be okay.

Unable to do anything but follow orders, I rush past him without saying a word and pull some clothes on.

Kieran then drives me silently to the care home.

It's awful.

The whole journey, his phone is going off. If it's not calls from Kat, it's messages from his brothers or teammates.

I haven't looked at mine, but I fear it'll look similar.

Sure, we've had a handful of arguments over the years; none of them were serious, though. We've certainly never fallen out to the point of not talking before.

By the time we arrive, I jump out of the car like my ass is on fire and rush into the building.

I have no doubt that he will follow me eventually, but I just need a few minutes.

Inside, I find Grams sleeping, and I collapse in the chair beside her.

"I've screwed up," I confess. "All I wanted to do was make you smile, and now I've hurt the one person I need more than ever."

Dropping my head into my hands, I cry for all my stupid mistakes.

I have no idea how long I sob for, but by the time they subside, my eyes are sore and my throat hurts.

Every time I think that life can't get any worse, it does.

Still curled up in the chair, I begin talking to Grams. She can't hear me, but I still blabber away about nothing. If there is any chance that she can hear my voice, then I want her to know that I'm here and not totally falling apart. Even if that is just another big fat lie.

Laura comes in and out a couple of times, but other than offering me a hot drink and her sympathies, she doesn't have a lot to say.

It's just a waiting game now. I get that. There really isn't any kind of positive spin anyone can put on this situation.

Kieran never comes, and I'm too scared to see if that's just because he's outside, lost in his own thoughts, or if he's gone.

He'd have every right to go back to Chicago and have Kat deal with the shitshow that I've brought on his life. It sure wouldn't be the first time he's needed the help of the team's publicist to get him out of trouble.

The thought of calling an Uber and going home to a silent, empty house tonight guts me.

I'd rather stay in this chair until they kick me out than return without him.

Hours pass. My stomach grumbles, but I don't make a move to fill it with anything.

Grams' eyelids flicker, but she never wakes or shows any other promising signs. And when the doctor does his rounds, he repeats what I've heard for the last few days.

The end is coming.

I don't leave the room until two nurses come in to do Grams' personal care.

I walk out of her room on shaky, weak legs and look up and down the hallway, wondering what I'm supposed to do now.

I used to make their visits my excuse to head off for the night. But as hard as it was going home then, it's going to be a million times worse now.

Deciding that some fresh air might help, I head for the double doors that lead outside.

Long before I get there, the soothing sound of torrential rain hits my ears.

A cold waft of air envelops me as I sit outside. I stand there for a few seconds as my skin prickles with goosebumps, watching the raindrops bounce across the parking lot.

A trickle of unease runs down my spine, and I look to the right where a bank of benches sits under the canopy.

I expect to find a stranger sitting there contemplating life without a loved one, but I quickly discover that I'm very wrong.

"Kieran," I whisper, the sound swallowed by the downpour.

He studies me as if he's seeing me for the first time.

"I thought you'd left."

He shakes his head, and I can't help but think he's disappointed in me.

Hesitantly, I walk over and perch at the other end of the bench.

My skin continues to burn with his attention, but I keep my eyes focused on the parking lot.

"I don't care that you made all of this up to make Grams happy," he tells me. "If I were in your position, I'd have done the same thing." A little relief trickles through my veins, but his next words squash it faster than I thought possible. "I'm really fucking pissed that you lied to me about it, though. That you allowed me to find out the way I did."

65

I cringe, unable to do anything but agree with him. I'm pissed at myself too.

I close my eyes and slump in the chair as the weight of my regrets gets too heavy.

"I'm sorry."

"You might be. Doesn't mean it didn't happen, though, did it?"

I swallow down any response I might have had.

"How's Grams?"

"Asleep. Peaceful."

"Good. Th-that's good."

"Is it?" I sigh.

9

KIERAN

My cell has finally died, and I have no intention of turning it back on.

I've spoken to my brothers and attempted to explain, but everyone else can get fucked.

I've had over ten missed calls from Kat, probably wanting to scream at me for not warning her about this huge development in my life, but I don't care.

The only person who matters is sitting right beside me. That'll always be true, even if I want to throttle her for lying to me.

The reason our friendship has lasted for so long is because we've always been honest with each other.

It hurts more than I'm willing to confess right now that she didn't talk to me about this.

Would I have thought she was crazy if she'd brought it up? One hundred percent, yes. But I'd have understood.

I'd have done anything to make Grams' final weeks happy ones as well.

If she'd have explained, I'd have agreed. It might have freaked me the fuck out, but I'd have agreed.

TRACY LORRAINE

I'd do anything for both of them, including going along with this farce of an engagement.

Suddenly, all the weird comments from both Grams and the whistleblower nurse make sense.

If the whole thing wasn't so unbelievable, I might have figured it out.

I glance down at the ring on Effie's right hand and wince.

Did they really think I'd have given her that?

Sure, it's pretty. But Effie deserves something so much better.

She deserves the world, and a man who can buy her the ring of her dreams, amongst many, many other things.

There's so much I want to say to her, but I can't find the words. They're trapped under a thick layer of hurt.

I've told her so many times this week that I'd do anything for her and Grams. Anything. I meant it too.

And yet she still didn't tell me.

I let out a sigh as the rain continues soaking everything around us.

"Do you want to go and see her?" Effie suddenly asks, breaking the uncomfortable silence.

I know that I should just forgive her and move on.

But it's not that easy.

"The nurses should be finished now."

Pushing to the edge of the bench, I agree.

"I'm going to go to the bathroom," she explains as I walk toward the main doors.

It pains me to leave her behind, but I do it.

Thankfully, Grams' room is empty when I slip inside. I'm annoyed with the nurse who sold her story. I have a few words I'd like to say to her, but at the same time, what's the point?

She's already done the damage and had her five minutes of fame. It's too late to do anything about it now.

"Hey, Grams," I say, hating that she doesn't react to me in any way.

I lower myself to the chair that Effie has been sitting in for hours while I was outside deep in my own thoughts.

For a few minutes, I can't muster up any words.

What is there to really say in this situation?

But after a while, something bubbles up.

"You don't need to worry about holding on. I know you're worried about Effie. But I promise you that she'll be okay. You've raised an incredibly smart and strong young woman."

I try to swallow the lump that crawls up my throat, but it doesn't shift.

"No matter what happens, or where life takes us, I'll always be there for her."

It's no lie. I will. I don't care if she meets someone, gets married, and has kids. I will always be there if she needs me.

The thought of her with a serious man in her life causes a weird reaction that I can't identify. I shove it away. It's not exactly close to being a reality right now, so I figure it doesn't need worrying about.

"I love her. I always have. She's my girl. But you know that, don't you?" A sad laugh spills from my lips as I try to imagine how she reacted when Effie told her our fake news.

I bet she was beside herself with happiness.

A noise at the door catches my attention, and I startle when I find Effie standing there with tear-stained cheeks.

"Speak of the devil and she shall appear," I tease. "Here," I say, getting up so she can retake her seat.

She looks unsure as she joins us, but she ignores the empty seat in favor of perching on the edge of Grams' bed.

Effie takes her delicate hand in hers and lifts it to kiss her knuckles.

"Kieran is right, Grams. I'll be okay. D-don't hold on because of m-me. It's t-time to find peace."

Stepping up behind her, I wrap my arms around her as her first sob breaks free.

Grams' breathing is shallower than ever. She's really struggling.

As much as I hate everything about this and how much Effie is about to lose, it's time. Effie knows it too.

I hold her as tight as I dare in an attempt to keep her together.

I might be annoyed with her, but she'll always be my best friend, and I will always be here.

It's long, heartbreaking minutes later when her broken whisper fills the air. "We should go."

It's the first time this week I haven't had to drag her out of here kicking and screaming.

"Okay," I breathe, relieved that she isn't going to make me fight her tonight.

Releasing her, I step around her to say goodbye to Grams before telling Effie that I'll meet her outside.

In only a few minutes, she joins me in the hallway with her head bowed.

"It's going to be okay," I say before wrapping my arm around her shoulder and pulling her into my body.

"I know," she whimpers, hugging my waist tightly.

When we get outside, the rain has subsided, and after opening her door for her, I climb in and sit in silence with her, staring at the building we just emerged from.

"I don't know if I can do what comes next," Effie confesses as she pulls her knees to her chest and wraps her arms around them.

"Of course you can," I assure her sadly. "I'll be with you the whole way."

She glances over. "Will you?"

The simple question makes my chest ache.

"Of course." I give her a small smile and start the car.

We need to talk, but right now isn't the time.

We stop at the drive-through for dinner on the way home, and I'm forced to sit in the car with the scent of burgers and fries taunting me. My stomach growls loudly, but I force myself to wait until we're back.

As soon as we're in the house, I make a beeline for the kitchen table and rip open the bag.

Effie moves much slower. I glance up as she finally makes it to the kitchen and concern rushes through me. Her legs look like they're going to buckle beneath her any minute.

"Come and eat," I demand, pushing her food toward her.

She lowers herself to the chair opposite me and just stares at the fries.

"Please, Effie," I beg.

"I-I can't," she whispers, pushing the food away.

"I can't watch you do this to yourself. Grams would never forgive me. I promised her I'd look after you, remember?" I say, my cheeks heating as I recall her listening to my words earlier.

I meant them, and I'll happily tell her to her face, but overhearing me telling her dying grandmother feels more intimate somehow.

"You said that I was your girl," she says quietly, ignoring what I said about looking after her. "But that's not true. I've never been yours."

I want to point out that it didn't stop her from pretending that I asked her to marry me, but I bite back the words. Now is not the time.

"Effie, you'll always be my number one girl. Now, please, please, eat something. If you won't do it for me, do it for her."

She narrows her eyes at me, unimpressed by my blackmail attempt.

I know everything feels bad right now, but something tells me that it's going to get worse before it'll get better, and I need to help her somehow. Attempting to keep her body functioning is going to be easier than trying to stop her from drowning.

It takes a few seconds, but she reluctantly reaches out for a fry and bites it in half.

"Good girl," I praise, and when her wide eyes jump to mine, my heart skips a beat.

"I bet you say that to all the girls," she mocks, trying to lighten the mood.

"Nah, all the ones I spend time with are bad."

She rolls her eyes. "Of course."

It takes her ages, but she eventually eats half her fries and two chicken tenders before she admits defeat and pushes everything in my direction to finish for her.

As much as I want to refuse and make her eat it, I know she's done.

I've got a mouthful of her almost-cold fries when she pushes her chair back and starts searching through the cupboards.

"What are you looking for?" I ask, but other than a glance over her shoulder, she doesn't respond.

I soon get my answer a few minutes later when she pulls out a bottle.

"What is that?" I ask with a frown, not recognizing it.

Effie shrugs as she twists the lid off and lifts the neck to her lips.

Whatever it is isn't very nice if her face is anything to go by.

"Eff," I warn, hating that she feels she needs to turn to alcohol to help with everything.

"It'll help me sleep. I just...need some rest."

"Shit," I whisper, scrubbing my hand down my face.

She swallows down another shot, her face twisting with just as much disgust as the first time.

Throwing the final chicken tender into my mouth, I gather up our wrappers and dump them in the trash before walking over to her.

"This isn't going to help, but I know what will," I say, tugging the bottle of...sherry—gross—from her grip and walking out of the room with it.

I go straight to the bathroom and begin running the bath. I search the small cupboard for a very different kind of bottle before pouring a generous amount of bubble bath into the water.

Her light footsteps move closer; her curiosity too much to ignore. The very moment she steps into the doorway, a tingle of awareness runs down my spine.

"Kieran," she whispers.

"Go and get ready. It won't be long."

"You don't have to do this."

Hanging my head for a beat, I push to my full height and walk over to her.

Wrapping my hand around her ponytail, I give her little choice but to look up at me.

Seeing her standing there at my mercy does weird things to me. But I quickly chastise myself. Now isn't the time or the place.

"There isn't much I can do to help right now. But I can do this. Relax, and I'll make you something to drink that actually tastes nice and might help you sleep."

Her eyes bounce between mine. They're glassy and bloodshot, showing the pain that's hiding behind them.

"Don't leave," she whispers.

A sad laugh spills from my lips.

"Who said anything about leaving?"

"You're mad at me," she says, attempting to break our connection, but I force her eyes to return to mine.

"Yeah," I agree. "I am. But that will never stop me from caring or wanting the best for you."

"I don't deserve you."

"No, what you don't deserve is all this shit. You deserve the world. And," I say, reaching for her right hand, "if a man ever proposes to you with a ring like this—" I tug it from her finger. "Then I'll fucking end him. Is this even a diamond?"

She shakes her head. "I grabbed it at the store. It's—"

"Not worthy of you. Effie," I whisper with every intention of following it up with something, but the words die.

Her bottom lip trembles, and I kick myself for upsetting her, but everything I just said is true.

Sliding my hand to the side of her neck, I drag my thumb along the line of her jaw.

My heart pounds harder in my chest as I think about the man who is one day going to ask her to be his wife.

That feeling from earlier returns.

"Give me two minutes to finish this off," I say, forcing myself to take a step back from her and passing her ring back.

"O-Okay."

Slowly, she backs away and disappears down the hallway, leaving me standing in the middle of the bathroom.

What the fuck was that?

10

KIERAN

I leave Effie standing in the middle of the bathroom with candlelight flickering around her.

Closing the door, I pray that it's going to help her relax and get a good night's sleep. Hell knows she needs it, and that sherry she started downing is going to help no one.

With the bottle in hand, I take it to the kitchen and immediately pour it down the drain. The bottle is dusty and the label is beginning to peel; I dread to think how old it is.

After tidying up a little, I head toward the guest room, stopping at the bathroom door for a beat to listen to her inside.

It's quiet, and I can only hope that she's okay.

As much as I might want to sit next to her, we both need a little space. Or at least, I do.

The revelations of the morning are still running rampant in my head.

I get it. I understand why she did it. But I still can't get over the fact she kept it to herself, even after I showed up here.

With my teeth gritted in irritation, I continue forward.

Pulling my cell from my pocket, I put it on to charge and wait for it to power up.

I dread to think how many notifications will be on it and how far the gossip has spread.

I no longer care as much about the things that are written about me. Most of it is bullshit made up by pointless reporters, football "experts" who think they can criticize my performance like they have any fucking experience doing what I do, or women who think they can make a quick buck by selling their stories about spending the night with me.

In the beginning, I used to read it all, mostly for amusement value, but as the years have passed, I've learned to ignore it more and more. After a while, the stories begin to linger. The negative reactions to games and how I live my life started to impact my day to day, and I very quickly cut myself off.

The internet, while really fucking useful for many things, is also a cesspool.

After changing into a pair of sweats and a t-shirt, I sit on the bed and reluctantly reach for my cell.

I have more missed calls and voicemails from Kat, Daniel, my agent, and Mom.

My group chat with the guys has blown up. There are more notifications than I can count, but without opening a single one of them, I know exactly what they're talking about.

I have separate messages from a number of them, but it's my teammate, Braxton's, that I open.

He's good people, and the words in the preview remind me of that.

> Brax: Am I right to be suspicious? Here if you need anything.

I bite down on my bottom lip as my finger drums against the side of my cell.

He gets it.

It probably helps that he knows Effie fairly well too.

I wonder if he believes it. Probably not. He knows that we're good friends. He's ribbed me about it enough over the years. Even asked for permission to ask her out once, which I swiftly declined before punching him in the arm.

I'm cool with Effie dating. She's been with a few guys over the years. None of them have been serious, though, mainly because none of them have been worthy of her.

She doesn't have great taste in men. Her best friend aside, obviously.

I have messages from not only King and Kian, but also their girls, too.

The final one from Tate makes me laugh.

> Tate: You need to ring your mother; she's driving us all crazy wanting to know if she needs to go hat shopping.

> Kieran: I'm amazed she hasn't already got one just in case of a shotgun wedding.

I smirk as I hit send. I am known for being the unpredictable one, so I wouldn't put it past her.

It shows she's typing instantly.

> Tate: She needs confirmation of a color theme first.

I laugh at the message, but I don't reply. Instead, I open the thread from Kian's girl.

> Lorelei: As much as I really, really want to believe all this... it's not true, is it? 🌚

I shake my head. Of course she wants it to be true. Lorelei is nothing but a romantic. How she ended up with Kian, who wouldn't know romance if it slapped him in the face, is beyond me.

I'm looking through my other notifications when my cell

starts ringing in my hand and Mom's name and photo appear before me.

"No time like the present, I guess," I mutter to myself.

Swiping the screen to answer the call, I press it to my ear and wait.

"At last. I've been trying to call you all day," she says without any kind of hello.

"My battery died," I lie.

"I've been going out of my mind, Kieran."

Tell me about it.

"Oh, I'm just so happy for you. I never thought it would happen, but—"

"Mom," I interrupt to stop the verbal diarrhea that I know is coming.

"Don't 'Mom' me. This is huge, Kieran. I'm so mad that you didn't tell me yourself and let me find out online, but I'll shout at you about that later."

Flopping back on the bed, I let my hand and cell fall to the mattress as she continues telling me exactly where and what our ceremony should be like.

While King, Kian, and my closest friend have taken this news with a pinch of salt and more than a bit of skepticism, it seems that Mom is running full speed with it.

I let her talk. I know from experience that it's better to let her run out of steam than it is to attempt to stop her. She's been working on this all day; if she doesn't expel it...I dunno, she might explode, maybe.

I have no idea how much time passes with her voice filling the guest room. I also have no idea what she's saying.

It's not until the sound of water running from the bath that I come back to myself.

"Mom," I attempt, already knowing that I'm going to fail.

"It will be the perfect time. It's the off-season and the weather will be beautiful. Just let me know when you want to book Effie an appointment with my designer. I just know that she'll create the perfect—"

"MOM," I shout.

"Oh, Kieran," she sighs, finally taking a breath. "I know I'm a little over-excited, but I've been waiting for this since you were both fifteen."

I cringe.

"Mom, it's not—"

"The two of you...you've always been so perfect together. And the way you look at her...I've known for years that she's the one for you. I've just been waiting for you to figure it out."

"No, Mom. Effie and I are just—"

"Perfect. Of course, she's already one of the family, but I always knew she was going to be my daughter-in-law one day. I'm so excited," she squeals again.

"Mom, you're not listening to me. Effie and I aren't getting married. This is all tabloid bullshit. I'm not in love with her. Effie is my best friend. That's it. There is nothing else."

"B-but you love her."

"As a best friend, yes. But I'm not in love with her. I've never been in love with her," I say, a little more forcefully than I intended.

A noise a few feet away catches my attention, and I lift my head just in time to see Effie fleeing down the hallway.

"Shit," I hiss as I fully sit up. "Mom, I've got to go," I say as she babbles in my ear.

Cutting her off, I jump to my feet, abandoning my cell on my bed as I chase after Effie.

Her door is ajar, and I press my palm against it as I whisper her name.

I cringe at myself for talking to her like she's a cornered animal, but it doesn't stop me from inviting myself in.

"Kieran," she gasps, quickly gathering her towel back around herself.

"I'm sorry," I say, stepping farther into the room.

"For what? You haven't done anything wrong."

Combing my hair back, I watch her as she awkwardly pulls a pair of sleep shorts on under her towel.

My mouth opens and closes, but no words spill free.

"Thank you for the bath. It helped."

"It was my mom," I explain.

"It doesn't matter. Turn around, please," she demands before glaring at me over her shoulder.

Doing as I'm told, I spin on the balls of my feet.

She's already got her back to me; I can't see anything.

Rolling my eyes at her over-the-top reaction, movement to my left catches my eye.

The mirror on her vanity.

I should look away. I know I should.

But...I can't.

I also can't breathe properly as I stare at her.

My heart, though, is in overdrive.

She really is beautiful.

As soon as she tugs her tank into place, I rip my eyes away and stare at the cream wall ahead of me, trying to ignore the guilt that wants to swallow me whole for watching my best friend get dressed.

"Okay," she says, and I spin back to find her crawling into bed.

"She's already planned the whole thing," I explain.

"Who has?" she asks, clearly lost in her thoughts.

"My mom. She believed it and has spent the day planning everything."

"Oh," she breathes, a deep frown between her brows. "That's...weird."

"Yeah, well. You've met my mom, right?"

"Hmm," she mumbles, and she sinks lower into the covers.

"Shit, I was going to make you a hot chocolate."

"It's okay," she whispers before falling silent.

I don't know if she's fallen asleep or if she's pretending.

Either way, I stand there at the end of her bed, watching her like a creep.

Every other night I've been here, I've slept with her. But everything feels different today.

I glance at the door, trying to decide what to do.

Ultimately, I turn away from her and close her door to give her some space.

I make myself a drink before taking it to the guest room.

Finding a series on Netflix, I rest against the headboard and grab my cell.

I don't watch or hear anything from the TV. Instead, I lose myself in the gossip about me and Effie.

Somehow, people have managed to get hold of younger pictures of the two of us. They've even been to our old school and interviewed some of the teachers who apparently "fondly remember our special friendship" and just like Mom, thought it was only a matter of time before we took things to the next level.

The endless notifications continue. In the end, I turn them all off. I'm not interested in talking to anyone.

I look at the closed door more than once, wondering if I should go to her.

Is she asleep? Or is she lying there crying?

Does she need me, and I'm not there?

At some point, I must fall asleep, because I find myself waking up to a loud, agonizing scream.

I'm on my feet in a heartbeat and racing down the hallway.

Effie's door crashes back against the wall as I fly into her room. But I come to a very abrupt stop when I find her sitting in the middle of her bed with her cell in front of her and tears streaming down her face, dripping onto the sheets beneath her.

"Effie, what's—"

She looks up at me with tear-filled eyes, and my heart jumps into my throat.

Devastation and heartbreak are written all over her face.

I know what she will say long before she opens her mouth.

"She's gone," she whispers so quietly I barely hear it, even in the silence.

"Effie," I breathe, immediately crawling onto her bed and wrapping her in my arms.

11

EFFIE

Pain explodes through my body; I swear, I feel it all the way down to my toes. But nowhere as agonizing as in my heart. Sobs rack my body, and I fight to suck in breaths as everything shuts down.

I knew this was going to happen. I thought I was prepared for it.

Turns out, it's impossible to be prepared for something that shatters the foundations you've built your entire life on, however inevitable it is.

Kieren's deep voice rumbles, but I'm unable to register what he's saying. Blood is rushing past my ears so fast, stopping me from focusing on anything but my own devastating thoughts.

His arms are locked like a vise around me. It's like he's holding me together. To be fair, he very well might be.

Everything is falling apart, including me.

Eventually, my sobs lessen, but the agony never leaves.

My eyes burn from the tears, and my throat hurts from crying, but at no point does he even attempt to release me.

All I can think about is the fact that Grams was alone.

I promised that I'd be there throughout this whole journey. Okay, so I didn't specifically say that to her face, but I had every intention of doing so.

She's been with me, supporting me, throughout everything I've ever been through. I owed it to her to do the same.

Keiran's arms loosen, making my heart jump into my throat, and my eyes fill with tears again at the thought of him releasing me.

I have no idea if he senses it or if he never intended to let go, but instead, his large, warm hand begins gently moving up and down my back.

"I'm so sorry, Effie. I'm so fucking sorry."

As much as I appreciate his support, the words don't really mean anything.

None of this is his fault. There was also nothing he could do to prevent it.

I let out a shaky breath, but it does little to calm the riot of emotions raging within me.

"Tell me what you need," he whispers. "I'll do it. Whatever you need."

The room falls silent around us as I try to get my brain to function, but there is only one thing I need right now.

"I need to go there. I-I n-need to—"

"Okay," he agrees before I've even been able to tell him. "You get dressed, and I'll go and grab my sneakers."

"No," I cry the second he lets go of me and begins to climb from the bed. "Don't leave me."

My bottom lip trembles. I fight to stop it, but I have no control.

Stepping forward so his shins hit my bed, he reaches down and takes my face in his hands.

Both of his thumbs wipe away the tears I wasn't aware were still falling as he stares into my eyes.

He feels my pain; I can see it in his dark depths.

I also know that if he could, he'd take it away from me.

If only that were possible.

"You need pants and a hoodie, Eff," he tells me.

"B-bottom drawer," I stutter as I point at my chest of drawers. "Hoodie on the chair."

He nods once before lowering his lips to my forehead and pressing a sweet kiss on my skin.

I squeeze my eyes closed to try to stop the onslaught of more tears, but it's pointless. There is no controlling them.

"I know it hurts, Effie. But it'll get easier. I promise."

How? How is it ever going to get easier?

I've just lost the only parent I've ever had. Sure, she was my grandmother, but she was everything. She was my person.

"I'm right here, and I'm not leaving. I'll be by your side for everything, okay? Lean on me; it's what I'm here for."

I nod, unable to force out any words through the gigantic lump in my throat.

He waits for another two seconds before releasing me and walking over to my bottom drawer. He pulls out a pair of grey sweatpants before swiping his old hoodie from my chair and returning.

Deciding that I'm not capable of doing anything, he takes my hands and pulls me to stand.

I've always felt tiny compared to him—I mean, I am tiny; there is well over a foot between us—but I've never felt it as viscerally as I do in this moment.

"Okay?" he asks as if he's waiting for me to do something, but I just stand there immobile.

He lets out a sigh, his warm breath rushing over my face and making the hairs on the back of my neck lift as a shiver runs down my spine.

Dropping to his haunches, he tugs my sleep shorts down

my legs before tapping one ankle and then the other to free the fabric before replacing them with my sweatpants.

Usually, I'd be self-conscious about my huge, unsexy cotton panties, but right now, I couldn't care less.

In seconds, he has the waistband in place and is gently tugging the hoodie over my head and letting it fall almost to my knees.

He finds my sliders—not what I would usually choose to pair with this outfit—and then takes my hand and pulls me along.

Numbly, I follow behind him as he walks toward his room.

He leaves me in the doorway, and a memory of only a few hours ago niggles at the back of my mind.

"As a best friend, yes. But I'm not in love with her. I've never been in love with her."

I don't know why the words stung as much as they did. I know they're true. But still...

I watch as he zips up his hoodie and shoves his feet into his sneakers, then he tucks me under his arm and ushers me out into the cold, dark night.

Silence fills the car, but I don't have it in me to break it.

Distraction seems like it would be a good idea, but just the thought of focusing on something other than Grams right now feels wrong.

When Kieran signals to turn off the freeway that will take us to the care home, I don't question him.

I trust that he knows what he's doing.

Less than two minutes later, the lights for a twenty-four-seven drive-thru Starbucks come into view, and my stomach knots.

There's no way I can handle anything right now.

He turns in and lowers his window.

He doesn't ask what I want; instead, he rattles off an order that includes all my favorites.

I love him so much in that moment, even if I don't want any of the things he's about to pay for.

With everything loaded on the center console, he continues toward where I need to be.

"Please, Effie. At least drink some water," he says, holding out a bottle for me.

Absently, I take it and twist the top, but as soon as I take a sip, my stomach turns over, and I lower it back down.

Blowing out a long sigh, I rest my head back and lift my feet to the seat so I can curl up in a ball.

Kieran reaches over and entwines his fingers with mine, silently supporting me and reminding me that he's right beside me, just like he promised.

After what I did, I wouldn't be able to argue if he turned his back on me and returned to Chicago.

I hurt him. I hurt him badly.

And it wasn't just a simple lie, either. I mean, it was when only Grams and I knew.

But it's out in the open now. The whole world knows about our "engagement," and they all want to know more.

I didn't unlock my cell once yesterday. I couldn't.

Of course, no one knows who I am; my socials are locked down as best I can, but I still exist, and I have no doubt the press and the fans have found me. I can only imagine the kind of comments and messages I've received.

Another sigh passes my lips as I slump lower in the seat. I'm so numb; it's almost possible to forget what we're about to go and do.

The moment the care home sign comes into view, though, everything comes crashing back.

She's gone.

A sob erupts as Kieran takes the turn that will lead us to the parking lot and the very last time I'm going to see Grams.

By the time he pulls the car to a stop, I'm trembling violently.

Kieran kills the engine and turns to me, his brows pulled together in concern.

"You don't have to do this," he says softly.

Licking my lips, the salty taste of my tears floods my mouth.

"I know," I whisper, my voice cracked and barely audible. "But I want to. I need to say g-goodb-bye."

He blows out a breath before nodding.

"Okay. But the second you want to leave, tell me."

I nod, unable to say another word as my chest tightens to the point I can barely suck in a breath.

My eyes track Kieran as he walks around the hood of the car before he opens my door and helps me out.

Together, we walk toward the doors, but as soon as we step inside, my legs freeze when reality hits even harder.

Knowing I need more than just his hand in mine, Kieran stands in front of me and takes my face.

"I'm right here, Effie. You're not doing this alone."

'I know,' I mouth before sucking in a deep breath and taking another step.

Tucked into his side, we walk toward Grams' room.

Laura, her main nurse, spots us from her station and rushes over with a morose expression on her face.

Kieran's grip on me tightens, but I don't have the brain power to figure out why.

The staff here deal with loss on a weekly basis, I'm sure. I have no idea how they do it.

Their patients might not be their relatives, but losing them, especially those who've been here for a significant amount of time, must hurt. I don't know how I could keep going through that.

"Effie, I'm so sorry for your loss," she says without breaking eye contact with me. "Would you like to see her?"

I nod, and she instantly spins around and walks toward Grams' room.

"She's all ready for you. Take as much time as you need."

"Thank you," Kieran says curtly, following me inside when she holds the door open for us.

I've barely crossed the threshold when I stop dead.

I can't do this.

The warmth of Kieran's body sears into my back as his arms wrap around my waist and his chin rests on top of my head.

"You don't have to do anything you don't want to," he says softly. "No one has any expectations of you right now."

His words mean everything to me, and they give me the strength to keep moving forward.

He releases me but stays just a step behind as I walk deeper into the room.

My breath catches, and the tears that were trapped in my lashes spill over at the sight of Grams lying in bed.

She looks like she has every other time she's been sleeping.

Peaceful.

My heart clenches painfully, but a little bit of relief also trickles through my veins.

She's no longer fighting, no longer suffering.

She's at peace.

It's all I've ever wanted for her.

But also...I miss her.

My entire body trembles as the grief tightens around my chest, making it almost impossible to breathe.

I don't move. I can't. I'm frozen as I stare at her.

All the medical equipment has been removed, and the room just looks... like a room now.

The only clue that it's a medical facility is the bed, but I can see past that.

My lips part with my need to say something, but for long, painful seconds, nothing happens.

When I find my voice, it's so quiet I barely hear it.

"Hi Grams."

12

KIERAN

It took everything I had not to break down as Effie said her final goodbye to Grams. My eyes were full of tears, my own grief ripping at my insides.

Losing my own grandparents didn't leave an impact on me, but losing Grams will.

But as much as it hurts, I need to be strong for Effie. She needs me to be her rock.

I know death is inevitable. It's going to be a part of everyone's life at some point. But fuck...it's devastating and life-changing. No, life-destroying.

Effie will get through this. But it's going to impact the rest of her life.

We stayed at the care home with Grams for almost an hour before she decided that she'd said everything she needed to.

Thankfully, Laura kept her distance. I'm not sure if that's because of her guilt or the look I gave her earlier, or a little of both.

Whatever the reason, I'll happily never see her again.

I don't care about the lies, but the way she's used Effie and Grams for her own gain is something I really fucking care about. And one way or another, I'm going to make sure she knows exactly how much I dislike it.

It may not happen today, or even next week, but she will learn a very important lesson over this.

Effie is one of the most important people in my life, and you do not mess with my family. Ever.

The drive back home was as quiet as the journey there. A couple of times, I thought Effie had fallen asleep, but every time I glanced over, I found her staring out of the window blankly.

As soon as we stepped into Grams' house, she slipped her sliders off and headed straight for her bedroom.

I made a pit stop by the kitchen for the hot chocolate I failed to make for her earlier and then joined her under the covers.

She may not have invited me, but right now, words are not necessary.

"Please," I beg as I pass the mug toward her.

She hasn't had anything since the sip of water in the car. I understand that she doesn't want anything right now, but I won't take no for an answer.

Her eyes find mine, and her lips part to argue, but whatever she finds stops her from saying the words teetering on the tip of her tongue.

"Thank you," she finally whispers, taking the mug and holding it close.

Side by side, we sit silently, sipping on our drinks.

There's so much that needs saying, but also, there aren't enough words in the world to capture what we're both going through right now.

As soon as she's had enough, which thankfully is more than I was expecting, she places her mug on the nightstand and slides lower in the bed, pulling the covers up to her chin.

A few seconds later, I follow suit and lie in front of her.

Her eyes are open, but they're not focused. She's too lost in her grief.

Unable to do anything else, I reach out, wrap my arm around her waist, and tug her closer.

If the only thing I can do right now is to make her feel safe and protected, then I'll take it.

She whimpers as I hold her tighter, her nose only an inch from mine.

"I've got you," I whisper. "Get some sleep. I'll still be here when you wake up. I promise."

It takes a long time for her eyelids to lower, but when they do, it only takes seconds for her breathing to get heavier and for her body to relax against mine.

I, however, don't manage to drift off for the longest time as I run through the endless things she's going to have to deal with in the coming days.

I wouldn't wish it on my worst enemy, let alone my best friend.

My body is heavy, my limbs still fully asleep, but something wakes me, and when my eyelids lift, I discover why.

Effie is sobbing right next to me.

She's doing it silently with her back to me so I can't see the tears, but the way her body trembles is a dead giveaway.

Just like last night, I reach out and pull her tiny body into mine. Locking one arm around her waist, I slide the other beneath her and wrap it around her shoulders before pulling my knees up so I'm spooning her.

Wrapping her arms around mine, she clings to me as she cries.

I hate this. I fucking hate that she's hurting and all I can do is hold her.

But as much as I hate it, I'll do it for as long as she needs me to.

Eventually, her sobs subside and she sucks in a ragged breath before wiping her eyes and whispering, "You're still here."

"Of course. I promised I would be."

"I know, but you get up early."

"Not today. My girl needs me."

Her breath catches and she spins in my arms so she's facing me.

Her eyes are red and puffy. They look sore as hell, and the dark bruising beneath them lets me know just how little sleep she actually got.

She smiles, although it's forced.

"I'm not ready for today," she confesses quietly.

My knee-jerk reaction is to say that it'll be okay, but I'd be lying. There is going to be nothing okay about today.

Staff at the care home offered to call Effie's father to let him know, but Effie refused. I thought they should do it to save her the dual pain of saying the words out loud and having to talk to her father.

The man is an asshole, and I'd happily never see him again in my life.

But I also understand Effie's desire to do it herself.

"I'll be right beside you. We'll do it together."

Her hand lands on my forearm, and she squeezes in a silent thank you. The—fake—diamond in her ring catches the light, and my eyes focus on it.

It's on her right hand, but I know for a fact she was wearing it on the other one before I arrived. Grams would have noticed otherwise.

"I guess I can take this off, now."

Her words make me suck in a sharp breath, and my eyes jump to her.

I shouldn't care about her putting an end to the lie. I should be relieved that we can go back to normal. Not that anything has really been normal since I arrived in St. Louis.

I want to say that it's the thought of having to deal with all the media attention that's still rampant outside of our little bubble here, but honestly, I think it's more than that.

There's something reassuring in knowing that we're connected on a deeper level while she's going through this.

Fucked up? Maybe.

But I want to be by her side, and I want people to know she has someone in her life.

Her face will have been all over the internet this week, and now that she's grieving, she'll be a prime target for the scumbags out there who think they can prey on a woman while she's weak.

Yeah...that is not fucking happening.

I promised to protect her, and I will in any way I can.

"No," I state, a little harsher than I intended. The thought of her being used as a pawn in some money grabber's game has anger and fear surging through my veins.

Reaching out, I pinch the ring between my thumb and forefinger and slide it from her hand.

"What are you doing?" she asks weakly as I lift the covers, searching for her other hand.

"I need the other one," I state as if it's obvious.

Her brows pinch, but she raises her left hand from the cover, her eyes holding mine as I slide the ring back into place.

"W-what are you doing?" she whispers, her eyes wide as she stares at her finger.

Reaching out, I tuck my fingers under her chin, forcing her to look back at me.

"The next week is going to be hard," I explain—not that I

need to; she's more than aware of what's ahead of her. "Everyone out there thinks we're engaged, and correct me if I'm wrong, but I'm not sure either of us is going to have the time or energy to try and convince the world otherwise.

"We need to be focusing on Grams and giving her the send-off she deserves, not arguing with everyone about our upcoming nuptials."

"B-but—"

"I'm going to be standing right by your side through all this. We'll never convince them, Effie. It's pointless trying. We have time to figure it all out. It's not important right now."

"But everyone thinks you're engaged. Surely you're not happy about that."

I shrug the shoulder I'm not lying on.

"You, Effie Campbell, are more important than what everyone out there thinks of me."

Leaning forward, I press a quick kiss to the tip of her nose.

"And right now, you need coffee and food," I announce before throwing the covers off and rolling out of bed.

I keep my back to her as I sink my hand into my sweats to rearrange my morning semi before taking off across the room.

"I'm not hungry," she whispers predictably.

"That's okay. It'll take us a while to bake the cinnamon buns anyway," I shoot over my shoulder as I leave the room.

I'm sure she wants to argue, but I don't hear anything as I make my way to the bathroom.

By the time I emerge again, there's movement in her room. I pause at the doorway to find her sitting at her vanity and staring blankly at a photograph of her and Grams when she was a child.

"I'll be right there," she says, her eyes lifting to the mirror so she can see me.

"Whenever you're ready. No rush."

She nods. "There are things I need to do."

With a nod, I duck around the corner and head toward the kitchen.

I might want to be beside her every second of the day, but the reality is that she needs some time alone to try and figure all this out.

Hopefully, once everything here is finalized, she'll move back to Chicago. But even if she does that, she has her own life, her own apartment. There are going to be plenty of times when I'm not there, especially once the season starts again.

Questions about how we're going to handle the next few weeks spin around my mind, but I don't have answers for any of them.

If we don't immediately deny the rumors, we're as good as confirming them. But right now, that feels easier than fighting when we should be grieving.

With a loud sigh, I move toward the coffee machine and turn it on before pulling out the ingredients I've become all too familiar with since arriving here.

I can make these buns without the recipe now, and even better than that, I can't remember the last time I burned one. Grams would be so proud.

Not as proud as I know Effie will make her in the next couple of weeks. I do not doubt that her granddaughter is going to give her a send-off full of love and happy memories.

13

EFFIE

My heart is racing and my hand trembles as I lift my cell to my ear and wait.

I hate calling my parents. But it's definitely preferential to seeing them. That's a whole level of hell I don't need in my life.

My body locks up as the first ring pierces through my ear. Kieran hears it too, because his hands tighten around my free one.

One of the nurses at the care home offered to make the call for me. Kieran did as well only minutes ago. But this is something I need to do.

I don't know why; it's going to cause me even more pain, but I'm doing it anyway.

It rings and rings, and I start to think that I've psyched myself up for this conversation for no reason when it finally connects.

There's a part of me that expects the soft voice of his assistant to fill the line. It wouldn't be the first time he's pawned me off on her, and I'm sure it won't be the last. But to my surprise, Dad's voice hits my ear.

"I've got a meeting in two minutes," is his greeting.

My teeth grind with irritation as disappointment floods through me. I don't know why I bother to hope that each time will be different. A deep growl rumbles in Kieran's throat. I know his face is going to be tight with anger, but I can't look at him for fear I'll burst into tears again.

Be strong, Effie. You can do this.

"O-kay, well...I was just ringing to tell you that Grams p-passed in the n-night."

Letting the words flow past my lips is akin to pulling my fingernails off. But I'm proud that I managed it with only a few emotional stutters.

"Thank you for letting me know. I'll instruct Sharon to make the necessary arrangements."

My chin drops at his coldness. It was to be expected, but still, I'm shocked.

Straightening my spine, I roll my shoulders back, ready to do something I've never done in my life.

Stand up for myself.

Or maybe for Grams; I'm not sure.

"No," I force out. Surging to my feet, my hand slips from between Kieran's and I begin pacing. "Sharon isn't planning Grams' funeral. She never met her. You don't even know what she wants, so there's no chance Sharon will."

There is nothing but silence down the line.

Good. I hope I've knocked him on his ass.

"I'll be planning Grams' funeral," I state, leaving no room for argument.

"Fine," Dad says. "Just send me the invoices."

The laugh that erupts from me doesn't sound like my own.

"That won't be necessary. I'll just send you the date. Enjoy your meeting."

Both my hands are trembling violently as I lower my cell and hang up.

My chest is so tight I can barely breathe.

But I did it.

I stood up to my father, and for once in my life, I didn't let him steamroll over me with his own bullshit.

"Effie," Kieran breathes, moving closer to where I've stopped in the middle of the room. "I'm so fucking proud of you," he says, engulfing my small frame in a hug.

I suck in a deep, steeling breath as I replay the events of that short phone call in my mind.

"He was going to have Sharon plan it," I whisper in utter disbelief.

I had every suspicion that he'd just throw money at it and make it go away. But to pass the entire thing off to his assistant...

"I know," Kieran whispers. "You did so good, though. Grams would be so proud of you."

I can't help but smile. It feels alien after the last few hours of complete misery.

"She'd want me to do this for her."

"Absolutely. You're doing the right thing."

I give myself a few minutes to allow the adrenaline from that phone call to lessen, then I tap in the number of Grams' lawyer and lower myself back to the couch.

"What do you mean, she's planned it all?" I balk after the person I'm talking to has pulled up Grams' files.

"It's all here. Everything she wants. Her casket, her flowers, the songs, and readings. It's all been paid for."

My mouth opens and closes like a fish as I try to process what I'm hearing.

"All you need to do is arrange the date and let family and friends know," she continues.

"Wow," I finally breathe. "When?"

"A year ago."

That was before her health really declined.

She knew.

She knew what was coming, and she did this.

She did this for me.

Tears burn my eyes, and my nose itches with emotion.

Shaking my head, I fight to find something to say.

"We also have her will here," the lady on the phone informs me softly.

"O-okay."

"Would you like to book an appointment for it to be read?"

"Umm...yeah, I guess."

Honestly, Grams' will has been the last thing on my mind.

"Shouldn't my father be there for that?" I ask. Technically, he's her next of kin, not me.

"Effie, your grandmother made her wishes very clear. If you'd like your father to attend with you, then that is your choice, but there is no need for him to be here. Just you."

My heart rate picks up.

Grams, what have you done?

After agreeing on a time, I finally hang up the phone after she's promised to email me with all of Grams' wishes.

"Is everything okay?" Kieran asks, not able to hear the details of that call as easily as the one with my father's booming voice.

"She did it all," I say in disbelief. "Planned it, paid for it, everything."

Kieran shakes his head, a small smile playing on his lips.

"Of course she did. I don't know why we didn't see that coming."

"Yeah," I agree. It really is a Grams' thing to do."

"Are you okay?" he asks.

I nod, although it's not the real answer. I'm not okay, I'm not sure I ever will be again, but I feel better now I've gotten through speaking to Dad, and having Grams lift the weight of planning everything myself sure helps.

"Are the buns ready to eat?" I ask, knowing it'll make him happy. I'm not hungry, but he's right; I need something.

His smile grows. "Yes. Stay right there," he says, pointing to my place on the couch before rushing out of the room.

I listen as he crashes around in the kitchen, taking in my surroundings.

This place has been home to me for so long. I'm not sure how I'm ever going to get it ready to sell. How am I going to decide what to keep and what to get rid of?

Her entire life is under this roof. How do you just dispose of that?

W e spend the rest of the day sitting on the couch and reminiscing about old times with Grams. It's nice, even if it makes my chest ache more than I thought possible.

As the sun begins to set, Kieran announces that we should go for a walk to get some fresh air.

The thought of leaving the house and facing the real world terrifies me, but I know he's right.

After getting dressed, we head out. It's a warm evening with the sun casting a soft orange glow on the city Grams loved.

Kieran takes my hand, and together we embark on a walk we've done many, many times before.

I know his plan long before the bakery comes into sight. I know him and his scheming ways too well.

"Dinner?" he asks as we approach.

"Sure," I agree, smiling up at him, letting him know that I can see through him.

He shakes his head before pulling me inside.

"What do you want?" he asks, his eyes scanning the homemade subs like they're the best things he's ever seen.

"Whatever. You pick." I might know him well enough to predict his thoughts, but it goes both ways. He knows what I like, and I trust his choice.

I stand to the side as he orders, and only a minute later, we're walking out with takeout coffees in hand and subs in a paper bag.

We keep walking. It might appear aimlessly to many, but I know exactly where we're going.

The thought of what we're about to do makes my heart begin to race, but it's nowhere near enough to stop him.

We approach the park just like we did many times as kids.

The gates are locked every night at eight o'clock sharp. They have been for years. It's to stop kids from getting in and trashing the place. And it works, for the most part.

This park at night has always been mine and Kieran's place.

I'm pretty sure we were fifteen when Kieran first came to stay with Grams and we scaled the fence after dark. We've been nighttime visitors ever since.

We follow the fence around the perimeter until we get to the spot that allows us to break in.

Just like always, my palms sweat, and my anxiety spikes.

I've never done anything wrong or broken the law in my life. This is the extent of it, and every time we do it, I'm terrified someone is going to catch us.

Kieran laughs at me as he throws our sandwiches over the railing.

"Ready?" he asks, holding his arms out to help give me a boost.

"Aren't we too old for this now?" I ask hesitantly.

"Never. We'll still be doing this in our sixties," he says confidently.

"Is that a promise?" I tease as I turn my back on him so he can lift me.

His large hands wrap around my waist, and not a second later, my feet leave the floor.

He's always lifted me as if I'm as light as a feather. Maybe that was true when I was fifteen, but I've gained a few curves since then.

"Got it?" he asks as my fingers curl around the top of the railing.

"No," I cry, suddenly even more terrified that I'm going to break a leg.

He chuckles before shifting his hands.

I let out a shriek so loud a couple of birds take flight out of the closest tree, scaring me even more.

"Kieran," I cry when his hands land on my ass.

"Just pull yourself over before I throw you," he warns lightly.

"You wouldn't."

"Do you want to find out?"

Rolling my eyes, I make the most of the added height advantage and throw my leg over.

I pray that I'm going to survive this with all my limbs intact. My other leg follows the first, and I jump.

I cry out as I land awkwardly, my ankle rolling painfully causing me to crash to the ground in a heap.

"Oh shit," Kieran grunts. I don't look up to see how easily he jumps the railing; it's just not necessary.

I do see the moment he drops to his knees before me, concern written across his face.

"Are you okay?"

"Twisted my ankle," I say sadly, pushing myself up so I'm sitting.

"Can't take you anywhere," he mutters before falling to his ass and lifting my foot from the ground.

He pushes my sweatpants up my calf before I can stop him.

"Ow," I complain as his fingers begin massaging my ankle in the most incredible way.

He hits one particular spot, and I can't help myself, a filthy moan spills from my lips. It's not a sound I've heard myself make in a very, very long time.

His fingers still, and my cheeks burn.

"I think it's okay now," I say in a rush as I pull my foot from his lap and gingerly get to my feet. "Shall we go?"

We walk toward our favorite place in the park in silence, her moan on repeat in my ears.

It was...

I close my eyes for a beat, trying to force the thoughts away.

I'm meant to be looking after Effie right now, not having these wild ideas about what it might have been like to keep going, to work my way up her leg and—

"Here we are," she says.

My feet stop moving of their own accord, and when I look up, I find she's right.

It took us quite a bit of time to find this place, but it's perfect.

Quiet and secluded.

Even if someone saw us jumping over the closed fence, there's only a slim chance they'd find us here.

Effie lowers herself to the leaf-covered ground. She doesn't care that she might get a little muddy, or that there are bugs down there. Effie isn't like any of the women I spend time with. She doesn't care if her makeup is on point or not, or if the dress or shoes she's wearing are designer. There is no fakeness or pretense; she's always just one hundred perfect herself. I love it, and I wish there were more people like her.

"Are you joining me or..." Effie trails off as she gazes up at me.

The sight of her puffy eyes is exactly what I need to drag me back to reality.

"Of course," I say as I drop to the ground. "Hungry?"

She wants to say no, I can hear the refusal dancing on the tip of her tongue, but she fights it.

"Yeah," she muses, making me smile.

Pulling her sub from the bag, I pass it over and watch as she unwraps it.

After a few seconds, I drag my eyes away and do the same. The only difference is that I instantly devour mine like I haven't eaten for a month, not just a few hours, while she nibbles at hers.

Once I'm done, I ball up the paper bag and lie back on the leaves.

It's dark, and the trees above us almost completely cover the sky, but every now and then, the wind blows, revealing some stars.

There's nothing but silence between us, and while I might still be feeling weird about that little moment between us earlier, it's not uncomfortable.

I replay the events of the day, thinking about the vast differences in the reactions of everyone she spoke to.

Her father being the worst of them.

Anger pulses through my veins as I think of his dismissive tone.

If I ever get the chance to become a father, there is no way on Earth I would ever speak to my child like that. Hell, I wouldn't even speak to someone else's child like that.

I give Prince more respect, and he's just a baby.

But then there were Grams' friends and neighbors. All of

them were so sweet and supportive of Effie, offering to help in any way they could.

That's what it should be like. In hard times like this, people should come together. I know it took me longer than it should have to get here. But I'm here, and I'm not going anywhere. And I'm hoping that when I do, Effie will be coming with me to return to her life in Chicago.

As much as I'd like to think that she'll be able to walk away from all this after the funeral, I'm not sure it's very realistic. Her heart is here in St. Louis right now, and it's broken beyond belief.

She needs to figure out how to put it back together before considering returning to work.

She's barely finished a quarter of her sub when she wraps it back up and puts it in the bag.

With a sigh I feel all the way down to my toes, she lies back with me.

"I know that losing someone is meant to hurt. But this...I never thought it would be like this," she confesses quietly. "I've never felt anything like it. It's...excruciating."

I don't respond. How can I? Everything I could say to that would sound patronizing. As much as I can sympathize with her, I don't really know what she's feeling right now.

All I can do is just be here.

So that is what I do.

Reaching out, I find her hand and hold it tight.

She releases a shaky breath, and I roll onto my side to see her.

Silent tears fall from her eyes.

My chest tightens, my own emotion clogging my throat.

We stay like that for the longest time with the cool evening air blowing lightly around us.

"Do you think what they say about stars is true?" she suddenly asks, her cracked voice startling me.

"W-what do they say about stars?"

"That those..." She sucks in a breath, trying not to break down again. "That those who leave us are up there, watching."

"She'll always be with you. Whether she's up in a star or haunting you as a ghost and judging your cooking."

A smile pulls at her lips, and I give myself a mental high-five.

"She'd make a great ghost," she says lightly. "Spying on everyone. Learning all their secrets. She'd finally find out if the couple at the end of the street are swingers."

"What?" I blurt.

"Oh," she laughs. "They moved in a couple of years ago, and apparently, they have a lot of guests. Grams put two and two together and—"

"Probably came up with twelve?" I ask.

"Probably. For someone who claimed not to be nosey like all the others, she sure did see a lot."

"Explains where you get it from," I tease.

"What?" She gasps.

"Oh, come off it. How long have you been trying to figure out if the two guys in your building are fucking?"

Finally, she turns to look at me.

"They totally are. I've never seen either with a woman."

"Must be gay then," I mock. "Can't be any other explanation."

She laughs, and my smile grows.

"You're a nightmare."

"I'll be anything that makes you smile like that, Lucky."

"Kieran," she teases, but before she can say anything else, I jump to my feet.

"Come on," I say, holding out my hand.

"We're leaving?" she asks, her face dropping.

"Not yet. Trust me?"

She pushes herself up so she's sitting and shakes her head.

109

"Too much," she laughs, holding her hand out so I can pull her to her feet.

"You love it," I say before swiping the bag with her remaining sub from the ground and then taking off, dragging her along behind me.

"Kieran," she squeals as she tries to keep up with me. "What are we—"

I come to an abrupt halt, and she crashes into my back.

Stepping around me, she looks up to see where I've brought her.

"Uh..."

Taking off again, we climb the steps to the bandstand, and once we're in the middle, I tug her into my body.

"Kieran," she whispers, staring up at me with tear-filled eyes.

Pulling my cell from my pocket, I find the song I want before turning it up.

Effie's breath catches the second she hears the opening beats.

She shakes her head in disbelief. "What are you doing?" Her voice is so quiet I barely hear it over the music.

"Dance with me."

Sliding one arm around her back, I lift the other into the air, still holding her hand.

I start moving, but she doesn't immediately fall into step with me.

Instead, she laughs. It's emotional and full of pain, but there's also so much joy and happy memories in there.

The song is the one Grams and her late gramps chose for their first dance. And our moves... they're ones we learned when Grams taught us all those years ago.

Leaning closer, I whisper in her ear, "If she's looking down at us, then don't miss a step."

She laughs harder, but she finally begins moving.

She smiles up at me, her joy and sadness colliding. But that smile gives me hope that her pain will subside. It won't be today or tomorrow, or even next week. But she'll get through it.

"I'm sorry about what you overheard on the phone last night," I say, the memory of what I snapped at Mom coming back to me.

Effie sighs and looks down at my chest.

"It was nothing. No need to apologize for anything."

"It hurt you; there is everything to apologize for."

Leaning forward, she rests her head against my chest.

"I'm an emotional mess, Kieran. That's on me, not you. You did nothing wrong. I know you're not in love with me."

Releasing her hand, I wrap my arms around her.

"My mom was freaking out about what color hat she needs to buy," I confess. "Anyone would think she hasn't lived her life surrounded by lies in the media."

"Well, it's humbling to know she approves of me."

"As if you didn't already know that. She loves you like a daughter."

Effie spills a bitter laugh, and I know exactly why, but neither of us says it. The less time and effort we give to her parents, the better.

The song ends and quickly transitions to another, but we don't stop moving.

"Effie?" I say after long, silent minutes.

"Yeah," she whispers.

"You're going to get through this. I know life will never be the same again, but you'll find a new normal and things will get easier."

Pulling her head away from my chest, she looks up at me with a sad smile.

"I know," she breathes, although she doesn't sound very confident. "Thank you for today. After what I did, I know I don't deserve—"

Releasing her, I press two fingers to her lips, stopping her from saying anything more.

I've already told her that I understand, and any hurt I felt after discovering her lie has now been overshadowed by something far more serious.

"Forget about it. Right now, we focus on Grams. Then we'll deal with the fallout of that."

"But..." She begins to argue, lifting her hand with her ring back in place.

"One day at a time," I say, bringing her hand to my lips and kissing where her ring sits.

The move comes so naturally that I don't even realize I'm doing it until my eyes meet hers.

I swear I stop breathing.

"Kieran," she whispers before a loud bang echoes around us, forcing her to jump back. "What was that?" she asks in a rush, looking around as if someone is about to jump out with a gun and arrest us for breaking into the park.

I look up into the distance and wince when I see dark clouds engulfing the stars we were staring at not so long ago.

Thunder rumbles again, only louder this time.

"I think it's time to go home," I say, turning the music off and collecting the bag.

"Yeah," Effie muses, following me as I descend the steps of the bandstand.

The wind blows cooler, and the rumbles get closer and faster.

The first crack of lightning illuminates the park just before we get to the gates.

"We're going to get soaked," Effie points out as the light from the almost full moon is engulfed by the storm clouds.

"It wouldn't be the first time," I point out, thinking of more than a few occasions when we've been caught out before, both here while visiting Grams and at school when we snuck out after curfew.

Effie was such a good student. I hate to admit it, but I think I was a bad influence on her.

The first raindrops hit the ground as we approach the fence.

"I can't believe I've got to do this again," Effie complains as she glares up at the top.

I guess it does look a hell of a lot more scary when you're so small.

"Come on, we've got this," I say, holding my arms out to help her up.

She huffs, but there's a smile playing on her lips.

She loves it really, being wild and doing things that no one would expect from her.

With my hands around her waist, I lift her from the ground and sit her on my shoulder.

"Ready?" I ask.

"Nope." But that doesn't stop her from reaching for the fence. "Kieran," she shrieks when my hands slide to her ass.

"What? I'm just helping," I say innocently.

"Just because everyone thinks we're getting married, it doesn't give you a free pass, you know," she teases.

15

EFFIE

My lungs scream and my legs ache as I try to keep up with Kieran as he runs down the sidewalk.

Each raindrop hits the ground with a splash. It's torrential, and we're both soaked through.

He's nowhere close to moving at full speed, but even still, I can't keep up.

Spinning around, he smirks at me.

"Shut up," I pant.

"Didn't say a word," he says innocently.

As I roll my eyes, the world around us lights up with another crack of lightning, closely followed by booming thunder.

We really need to move, but I'm not sure my legs can take it.

"Go without me," I say, sounding way more dramatic than necessary.

A violent shiver races down my spine and my teeth begin to chatter.

"You think I'm going to leave you here alone?" Kieran asks in disbelief.

I already know he's not, but I'm slowing him down.

Reaching up, I try to drag my hair back from my face, but it's soaked and sticking to my skin, just like my clothes.

He does the same, but because he's Kieran freaking Callahan, he looks like a god as he drags his fingers through his soaked hair. His muscles ripple beneath his skintight, long-sleeved t-shirt.

Water runs down his face and drips from his chiseled jaw. He looks like he should be on some TV commercial right now, whereas I look like a drowned rat.

Suddenly, he moves forward, and before I know what's happening my feet have left the ground and my ass is up in the air.

"Kieran," I scream as he takes off running again.

I bounce around upside down with his arm locked around the backs of my thighs.

My hoodie and shirt ride up, exposing my back to the ice-cold rain that's lashing at us.

My teeth chatter violently as rainwater runs toward my shoulders.

I attempt to wrap my arms around him, but I don't stand a chance. His body is too massive.

"I'm not going to drop you, Ef," he shouts back when I settle for twisting my fingers in his soaking wet shirt.

By the time he slows, all my blood has rushed to my head, making it feel like it's seconds away from exploding.

Glancing to the side, I discover that we're on Grams' street and I let out a sigh of relief.

"Holy crap," Kieran says after walking past his car and toward the front door. "Look," he says before putting me back on my feet.

The world spins around me, and thankfully, his hands don't leave my waist as everything settles.

When I see what caused his reaction, my breath catches.

115

We have bouquets of flowers, plants, and containers of all shapes and sizes in front of Grams' front door.

"What is all that?" I ask in confusion.

The flowers are self-explanatory, but the rest...

I stand there with my head still spinning while Kieran gathers it all up.

"Are you going to let us in?" he asks with his arms full.

I jump into action and pull the key from my pocket.

No sooner does he releases everything, than I begin pulling lids from containers.

Cookies. Cakes. A casserole.

I shake my head, unable to believe what I'm seeing.

I know that Grams had great friends and a support network. I've spent time with all of them at the care home over the last few months. They're always inviting me to dinner, or offering to cook for me, but I've never taken them up on the offer.

Sure, a few came to see Grams with goodies to share, but I never expected this.

With my hand covering my mouth, a sob breaks free.

Their kindness and generosity floor me. And I haven't even opened the cards that accompany the gifts.

I stand there shivering and staring at it all in shock.

"Effie, you need to go and shower," Kieran says, dragging me back to reality.

Another violent shiver rips through me, proving that he's right.

"Come on," he says, once again gathering me up and leading me toward the bathroom.

I'm aware of how much I'm leaning on him right now, but I can't help it. If it weren't for him, I'm not sure I'd be functioning at all.

He's giving me a reason to fight and to keep moving. I'll take everything he's offering me while he's here and willing.

At some point, he'll have to return to Chicago. I should probably go with him. It's where my life is. My job. My apartment. But right now, I can't imagine being anywhere but here.

He leaves me in the middle of the bathroom as he turns the shower on.

In only seconds, steam fills the room, and warmth rushes over my cold body.

"Can you take it from here?" he asks, ducking down to look into my eyes.

I hate to consider what he sees when he looks at me.

Unable to hold his stare, I look down at the floor and nod.

I might be broken, but surely, I'm capable of undressing myself.

"Call me if you need me," he says before kissing my brow and stepping out of the room.

I release the breath I didn't realize I was holding the second the door closes behind him.

Needing to get out of these wet clothes, I let out a shaky breath and embark on the challenge of stripping down.

It's harder than I thought possible, and I almost call Kieran back to help at one point. But I summon some strength from somewhere, finally abandoning everything in a soggy pile on the floor and stepping under the hot stream.

A blissful sigh falls from my lips, and I stand there unmoving as I soak up the warmth.

Spinning around, I close my eyes and tip my face toward the water.

Tonight was...I shake my head, unable to find a word that sums it up.

Painful. Beautiful.

Everything I needed.

Kieran is everything I need.

He seems to know exactly what will help, and tonight was it.

And dancing on the bandstand.

There is a photo on the mantlepiece of Grams and Gramps doing the exact same thing a few decades ago.

He made me feel so close to both of them tonight.

Tears fall as I think about their lives and how quickly their presence has been wiped from the world.

I manage to clean up, but I move slowly, enjoying the escape the shower provides me.

It's not until the water begins to run cold that I finally reach for the dial and shut it off.

With a huge fluffy towel wrapped around me, I make my way to my room to find some pajamas.

I'm dressed and sitting at my vanity, brushing my hair, when his footsteps move closer.

I look up just in time to see him fill my doorway with his massive frame.

My breath catches at the sight of him standing there in nothing but a pair of tight boxer briefs.

Holy hell.

My mouth runs dry and I fight to swallow.

"Finished in the bathroom?" he asks, as if he hasn't just knocked me on my ass.

It's not the first time I've seen him wearing barely anything. But it's been a few years since I've seen it this up close. It's usually on a screen on some advertising campaign.

Dragging my eyes up his body, I find a smirk playing on his lips.

Asshole did that on purpose.

"Y-yeah," I stutter like a teenage girl with a stupid crush.

He nods once and then disappears, leaving me with burning cheeks and a racing heart.

It was the same when he slid his hands to my ass earlier.

Something I haven't felt in a very long time shot through my body, leaving my nerves tingling and my blood heating.

The shower starts running thirty seconds later, and I shamelessly imagine him pushing his thumbs into his waistband of those tight boxers and letting them drop down his legs.

Do not think about anything else, Effie...

"Motherfucker," Kieran barks, and I gasp.

I didn't tell him there wasn't any hot water.

A cackle erupts as I think about him hopping around in ice-cold water.

It's evil, but I can't help it.

Forcing myself to move, I pad through to the kitchen in my fluffy socks, shorts, and zip-up hoodie.

Putting some milk in a pan to heat, I hop up onto a stool at the island and stare down at the pile of cards that accompanied the gifts Kieran brought in earlier.

They're all addressed to me. It's humbling to know how many lives Grams affected, and also how many people care enough to reach out, to send me their love and support.

I'm still trying to decide if I want to open them or not when Kieran appears in the kitchen, wearing a pair of sweats and a t-shirt.

I don't want to say I'm disappointed that he's covered up, but...I am a little.

"Good shower?" I ask, putting on my best innocent face.

"Hmm," he mumbles before walking toward the stove to check the milk. "Are you going to open those?" he asks, distracting me.

"I don't know," I confess, staring back down at them. "I really appreciate that people have sent them, but..." I sigh. "It's just another bit of evidence that she's really gone."

He turns back to me. My skin tingles with his attention, but I don't look up.

"Then don't. Wait until you're ready. There is no right and wrong right now."

"I know," I mumble as he makes our hot chocolate.

"What do you want to do?" he asks, bringing two steaming mugs over.

It's late now, but while I might be exhausted, I don't want to go to bed. I'll only lie there thinking.

I shrug. What is there to do?

"Movie?" he asks. "I'll let you choose."

"Sure," I say, slipping from the stool and walking out of the room.

We settle on the couch, and Kieran passes me the remote control.

"Oh, the power," I tease.

"Make sure you choose wisely," he mocks, knowing full well the kind of movie he's going to end up watching.

I don't need to search very far; Grams and I used to watch old romcoms whenever I visited, and they're all there in her recommended section.

Kieran groans as I scroll through, and I can't help but laugh.

"We can just watch ESPN if you want," I offer.

"Absolutely not," he states firmly.

"Okay then. Miss Congeniality it is," I say, pressing play on mine and Grams' most-watched movie. Grams used to fantasize about being a badass like Gracie Hart. She'd have made a great FBI agent.

"Wonderful."

"Careful, I know all of Gracie Hart's moves. I could take you down if necessary."

Kieran chuckles. "Is that right?"

"Yep. You wouldn't even see it coming."

"Now that I want to see."

"Shhh," I hiss. "It's starting."

He laughs again and wraps his arms around my shoulder, pulling me into his body.

Snuggling against him, I relax as I lose myself in Grams' favorite movie.

Tomorrow, I have a long list of things I need to do to ensure her final send-off is worthy of her, but right now, I'm going to reminisce on the good times with my best friend.

She may be gone, but her spirit will live on through us forever.

16

KIERAN

I spend the next three days following Effie around town as she meets with the funeral directors, the florist, and the reverend who is going to perform the service for Grams.

Every time we return home, there are more flowers, condolence cards, and food waiting for us.

I can't say that I'm disappointed, especially when it's cookies, but I know they make Effie feel weird. Of course, she appreciates them and all the gestures from those who cared about Grams. But she's struggling with the fact that people want to help her. I genuinely think she expected that everyone would forget she existed once Grams left us.

It's just another thing that shows what an awesome person she is.

The KC Foundation sent her a huge bouquet of flowers and a card expressing their condolences and how much they miss her in the office.

Out of all of the gifts, that was the one that affected her the most. I think it was because it was from people who know her, not just Grams' friends. A reminder that she has a life, a home outside of here.

"Ready for this?" I ask as I kill the engine outside the lawyer's office.

It's the second time we've been here this week. But today, we're hearing the will reading.

Effie blows out a long, calming breath as she focuses on the building before us.

"Yeah," she says, sounding a little more confident than she looks.

She's put makeup on today to cover up her reality, but I'm not sure it's possible to conceal the dark circles under her eyes.

She stays in the car, putting this off for as long as possible, as I round the front and open the door.

Taking her hand, I pull her out and we walk into the building together.

We're right on time, and no sooner has Effie said hello to the receptionist than Grams' lawyer emerges to invite us into the back room.

I sit awkwardly beside Effie, feeling completely out of place as the lawyer goes through the formalities of the reading.

"She's left everything to you, Effie," the lawyer says softly, clearly able to tell that my best friend's emotions are balancing on a knife's edge.

Effie doesn't react. She remains sitting ramrod straight in the chair, her eyes locked on the woman sitting behind the desk.

"Effie," I whisper, squeezing her hand to get her attention. "Did you—"

"Everything?" she whispers, proving that she was listening.

The woman nods. "Her estate is fully in order. One bank account with everything in it, and the house she owned. It's all yours."

"But my dad..."

"Not mentioned."

"Wow," Effie breathes, shaking her head in disbelief.

I wonder if she had any inkling this was likely to happen—she must have known. But thinking it and hearing it are two very different things.

The lawyer begins explaining the probate process and how everything works, but I don't hear most of it. I'm too focused on Effie.

Her tiny body trembles in the seat beside mine, and her eyes are full of unshed tears.

She doesn't need any of this money from Grams. She has more than enough from her parents, and from her own income, but something tells me that this means so much more to her any cent that's come from them.

Only a few minutes later, we say our goodbyes to the lawyer, who promises to contact us soon, and make our way out of the office.

Effie is in a daze as I guide her back to the car, and we sit there in silence for long minutes. But as much as I want to give her time and space to process all this, we can't sit here all day.

"Did you want to just go home?" I offer.

We'd made plans for this afternoon, but I understand if she no longer feels up for it.

She considers for a moment before tucking her loose hair behind her ear.

"No. We're going out for lunch, remember?"

"We don't have—"

"We do," she argues. "You've done so much for me recently. You deserve that steak."

"It's not important," I argue. I mean the words, but my stomach grumbles in complaint.

"Kieran...we're going for lunch, and then we're going shopping," she reminds me.

Grams explained in her funeral plan that she didn't want

anyone wearing dark and drab colors. She wants bright and colorful. She wants it to be a celebration, not a dreary occasion.

It didn't surprise me. Grams lived her whole life in color, and it's only fitting that we say goodbye in a similar way.

I found Effie standing at her closet not long after she got confirmation about Grams wishes for her send off. When I asked her what she was doing, she tearfully told me that she didn't have anything suitable to wear, so we're rectifying that this afternoon.

I smile at her. Most guys would probably hate the prospect of a shopping trip with a woman, but I'm not most guys. I enjoy trailing Effie and giving her my opinion on the things she picks up and tries on.

Only with Effie, though. I don't have the patience to do it with anyone else.

"Okay then," I say, starting the engine and backing out of the space.

I make my way across town toward the best steak house in St. Louis. It's my second-favorite place to eat.

"Good to see their portions haven't gotten smaller," Effie mocks when one of the biggest ribeyes I've ever seen is placed before me.

My stomach growls appreciatively as her slightly more modest filet is lowered to the table.

I watch her stare at it in horror. It's barely a quarter the size of mine, but it's probably more than she's eaten all week.

After checking if we need anything, our server leaves us to our food.

We both dive in, but only one of us eats like they've been starved.

Effie mostly pushes her meal around her plate, only eating a few mouthfuls.

While I might be concerned, I don't say anything. I know I'm driving her crazy, and I'm trying to lay off, but I hate seeing her like this.

"How are you feeling?" I ask, opting for just being upfront. On top of the recent revelation, her parents flight landed not so long ago, and I know she's already anxious about seeing them.

She shrugs. "I don't know. I guess I should have seen it coming. Maybe I did...I don't know," she rambles, focusing on the will reading.

"Your dad doesn't need or deserve any of it," I state firmly.

"No, I know that. But he'll expect—"

"Will he?" I argue, cutting her off.

"He's a chauvinistic man who thinks women are the lesser sex. Of course he will," Effie says, with more than a hint of bitterness.

"Well, fuck him. He's wrong. You're worth two of him, if not more. You deserve everything Grams has given you and then some."

"I don't need any of it."

"That's not the point. She wants you to have it because she loves and appreciates you."

"I work for my money. Or at least, I did."

"You still do. You're on a sabbatical; you haven't left." She looks up at me through her lashes, and my heart sinks into my stomach. "You're not, are you?"

"Not what?" she asks, her brow crinkling.

"Leaving."

Her eyes widen and I relax back into my seat, relieved.

"No. Not unless you want me to."

"Hell no. Your job will be waiting for you whenever you're ready to return."

"As much as I appreciate that, I really hate that I get special treatment because we're friends."

"That's not—" I shake my head. "I'd do the same for anyone as good at their job as you are."

She smiles weakly at me.

It's true, though. She's amazing—the best thing to ever happen to the KC Foundation. Hell, it wouldn't exist if it weren't for her. She is the beating heart of that place; it wouldn't be the same without her.

"I mean it, Effie."

Her lips curl up as more tears fill her eyes at the compliment.

I hate that seeing her upset and emotional is becoming normal.

She's always been such a happy, joyful person. I miss that.

'Thank you,' she mouths before admitting defeat and pushing her almost full plate away before we pay the check and head out for our shopping spree.

The sun is shining when we emerge from the restaurant, and I put the windows down and turn the volume up on our playlist as I take the freeway toward the mall.

Before we exit the car, I reach into the glovebox and pull out a baseball cap. The last thing we need is someone spotting me. It's fairly uncommon here. It's not like being in Chicago, where everyone is on the lookout, but it does happen occasionally. After all the media attention our fake engagement has caused, it's the last thing either of us need.

Allowing Effie to take the lead, I follow her to one of her favorite stores and give her my opinion on everything that steals her attention.

"This one," I say, picking up a full-length bright floral dress.

Effie spins around, her eyes landing on the material in my hand.

Her brows pinch. "Uh..."

"It'll suit you," I say, holding it up to her body.

"Maybe on a beach holiday. It's not exactly...funeral wear"

"Bullshit. Grams would totally back me with this."

Effie rolls her eyes, but she doesn't argue. She knows I'm right.

"Fine," she sighs. "I'll try it on, but I'm promising nothing."

By the time we get to the dressing room at the back of the store, I have at least ten dresses of all different styles and colors draped over my arm.

I hand them over to the assistant, who counts the hangers before gesturing for me to sit on the couch to wait while directing Effie into the first dressing room.

Sinking into the cushions, I spread my legs wide and slip the cap off my head, running my fingers through my hair.

I don't see the store assistant return until she gasps, trips over her feet, and almost ends up in my lap.

Thankfully, my reaction time is better than hers, and I catch her before she faceplants in my crotch.

"Oh my god, I'm so sorry," she says in a rush as I place her back on her feet. "Y-you're... you're...Kieran Callahan." She stares up at me with bright eyes and a wide smile on her face.

"Uh...yeah," I say reluctantly.

"Oh my god, I can't believe this. I'm a huge fan. Go Chiefs," she says, punching the air, her cheeks immediately heating in embarrassment when she realizes what she's doing. "Sorry, I mean...I had pictures of you all over my college dorm."

"Had?" I ask with a smirk. "Did you get a new favorite player?"

"O-oh n-no. I moved in with my boyfriend and—"

"He didn't appreciate them?" I ask lightly.

"No. Not so much. Plus, he's a Saints fan."

"And you're still with him?"

She throws her head back and laughs like it's the funniest thing she's ever heard.

17

EFFIE

Irritation rolls through me as the fake laugh of the shop assistant fills the air.

A huge Chiefs fan...I can't help but roll my eyes.

I bet she's never seen a full game in her life.

She's just a fan of the players and the lavish life they'd be able to provide her if one were stupid enough to fall for her moves.

As much as I want to think that Kieran isn't one of them, I've had firsthand experience of the kind of women he goes for.

My best friend doesn't always have the best taste.

She laughs again, and my teeth grind.

"How long are you in town for?" she asks as I reach for the dress Kieran chose for me.

Don't get me wrong, it's beautiful. The colors and the cut are incredible, but I'm not sure it's suitable for a funeral.

That's precisely why you should wear it, a little voice says.

Grams would love it. It the exact kind of thing I'm sure she had in her mind for me when she wrote down her wishes.

But that doesn't mean it's going to be the one.

It looks like it's going to be incredibly tight—unable-to-wear-underwear tight—and I refuse to go commando for Grams' funeral. That's just wrong.

Before stepping into the fabric, I have little choice but to lose my bra. But as I slide the dress straps over my shoulder, I discover that the garment has much more structure than I'd expected.

"Wow," I breathe when I look up at myself in the mirror.

It isn't zipped up yet, but even still, it does incredible things for my boobs.

Another reason I can't wear it for a funeral.

The cowl neck is low, and the girls are very much high.

I'd probably give some of Grams' male friends a heart attack.

"I know this little place that you'd love," the shameless woman continues. "Are you busy say...tonight?"

Anger, disbelief, and—I'll admit it—an unhealthy dose of jealousy rush through me, and before I know what I'm doing, I've thrown the curtain back and stepped out of the dressing room I was hiding in.

Unsurprisingly, she doesn't notice.

Kieran, however, turns his wide, shocked eyes on me.

"For such a big fan, it seems you've missed the most recent news about your favorite player," I state bitterly.

It's wrong. I should have kept myself hidden away and let her continue to make a fool of herself.

The thought of him taking her up on her offer shouldn't bother me. It wouldn't have in the past.

But the memory of him sliding a ring onto my finger only days ago is still too vivid. He told me that we would continue as if the rumors were true, that we'd deal with it all later.

He said that we had to play the game.

Well, here I am, making my winning move.

I take another step forward and hold my head high.

"You should probably go and message your boyfriend. Remind yourself he exists."

Her mouth opens and closes as if she has something to say but can't find the words.

"She's right," Kieran agrees, although she doesn't immediately jump into action.

Instead, she stands there like a deer stuck in headlights until some kind of bell rings from out on the main shop floor. The second she hears that, she scurries away like her ass is on fire.

"Well, that was—"

"Don't," I warn as he pushes from the couch and steps toward me, my face burning with embarrassment.

"Who knew my little Lucky could be so possessive?"

"I mean it, Kieran. Don't."

"She was—"

"Beautiful and exactly your type?" I ask coldly.

He shakes his head.

"Nothing. She was nothing."

"Let's just forget the whole thing," I say, attempting to wave him off.

"Effie, I didn't even really see her. I don't know what color her hair was, or what she was wearing."

"So? None of that matters."

He studies me closely before his eyes drop to the dress I'm wrapped in.

"You, however..." He moves closer. "This dress was made for you."

When his eyes return to mine, I find something in them that I don't think I've ever seen directed at me before. Something that makes my stomach knot and my thighs clench.

"I-it's not done up," I blurt, saying the first thing that comes into my mind.

Breaking eye contact with him, I spin around, giving him my back.

His breath catches, and my eyes jump to the mirror in front of me.

I find him staring down at my exposed skin like it's something he's never seen before, and my heart rate picks up as I wait for him to do something.

Anything.

"Kieran," I whisper.

"Shit," he mumbles under his breath, reaching for the zipper that sits just above my ass.

I suck in a breath as he slowly pulls it up, and I don't release it until it gets stuck at my waist.

"It's fine. Leave it th—" His eyes lift, meeting mine in the mirror, and my words cut off.

His face is set with determination, stopping me from saying another word.

Returning to the task, he pinches the fabric tighter around my waist and tugs harder.

The zipper moves, and I breathe a sigh of relief—until he tucks two fingers under it so he doesn't catch my skin.

A gentle shiver goes through my body as goosebumps cover my skin and my nipples pebble behind the light fabric of the dress.

Thank fuck for the built-in bra.

"There," he says once it's fully fastened. "What do you think?"

He takes in my reflection; I don't look down, though.

I can't.

I'm too enthralled watching him.

When I don't immediately respond, he looks up, and our eyes collide in the mirror again.

"You have to buy this dress," he states after clearing his throat.

"Um..." Ripping my eyes from his, I finally look down. "I can't wear this to a funeral." I balk.

"Sure you can."

Spinning around, I look up at my best friend.

"I absolutely cannot. It's in a church, Kieran."

"God won't argue about this," he says, his eyes dropping to my chest.

"Oh my god," I mutter, covering my face with my hands.

He moves closer, his breath rushing over my skin before his fingers curl around my wrists.

Tugging my arms behind my back, he holds my hands captive before ducking down and staring into my eyes.

The move makes my breath catch and my heart slam against my ribs.

"You're buying this dress even if you don't wear it for the funeral. Hell, even if you never wear it outside the house. It was made for you."

My chest heaves as he gives me a look that dares me to argue. I want to, but the words dry up on my tongue.

His grip on my wrists tightens, and he moves closer. So close that my breasts almost brush his chest when I breathe.

"Kieran?" I whisper, praying that he moves closer and steps back at the same time.

We're a second away from doing something we've never done before, something we're likely to regret, when a voice suddenly shatters the moment.

"Is there anything I can help you with?"

Kieran jumps back as if burned, and we both turn—I'm sure looking guilty as hell—at the new assistant.

She's older and looks much less star-struck and more shocked that she's found us in what was about to be a compromising position.

"She needed help with the zipper," Kieran states, and unlike a few moments before, his voice is emotionless.

"Right, well, I'm here now to help where needed. If you can go and sit down..."

Kieran takes a step back and coldness rushes over me.

"Of course."

The assistant watches him go before turning to me with a disappointed expression.

What the hell did I do?

With a tut and a shake of her head, she disappears, pulling the curtain closed behind her.

I stand there for a minute, trying to understand what just happened.

Was...was Kieran going to kiss me?

No. Surely not.

That assistant just gave him ideas, and then he had my boobs all up in his face.

It was because of her. It had nothing to do with me.

Well, the fact he can't do anything with her has a lot to do with me.

The guilt I felt when he first arrived and didn't know what I'd done returns.

It doesn't matter that he understands and is fully on board.

It's still my fault he couldn't take her up on her offer. He could be heading out tonight and enjoying himself. But because of me, he'll be at Grams', probably holding me while I sob on him. Again.

Spinning around, I stare at myself again in the mirror.

He isn't wrong. The dress really is incredible.

Reaching behind me, it takes a little work to pull the zipper down, especially over the bump of fabric that caused Kieran some trouble, but I manage it and let it float to the floor around my ankles.

The price tag catches my eye as I bend down to get it, and I gasp. "Holy cow."

Feeling a little disappointed that it's not going to be mine after all, I try on the final two dresses, and without showing Kieran, I decide to go for the first one I saw when we walked in. Isn't that always the way?

It's beautiful, fits me well, and, most importantly, it covers everything it needs to cover. It's both funeral-worthy and something I'm sure Grams would have appreciated—even if she would be longing for Kieran's choice.

"Okay, let's go," I say in a rush as I pull the curtain back. "This is the one," I say quickly, thrusting the dress at Kieran before unloading the others onto the judgy assistant.

"I thought you were going to show me," Kieran sulks as if that moment between us didn't happen. "And what about my one?"

"It's not right," I shoot over my shoulder as I walk away from the dress.

"But..."

I don't hear what he says after that; I'm too busy trying to get away from him so I don't have to look into his eyes.

That dress...the way he looked at me in it...that moment between us...it was as exhilarating as it was terrifying.

Kieran is the most important person in my life.

I can't risk that.

If I were to lose him—especially now—it would kill me.

He catches up to me at the register just as the assistant who hit on him awkwardly folds my dress and places it into a carrier bag.

"You need shoes and a purse for that, darling," he says before wrapping his arm around my waist to prove a point. Not that the woman risks looking up.

"N-no, it's okay. I have something at home," I argue, just wanting this little trip to be over.

"Nonsense. My girl deserves better than that."

I glance up at him to find him staring down at me with an intensity similar to inside the dressing room.

I don't respond. Instead, I take the bag when it's offered, duck away from his arm, and make a beeline for the exit.

The dress I didn't choose taunts me on the way out, and the memory of how I felt when he looked at me in it hits full force. But I lock it down.

It's better left in the past where it belongs.

18

KIERAN

I sit on the couch with Effie as another of hers and Grams' favorite movies plays on the TV before us.

She's lying across the cushions with her head in my lap. She hasn't said anything or moved for the longest time; if she weren't so tense, I'd think she's fallen asleep.

But I know it's not the case. As much as I wish she'd relax, she can't.

She offered for her parents to come over, said she'd cook for them, but they refused, making the excuse that they'd be tired after their trip and would rather stay at the hotel. Alone.

Although it was to be expected, their words still hurt.

Honestly, I would be shocked if they turned up here. We already know they're flying out again tomorrow night. Mr. Campbell's meetings are just too important to put off for more than a day, apparently.

How Grams managed to end up with such a selfish prick like him is beyond me. Both her and her late husband were such wonderful people; they deserved so much more from their only son.

Reaching out, I gently pull a lock of Effie's hair from her face and tuck it behind her ear.

I'm not surprised when my knuckle runs through tear tracks.

I don't say anything. There is nothing to say.

Nothing can make any of this better.

She snuggles against me, and I continue stroking her hair softly.

Closing my eyes, I rest my head back against the couch, and instantly, my mind goes back there.

To the dressing room.

Fuck.

I was seconds away from doing it.

I was going to kiss her.

Effie has been my best friend for over a decade, but I've never felt that magnetic pull toward her before.

Hell, I've never felt that pull toward anyone before.

Certainly not the jersey chaser working in the store.

I wasn't lying when I told Effie that she was nothing.

I humored her, sure. But only because I have to.

Watching Effie's reaction though...that was fucking priceless.

She's been my wingwoman more times than I can count. But she has never before shown any true jealousy.

It was...incredible. Terrifying. Confusing. But incredible.

It messed with my head. That's the only reason I can come up with for why I nearly lost my mind.

I can't kiss her.

She's my best friend.

My ride or die.

The one genuine person I know I can always count on to be there for me.

I can't ruin that. I would never forgive myself.

But that doesn't stop the tingles from racing up my arm

139

every time I touch her, or halt my mind from running away with itself and trying to imagine what it would have been like to close those final few inches between us yesterday.

It was the dress, a little voice says.

It was a good thing she didn't buy it. I wouldn't have gotten through tomorrow if she wore that.

It might have looked killer on her, but it would have been a disaster.

She shifts on my lap, and my nostrils flare when she slides her head back a little and places her hand on my thigh, squeezing gently.

She says nothing, but I feel her gratitude through her touch. That and a few other things that I shouldn't.

This is wrong.

So incredibly wrong.

She's hurting. Suffering. Grieving. And here I am, thinking of things that I'm sure are the furthest from her mind right now —especially involving me.

Forcing my attention back to the movie, I try to forget the lingering memories.

Eventually, Effie's breathing does even out and her body relaxes into the couch as she drifts off.

All I can hope is that it provides her some escape from the pain and thoughts of what tomorrow will bring.

Once I'm confident that she's in a deep sleep, I shift beneath her and lift her into my arms as smoothly as I can.

I carry her to her room and lay her down in bed before returning to the living room to tidy up and turn everything off.

I have every intention of slipping down the hallway to my own room. The last thing I need while my head is cluttered with thoughts of what-ifs is to lie beside her.

But instead of walking to my room, my legs force me to stop when I get to her doorway.

She's lying on her side with one hand tucked under her

cheek. The other arm is stretched out like she's searching for something.

It only takes two seconds to discover what—or who—she's looking for.

"Kieran," she whispers, wiggling her fingers as if I'll suddenly appear beside her.

My chest tightens as if someone has wrapped a rubber band around it.

She shifts into the middle of the bed, still searching, and I cave.

Her eyes never open. I don't think she's awake, and if anything, that makes it worse.

Even in her slumber, she needs me.

With my heart slamming against my ribs, I drag my hoodie over my head and then step up to the bed.

She's asleep; what's the worst that can happen?

No sooner has my body hit the mattress than she wraps herself around me like a koala.

Her head rests on my shoulder, her arm wraps around my waist, and her leg hitches up on my thigh.

It's incredible.

Incredibly terrifying.

I lie there for hours, lost in my thoughts about my best friend, but at some point, my exhaustion claims me.

"Effie," I moan as her warm, soft palm slides down my stomach, heading for the waistband of my sweats. "Oh god."

My heart thunders as I fight to suck in the air I need.

We can't do this. We can't—

"Fuck," I grunt as her hand slides over the fabric of my sweats and my hard length.

It's been aching for hours.

Lying here next to her, it's been impossible to contain it.

Thoughts of her in that dress...how close we came to fucking up our friendship...how fucking insane her tits looked...

I grit my teeth, trying to fight against my body's natural instinct to thrust into her touch.

It's been so long since I've had any action.

My body craves it.

Her delicate fingers wrap around my shaft, and she strokes me again.

I'm fucking powerless but to give into my baser instincts.

My hips thrust forward, and a filthy groan spills from my lips.

So good.

She grips me tighter, and I shamelessly use her hand to get off.

I feel like a teenager again, but I don't care.

It's good. Too fucking good.

All too soon, my release is surging forward.

I want to be embarrassed, but I'm not. I'm burning too hot and soaring too close to orgasm to care.

"Shit," I hiss when my release barrels into me.

My cock jerks violently in her hold as I come in my pants.

Fuck.

My breathing is erratic as I fight to come down from my high.

My sated body relaxes into the mattress, but it all changes when the warm body behind me suddenly tenses, and she pulls her hand away so fast, I startle.

My eyes fly open, and I stare at the ajar door of Effie's bedroom.

That...that was a dream...right?

Just a dream.

Sucking in a deep breath, I turn over and risk looking at Effie.

She's lying on her back with her hands over her face.

My heart lurches.

It wasn't a dream.

Reaching down, I readjust myself and cringe.

Nope. Not a dream.

"Effie?" I whisper, not knowing what to say.

This isn't a position I ever thought I'd find myself in.

Letting her hands fall away, she stares up at the ceiling.

"I need to start getting ready," she says, quiet and hesitant.

"There's time," I assure her despite the fact I haven't looked at a clock. We could be late, for all I know.

"No, there's not. Everything today needs to be perfect."

Before I can say anything else, she throws the covers back, jumps from the bed, and races from the room.

Mimicking her previous move, I cover my face with my hands and shout, "Motherfucker."

With only one bathroom in the house, I have little choice but to wait for her to finish getting ready before I can properly clean up. Not ideal, but it's sure a great reminder of how our day started.

By the time she emerges, I've already had two coffees and there are cinnamon buns in the oven.

We don't need more. Some from the other day are still in a container, but I needed to do something.

"Buns will be seven minutes," I tell her when she makes a beeline for the coffee machine without glancing in my direction.

"Effie, please can we—"

"Don't, Kieran," she sighs, tipping her face to the ceiling and closing her eyes. "Can we just forget everything and focus on Grams today?"

"O-of course. That's what I was going to say," I lie as I push from the stool and walk closer.

This morning was an accident. A happy one, but an accident all the same.

Hell, maybe both of us were dreaming.

Neither of us meant to do that.

We were just being human—humans who have needs.

Stepping up beside her, I reach out and turn her to face me. Tucking my fingers under her chin, I force her to look up at me.

"Today will always be about Grams," I promise her, my eyes searching hers to discover how she really feels about what happened.

Thank you, she mouths.

"You look beautiful, by the way," I tell her, stepping back and holding her arms out. "Good choice."

I smile as she blushes.

"I mean, it's not quite the one I chose."

She rolls her eyes.

"Go and get ready," she instructs, tugging her hands from my grasp and lifting her mug from the machine.

"I'll be right by your side today. Lean on me, okay?"

She nods but doesn't look me in the eyes again.

The thought of her regretting this morning kills me. But I guess it's to be expected.

I'm just her manwhore best friend.

She doesn't think of me like that.

Just like I shouldn't think of her...

Probably best not to tell her that this morning was one of the best things that's ever happened to me.

Without saying another word, I walk out of the kitchen and directly to the bathroom.

"Fuck. Fuck," I grunt, slamming my palms down on the tiled wall in frustration.

I'm fucking this up.

She needs me to be her friend right now.

Nothing more.

Just a friend.

Lifting my hands to my hair, I comb my fingers through, dragging the wet locks back until it hurts.

Just a friend, Kieran.

Be what she needs. Help put her back together, and then you can both return to Chicago and your lives, and things can continue as they're meant to.

19

EFFIE

I stand straight with my shoulders back. There have been a few times in my life where I've had to put my emotions to one side and pull on my game face, but never more so than today.

My heart is racing, and my palms are sweating.

It's going to be okay. I know it will.

Today is going to be the kind of day that Grams wanted. But that doesn't mean it isn't going to hurt.

The pews behind me are already beginning to fill with people whose lives Grams touched. Many of them I met at the care home when they visited, but there are still loads I've never seen before. Knowing that they cared enough about Grams to be here today fills me with pride. She was such an incredible woman; she deserves for everyone to remember her as the selfless, caring person she was.

But the two I'm dreading to see still aren't here.

I can't say I'm surprised.

If this were a business meeting, he'd have been here fifteen minutes ago. But this is a family event, so punctuality goes out of the window.

As if he knows exactly where my head is at, Kieran's hand slides down my back before resting it just above my ass, a warm, strong presence.

I haven't been able to look him in the eye since this morning.

How he's acting as if nothing happened is beyond me.

"Effie?" he whispers.

I don't want to look up.

Hell, I don't want to be here, dealing with all of this.

But I don't have any choice.

Woman up, Effie. Things could be worse.

"Ef—" His words are cut off when I finally look up.

My breath catches at the darkness in his eyes. The green that's usually there has almost been engulfed by it.

"I'm okay," I whisper weakly, proving that I'm very much not.

His smile is forced and sad.

I love that he's here with me, but I also can't help feeling like I'm holding him back from doing something better.

It's the off-season. He could be on some exotic island spending his days with girls in bikinis and grass skirts. He could be doing charity projects, bringing in much-needed funds for the KC Foundation. Hell, he could just be at home, chilling out.

But no, he's here wiping my tears and holding me together.

If he didn't want to be here, he wouldn't be, a little voice says.

I blow out a long, slow breath as his eyes hold mine captive. Embarrassment stains my cheeks while my chest continues to ache.

As much as we need to deal with what happened this morning, I don't have the energy or the brain power to even try.

His lips part and my stomach twists with anxiety, but

before he manages to get a word out, another voice floats through the air.

"Good afternoon," my father booms, his deep voice echoing around the modest entrance to the church.

Kieran's jaw ticks with irritation before he pulls on a mask of his own and turns to face the two people who brought me into the world.

"Mom, Dad," I greet through gritted teeth.

Neither of them says anything as they look me up and down with distaste.

"What on Earth are you wearing, Effie?" Mom chastises with her nose in the air like she's something special.

"This is a funeral, not a tea party," Dad snaps.

My natural reaction would be to slink away and let their comments weigh me down.

But today is different.

Today isn't about me. And for once, it isn't about them. It's about Grams.

If she wanted me to turn up wearing a Teletubbies costume today, I'd have done it just to make her smile.

Holding my head high, I take a step forward.

"Grams specifically requested we all dress in bright colors. A request you both clearly ignored."

As my father glowers at me and my mother's mouth drops open in shock, Kieran steps up behind me.

His arm wraps around my back and his hand squeezes my waist in support.

"Mr. and Mrs. Campbell," he says tersely, holding his hand out for my father to shake.

"Kieran," Dad greets, although there is no joy in his voice. My brows pinch in confusion. Dad has never cared about anyone other than himself and my mother, so his distaste of Kieran comes as no surprise, but there is a bitterness in his tone I wasn't expecting. "Am I to assume that you merely forgot to ask my permission?" Dad questions, his brow lifting.

Permission?

Oh.

If I weren't so shocked by the question, I might be pleasantly surprised that he's taking some kind of interest in my life.

"My apologies, Mr. Campbell. It was all rather fast," Kieran explains.

I hate that he does. He doesn't have to answer to my father.

Not for a single thing.

"Can I assume that it's the only thing that is going to be rushed when it comes to my daughter? It's always distasteful to see pregnant women walking down the aisle."

All the air in my lungs comes rushing out.

"I'm not pregnant," I hiss, my fists curling at my sides.

"At least that's something," Mom starts, but just before she goes to continue, her words are cut off.

"We're ready to begin when you are," the reverend says, coming to step up beside us.

"Come on," Kieran says, taking my hand and leading me away from my parents.

My entire body trembles in anger as we make our way down the aisle.

I look around, trying to focus on Grams and all the reasons why she loved this church.

My parents won't approve. It's too small. Too old. Too understated.

But to Grams, it was everything. And being here will bring her back to Gramps. Exactly where she belongs.

Kieran leads me to the very front pew before walking to the end and tugging me down.

Leaning close, he whispers, "Ignore them."

Blowing out a shaky breath, I turn to look up at him.

"I'm trying," I confess, my voice barely audible as the organ begins to play.

He gives me a sad smile before a shadow falls over us.

Glancing up, I find Dad with his signature scowl on his face, and no doubt Mom is behind him like the doting wife she is.

Scooting closer, Kieran presses his right side against me and wraps his arm around my shoulder.

Keeping my eyes focused on the lectern, I do my best to ignore the other two in our row.

I expected them to join us. There is no way on Earth that Derek Campbell would sit anywhere but the front row.

The music changes, and the reverend gestures for everyone to rise.

My heart sinks and I close my eyes.

I don't want to do this.

"It was a beautiful service," one of Grams' friends says before she leaves. "You did her proud today." She takes both of my hands in hers and squeezes tightly.

The ball of emotion only grows larger in my throat as my nose itches and my eyes burn.

"Thank you," I whisper, barely able to force the words out.

She pulls me in for a hug, and it's all I can do to hold myself together.

Today has been a lot. I'm not sure I've ever been so drained. Both physically and emotionally.

Every inch of me hurts. All I want to do is curl up in a ball and fall asleep.

If only I could.

I can count on one hand the number of full hours of sleep I've had this week. I'm feeling it today.

The older lady—Rosa, I think—releases me and gives me a soft smile.

"Get some rest."

I will, I mouth.

Turning to Kieran, who's still exactly where he promised he would be—right by my side—she looks up at him.

"Look after her," Rosa instructs.

"Don't worry. I intend to," he assures her before also accepting a hug.

Seems like it's not only the young women my best friend has a way with. He can wrap the elderly ones around his little finger too.

We say a few more goodbyes before we close the door to the church hall.

Thankfully, Mom and Dad left not long after the committal.

I'd hoped they might have stayed a little longer. Introduced themselves to Grams' friends. But it was always unlikely.

I should be grateful they turned up at all.

"Right," I say, finding some strength from the very depth of my soul. "I guess we've got some cleaning up to do."

Empty glasses and plates litter the tables from our buffet. The thought of having to tidy it all up makes me want to cry—again.

"No."

Spinning around, I narrow my eyes at Kieran as he closes the space between us.

My heart begins to race and my temperature rises.

"W-what do you m-mean, no?" I ask quietly.

"I've booked some cleaners to come in and take care of it," he confesses. "You've done enough."

Ripping my eyes from his, I take in the room around us.

"Really?"

"Really," he says softly. "Let me take you home."

The sob I was desperately trying to hold back erupts and he pulls me into his arms.

Any awkwardness from this morning has gone, and I couldn't be more grateful.

His arms engulf me, and a heavy sigh falls from my lips as I cling onto him.

"It's okay, Effie. I've got you," he says softly, his lips in my hair as he holds me tighter. "I promise. I've got you."

Unable to hold it together any longer, I fall apart in Kieran's arms again.

He doesn't release me for even a second. I couldn't love him more.

He is hands-down the best friend anyone could ask for.

As my sobs and tears subside, reality begins to slip back in.

The scent of his cologne and the hardness of his chest that I'm pressed against make itself known, distracting me from the grief for a few blissful seconds.

"Kieran?" I whisper before pulling my tear-stained face from his chest and looking up at him.

My vision is blurry, but it doesn't matter. He's still as devastatingly beautiful as ever.

He stares down at me with his dark eyes. His tongue sneaks out and runs along his full bottom lip, and my stomach tumbles.

This morning comes flooding back, and I can't deny that there was a moment when I first woke up where I wanted more.

I wanted him to turn around, take me in his arms, and kiss me.

Make everything else in my life disappear. Just for a few moments.

My heart slams against my ribs as time seems to cease.

Without any thought, I stretch up a little, attempting to lose the space between us.

I swear, I'm not the only one who moves. I'm sure he lowers toward me.

Kiss me.

Please.

I close my eyes, waiting for that moment when our lips touch.

But it never comes.

20

KIERAN

Effie slams the car door and marches toward the house before I even have time to kill the engine.

"Fucking hell," I groan, tipping my head back and slumping lower in my seat.

Today has been...a clusterfuck of emotions.

I've gone from horny, to embarrassed, to angry, to sad, and back to horny again.

Reaching down, I tug at my slacks, giving myself a little extra space.

I've been hard since she looked up at me with wide eyes full of longing.

My blood rushes past my ears just thinking about us standing in the middle of the church hall thirty minutes ago.

I knew what she wanted. It was written over every inch of her.

But I couldn't.

Not there.

If we...

Fuck.

I drag my hand down my face, unable to believe that I'm contemplating this.

I've never thought about doing anything with Effie before. Sure, she's beautiful and sexy and a whole host of other attractive things. But she's Effie. She's been my best friend forever.

Does she even really want me? Or am I just an easy distraction for her?

If I were to throw caution to the wind, would she regret it in the morning?

Would it change everything we know about life? And not for the better...

She sure didn't react very well to what happened this morning.

Not that she's in any kind of mental state to deal with this huge change.

Hell, I'm not exactly in the right frame of mind either.

I curl my fists, remembering how close I came to knocking her father out earlier.

The way he spoke to her...

My teeth grind.

No one gets to speak to my girl like that.

With a renewed fire burning through my veins, I throw my door open and climb out.

"Effie?" I call once I've locked us inside Grams' home.

I expect her to have shut herself in her bedroom, but to my surprise, when she responds, her voice comes from the kitchen.

"Yeah."

My brows pinch, but I don't stop to question it. Instead, I stalk through to where she is.

"What are you doing?" I balk when I come to a stop in the doorway.

She's already shed her dress and is standing in one of my T-shirts. It swamps her, but it looks sexy as hell. Of course, it helps that it has my name and number on it.

She's not playing fair.

"I just need something," she explains as she messily pours vodka into glasses.

They're not shot glasses; they're tumblers. I dread to think how much she's just poured.

"Haven't you already had enough?" I ask, thinking of the numerous glasses of prosecco I've seen her drink today.

"Just one," she states before lifting the glass to her lips.

"Or five," I point out, eyeing the glass.

"Come on. I'm not drinking alone. Not tonight."

Shrugging off my suit jacket, I fold it on the counter before moving closer.

Her hair is still styled, and the makeup lingers. Her eyes are red and swollen from crying, but she still looks beautiful.

Lifting the glass, I clink mine against hers.

"To Grams," I say.

Effie swallows thickly, fighting her emotions again. I kick myself for upsetting her, but what else are we raising a glass to?

"Today was perfect. She'd have loved it."

Lifting her glass to her lips, she takes a sip, and I breathe a sigh of relief that she doesn't swallow it all down in one go.

"I hope so," she finally says before drinking more.

I can't help but copy her, but I don't take it so slowly. I've only had soda today, and I can't deny the need to drown some of it out.

I swallow the huge shot in one go, making Effie's eyes widen as she watches me.

"Fuck," I grunt as the vodka burns down my throat.

"Where did you get this?" I ask. I thought the sherry I tipped down the drain was the only alcohol in the house.

"I ordered it," Effie confesses before throwing the rest of hers back.

She winces as it burns before slamming her glass down.

"Kieran?"

"Yeah?"

Despite wanting to say something, she keeps her eyes downcast.

Silence follows as she decides against saying whatever is on her mind.

Instead, she reaches for the bottle again.

"Effie," I warn, but it falls on deaf ears. She picks up the bottle and pours herself another vodka. "No," I bark, grabbing her wrist before she gets it to her lips.

The clear liquid sloshes in the glass and spills over the side, landing on her t-shirt.

My eyes drop.

The vodka soaks the fabric, instantly making it stick to her skin...to her breasts.

Her nipples pebble, pressing against the thin t-shirt.

My jaw pops as my mouth runs dry.

She's messing with my head.

"Kieran," she hisses when I don't release her.

"I'm not letting you get wasted," I tell her, dragging my eyes back up to her face.

She stares at me, her face clearly showing her pain.

If I thought for even a second that drinking the entire bottle would help, I'd tell her to have at it.

But the only thing it'll leave her with is regret and a massive hangover.

Sure, it might help her forget for an hour or two, but it won't be worth it.

She'll hate herself for it tomorrow, and I'd much rather she hate me now for not letting her drown her sorrows in alcohol.

"I just need to forget," she pleads, attempting to move the glass closer to her face. All she achieves is another slosh of vodka on her chest.

"I know, but this isn't the way," I argue, easily overpowering her and removing the glass from her grip.

"Then what is? It hurts, Kieran. It hurts so fucking much. I need some relief. I just need some—"

I act on instinct.

I cut her words off with my lips.

Talk about doing things you'll regret tomorrow…

She freezes against me, and I panic.

Did I read her wrong earlier?

No. There is no way.

She wanted this.

Me.

My heart races so fast, my head spins a little. To be fair, it could also be the vodka.

I open my eyes and find her staring back at me.

"Tell me to stop," I demand against her lips.

If she does, I can take a step back and go and shower.

I'll take care of business and then come back out here and be the friend she needs.

But if she doesn't…

"Please," she whispers, squeezing her eyes closed. "D-don't…stop."

"Look at me," I demand, pulling back a little bit.

She drags her heavy eyelids open, and her eyes immediately find mine.

"Don't stop," she repeats.

So I don't.

Surging forward, my lips crash against hers and my hands grip her waist.

I lean into her, my lips parting at the same time hers do, and our tongues meet.

Her hands slide up my chest before her fingers twist in the short hair at the nape of my neck.

A deep groan fills the kitchen, and it takes a couple of seconds to realize it came from me.

"Kieran," she gasps as my hands slide lower so I can lift her from the floor.

The second her ass hits the counter, her thighs part, allowing me to step between them.

"Shouldn't be doing this," I mutter as I kiss down her throat.

"Don't stop," she begs, tugging at my tie.

In seconds, she pulls it through my collar and lets it float to the floor.

Her fingers then begin working on my buttons.

"Fuck, Effie," I groan, diving for her lips again as she relieves me of my shirt.

Her hands sliding down my chest feel insane.

My skin prickles and my dick gets harder, pressing painfully against the zipper of my pants.

"Yes," she cries when I skim my hands up her body until I squeeze her braless tits. "Kieran."

Fuck. My name has never sounded so good before.

As she tugs at my waistband, I twist my fingers in the fabric of my shirt and drag it over her head.

Our lips part for a beat as the t-shirt passes our mouths, but we quickly reconnect.

My hands roam, learning every inch and curve of her body.

Her skin is so soft, and something tells me it'll be deliciously sweet as well.

With her nails scratching over my shoulders, I kiss down her throat, needing to taste her.

Leaning into her, I give her little choice but to let go of me and lean back on her hands.

I pause as my lips brush over the swell of her breast and look up.

Her lips are swollen and her pupils are dilated, and miraculously, the pain etched into her features has gone.

It won't last forever. But right now, she's not consumed by it.

I'm doing that.

I'm helping her forget.

I'm giving her some relief.

It's all I've wanted to do since she got the call that Grams had passed.

Her chest heaves as her warm breath rushes over my face.

"Beautiful," I whisper before moving lower and flicking my tongue over her nipple.

"Fuck," she gasps.

But it's not enough.

It's nowhere near enough.

I suck her nipple fully into my mouth, and she throws her head back and mewls.

It is fucking everything.

I tease her, licking, sucking, and nipping until she's panting and grinding her hips in her need for more.

Switching to the other side, I give it the same treatment.

"Kieran, please," she begs.

It's like music to my fucking ears.

Panic covers her face when I take a step back, but she doesn't need to worry; I'm not going anywhere.

Reaching for her hips, I hook my fingers into her panties and tug.

"Lift up," I demand before sliding the final item of clothing from her body.

She shudders on the counter as my eyes take her in.

Letting her underwear drop to the floor, I rest my hands on her knees.

"One last chance," I warn her, although I'm not sure I'd be able to walk away now even if she asked me to.

She sucks in a deep breath that makes her chest rise and her glistening nipples catch the light.

"Please." The word is barely audible, but it hits me in the chest like a fucking sledgehammer.

"Lie back," I demand before pushing her legs wide.

My eyes drop to her pussy and my mouth waters.

"Kieran?" she questions nervously as she looks up at me with caution in her eyes.

"Have you always been this wet for me, Luck?" I ask cockily before reaching out and dragging my fingers through her folds.

She cries out as I find her clit.

"Oh yeah, you've been dreaming about this, haven't you? Dirty girl."

"Kieran, please."

"Please what?" I ask, dropping my fingers back down and teasing her entrance. "Use your words, Effie. Tell me exactly what you want."

"Y-You," she stutters. "I-I want...I want you to make me come."

Fuck me. How I don't come in my pants for the second time today as she demands that of me, I don't know.

"Your wish is my command, Luck," I growl before sliding my hand down the soft skin of her inner thighs, holding her wide open for me before I duck down and lick up the length of her pussy.

Her taste explodes on my tongue and I lose my goddam mind.

She's always been so perfect.

But I think I underestimated just how much.

21

EFFIE

O h my god.
Oh my god.
Oh my fucking god.

My eyes are so wide I don't know how they don't pop right out of my head as I watch my best friend's head descend toward my pussy.

Surely, he's not.

He won't.

He—

My breath catches as he drags his tongue up my sensitive skin.

His eyes never leave mine as sensations I haven't felt for the longest time flood through my system.

It's so good. So intense that I forget anything else exists.

"Yes," I cry, my arms giving out as he focuses on my clit.

I fall back onto my elbows; my eyes still locked on him.

I'm dreaming. I have to be.

This can't really be happening.

Kieran, my best friend in the entire world who's never looked at me like he wants me, is going down on me. And despite the fact he's only just started, I'm pretty sure it's going to be the best head of my life.

He licks and sucks at my clit. It makes my head spin. But it gets even worse when he bares his teeth and nips me.

Finally, I fall back, unable to hold myself up any longer.

"That's a good girl," he praises before diving back in.

That's it. I'm gone. So fucking gone.

His palms spread my thighs even wider, and he indulges like a man who hasn't feasted for a month.

"Kieran, oh my god," I pant as my back arches from the cool countertop of the kitchen island.

I'm in the middle of the room; the blinds are open, and I'm exposed for anyone to see.

It should be enough to make me run and hide. Any other time it would, but right now, I don't care.

Let the fucking world see.

Needing more, I reach for my breasts.

"Christ," Kieran grunts between my thighs, watching as I squeeze my aching breasts and pinch my hard nipples.

The added sensation makes me whimper.

"So fucking hot," he muses. "And you taste like the sweetest sin."

"Please," I whimper. "Please, Kieran."

He chuckles, although hell knows what's funny.

He's stopped and left me high and—

"Holy—"

My words are cut off as he pushes a finger inside me.

My muscles ripple around his digit, reminding me just how long it's been since I felt this.

I've got myself off, sure. But nothing compares to this.

No one has ever compared to this.

My hips lift from the counter in a silent plea for more.

Thankfully, it works. Not a second later, his lips return to me and his finger slides deeper.

He has me panting and writhing on the counter, building me higher and higher toward one hell of a release.

With my eyes squeezed closed and my body flying high, I let go of my breasts and reach for him.

My fingers twist in his hair, dragging him closer, silently telling him that I need more.

He groans as I pull his locks, and it only spurs him on.

"Kieran, Kieran," I moan as he adds another finger, curling them to find my G-spot. "Yes. Oh god."

"Come for me, Luck," he demands against my pussy.

My legs tremble and sweat covers my body.

I'm right there.

I just need...

"K-Kieran," I cry when he does something that pushes me over the edge.

Pleasure rushes through my body, exploding from my core and spreading out to every nerve ending.

Lights flash behind my eyes as I convulse on the counter.

I'm no longer in control of my body.

He is.

And that is perfectly okay with me.

His tongue laps at me and his fingers continue working until I come down from my high.

My chest is heaving, my breathing erratic.

And it only gets worse when he stands upright and looks at me.

His mouth and chin are glistening with my arousal, and he's got the widest, smuggest grin I think I've ever seen playing on his lips.

But it's not his reaction that hits me hardest. It's the reality of what he just did.

"Kie—"

"No," he states, his smile dropping as he steps between my legs. "Don't do that. We're not done yet."

Before I know what's happening, he's lifting my weak, trembling body from the counter, carrying me effortlessly through the house.

I cling to him like a monkey, the heat of his bare chest singeing my skin.

His hands are on my ass, holding me tightly against him. So tight that it's impossible to ignore how hard he is.

Heat rushes to my core.

I did that.

"W-what do you mean, we're not done?" I ask, gazing up at him as if he's God.

After what he just did, he might as well be.

"We're not done until I say so," he states, making my pussy flutter.

"A-and when will that be?" I whisper.

I could have predicted that Kieran would be assertive and dominant in the bedroom, but that doesn't mean I'm not shocked hearing it in person.

"When you can't take any more."

My chin drops, but his intense stare stops me from responding.

Instead, I cling tighter as he steps up to my bed and gently lowers me down.

I stare up at him in disbelief.

"Kieran?" I whisper, waiting for this dream to come to an end.

But it doesn't.

Instead, he pushes his hand into his pants pocket and pulls his wallet out.

My mouth runs dry as I watch him flip it open and pull out a number of condoms.

I gasp as they drop on the bed beside me.

Holy shit. He really does mean business.

I look back at him just in time to see his hands drop to his waistband.

Oh my god.

I might be lying here naked after coming all over his face, but the thought of him stripping down suddenly has me nervous.

Once I see him...all of him...there will be no turning back.

Time seems to slow as he rips his fly open and tucks his thumbs under the fabric.

"Kieran?"

I don't realize I said his name until his eyes meet mine.

A smile kicks up the corner of his mouth, and I instantly relax.

My heart pounds steadily in my chest, but as curious as I am about what he's hiding, my eyes don't drop as his pants do.

Is this really happening?

"Yes," he rasps as his knees hit the mattress and he crawls between my legs.

Wrapping his hands around my ankles, he places my feet flat on the sheets and spreads my legs wide.

"You're beautiful," he says quietly.

A laugh erupts from me without permission.

"What?" he asks, his brow furrowing.

"Have you seen yourself?"

"I don't hold a candle to you," he murmurs before placing a hand on either side of my head and ducking down to kiss me.

The moment we connect, all of my anxiety and unease falls away.

Why does this feel so right?

My hands slide up his arms until I can anchor myself around his neck.

His body folds over mine, his dick brushing against me.

I gasp as my muscles contract, desperate to have something to grip.

Our kiss goes on forever, and the emotion behind it brings tears to my eyes.

Thank God I keep them closed.

If he were to see them, it might bring this to an end.

Tomorrow, I might well regret this. But right now, I am all in.

"Kieran, please," I beg when he finally drags his lips from mine in favor of kissing across my jaw and down my neck.

My hips lift as I search for the friction I need.

"Jesus, Luck." He groans. "Tell me what you need."

My eyes open and I find him staring back at me with dark, hungry eyes.

I blink a couple of times, trying to get my head on straight.

It's really freaking hard when his erect dick is brushing up against me.

"You. Inside me."

His eyes blaze even hotter.

"Which part of me? My fingers again? My tongue?"

Yes, yes. I'll take both, I want to cry.

I'll take anything at this point.

"Your dick. Please. Inside me."

Blindly, he slides his hand across the bed, searching for the condoms he abandoned a while ago.

The instant he finds one, he lifts the packet to his mouth and rips it open.

He sits up between my legs, and finally, I let my eyes drop to take him in.

My core clenches with a mixture of excitement and fear.

Something tells me that this is going to hurt. In the best kind of way.

I watch in awe as he rolls the condom down his shaft. Once he's done, he holds himself and drags the tip of his cock through my folds.

My body sings, and it only gets better when he nudges against my entrance.

"More," I beg, not giving a single shit about the fact I sound like a needy whore.

If you'd have asked me yesterday if I missed sex, I'd have said no.

But right now, I'm wondering how I've gone without it for so long.

He smirks, his hair falling forward as he stares down at me.

Fuck. I don't think he's ever looked hotter.

And right now, he's all mine. In every single way.

Suddenly, he thrusts forward, dragging me from my head and forcing me back to the here and now.

My entire body tenses at the invasion.

Yep, it's been a very long time since I've done this.

Kieran's hot hand slides against my face, his thumb brushing over my bottom lip.

"Look at me, Luck," he demands.

Unable to deny him, my eyelids flutter open.

"Relax. It's just me."

I'm not sure if that's the best or worst thing he could have said.

Kieran Callahan—my best friend—is currently pushing his dick inside me.

My heart rate increases even more as I stare back at him.

"Baby," he breathes, leaning closer and kissing me.

As his tongue slides against mine, I relax, allowing him to push deeper.

He groans in delight. It's deep and filthy, and everything I needed to hear.

Lifting my feet from the bed, I wrap my legs around his hips, pushing him deeper.

"You feel incredible. So wet for me. So tight," he mutters into our kiss.

"Slow," I demand, feeling like I'm being ripped in two by his size.

"I've got you, Luck. I'd never hurt you."

Slipping his hand under my ass, he lifts my hips slightly, changing the angle, and I cry.

"That's it. Let me in farther and it'll get better."

There's no cockiness to his words, but a promise that I have little choice but to believe.

Deepening our kiss, he takes his time opening me up for him.

"Oh my god, Kieran," I gasp, ripping my lips from his and sucking in deep lungfuls of air.

My nails drag down his back until I grip his ass, trying to keep him closer, deeper. Just more.

"That's it, baby," he groans, sliding his hand down my body until his fingers find my clit.

"Yes," I breathe, my second release surging forward.

"I want you to come all over my dick. Show me how good it feels inside you."

Christ.

"You look so hot when you come, Luck. Come for me."

He grinds his hips as he circles his finger over my clit and I fall.

"Eyes," he demands as they fall closed.

Forcing them open, I hold his gaze as fireworks explode inside me.

His jaw pops as if he's holding himself back. As much as I wish he wouldn't, I'm also delighted that this isn't over yet.

If this is going to be a one-time thing—which I can only assume it is—then I want to make the most of it.

And maybe, just maybe, he'll fuck me into a good night's sleep.

22

KIERAN

"That's it, come all over my dick again," I demand.

I've no idea how much time has passed since I carried her in here and kicked the door closed, but it hasn't been long enough.

The sun has long set outside, but that's not stopping me.

I made myself a promise after she told me not to stop to do whatever it takes to make sure she gets a good night's sleep tonight.

Tomorrow is going to be just as hard for her as all the other days since Grams has died—possibly even more so now—and I want to give her the best chance of being able to deal with it.

Her body trembles, her skin glistening in the light from the bedside lamp I leaned over and turned on not so long ago.

She was happy to continue in the dark, but there was no way I was missing a second of this.

"Kieran," she whimpers, her nails dragging down my arms.

I shudder and grind my teeth, trying to stave off my release.

I've already come inside her once. It was fucking outstanding.

But three for her and one for me wasn't where we were stopping.

"You're such a good girl," I tell her, loving the way she reacts to the praise.

Her hips lift and her pussy sucks me deeper.

Fucking heaven.

Releasing one of her hips, I grab her breast and squeeze a little harder than previously.

I thought I knew my best friend. But I'm learning a whole lot of new things tonight.

Her eyes pop open in surprise, and I grin down at her.

"Eyes on me," I say.

While I love that she's so consumed with pleasure she needs to close them and focus, I need her to know exactly who is giving it to her.

Her swollen lips are parted as she tries to suck in greedy breaths.

My eyes drop to her slender throat, ideas of all the things I want to do to her spinning around my head.

Sliding my hand up, I drag my fingers over the delicate skin, testing her to see how she'll react.

Being in the position I am, and fucking the kinds of women I usually do, means I have to keep many of my fantasies locked down.

Having the jersey chasers sell stories of their vanilla nights is bad enough. The last thing I need is one diving into the dark depths of my true fantasies.

But with Effie...

Testing the water, I slip my fingers around her throat.

Her lips open and close like she wants to say something. But she doesn't, and other than resting her hand on my forearm, she doesn't try to pull me away.

In fact, as I squeeze gently, her grip on my arm tightens as her pussy clenches around me.

"Such a good girl for me," I praise again, and it's the final straw; she shatters all over me, dragging me along with her.

Releasing her throat, I flip onto my back, taking her with me as she tries to catch her breath.

My softening dick slips from her and she whimpers as if she misses it already. Reaching down I pull the rubber off and drop it over the side of the bed.

"Look at me," I demand, giving her little choice but to lift her head from my chest.

Her eyes are heavy with desire, and it hits me right in the chest like a baseball bat.

She wants this. Wants me.

It's a heady feeling.

"You're incredible," I tell her.

She licks her lips, dragging my eyes back to her mouth for a beat.

Fuck.

How is it possible that I already need her all over again?

Reaching up, I cup her jaw. She leans into my touch, and it makes my heart beat faster.

There are so many things I want to say to her, want to ask her, but they all get stuck in my throat as we just stare at each other.

Surging forward, we sit chest to chest, our breaths mingling, our eyes locked.

This is...

I blink, shutting down whatever the end of that thought was going to be.

There will be plenty of time to dissect this later. Right now, I have a promise to follow through on.

Her lips part as if she's about to say something, but before she gets a chance, I wrap my hand around the back of her neck and crash my mouth to hers.

She groans as we fall into our kiss.

It starts slow, but it doesn't stay that way for long.

The fire that blazes between us shows no sign of going out, and I am here for it.

Although, I can't help but wonder if it always would have been like this between us. If I didn't take that leap in the kitchen, how long would we have continued to miss out for?

Her fingers twist in my hair, her nails scratching my scalp as my dick hardens again.

I've always had a fairly fast recovery time, but this is insane.

I can't get enough.

And from the way she's grinding down on me again, I'd predict she feels the same way.

Fuck. I hope she feels the same way.

Reaching for her wrists, I wrap my fingers around them and pull them behind her back, securing both in one of my hands.

The move forces her to push her chest out, making her nipples brush against my chest.

She whimpers, her hips moving faster, her wetness coating my cock.

"You want my dick again, don't you, baby?" I ask, tugging on her wrists and forcing her away from me so I can look at her.

She licks her lips and then nods.

"Fuck, you're hot when you're desperate," I muse.

"Kieran, please," she begs, shifting her hips in search of the relief she needs.

"Wasn't four enough, baby?" I taunt.

"No," she cries as the head of my dick brushes her clit. "More, please."

"Greedy girl."

Her cheeks blaze, but something tells me it has more to do with the temperature of her body than embarrassment. For someone who can overthink a lot, it seems that Effie is able to put everything aside when she wants to.

It's hot as fuck.

Reaching between us, I drag my fingers through her folds. She's soaking wet and desperate.

Fisting my cock, I hold myself for her.

"Sink down on me, baby," I demand.

I might prefer to be the one in charge, but every now and then I'll hand it over. It's all for my own gain, though. I want to see her tits bouncing as she rides me.

"K-Kieran," she whimpers as I press against her entrance, desperate to feel her sucking me in again. "C-condom."

I freeze with the head of my dick inside her.

Her muscles ripple, trying to pull me deeper as my heart pounds against my ribs.

I've never taken a girl bare before.

But this isn't just a girl.

This is Effie.

I search her blue eyes, and I relax in a way I wouldn't with anyone else.

"I'm on birth control," she suddenly blurts.

"I-I—"

"I trust you, Kieran. I trust you more than anyone else on this Earth."

All the air comes rushing out of my lungs at the same time she takes the decision away from me and sinks down on my length.

"Oh fuck. That's—"

"Yesss," she hisses, circling her hips.

Keeping her wrists locked in one of my hands, the other grabs her ass, helping her to move as I thrust up into her.

Her heat. Her wetness. Her velvet walls.

Fuck.

"Oh my god," she gasps as I fuck her.

Her tits bounce just like I wanted, and I can't help but pull her farther backward and suck one and then the other into my mouth.

Her entire body trembles as she tries to hold herself up. It's not necessary. I'm not going to let her fall.

"I've got you," I promise her, my grip on her body tight enough to leave bruises.

The thought of looking at her covered in my marks tomorrow makes my chest swell.

Fuck. I want her wearing them for days.

"Let go, Effie. Give it to me."

Leaning forward again, I suck her nipple hard into my mouth.

"Kieran," she cries before I push her over the edge again.

This, hands down, is the best thing I've ever seen.

She's barely come down from her high when I flip our positions again, putting her on her stomach.

Pulling out of her, she whimpers at the loss as I lean over the side of the bed and pull my belt from my pants.

She twists to the side, trying to see what I'm doing as I crawl between her legs and recapture her arms. Wrapping the leather around her wrists, I secure them behind her back.

"Kieran?" she whispers.

"You said you trusted me, remember?"

"I-I do."

Leaning over her, I kiss up her spine, loving the way she shudders.

"I'll never hurt you," I whisper in her ear. "But I promise to make it feel better than you've ever experienced before."

Fuck any of the men who have come before me. None of them were worthy of her.

Hell, neither am I. But I'll try my best to make her think I am.

"Okay," she whispers as I sit up, wrap my hands around her hips and pull her ass up.

My eyes focus on her wet, swollen pussy, and my cock jerks.

Palming her ass with one hand, I press two fingers from the other against her clit, teasing her until she's trembling again.

Dipping my fingers inside her, I coat them with her cum before lifting them to her ass.

"Kieran," she shrieks as I tease her, her body flinching in shock.

"Anyone been here before, Luck?" I ask, dying to know.

Effie and I might be close, but we've never really dived into the details of our sexual encounters. Of course, if she's read any of the stories about me then she probably knows more than I do about her. Although, those tales barely scratch the surface of what I really want.

"No," she whispers—not that I needed the verbal response. Her body tells me everything I need to know.

"You're missing out," I muse, watching as I push the tip of my thumb inside her unused hole.

"Oh god," she cries.

"One day," I promise before pulling it out again and taking my cock in my hand.

Honestly, I have no idea if that's a promise I'll be able to keep or not.

Tonight might be my only time to indulge like this. It won't stop me from dreaming about it, though.

As I slip inside her again, she pushes back against me.

Holding the belt that's binding her wrists, I pull her arms back as I fuck her.

"Yes. Fuck. Kieran," she cries as my hips pick up pace.

"That's it. You take my cock so well, baby."

My eyes are locked on where my cock disappears inside her.

We look so perfect together. I'm addicted.

I fuck her hard and fast, my new obsession with her getting the better of me.

She comes again before I flip her onto her back and spread her thighs wide.

"Kieran," she cries, and when I look up, I find she's got tears leaking from the corners of her eyes.

"So fucking beautiful," I tell her, watching as her makeup runs down her face. "I want one more."

She cries out as I thrust back in.

She's exhausted and overstimulated.

But that's what I need. No, that's what she needs.

With her arms beneath her, it makes her hips lift to the perfect height for me to take her.

"You're going to come for me again, and then I'm going to fill this pussy with my cum."

She whimpers again, her eyes barely open as she tries to follow orders to keep them on me.

With one hand on her hip, holding her exactly where I want her, I reach for her throat.

She doesn't startle. Instead, she lifts her chin, encouraging me.

Wrapping my hand around her, I squeeze harder than I did last time.

Her pussy tightens around me, and it's almost all over.

"Look at you, Luck. Who knew you'd be such a good whore."

I have no idea if it's my words or my actions, but she shatters before me. I release her throat, and she sucks in greedy gulps of air as my dick jerks.

Pleasure slams into me as her body trembles in my hands, and I do exactly as I promised and pump her full.

The second we're both done I pull out and watch as my cum dribbles out of her.

It's a sight I've never seen before, but one I want to see every fucking day of my life.

Reaching out, I push it back inside her.

She whimpers, but even though she's exhausted, it doesn't stop her body from trying to suck me deeper.

"My dirty girl," I muse as I pull my finger free and then paint her lips with our combined release.

23

EFFIE

Warm water surrounds me, and I blow out a breath.

My arms are aching, and every muscle in my body is quivering.

I know what just happened, but at the same time, I'm struggling to get my head around it.

Kieran was...

Kieran was mind-blowing.

I still can't quite believe we did that.

I fucked my best friend and it was the best sex I've ever had.

Things between us were so easy, so relaxed.

I guess that's what you get from years of friendship.

Usually, I'm self-conscious about my body when I'm with guys. More often than not, it's a lights-off, hide-under-the-sheets situation.

I have never, ever been as brazen as I was tonight.

I should probably be embarrassed about the way I threw my head back and begged for more of his dick. But I'm not.

Just like he wasn't when he wrapped his hand around my throat.

Fuck, that was hot.

My body heats up just thinking about the possessive move.

And then there was his belt...

I had no idea that Kieran was kinky like that, but hell, I'm glad he was.

He opened up something inside me.

Something I want to explore.

A rush of hot water tickles down my back, and I crack my eyes open to find Kieran sitting on the edge of the tub, taking care of me.

"W-what are you doing?" I ask, my voice rough and my throat sore.

Jesus, how loud was I?

"Looking after you before I carry you to bed."

A lump of emotion crawls up my throat as I stare up at him.

Tears fill my eyes before they spill over again.

I can only imagine how awful I must look right now. But it doesn't seem to matter to him. He still gazes back at me just like he did in bed.

There's awe in his eyes. I don't understand why, but it's there.

I shouldn't complain. At least it's not pity.

A sob erupts before I can catch it.

Dropping my face into my hands, I try to hide my reaction.

I might be crying, but they're very different tears from the others I've cried this week.

Of course, the grief lingers, but it isn't so all-consuming.

I just wish I could grasp why.

"Effie," he breathes.

I sense him move, but I don't look up to see what he's doing.

I soon find out when his large, hard body slides behind mine, his toned legs encasing me.

Instinctively, I lean back into him.

His arms wrap around me and I snuggle into him, feeling safe and protected.

I wake feeling better than I have in a long time.

I slept. And not just for an hour or two—for the whole night.

But while I might be well rested, my limbs are heavy, as if I ran a marathon before crashing last night.

I lie there for another few seconds, enjoying the level of relaxation I haven't felt in a very long time, but all too soon, there's movement behind me and everything that happened last night comes back me.

My eyes pop open as filthy images from the night before flash through my mind like a porno.

Oh my god.

I slept with Kieran.

Multiple times.

And—

Something squeezes my breast, and my breath catches.

Aware I'm awake, he shifts his hips, and it reveals something even more surprising than his hand on my bare skin.

"K-Kieran?" I whisper as heat surges through my body.

"Morning, Lucky," he groans as he thrusts his hips again.

I'm sore. Sorer than I think I've ever been before. But it's not enough to mask the pleasure I get from him moving inside me.

Holy Christ; I've just woken up with my best friend inside me.

My heart races, and my hands begin to tremble.

My eyes close as warmth and contentment flow over me hearing him call me that.

It's a nickname he's called me for as long as I can remember, and I love it.

I love being his lucky charm.

I shiver when his warm breath rushes over my neck, making my skin erupt in goosebumps before his lips press against my shoulder.

"How are you feeling?"

My mouth opens and closes, but I can't find any words.

But when he moves again, the moan that spills from my lips says it all.

"Do you have any idea how amazing you feel?" he groans.

"Kieran," I gasp as he pushes deeper.

"Fuck, baby."

My eyes fall closed as heat surges through me.

I've never felt like this with a man before, and something tells me I won't feel it again with anyone but Kieran.

His hand moves from my breast and slides down my stomach in favor of my clit.

"Oh god," I gasp.

"You squeeze me so goddam tight. I can't get enough."

The feeling is mutual.

He moves slowly, his thrusts so much gentler than anything I remember from last night.

He knows I'm sore; I don't even need to say the words. He's still taking care of me.

Reaching back, I find his ass and squeeze in encouragement.

No more words are said as we move together, the morning sun streaming through the open curtains.

My release builds, but he doesn't allow me to get there in this position. Instead, he pulls out and rolls me onto my back.

He crawls over me, and the instant I see his beautiful face staring down at me, my cheeks burn red hot. And it only gets worse when he slides back inside me.

"K-Kieran," I stutter, my emotions colliding and leaving me lying here a horny, hot mess.

Reaching out, he presses his fingers against my lips to stop me from saying anything.

"Let go, baby. Forget everything and just enjoy."

I stare up at him in disbelief as he slowly fucks me.

Reaching up, I wrap my hand tenderly around his neck.

He lowers and rests his forehead against mine and stares into my eyes.

Tears threaten and as he makes me fall apart beneath him, they spill over.

The groan of pleasure as he comes is pure filth and sends little aftershocks from my release shooting around my body.

Pulling me into his arms, he drops to his side and tucks me into his body.

His lips descend for mine, and I'm powerless but to fall into the kiss.

My head spins and my heart races.

What are we doing?

He kisses me until both of us are ready to go again. But this time, he doesn't make a move.

When my stomach rumbles, reminding me that I've barely eaten anything for days, he pulls back.

His eyes search mine for a beat before he kisses my nose and then rolls out of bed, announcing, "I'm going to make you breakfast." Then he walks away with his firm butt on full display.

Unable to rip my eyes away from his body, I'm staring at him when he pauses at the doorway and turns around, making my view even better.

I always knew Kieran Callahan was a god, but seeing him in all his glory...well, I'm speechless.

"Take your time, Luck. I'm not going anywhere."

My stomach knots at his words, but as soon as he walks away, I begin second-guessing everything.

Rolling onto my stomach, I press my face into the pillow Kieran slept in, and the moment I breathe in, I realize my mistake.

Last night when he kissed me, I was powerless but to dive headfirst into it.

I needed the escape, and oh boy, did he give me one.

He gave me so much more than the bottle of vodka I ordered ever could.

Sure, things hurt this morning, but it's not anywhere close to being a hangover.

My thighs rub together as I vividly remember everything he did to me last night.

I know he promised me that he'd do anything he could to help, but I never in a million years thought he'd go to that extreme.

Sure, I got him off—accidently—yesterday morning.

I could barely look at him all day because of it.

How am I supposed to go out there and face him now?

He's had his face between my thighs, for fuck's sake.

Heat surges through me as one specific memory comes back to me.

"Anyone been here before, Luck?" he asked while teasing my ass.

Oh my god.

I scream into the pillow as my confusion over all of this gets to be too much.

I guess he has managed to achieve one thing—the pain I was feeling over losing Grams now isn't my only concern.

She's gone; there is nothing I can do about that. I just have to go through the motions of coming to terms with it.

But what happens next between us is anyone's guess.

Kieran's heavy footsteps move past my door as he makes his way to the kitchen, but as he slows to check on me, I can't bring myself to look up at him.

The fear that we've made a huge mistake is crippling.

I might be able to survive losing Grams. But losing Kieran...

I give myself another five minutes of wallowing before I force myself to crawl out of bed.

As I stand, the evidence of what we did this morning begins to run down my thigh.

Gross.

Reaching for one of his T-shirts that I've stolen over the years, I drag it over my head and then race toward the bathroom to clean up.

The moment I step into the room, my eyes land on the bathtub, and the image of us sitting in it last night hits me hard.

I stumble toward the toilet, and the second I sit down, my head falls into my hands as my regrets grow.

Where the hell do we go from here?

I move in slow motion as I brush my teeth and shower. I even dry my hair in my need to put off walking into the kitchen and seeing him.

This morning, he didn't show a single sign that he was regretting what he did. Hell, he was there doing it again. Something I am not complaining about. It was hot, just like everything he did last night.

But how hot it was or how connected we felt isn't the issue.

Eventually, I can't put off facing him any longer, and once I'm dressed, I reluctantly make my way to the kitchen.

The scent of his breakfast makes my stomach growl loudly. But despite feeling hungry for the first time this week, I'm not sure I'm going to be able to eat it.

"I thought I was going to have to come and drag you out here," Kieran says the second I step into the room, as if everything is normal.

Risking a look up, I find him standing at the island, sipping on a cup of coffee as if he didn't eat me out right there for dinner last night.

My cheeks blaze red hot and I avert my gaze fast.

"Take a seat; I've been keeping it warm for you."

Unable to do anything but what I'm told, I move to the stool closest to me and hop up.

Reaching for my mug of coffee, I stare down into it while Kieran plates up our food.

A couple of minutes later, pancakes, bacon, and eggs appear before me.

My stomach turns over and I close my eyes.

"Effie," Kieran warns.

"I...I don't think I can do this," I blurt before slamming the mug down and fleeing down the hallway like my ass is on fire.

24

KIERAN

"Shit," I hiss as the sound of her retreating footsteps fills the air before her bedroom door slams hard enough to shake the entire house. "Fuuuuck."

My kneejerk reaction is to jump and run after her. But no sooner am I on my feet, do I second-guess myself.

She doesn't want me right now. That realization hurts. But not as much as knowing that I'm the reason.

Last night, I...

Last night, I clearly fucked up.

I fall back on the stool and stare down at my breakfast.

If I weren't so fucking confused and lost, I'd be impressed. I even made waffles.

I thought it was time to break free from the cinnamon buns.

As hard as it is to accept, Grams is at peace now, and it's time to help Effie move on so she can return to her life.

Her team misses her in Chicago.

I miss her.

I know she feels at home here, but it's not her home. It's Grams'.

Her life is in Chicago. It's where she needs to be.

She's going to drown if she stays here. And I refuse to let that happen.

Ignoring my instincts to go after her, I force myself to eat some of my breakfast before I finally push the plate away.

Just like earlier, my footsteps slow as I get to her door, but I don't stop. I can't. If I hear her crying inside, it'll shatter my resolve to give her a moment.

My fists curl at my sides. Walking away from her feels wrong.

So wrong.

But getting close was also wrong.

I'll stand by my decision. In the moment, it helped.

And fuck, it was everything I didn't know I was missing in my life.

Combing my fingers through my hair, I haul my ass to the guest room, stuff my feet into my sneakers, and drag a hoodie over my head.

If I can't be with her, then I need to move.

Standing at the front door with my muscles screaming for me to do something, I debate how to leave.

Maybe I should have left a note or knocked to tell her I was going for a run.

Shaking my head, I force myself to slam the front door so she stands a chance of realizing I've left.

However, as I jog down the driveway, I question that decision.

What if she thinks I've left? Not just for a run, but for good?

"Get a fucking grip, Callahan," I mutter to myself before taking off.

I push myself as hard as I can in some kind of fucked-up punishment for last night.

What the fuck was I thinking kissing her?

I should have known that it was a bad idea.

Did I really think she'd wake up this morning, turn to me and everything would be okay?

I'm such a fucking moron.

A moron who is now hard as fuck for his best friend.

Jesus, she was incredible.

The way she accepted everything...how her insecurities fell away and she embraced the incredibly sexy woman I've always known her to be.

She was perfect, and something tells me that she has no idea.

Being with her was so easy, but not in a boring kind of way.

I'm so used to fucking strangers that I wasn't expecting the connection.

One look at her and I knew what she wanted, what she needed...and fuck did it bring me to my knees when I realized it was what I needed as well.

Everyone has been telling you for years that she's your perfect woman...

Shaking that thought from my head, I keep running.

By the time I get to the top of the hill, sweat runs down the side of my face and my hoodie sticks to my back.

The sun is now high in the sky and beating down on me. I love it just as much as I hate it.

Mornings like these bring hope.

I just wish Effie could feel it.

Something tells me that she's currently locked inside her dark bedroom, refusing to feel any kind of hope.

I bring myself to a stop and press my palm against my pounding heart as my chest tightens.

"Fuck," I pant, tipping my face toward the sun and sucking in deep lungfuls of air.

Spotting a small park on the other side of the road, I cross over and walk through the gates.

Dropping my ass onto a bench, I stare ahead of me as my brain runs at a mile a minute.

People come and go, but I don't see any of them as I relive last night and this morning over and over in my head.

What I wouldn't give to have a do-over.

I consider all the things I'd do differently. All the different ways I could pleasure her. All the things I could teach her...

Dragging my hand down my face, I pull my hoodie up, slump lower, and spread my legs wider, trying to ignore the fact I'm rocking a semi while sitting alone in a park.

The minutes tick by, but they don't help. They don't give me any clarity.

In the end, I don't have any other choice, and I pull my cell from my pocket.

Ignoring all my notifications, I pull up the contact I need and hit call.

It rings twice before the line connects. I don't give him a chance to speak before I blurt, "I fucked up."

A deep chuckle fills the line.

"Good morning to you too, little brother."

I groan, questioning my life choices.

"What did you do?" he asks when I don't expand on my opening line.

Dragging my hand down my face, I close my eyes and spill.

"I slept with Effie."

Silence.

"And now she's hiding in her bedroom refusing to talk to me."

"Honestly, Bro. I'm not sure you're talking to the right person. But thankfully, you're on speaker, and I've got just the woman for the job."

"Hey, Kieran," Lori says.

"Hey," I say, cringing. It's bad enough I'm confessing to Kian. Sure, he'd have told Lori the second we got off the phone, but still.

"I'm going to need more details," Lori says innocently.

"Really?" I ask.

"Really. I need to know what I'm dealing with."

"Okay so, she was sad and wanted to down a bottle of vodka. I decided that I had a better way to distract her, and I fucked her with her hands bound behind her back while I choked her."

Lori splutters on the other end of the line.

"My little brother, ladies and gentlemen," Kian announces like an asshole.

"I didn't mean quite that many details, but thanks."

"I just wanted to help," I explain. "She's so sad, and I hate it. Getting drunk isn't going to do anything."

"But pushing your penis inside her will?" Kian quips.

"I knew I should have called Kingston," I hiss.

"Charming."

"Ignore him," Lori mutters, her voice getting louder as she moves closer to the phone. "Go and get us some coffee."

Assuming she's not talking to me, I remain quiet.

"Me? Go and get coffee? I think you're forgetting who's in charge here," Kian scoffs.

"A grande caramel macchiato would be fantastic. Thank you."

I shake my head, picturing them glaring at each other inside Kian's office.

After a few seconds, he huffs. "Fine. Would you like anything else?"

"Surprise me."

"Trust me, Temptress, you already do. Daily." He continues muttering for a few seconds before the door slams closed and Lori laughs.

"Okay," she says. "Let's figure this out."

I want to say that talking to Lori helped. But...I'm still just as confused as ever when I hang up and drop my cell to my lap.

She asked me if I wanted a serious relationship with Effie.

No. I don't want a serious relationship with anyone.

She asked if I was happy to walk away and let her meet someone else.

Secretly, my answer was no. After last night, I don't want any man seeing her like that. She's mine.

But I lied and said yes.

I told Lori I thought Effie deserved to find a decent man who could give her the world.

That's not a lie. But right now, I'd kill any motherfucker who tried to give her anything.

I've never been a jealous man, but I'm pretty sure that is what bubbles up inside me every time I think about her with someone else.

Ultimately, Lori told me that I needed to figure out exactly what I want and then talk to Effie.

Not exactly the kind of rocket science advice I was hoping for that would fix all this, but I guess the most logical.

Knowing that I'm not going to find the answers I need in a park, I push to my feet and walk back toward the street.

It's lined with shops, and after grabbing a coffee, I begin wandering in and out of them in the hope inspiration might strike.

And it does—just not in the way I was hoping for.

I stop in a deli to buy ingredients for lunch. Effie will probably refuse to eat it, but I have to try.

As I begin walking back toward the house, my cell dings.

Hoping it's going to be Effie, I pull it free.

Sadly, the name I find staring back at me isn't her; instead, it's my agent.

> Daniel: Can I trust that you'll be in town for the photoshoot Tuesday?

My heart slams against my chest. Fear that Effie isn't ready to leave yet flooding through my veins.

I have to go back though. I have a life and commitments I need to see through. And if I'm being honest, she needs to return too.

It's time.

The trip back to Grams' house takes a lot longer than I was expecting, but the time away doesn't bring me any clarity.

I still feel the same way I did when I slammed the front door hours ago.

Confused and horny.

She blew me away last night to the point that a part of me thinks I may have dreamed it.

That's why I did what I did this morning.

I couldn't help myself. I woke up with her hot little body pinned against mine. For a second, I thought she was still, but then her hips moved and I discovered that my hard cock was between her thighs and she was grinding down on it. Not only that, but she was soaked.

It seemed that it didn't matter how many times I made her come the night before; my dirty girl was still desperate for me.

I was too.

It was a risk. I knew that when I slipped inside her.

Hell, everything we'd done the night before was a massive fucking risk, but if we'd already fucked everything up, what was one more time?

I can't lie, sliding back inside her was pure bliss.

I felt like I belonged in a way I've never experienced before.

Hearing her moan, feeling her body shudder...

I'm never going to forget last night or this morning.

It doesn't matter how much she regrets it. I'm pretty sure it'll forever be the best night of my life.

Do I want more? Of course I fucking do.

But I'm not stupid. I can't offer her the life or the kind of relationship she wants.

Even at my best, I'd be a part-time boyfriend.

Things could be great during the off-season, but then the season would kick off and she'd no longer be my priority, and that would fucking kill me.

But football is my life. I made that decision a long time ago.

I was happy to forfeit anything for it.

I still am.

It's the reason I was put on this Earth.

I have to be honest, though...this is the first time ever that I've questioned my decision.

If things were different and I had a normal job, would things between me and Effie be different?

Could I be that man for her?

As I approach the house, I figure that it doesn't really matter.

They're bullshit questions.

That isn't my life.

My life is football and fucking random women, because having anything serious is terrifying.

It's just the way it is.

25

EFFIE

The instant the front door slams, I panic.

Surely, he won't leave.

With my heart in my throat, I jump from the bed and rip my bedroom door open.

As I race toward the living room, I berate myself for being so pathetic.

Knowing Kieran, this is probably a trick and he'll be standing at the front door, aware that hearing it slam would have forced me into action.

Dread and excitement collide as I round the corner, but as soon as the hallway beyond comes into view, I realize I'm wrong.

This isn't a game. He really has left.

My chest tightens painfully as the silence around me becomes deafening.

"No," I breathe. "No, please."

Wrapping my arms around myself, I stand there staring, begging for him to come back and pull me into his arms, promising me that everything is going to be okay. That us sleeping together wasn't the worst possible thing we could have done last night.

Kieran has always been my closest friend. But now we're even closer than ever, and I'm terrified it's going to rip us apart.

A sob erupts from my sore throat and my eyes burn as more tears spill free.

I'm so fed up with crying, of being sad, but I can't shake it off.

It's all-consuming and has engulfed every single inch of me.

Numbly, I pad through the house with dread sitting heavy in my stomach.

Ignoring my bedroom, I continue toward the guest room. With my heart in my throat, I reach for the door handle and throw it open.

My eyes don't immediately lift. I'm too scared.

Memories of the last time I stood here eavesdropping on Kieran's conversation with his mother come back to me, and it does little for my emotional state.

He doesn't love you, Effie. Last night—and this morning— didn't mean anything to him.

He doesn't do relationships.

Not that I want one right now.

I can barely look after myself. There is no way I could give someone else the attention and care they deserve.

Sucking in a deep breath, I count to three and then drag my eyes from the floor.

I need to know how badly I've fucked everything up.

All the air comes rushing from my lungs, and I stumble forward at the sight of his things still here.

He hasn't left.

"Oh my god," I sigh, continuing toward the bed and gathering up one of his hoodies on the way.

Crawling onto the bed, I lift the fabric to my face and inhale.

Everything between us might be up in the air right now, but he is still the best thing about my life.

Always has been, always will be.

———

I wake still clutching his hoodie. My eyes are so sore when I drag them open and look around.

It takes me a second to recognize where I am, and then another for the pain to hit.

Surely, it can't always be this bad?

Rolling onto my back, I stare up at the ceiling, still clinging to the little bit of Kieran I have.

I have no idea where he is or how long he'll be gone.

For all I know, he's just gone to the store. But deep down, I know that's not true. He'd be back already.

Despite the sleep I've had, my legs are still weak as I stumble down the hallway to the bathroom.

If I didn't know better, I'd say I was drunk. I might have had some vodka last night on an empty stomach, but I find it hard to believe it could still be affecting me.

I pee before washing my hands and pulling Kieran's hoodie on.

I should let him go and put my own clothes on, but I can't. His scent provides me with too much security and warmth.

The coffee and breakfast he made me are still sitting at my place in the kitchen. His is also only half-finished.

My stomach knots. He couldn't eat because of me. Kieran always eats. Some might argue too much.

A sad smile spreads across my lips as I think about him and his insatiable appetite, but it quickly drops.

Last night, he was...he was something else.

And the way he made me feel...

My hand instinctively lifts to my throat.

With a sigh, I pull a mug from the cupboard and place it under the coffee machine.

Once it's full, I take it and unlock the backdoor.

My dark mood lifts slightly as I walk through Grams' garden.

This was her favorite place. She used to spend hours tending to her flowers.

I've tried to do some weeding and make it look as beautiful as I remember it, but I haven't exactly done a good job.

Most of the flowers are looking a little sad. They weren't pruned like they should have been at the end of last summer, and they haven't come back. The bushes are overgrown despite my attempts to keep on top of them, and there are weeds everywhere. The problem is, I don't actually know which are weeds and which are flowers.

Gardening is not my forte. Much like cooking. And I'm not a very good cleaner, either.

Honestly, it's no surprise Kieran doesn't want to be with me. I'd be a shitty wife.

Making my way to the bottom of the yard, I squeeze through the arch that used to be cut so perfectly to get to the swing seat that hides down here.

Gramps made it when I was little. He and Grams used to spend all their evenings down here together. It was their happy place.

My eyes close as I think about the life they used to live before I curl up on the seat.

The cushions are in the shed, so it's not the most comfortable place to sit, but I don't care.

Pulling my knees up to my chest, I pull Kieran's hoodie over them and hold my mug in both hands.

A heavy sigh falls from my lips as the weight of the world presses down on me.

The sun beams down, but I barely feel the heat from it. Inside, I'm too cold. The birds overhead tweet their songs, but I don't hear it.

The world continues spinning around me, everyone else going about their lives, and yet I'm here, stuck in my own misery with no sign of a way out.

"Effie?"

I blink, the brightness making my eyes water.

I wince, and my face hurts.

What the—

"Effie?"

My breath catches at the sound of his voice.

He came back.

"Effie, where are you?" he calls.

He's getting closer.

My heart rate increases at the prospect of seeing him. Of looking him in the eye and trying not to remember how he looked between my thighs last night.

"Effie, you're starting to—" He bursts through the small gap that hides this part of the yard from the house, and he visibly relaxes. "Scare me." His expression softens as he looks down at me, but it only lasts for a couple of seconds. "We need to get you inside," he states firmly, making my brows pinch.

My face stings at the move, but I don't think anything of it.

"Effie," he warns, stepping forward and reaching for me.

Panicking, I sit up and shift to the other end of the seat.

I glance up. Hurt covers Kieran's face.

"Luck, you're sunburned. You need to get inside right now," he explains.

My mouth opens to argue, but my eyes catch sight of my bare legs.

Shit.

Reaching up, I press the backs of my fingers to my cheek.

It's red hot.

And I'm in the direct line of the sun.

Reaching down, he picks up my mostly untouched coffee and then holds his hand out for me.

I stare at it. Previously, I wouldn't have stopped to question it.

But now...everything is different.

"Effie?" he whispers, his eyes boring into the top of my head.

I swallow, trying to force down the lump of messy emotion that's crawled up my throat, but nothing happens.

"Please, Luck. Let me look after you."

A fire ignites inside me and I surge to my feet.

"I think you did more than enough of that last night, don't you?" I snap, placing my hand on my hips and glaring at him.

His lips press into a thin line as his eyes narrow.

"Are you serious? All I've done since I got here is try to help. Sure, I'm not perfect, and I don't know what the fuck I'm doing, but I'm trying my best. Last night...last night..."

Ripping his eyes from mine, he stares up at the clear blue sky as he tries to find his words.

The air crackles between us, and my skin prickles as I wait for what he's going to say next.

Finally, he lowers his face and his eyes find mine. His expression has softened, and it makes my stomach knot.

I preferred the anger. I could deal with the anger. I could meet it head on and give as good as I got.

The softness, the compassion...

"You were drowning, Effie. I either let you drink that entire bottle of vodka or...so, I did something. Was it the best option? I don't know. But it worked. For those few hours, you forgot. For the first time in...a while, I saw you, Effie. I saw your colors. Hell," he laughs, rubbing his jaw, "you were in fucking technicolor. It was—"

Surging forward, I reach up and press my fingers to his lips.

"Don't," I warn, my face heating. The only saving grace is that he won't be able to see it with the sunburn.

His mouth opens, but thankfully, no words emerge.

Instead, he wraps his fingers around my wrist and tugs my hand away from his face.

"Come on, you need moisturizer."

With my hand locked in his, he drags me up the yard and into the house.

The second we step inside and into the cool, I realize just how bad things are.

He doesn't stop until we're in the living room, and then he turns around, staring down at me. His bright green eyes are darker than I'm used to. They're...they're like they were last night as he gazed down at me.

"Sit down," he demands before rushing out of the room, leaving me sitting there with my head spinning.

He crashes around in the bathroom for a few minutes before his heavy footsteps get closer.

Coming to a stop before me, he lowers his ass to the coffee table and flips open the tub of Aftersun.

"Oh no, no, no," I start, attempting to get away from him, but he's having none of it.

Reaching down, he wraps his hand around my ankle and lifts it to his lap.

"Kieran, really. I can do this myself," I argue, trying to pull my leg away, but he's holding me too tightly.

"Luck," he growls before lifting his eyes from my leg and holding mine captive. I feel it all the way to my core. "I thought you were my good girl."

26

KIERAN

"Don't do that," Effie warns.

She doesn't mean it.

The moment those words rolled off my tongue, her entire body relaxed.

"Luck."

"Kieran," she counters. "You're not playing fair."

I can't help but chuckle.

"Life would be boring if we always played by the rules, don't you think?"

She shakes her head as she returns to trying to tug her foot from my grasp.

"I'm mad at you," she hisses.

"That's fine. I can deal with your anger," I tease.

"Kieran, I'm being serious. This..." she says, gesturing to where I'm touching her. "It's... it's..."

"The most fun you've had in a really long time."

"Christ," she gasps, throwing herself back on the couch and squeezing her eyes closed.

I make the most of the opportunity and squirt some cream onto her leg.

She shrieks as the coolness hits her before her eyes return to mine.

"Don't do this," she whispers. There is no conviction in her words, and I let them pass me by.

"Don't think you can control yourself, Luck? Trust me, I won't be complaining if you strip my hoodie off and get on your knees to beg me."

The visual alone makes my cock jerk.

Fuck, the thought of her on her hands and knees crawling to me drives me crazy.

I fucking bet she'd do it, too.

Smearing my palm through the cream, I gently rub it into her bright red skin.

I can only imagine how long she's been out there from the color of it.

Sucking her lip into her mouth, she bites on it as I work my way toward her knee.

"You good?" I ask with amusement as I watch her try to hold it together.

"I hate you," she seethes.

"Is that why your panties are soaked right now? Because you hate me?"

"Kieran, you can't say stuff like that to me."

"Why? Because it makes you want to beg for my dick?"

"Fucking hell," she complains, throwing one arm over her face to hide.

"You're cute."

"You're not," she counters.

"No, I'm not. I'm hot as fuck and rocked your entire world last night, and you know it."

"Modest too."

"Come on, Ef. We're grown-ups. We can talk about it without it being awkward."

She sighs. "Can we?"

"We had sex, Effie. It's not that crazy."

Suddenly, she sits upright.

I'm pretty sure her cheeks are burning up with embarrassment, but thanks to her sunburn, I can't see it.

"Not that crazy. Are you freaking joking? We had sex, Kieran. S-e-x. And not just the normal, wham-bam-thank-you-ma'am kind. Hot, and passionate, and kinky..."

"Go on," I encourage when she trails off.

"Y-you..."

"I what?" I ask, already predicting where this is going.

"You were rough, and you choked me and—"

"You loved it?"

Her eyes shutter, and she licks her lips.

Fuck. This conversation has me rock fucking hard.

The second she looks down, she's going to know as well. My sweats hide nothing.

My hand glides over her knee and up to her thigh, and she begins to tremble.

"It's okay to admit it. There's nothing wrong with kinky sex, Ef."

Her eyes fly open. "I know that. I've just never..."

My smile grows wider and wider, but to my disappointment, she doesn't finish that sentence.

"Had sex that good? Come so hard? Been with such a god?" I offer up.

"Handed control over quite like that," she confesses quietly.

Her words hit me right in the chest.

"Because you trust me," I tell her.

"Hmm...for my sins."

"Oh, baby. There were sins," I tease as I slide my palm higher, dipping under the hem of my hoodie.

Her breathing becomes labored and her fists curl at her sides.

My girl is desperate for a repeat.

She's not the only one.

I'm not going to make it easy for her, though. She's going to have to work for it if she wants my dick again.

She blows out a long, slow breath as I release her leg and reach for the other.

This time, though, I don't rest her foot on my thigh. Instead, I press it against my aching cock.

"Kieran," she gasps.

She might be shocked, but that doesn't stop her from rubbing her foot against me like the needy little whore she was last night.

Fuck. I think I love my best friend even more now that I've unlocked this side of her.

"What? I'm not the one moving it."

Her teeth grind and she tries once again to pull away from me.

Yeah, that's not fucking happening.

"Why are you doing this?" she whispers, ripping her eyes from mine in favor of staring down at my hand on her calf.

"Firstly, to get you out of your head. And now...because I can't think about anything but doing it again," I answer honestly.

Shock has her eyes jumping to mine.

She swallows before her mouth opens and closes, but no words come out.

"B-but you don't want a relationship," she blurts.

"Whoa, Luck. I never said anything about a relationship. Last night was fun, no?"

"I-I don't know."

I smirk. "Yes, you do."

She rolls her eyes.

"We don't do this, Kieran. We *can't* do this."

"Says who?"

"Everyone who's ever fucked things up with their best friend by letting sex get involved."

"Who do you know who's done that, then?" I ask, lifting a brow.

"Uh..."

"There are no rules or guaranteed outcome here. It's up to us," I say as if it's that easy.

"This is fucking crazy, Kieran."

I shrug, pushing my hand higher to massage her thigh.

"Maybe so. But do you know what's even crazier?"

"This entire conversation?"

"Cute, but no. What's crazier is the fact that you're sitting there soaking fucking wet for me, desperate for my dick, and yet you're arguing and trying to pretend you're not interested."

"I-I'm not we—Kieran," she cries when I suddenly grab her knees and spread her legs wide, exposing the fabric that's covering her pussy, and more importantly, the more-than-obvious wet patch on them.

Her hand drops to cover herself, but it's too late.

"Knew it," I muse, reaching for my hard dick and giving it a gentle squeeze through my sweats, making sure that she sees.

"Oh my god."

"Gonna try telling me that you don't want it again?" I ask, cocking my head to the side as I wait for her to lie to me.

"This isn't about what I want," she says fiercely. "It's about not losing you. Kieran, you're... you're the most important person in my life. My favorite person. I won't do anything to lose you. I-I c-can't lose anyone else."

"Baby," I say, releasing her knees in favor of cupping her face. "You're not going to lose me, that's not going to happen." I lean closer, pressing my forehead against hers. "You're my favorite person too, Lucky. I never want to live a life without you in it."

Her eyes instantly fill with tears.

"We can't do this, Kieran. It blurs lines."

"What if we draw some very firm lines?"

She blinks up at me, battling against what she should do and what she really wants.

I get it. I feel the same.

But I'm confident in our ability to be able to have a bit of fun and still remain close friends.

It's working for us right now, so why can't it work a few weeks, or a month from now?

"B-but—" she stutters.

"You trust me, don't you?" She stares up at me with indecision warring in her eyes.

Her head is saying one thing, but her body...that is on a very different page. I'm pretty sure I know which one is going to win out.

Releasing her face, I wrap my hands around her waist and lift her from the couch, switching our position.

She fits so perfectly, straddling my lap.

Reaching for the moisturizer, I squeeze a little more onto my fingertip before rubbing it onto her rosy cheeks.

Her eyes flutter closed, severing our connection.

"Eyes on me," I demand, and she instantly opens them.

"Yes," she whimpers. "I trust you."

Her confession makes my chest expand.

I already knew she did, but that doesn't mean I don't want to hear the words.

As I rub the cream into her face, her stomach growls.

"Have you eaten anything?" I ask, already knowing she hasn't.

She looks away, and I drop my hands to her bare thighs.

She flinches at my contact, her pussy grinding against my dick and making my breath catch.

She hasn't even touched me and I'm already riding a knife's edge.

"I bought ingredients for sandwiches," I tell her. "Why don't you go and make them while I shower." As much as I might want to push her for a decision and get down and dirty with her again, I've run for miles in the blazing sun, and I need to clean up. "And maybe think about what I said."

Sliding my hands under my hoodie, I skim them over the sides of her panties and grip her hips.

I'm desperate to strip it off her and see if she's got my marks on her from last night.

She wasn't wrong earlier; I was rough with her. Rougher than I probably should have been. But she can't argue with the fact she loved every second of it.

I know she did. So does her body. It's begging for more.

"Kieran," she whispers.

"I've got to be back in Chicago on Monday," I confess. "That gives us four days. Four days to forget about the world and enjoy ourselves. Then we can get in our cars and return to our usual lives."

"And you think you can do that?"

I search her eyes.

"It's just sex, Effie. No strings. A way for you to let go and burn off some steam."

"But—"

Reluctantly, I lift her from my lap and place her back on the couch before standing.

Turning to face her, I don't bother attempting to hide the way my dick tents my sweats.

Her eyes drop instantly, her pupils dilate, and her tongue sneaks out, licking across her bottom lip.

My cock jerks, and I only just manage to catch the groan that rumbles up my throat at the thought of her getting on her knees and—

"Think about it. No pressure. You don't want more, just say, and we'll continue as we were until Monday."

Without offering up the alternative, I spin around and walk away, dragging my hoodie from my body as I go.

Her heavy sigh fills the air as I walk around the corner and straight into the bathroom.

I don't close the door. It's stupid, but if I leave it open, then maybe she'll see it as some kind of invitation to join me.

Shoving my sweats and boxers to my ankles, I kick them off and step into the shower.

I turn it on without waiting for it to warm up, but the cold water does nothing to lessen the fire that's burning through my veins.

Reaching out, I press my palms to the tiles and hang my head, letting the water hit the back of my neck and run down my back.

I startle when a loud bang comes from another room, and I can only hope that she's followed orders and is making lunch.

She really needs to eat something.

As disappointed as I am that she didn't immediately follow me in here, deep down, I know that she's doing the right thing.

Last night—and this morning—was so good. I can only imagine how addicted I could become to her with another four days of it.

She's probably right.

It's a stupid thing for us to embark on.

It could change everything.

But as I'm trying to convince myself that I can put our time together behind me as if it didn't happen, movement by the door catches my eye.

I look up just in time to see her pull my hoodie and shirt she's wearing over her head before pushing her panties down her legs.

My heart jumps into my throat as my eyes drop down the length of her naked body.

My cock jerks and my hands fist as I discover I was right. Her hips are littered with bruises from last night.

She looks fucking spectacular.

"W-what are you doing?" I ask as she closes the space between us and steps into the shower.

Her eyes hold mine for a beat before she whispers, "Four days, yeah?"

I nod, unable to speak past the lump in my throat.

"Four days and then we move on like it never happened?"

I nod again.

"Okay. Deal," she says, sinking to her knees before me.

27

EFFIE

The second he walks away, everything changes again.

The heat coursing through my veins and the desire that pulled at my muscles ebb away, and the grief I'm all too familiar with creeps back in.

I had every intention of doing what Kieran suggested. I even make it as far as the grocery bag he'd abandoned in the kitchen.

I am hungry, I can't deny that, but still, my stomach knotted the instant I looked at the fresh baguette and all the fillings he'd bought.

I don't want to think about food. I don't want to be sad.

I don't want to be in pain.

He's shown me a way to make it stop, and he's offering it to me on a platter.

Without overthinking it, I abandon the food and walk down the hallway to where I know he is.

The image of him standing under the shower with water running over his muscular body is the only thing I can think about. Well, that, and the way his erection tented his sweats not so long ago.

I'd be lying if I said my mouth doesn't water at the thought of getting a taste of him.

He's had a taste of me after all.

It's only fair that I return the favor.

If we're going to do this, then I want the full Kieran Callahan experience.

Pressing my trembling hand against the ajar bathroom door, I suck in a deep breath before pushing it open and stepping into the steam.

If it were anyone else in here, I would probably be nervous. But I already know how he's going to react, and it's only spurring me on.

It's four days.

We can do four days.

Right now, the biggest issue I have is whether I'll be able to leave this place and go home.

That's going to be harder than giving him up and returning to normal.

I'll still have him in my life no matter what, but I'll be leaving Grams behind.

Squeezing my eyes closed, I refuse to allow myself to go there.

Look up.

My breath catches in my throat at what I find.

The sight of him with his head bowed hits me hard.

He looks...defeated.

Without thought, I move deeper into the room with my heart slamming against my ribs.

The nerves have hit, but I refuse to give into them.

I take my glasses off before reaching for the bottom of both his hoodie and the shirt I'm wearing. I begin pulling them up my body, exposing myself again.

I've got the fabric around my hips when he realizes that he's no longer alone and looks over at me.

My breath gets stuck in my throat as his eyes widen in surprise, watching as intently as I reveal inch after inch of my body.

They lock on my bare chest before I pull both items over my head.

I may no longer be able to see him looking at me, but I know he is. My skin is burning up and my breasts are already aching.

The second the fabric clears my head, I discover what I already knew.

Kieran has turned to face me, his eyes are now on mine and they are blazing.

"W-what are you doing?" he stutters once I've dropped my panties and moved closer.

A light mist of water from the shower covers me, and it makes my nipples pebble even harder than they already are.

Keeping my eyes on his, I suck in a deep breath and say what I came in here to say.

"Four days, yeah?" I ask, my voice firm and confident despite the riot of emotions warring inside me.

His chin drops in surprise, but he doesn't say a word.

Instead, he nods.

Not exactly the response I was hoping for, but I guess making him speechless isn't a bad thing.

"Four days and then we move on like it never happened?" I ask with a wince.

God. It's crazy.

We're crazy.

He nods again, his nostrils flaring and his fists curling at his sides.

"Okay. Deal," I say before doing what I was imagining when I stepped in here.

His sharp intake of breath hits my ears as my knees land on the tiles at his feet.

"Baby," he groans, suddenly finding his voice.

I shuffle forward, moving closer to what I really want before I reach out and wrap my hand around his hard dick.

My stomach flips and every muscle south of my waist pulls tight as I remember just how good he felt inside me.

My heart pounds so hard, I can feel it in every inch of my body as I lean closer to him.

His fingers sink into my hair, twisting tightly as I stick my tongue out and lick his tip.

His hips jerk forward the very moment we connect and the head of his dick slips past my lips.

Oh my god.

I'm sucking Kieran Callahan's dick.

My wide eyes roll up his body as he pushes a little deeper.

If I'm being honest, I don't rate my blow job skills. I've given a few in the past, but no one has ever been overly complimentary. But then, I can't say I ever really wanted to get on my knees and do it.

Right now, though...everything is different.

I want to blow his mind just like he did mine last night.

I want to be the best whore he's ever had. And that thought alone would be enough to put me on my knees if I weren't already there.

What the fuck has this man done to me?

"Christ, Luck," he groans, feeding me more of his dick.

I open wider for him, happily taking him.

He gazes down at me with awe in his dark green eyes, and my already slick pussy gets wetter for him.

"Look at you," he muses. "Such a good girl on your knees for me."

My eyes shutter as I embrace his words, desire pulsing through my veins.

"Can you take more?" he asks, his free hand reaching down to cup my jaw tenderly.

I nod as best I can, willing to do whatever he wants.

He smiles down at me, and I light up inside, knowing that I'm pleasing him.

"Good girl," he praises at the same time his grip on my hair tightens.

Tears prick my eyes as he drags me closer, forcing his dick deeper.

He hits the back and I gag.

"We'll take it slow. Build you up, okay?"

Hating that I'm not giving him what he needs, I suck in a deep breath through my nose and force myself to relax.

He moves again, but this time, I don't gag. I take him.

It's not all of him by a long shot, but it's more than I've ever dared take before.

He completely consumes my senses, and my breathing.

My lungs burn from lack of oxygen as he continues to fuck my face, drool running down my chin and tears spilling from my eyes.

But these tears are different from all the others I've shed recently. They don't come with a side of unbearable pain. They only come with pleasure.

My clit throbs with my need to come as he continues using me.

I rub my thighs together, trying to get the friction I need. I don't realize it's obvious until he barks.

"Spread your legs," he demands, his voice deep and unforgiving.

Without missing a beat, I do as I'm told.

"You're dripping wet for me, aren't you?" he rasps.

I stare up at him, aware that he can probably read the answer in my hungry eyes.

"Be a good girl and I might let you come."

I whimper around his dick and he curses.

"You only get to come when I say you can. For the next

four days, your pleasure belongs to me. You don't touch yourself. You don't get yourself off. It's my job and mine alone. And I will decide when."

Every single muscle in my body tightens.

Oh my fucking god.

Pulling his dick from my mouth, he allows me to suck in a couple deep breaths.

"Do you understand, Luck?"

"Y-yes."

He stares down at me with his dick in his hand and his chest heaving as water rains down on his back.

Hottest thing I've ever seen in my life.

"Good. You won't regret it."

My lips part to speak, but I don't manage to get any words out before he pushes his dick back inside my mouth.

"Goddamn, Effie," he groans, his pace increasing.

The tip of his dick pushes against my throat, but he doesn't go any farther. Not yet. Something tells me that might change by the end of these four days.

My kind and caring best friend has some serious kinks, and I am more than happy to indulge him and find out just how far they really go.

"Fuck," he grunts, his fingers twisting so tightly in my hair.

He stares down at me as his hips thrust his dick in and out of my mouth, and I can't take my eyes off him.

"That's it. Fuck. You look incredible. Fuck," he groans again before his loud moan bounces off the tiles around us and his dick pulsates in my mouth before he comes down my throat. "Effie, fuck."

He pulls back, his cock softening between my lips, but he demands, "Don't close your mouth," before he lets it drop.

My jaw hurts, and I'm desperate to swallow, but I do as I'm told.

I need him to tell me that I'm a good girl again like I need my next breath.

His eyes run over every inch of me before coming back to my face.

"Swallow," he finally commands, and I do in a heartbeat.

A smirk spreads across his lips before he mutters, "Who knew you'd be this perfect?" before reaching down and effortlessly lifting me from the floor.

But he doesn't place me on my feet. Instead, he wraps my legs around his waist and presses my back against the tiles.

Reaching beneath me, his fingers find my pussy and he groans.

"Look how much you loved sucking my dick, Luck," he says before pulling his glistening fingers free. "And you looked so beautiful doing it."

Pushing his fingers into my mouth, they hit the back of my throat as my taste explodes on my tongue, and I gag again.

"We'll work on that," he tells me before pulling his hand away and slamming his lips down on mine, tasting me on my tongue. "Delicious."

"Kieran, please," I beg when he finally pulls back, breaking our kiss.

I'm desperate, my body screaming for a release.

"Please, what, Luck?"

"I-I need to come."

His smile is nothing but pure filth, and it hits me right in the clit.

"Do you remember what I said?" he asks.

I lick my lips, my brain barely firing at this point.

"Tell me. Tell me what I said."

"Y-you said..." I swallow, my throat dry. "You said I only come when you decide I can."

His smile grows.

"Good girl."

He shifts me against his body, ensuring his dick rubs against my pussy before he spins us around and under the spray.

"What are you doing?" I ask when he places me on my feet. I look over at where he had me pinned only moments ago, mourning the loss of what could have been.

Reaching over my shoulder, he grabs something before bringing it in front of me.

"I'm taking care of you," he explains as he pours shower gel onto his and moves it to my chest.

"Not exactly what I had in mind."

He raises a brow.

"Be a good girl, Effie. You never know what might come next."

My head falls back and a moan spills from my lips when he teases my nipple.

He chuckles, and it makes my thighs clench.

"I like it when you're desperate, Luck. Makes you even hotter."

28

KIERAN

I caress every inch of Effie's body, loving the way she whimpers and leans into my touch, proving that this was the best idea I've ever had.

We can spend four days together. I can help her find herself again. And then we can return to Chicago, and our lives, with more than just sad memories of our time here.

I'm not naive; I know that losing Grams will always overshadow whatever we do here. I just hope that it softens the blow and gives her something positive to think about as well.

"Kieran," she moans as I drag my fingers between her legs, giving her just a taste of what she wants.

The sound of my name on her lips ensures my cock is rock hard again.

It makes me wonder if I'm going to be able to control it when our time is done.

Surely, after four days, I'll have whatever this is out of my system and ready to move on?

It's not like any woman has ever held my interest for that long before.

Hell, four hours can be too long, let alone four days.

Or, I guess, five, if you include last night.

"Oh god," she whimpers as I push two fingers inside her.

She's just as tight as I remember and my dick jerks, jealous.

"You want my dick, Luck?" I ask, ducking down so I can look her dead in the eyes.

"Yes."

I smirk. "Then don't come."

"W-what?" she stutters as if she misheard me.

"Then don't come," I repeat.

"But...please." She pouts and I reach out, dragging my thumb across her bottom lip before tugging it forward even more.

The image of her lips stretched around my cock only minutes ago fills my mind.

Her inexperience was obvious, but it was by no means off-putting. What she lacked in finesse, she made up for in effort.

She wanted to suck my dick, and she got off in doing so.

That means more to me than anything else.

Give it a couple of days though, and she'll be fucking outstanding. She'll know exactly what I like and just what to do to blow my mind.

"Good girls get rewarded," I remind her before copying her move from earlier and dropping to my knees.

She watches me with her swollen lips parted and her chest heaving erratically.

Leaning forward, I kiss up her thigh before lifting one foot from the floor and throwing her leg over my shoulder, leaving her standing on the other.

She reaches out to steady herself against the wall as I close in on her pussy.

Her scent fills my nose and my mouth waters.

I could eat her for a week and I'm not sure it would be enough.

With my fingers still curled inside her, I lick her clit.

Her entire body trembles, a needy whimper spilling from her lips.

"Kieran."

Her fingers twist in my short, wet hair, and she holds it tight as if it'll stop me from going anywhere.

I chuckle against her as her release begins to build in record time.

She hasn't said anything, but I have no doubt she's still sore from last night.

I'm going to fuck her again; it won't stop me, but I'll make sure she's nice and ready first.

"Eyes," I demand when hers close so she can chase her high.

She follows orders and something potent crackles between us as our gaze holds.

Her pussy grips my fingers tighter as her release approaches, and just before she crashes, I pull back and stand up.

"W-what—"

Turning the shower off, I step out and grab one of the towels on the rack.

I spin around and hold it out for her, but I can't help but laugh when I get a look at the expression on her face.

"Everything okay?" I ask, making her lips purse harder as I wrap her in the fluffy towel.

"Wonderful," she seethes as I grab her glasses and slide them onto her face before tucking my fingers under her chin. I tilt her head back so she has no choice but to look up into my eyes.

"That attitude won't get you what you want, Luck." It's bullshit. I'll give her exactly what she wants over and over, because I want to watch her coming just as much as she wants the relief.

Thoughts of her tied to her bed and writhing as she comes all over herself fill my head.

Shaking the images, I duck down and kiss her tempting lips.

But no sooner does she open her mouth to deepen it than I pull away and grab a towel of my own.

Leaving her standing in the middle of the bathroom, I march toward the guest room to grab a clean pair of sweats. I go without boxers because...well, you know.

By the time I emerge, I find her in her bedroom, brushing her hair and still wearing nothing but the towel.

Ignoring her heated stare, I go to her chest of drawers and grab another of my t-shirts from her collection.

This one is a Chiefs one, and it's got my name and number on it. I mean, why would I choose anything else? For the next four days, she's mine, and I want to make sure she knows it.

Stepping up behind her, I hold her eyes in the mirror before tugging her towel from her body.

As tempting as her curves are, I don't let my gaze drop.

"Arms up," I say, smirking when she follows orders despite the fact she clearly wants to argue.

Reluctantly, I cover her up. But it's only for a short while.

When I get her naked again, it's going to be for a very long time.

Picking up the hairbrush from her vanity, I continue with what she was doing when I walked in.

"Kieran, you don't need to—"

"Shush. I told you that I was taking care of you, now let me."

She falls silent as I drag the brush through her blonde locks.

Once I'm happy, I grab her hand and tug her out of her bedroom and to the kitchen.

She complains as I sit her on a stool, but the second I spin her to face me and pinch her jaw between my fingers, she stops.

She had to have known this was going to come before anything else.

I might have an endless list of things I want to do to her, but none of them are happening until she's eaten.

"Good girl, remember?" I say before kissing the tip of her nose and walking to the bag I abandoned when I got back earlier.

My skin tingles where she watches me work, but I don't look back or let her know I'm aware of her attention. Although, when I'm done and finally turn her way, I think it's pretty obvious by the tenting of my sweats again.

"You really love sandwiches, huh?" she muses as I walk toward her with two plates in my hands.

Walking behind her, I lower her plate before brushing my lips against her ear.

"It's not the food, Luck. It's everything I'm going to do to you once we've finished it."

All the air rushes from her lungs as she shudders on the stool.

"Eat up, baby. You're going to need your energy," I promise before pulling away and taking a seat beside her.

We eat in silence, but the air is charged with everything we want to say.

I demolish mine in only a few minutes, leaving Effie to nibble at hers.

To my delight, she eats more of it than I was expecting, and certainly more than she has for at least a week.

See...this little deal is good in more ways than one.

It's going to help her find herself again.

"Done?" I ask when she pushes her plate away.

She glances over but doesn't hold my eyes. She doesn't think she's done enough to please me.

Fuck. She's so fucking perfect.

"Y-yeah. I can't—"

"It's okay," I tell her, cupping her jaw and turning her to face me. "You did good, baby." Standing on the stool, I take her hand and help her to her feet. "Are you ready for dessert?" I ask.

She gasps, staring up at me with wide, desire-filled eyes before sucking her bottom lip into her mouth.

"Words, Effie. I need your words."

"Y-yes," she whimpers.

I search her eyes, looking for any hint of a lie.

I don't find any.

"This isn't going to be fast. And it might not be what you're expecting. But I promise it'll be worth it."

"Okay."

"If at any point you don't want to continue—"

"Stop," she says, stepping closer. "I trust you, Kieran. Do you worst."

Swallowing the lump in my throat, I retake her hand and lead her to her room.

My heart is racing as we step through the door, and irritatingly, my confidence wavers a little.

Suddenly, I feel like a teenager again who's about to attempt his first time.

I guess, in a way, I am.

For the first time ever, I have every intention of doing this exactly as I want to.

I'm not going to let my fear hold me back because, for once, this isn't about me.

It's about her.

Effie.

My best friend.

The one woman I know I can trust with all my darkest secrets and desires.

Releasing her in the middle of her room, I take a step back.

"Strip," I demand, pushing my hands into my pockets as I wait for her to follow orders.

She does instantly, revealing her body to me.

The bruises on her hips catch my eye again, and I can't help but hope that this time tomorrow, she'll have more.

She stands before me beautifully naked, waiting for my next command.

"Get on the bed, in the middle, arms above your head."

Her cheeks expand as she sucks in a deep breath before spinning and stalking toward the bed.

I watch as she crawls onto the middle, giving me a look at her ass and pussy before she flips over and does as she's told.

I stand there for a few more seconds before jumping into action.

"Where are you going?" she calls as I dart from the room.

"Spread your legs and wait," I call over my shoulder, rushing to the guest room.

Her eyes widen when I return with two leather belts in my hand.

She swallows nervously but doesn't say a word as I walk to the top of the bed, wrap the leather around her wrist, and then secure her to the bed.

I repeat the action with her other arm, loving the way her breathing gets more and more erratic as I restrict her movement.

Stepping back, I assess my handiwork.

"Beautiful," I muse before movement catches my attention. I frown. "I said spread your legs."

Instantly, she obeys, and I stalk to the foot of the bed, my eyes locked on her glistening pussy.

"You like being at my mercy, don't you?"

I don't need her confirmation; her body answers for her, but that doesn't stop her from whispering, "Yes."

"Has anyone ever tied you up before?"

She bites her bottom lip before shaking her head.

"Good." I love the idea of being the first to do this to her.

Ripping my eyes from her, I begin pulling her drawers open.

"What are you looking for?" she asks before slamming her lips shut when I give her a heated look over my shoulder.

Finally, I find something that will work.

I spin around with two scarves in my hand.

29

EFFIE

Blood rushes past my ears and my heart pounds in every inch of my body as I watch him wrap the scarves around each of my ankles and tie them to the foot of the bed.

I wasn't lying when I told him earlier that I'd never been tied up before. And I'm glad I haven't. I wouldn't want to experience this with anyone else.

"There," he mutters as he steps back to assess his handiwork.

My breathing is erratic and my skin is prickling with my need to be touched.

I've been buzzing since he got me close with his tongue and fingers in the shower, my pussy aching and clenching in its need for more. And now I'm lying here completely at his mercy, everything has only gotten more intense, more desperate.

"Kieran," I whimper, watching as he walks around the bed.

He's like a lion stalking his prey, waiting for the perfect time to strike.

Wrapping his hand around the back of his neck, he pulls on it as his eyes lift to the ceiling.

My heart jumps into my throat worrying that he's suddenly regretting all of this.

I'm not exactly in the best position if he's doubting everything.

"I...I don't show women this side of me, Effie. I've never—" He cuts himself off, and his eyes find mine. "I usually keep it locked down. But...I trust you. And I think...I think you get off on this too. My sweet, nerdy little lucky charm is secretly just as kinky as I am."

Am I?

His eyes blaze with fire at the thought of his statement being true.

I mean, it could be. He's not wrong; last night was wild. The way he touched me, the things he said...I burned for him like I never have for any other man.

"This is between us," I tell him.

I would never in a million years consider telling anyone anything about our friendship or anything we do or talk about.

My relationship with Kieran is precious. Always has been, always will be.

"I know. I just...I needed you to know that this—" He gestures between us. "—isn't what I usually do with women."

I raise a brow.

"I'm serious. I don't show strangers this side of me. Hell, I've never shown anyone this side of me."

A wide smile spreads across my lips.

It's fucking weird.

If you described this situation to me and told me that I'd be lying here feeling happier than I have in quite some time, I'd say that you were crazy.

But as it turns out, I might be tied up and unable to do anything but follow him with my eyes around the room, but I

229

feel lighter than I have since moving my life to St. Louis to be with Grams all those months ago.

"What are you going to do to me?" I ask.

I don't care what it is. I'll let him do whatever he wants.

He pauses at the end of the bed and turns, pressing a knee against the mattress.

"I'm going to make you forget your own name," he tells me honestly, his voice deep and raspy.

The promise makes my core throb, and I try to close my thighs to squash it, but I can't move them an inch.

He crawls between my thighs, his smirk growing.

"By the time I untie you, the only name you'll remember is mine."

"Cocky much?" I tease.

His expression hardens, his jaw ticking as he grinds his teeth.

"You don't have to have use of your mouth, you know."

My chin drops, but I can't deny that the thought of him gagging me doesn't make my already sky-high temperature increase.

"Remember what I said? Only good girls get what they want."

I flinch when his fingertips brush against my ankle. It's such a simple touch, but it affects me like he's just pressed a branding iron into my skin.

"Kieran," I moan.

"Right here, baby," he rasps as he slowly drags his fingers up my leg. "And I'm not going anywhere.

Turning his attention to my other leg, he bends over and kisses my shin, right above where my scarf is tied around my ankle.

I flinch again, tugging at my bindings, but none of them give.

Arching my back, I grind my hips, desperate for some relief, but it does nothing.

I'm useless like this and totally reliant on him. Something that he is loving if the tent in his sweats is anything to go by.

"Why aren't you naked?" I gasp as his lips trail up my leg.

"Because I'm the one in charge, and I've decided to remain dressed."

"B-but—"

"Keep arguing, Luck. See where it gets you," he taunts.

Slamming my lips shut, I fall silent and try to just enjoy the ride.

Fuck. I really hope there is a ride coming.

If he thinks he's just going to tease me and leave me here to suffer for the rest of the day, then he's going to regret it.

I don't know what I'll do to punish him, but I'll figure something out.

"Oh my god, yes," I moan as he gets to the top of my thigh and blows a stream of air across where I need him most.

He moves closer, and I hold my breath, waiting for the second his tongue connects with my sensitive skin.

But it never comes.

I cry out in frustration, tugging at the belts holding my arms hostage.

The entire bed rattles, not used to seeing any action, but I don't achieve anything.

Kieran chuckles as he kisses over my hips.

"Needy little whore," he muses before his hands land on either side of me and he dips his tongue into my belly button.

"Please," I beg. I know it won't help, but the plea falls free regardless.

"Tell me, how much did you like sucking my cock earlier?" He looks up my body as his lips move toward my ribs. "Are you already thinking about doing it again?"

"Yes," I whisper, licking my lips as if his taste still lingers.

"By the time we leave for Chicago, you're going to take all of it. I want to watch you swallow me down."

I nod eagerly, desperate to give him anything he wants.

"You looked so beautiful on your knees," he tells me as his nose bumps against the underside of my breasts.

I gasp, but as good as this feels, it's not enough.

"Kieran, please."

"Patience, baby. Good things come to those who wait."

I want to thrash and scream, but it won't get me anywhere.

He licks around the side of my breast before kissing up my chest and to my ear.

"Beg me," he whispers, making a shiver race down my body.

"Please, Kieran. Make me come. Plea—"

His lips claim mine, cutting off my words.

I stretch up the best I can to continue the kiss, but I don't have to worry because he has the same idea.

Resting on his forearms, he lowers over me, his chest brushing my nipples as he kisses me as if he'll die without it.

Time ceases to exist, but I never lose the desperate throb that has now taken over my entire body.

He leans forward a little more, and I cry out into our kiss as his fabric-covered cock brushes against my swollen clit.

He sits up, severing our connection, and stares down at me, his eyes almost black with desire.

His smile of accomplishment takes my breath away.

"I'm going to go out tomorrow and buy you some things," he explains.

"W-what things?"

"Things that will have you begging and pleading me to let you come."

I swallow nervously as my mind races with options.

He means toys. Sex toys.

My stomach flutters with a mixture of nerves and excitement.

I own a vibrator. Two, actually. But something tells me this isn't going to be as simple as a bullet vibe.

My mouth runs dry, but the pulsating of my clit gets worse.

I didn't think it could be like this.

I gaze up at Kieran, suddenly seeing him differently from every other time I've looked at him.

I appreciated him being here and looking after me before. But what he's doing now...this escape he's giving me...I'll never be able to thank him properly for getting me out of my head.

"O-oh."

His smile grows as he shifts his weight onto one arm and wraps his free hand around my throat.

My pulse pounds against his gentle grip.

I never thought I'd like a possessive move like this, but it turns out, I would have been wrong.

"Please," I whimper.

He shifts again, so he's sitting up between my thighs, his hand still on my throat. I would say he's pinning me in place, but we both know that I'm not going anywhere.

"You're soaked," he muses as his eyes drop between my legs.

I wiggle my hips, hoping to tempt him closer, to give me what I need.

"Do you think you deserve to come? Have you been good enough?"

"Yes, yes," I chant. "Please."

He nods, and all the air rushes from me as relief floods through me.

But instead of diving straight for where I need him, he grabs my breast, squeezing just enough to sting, not enough to hurt, which sends a powerful shot of desire straight to my core.

"You like a little pain with your pleasure, don't you?" he muses.

I don't respond. I can't.

'Please,' I mouth as he tugs on my nipple, driving me crazy.

"Christ," he grunts, although I have no idea why. He doesn't follow it with anything else.

But I can't complain, because his hand skims down my stomach and finally brushes over my pussy.

I whimper in relief as he gently traces his fingertip over my desperate skin.

The second he presses two fingers against my entrance, my body tries sucking him in, and he chuckles.

"Love how desperate you are for me," he muses.

Another noise spills from my lips, but I have no idea what it is.

"I'll give you what you need, but only if you do something for me," he says, refusing to give me any more.

His eyes hold mine hostage as he waits for me to respond.

"Anything," I finally manage to whisper.

"Count."

I frown, confused.

"C-count what?" I ask as he twitches his fingers.

"Orgasms."

My eyes widen as understanding dawns.

"Okay?" he questions when I don't respond.

I nod eagerly. I'll do anything if it means he gives me more.

I want everything he can offer me.

If we've only got four days to indulge, there won't be anything I'll say no to.

We only regret the things we don't do, as they say.

"Good," he states as he thrusts his fingers deep inside me.

My hips jump from the bed as pleasure rushes through me and his hand on my throat tightens enough to make my eyes open.

I didn't even realize they'd closed.

"Eyes on me, Luck. And don't forget to count."

He works me hard and fast, curling his fingers just so, and in only a couple of minutes, I cry out as he demands I begin counting.

"One," I gasp as I come down from my high.

"Good girl," he praises. "Now, let's see how high you can get."

My body trembles from the strength of my first release, but he barely gives me a second to recuperate before he goes for number two.

30

KIERAN

"Fuck," I grunt, falling back to the bed after untying Effie.

Slipping my arm beneath her back, I pull her into me.

Her entire body trembles, and I can't help but smile.

She was so fucking awesome.

She stopped counting at eight, but she had a few more. She's just lost the ability to talk after that.

"Good girl," I praise, gently rubbing her back as her breathing begins to slow down. "You're so beautiful when you come, Luck. Could watch you all day."

Her warm breath tickles over my chest, and despite only just filling her pussy full of cum, my dick jerks.

It can't get enough.

I'm just hoping that after another three days of this, she'll be ready to move on so I can keep my promise to her.

But before I get too comfortable, and before she succumbs to her exhaustion, I need to take care of her.

Slipping from beneath her, I pad naked to the bathroom to

get a washcloth to clean her up with before heading to the kitchen for a bottle of water and one of my expertly made cinnamon buns.

She's quiet as she accepts both, her eyelids heavy and her muscles relaxed.

Crawling back into bed with her, I accept her embrace once she's finished, and in only seconds, she's asleep.

If the only thing that comes out of all of this is that she finally gets some rest, then I can live with that. Rest and food, then she'll be able to start healing. Hopefully.

I lie there with her sleeping in my arms for the longest time, but eventually, I need to move.

Slipping from beneath her, I make sure she's still out before pulling on my sweats and silently leaving the room.

I clean up and then head for the kitchen. I'm washing our plates from earlier when my cell buzzes in my pocket.

Assuming it's either King—because he'll have been told the latest by now, no doubt—or Kian, I pull it free.

But to my surprise, it isn't my brothers.

Instead, it's my teammate.

Drying my hands, I swipe the screen and then walk out to the backyard to ensure I don't wake Effie.

"Hey, man. How's it going?" I greet.

"Yeah, good. The usual," Brax hedges.

I like it here in St. Louis. It's quiet and peaceful. But it's not home.

It's not Chicago.

Brax was just finishing up his rookie year as a Chief when I was drafted. We hit it off immediately, and he was more than willing to hand out advice when he thought I needed it.

He's a good guy. Effie likes him too.

There was a moment when they first met when I wondered if there could be something there. But clearly, I was wrong. As far as I know, he never asked her out, and there has never been anything between them.

I couldn't have stopped them if they did. I had—have—no claim on Effie. She's my best friend, and up until yesterday, nothing further had ever happened between us.

I've always wanted her to meet someone.

Did I want it to be one of my teammates? No, not really.

My stomach sloshes with something unpleasant at the thought.

"How are things there?"

I let out a heavy sigh, which I'm sure is enough to answer his question.

Slipping through the bushes, I lower my ass to the swing seat where I found her earlier.

"Yeah, you know." I scrub my hand down my face, trying to decide how much I want to divulge.

"The media is still full of stories," he warns.

My stomach knots at the reminder that I've still got to deal with all the false news that's spread through the country like a disease.

I've been running over things to say to put an end to it all, but it all sounds ridiculous.

I can't say that my best friend lied. I refuse to throw her under the bus like that.

She did it for a good reason. But I'm not sure the rest of the country—the jersey chasers—will be as understanding as I was.

So, if I can't tell them the truth, do I tell them we split up? But then, that'll cause another truckload of drama to surround both of us.

"Brilliant," I mutter.

"I was right, wasn't I? This isn't real?"

Brax has sent me a few messages since the news broke, but I haven't been very forthcoming with answers. I've been too focused on Effie. But he saw through it the instant the news hit the headlines.

"No," I confess. "It's not. Effie's grandmother's dying wish was for us to get married. So Effie—"

"Made her dream come true. That's cute."

"Yeah," I agree; the concept is really fucking cute. But the reality is a bitter pill to swallow. "It made Grams very happy. But the goddamn nurse leaked the story, and here we are."

"What are you going to do?"

"Well, I'm not about to walk down the aisle, that's for sure."

Brax laughs. "You could do a lot worse than Effie, man."

Don't I fucking know it.

My eyes lift to the house, or more specifically to where the bedroom hides behind the bushes. She's lying there naked with my cum running out of her.

Yeah, she's even more perfect than even I was aware of.

"Maybe so, but I couldn't commit to her for life."

"Understandable. You can barely look after yourself most days, let alone someone else."

"Speak for yourself," I laugh before falling quiet.

"You still there?" he asks after a couple of seconds.

"Yeah."

"You gonna be back here for the photoshoot Tuesday?" he asks, clearly having had the same reminder that I did earlier.

"Yeah, I'll be there."

"And Effie?"

"I'm hoping she'll come back with me. She's been here too long. Her life is waiting for her."

"Kat has been trying to get hold of you," he suddenly says, making me groan.

It's not news. I've seen and ignored her missed calls, voicemails, messages, and emails.

I just...don't want to deal with her or this, or anything, right now.

"You're gonna have to deal with it. Especially if you leave her there. That'll invite even more questions."

I drop my head into my hands. "I know."

"Speak to Kat. She might have the answer."

"She'll want me to throw Effie under the bus to make me look better."

His pause doesn't fill me with joy.

"I get that, Kieran. I really do. But at the end of the day, she lied. She might just have to face the consequences. She—"

"The fuck, Brax?" I bark, shooting to my feet.

"I know you want to protect her. I'd be exactly the same. But you can't do that all the time. Effie is a smart woman. She knew what she was risking when she tied herself to you like this. Have you spoken to her about how she might want to deal with it?"

"No," I confess, the adrenaline ebbing away.

"That might be the best place to start, don't you think?"

He's right. I know he is. But every time I mention the future and having to return to her life, shadows of pain flicker across her eyes. I hate hurting her. Brax is right; I do want to protect her. But maybe this just isn't a time where I'm able to do that.

She's going to need to stand up and rip the band-aid off if she stands a chance of moving on.

Which she has to do. I refuse to let her wallow here forever.

We spend a little longer chatting, our conversation thankfully drifting away from my current situation to Tuesday's photoshoot and other plans we have for the rest of summer. Or at least, plans he has. Other than some helping out at some of our summer camps, and appearances and endorsements, I don't have much. With Grams' health declining, I knew my summer would be spent with Effie.

My mind drifts to vacations. The temptation to whisk Effie

away from all of this is strong. But it would be irresponsible of me to convince her to go back to Chicago and then drag her away again.

She needs to find stability in her life, to return to her routine and not be pulled away again just as she gets settled.

Forgetting the idea of a week or two on a white beach, I consider shorter options.

I think about the cities we've always talked about visiting.

But will us jetting off together blur the lines again?

I'm going to have to tell the media that we're not a couple; how would us taking trips together look?

When we eventually hang up, my head is spinning even more than before I answered.

So much is up in the air right now. Coming here, I thought it was only my professional life that was in tatters after that tragic loss. I never would have thought that my private life would become headline news, or that I'd find myself engaged.

Leaning forward, I rest my elbows on my knees and let my cell hang between them. I close my eyes and try to make sense of my thoughts.

It doesn't take long to discover that it's completely impossible, and eventually, I give up trying and head back to the house to continue tidying up.

In my quest to ignore my thoughts, I pull the refrigerator open and attempt to come up with something for dinner.

It's already getting late, but I'm hoping Effie wakes up hungry.

Hell knows I already am.

By the time the sound of light footsteps moves toward the kitchen, it's dark outside.

Closing my emails and lower my cell, I look up as she steps into the doorway.

She's breathtaking.

Her hair is wild, her lips are still swollen from my kiss, and she's once again wearing nothing but my t-shirt. Her nipples harden the longer she stands there under my attention, and she begins to shift her weight from one leg to the other.

I smirk, loving how I can still affect her even after what we did a few hours ago.

"How are you feeling?" I ask, pushing to my feet and walking over to the fridge to get her a bottle of water.

"Good. Sore. Tired," she states as she takes the bottle from me but makes no move to lift it to her lips.

"Drink," I demand.

She stares at me for a moment before remembering how this is currently working between us.

As she lifts her hand, the red marks on her wrist from my belt catch my eye, and my cock swells.

She looked so fucking perfect tied up there for me.

I can't help but wonder if vanilla sex with random women is going to satisfy me when this comes to an end.

It won't, a little voice says in the back of my head, but I shove it down.

I'll worry about that when the time comes.

If the worst happens, there are clubs in Chicago that discreetly cater to such tastes. I'm sure I'll be able to get my kicks there while staying under the radar.

"I made pizza," I explain as I pull the tray from the fridge.

She blinks a few times.

"F-from scratch?" she asks, sounding impressed.

"Yes, from scratch," I state proudly. "You're going to eat, then I'm going to run you a bath, and then we're going to find something to watch."

Her eyes narrow on me.

"What?" I ask, a little too amused by her attempt to figure me out now that she's learned all these new things.

"You're not going to tie me up again and—"

"Oh, I will," I say, dropping the tone of my voice. "But not until you've recovered." Abandoning the pizza on the counter, I step up to her, tilting her chin back so she has no choice but to look up at me. "As much as I enjoy making you fall apart, I love putting you back together again just as much."

Her eyes study mine as her teeth sink into her bottom lip.

"Words, Effie."

"Will you...will you join me? In the tub, I mean."

31

EFFIE

The last three days have been...
Unexpected.
Surreal.
Incredible.
Educational.

God, there's a whole list of words I could use to describe it.

But the one that really comes to mind is easy.

Everything has been so relaxed and natural.

I guess that's what happens when you start fucking your best friend. You're already connected on a level. There is none of the awkwardness. Well, maybe not as much of it. Getting naked in front of him, knowing how stunning the women he chooses to spend time with are, was a little unnerving. But the moment I saw his reaction to my body, it was easy to push it aside.

I might not be tall and slim like those supermodels, but he wanted me, and the thought makes my head spin.

I've become too comfortable around him, too reliant on him.

I've been trying not to think about it, because I know I've set myself up for a fall here.

The idea that we could sleep together and have a little fun for four days before returning to our lives was a dream.

A dream I should have known would never work.

With a sigh, I drop my ass to the end of my bed.

Memories of everything I've experienced in the past few days makes my body heat.

I never in a million years would have thought I'd enjoy the things he's done to me.

Choked me. Tied me up. Withheld orgasms one moment and then forced me to have so many I could barely think straight. He's had his fingers in my ass, for fuck's sake. Something I had no intention of experimenting with. But damn, the release that dragged out of me was so freaking worth it.

I've certainly learned a few things.

And tonight...well, I can only imagine the things he has planned.

The water cuts off, and I jump from the bed, knowing that he's going to look in on me soon.

I'm supposed to be packing to return to Chicago tomorrow. I don't know how I feel about it.

There's a part of me that's ready to get back to normality.

But there is still a huge part that wants to be here. I love the comfort of Grams' home. I love being surrounded by her things. Leaving it all behind is going to kill me.

I know she'll be with me no matter where I am, but it won't be the same.

Glancing at my suitcase on the middle of the bed, I return to what I should be doing.

Kieran is buzzing to get home. I wish I could feel some of it.

But seeing his excitement is a harsh reminder that he'll be

able to walk away from this thing between us as soon as we get back.

That's the thing about men. Sex is an act. An epic one, but just an act all the same.

I know there are women out there who are able to view it that way, but I'm learning fast that I'm not one of them.

I wanted to be.

Hell, maybe if I weren't so broken, I'd have been able to keep my head.

I never should have agreed to this four-day fuck fest.

I squeeze my eyes closed as regret mixes with pain.

Footsteps moving closer has me dragging my head up and rolling my shoulders back.

Kieran...none of this is his fault. He promised to look after me, to find a way to help me. That's all he's done.

His shadow appears first, and I attempt to swallow down the lump in my throat and school my features.

"Hey," he says, magically forcing every single previous thought from my head the instant he reveals himself.

He stands there in my doorway in nothing but a towel, which is wrapped low on his hips.

My eyes drop to his body, watching as water droplets run over his skin.

Lifting his hand, he combs his fingers through his wet hair, making the muscles in his chest and stomach ripple and pull in the most delicious way.

My mouth runs dry.

That was why I never would have said no to him.

I've always appreciated how hot he is. But since being intimate with him, I have noticed everything.

"Are you almost packed?" he asks. The smirk on his lips lets me know that he's aware of my ogling and is more than happy for me to continue.

"U-uh..."

Ripping his eyes from me, he glances at the disaster around me.

"So I see." His smile widens, and it makes my stomach flutter.

How am I ever going to look at him again and not remember all the things he's done to me?

"You've got thirty minutes and we're going out," he declares, making my brows pinch.

"W-what?" I ask, disappointment tugging at me.

I thought we were going to spend our last night together here doing...my cheeks heat as my imagination begins to run wild.

"We're going out," he repeats.

"Yeah, I got that. Where?"

His face lights up with excitement, and I can't help but get dragged along for the ride.

"It's a surprise."

"Okay. What should I wear?"

"You can go like that," he says, glancing down at my leggings and hoodie.

I frown, although I must say that I'm a little relieved.

My first thought is that we're going to end up in the park again. But then I glance outside and take in the dark angry clouds. There's a storm approaching.

"Mysterious," I mutter.

"I like to keep you on your toes."

A laugh spills from my lips. "You've certainly done that."

Pride covers his face, and I shake my head.

"Finish up here and then we'll go."

"Do I need to bring anything or—"

"Just yourself." He grins before spinning on his heels and taking a step away; although before he disappears, he tugs his towel from around his waist, allowing me a shot of his bare ass. "I know you're staring."

"Because you want me to."

His laughter bounces around the hallway, and a smile plays on my lips.

Hands down, Kieran Callahan is the best person I've ever met.

As I continue packing the storm hits and the rain begins pounding on the windows.

By the time he comes to collect me for our surprise trip out, I've almost got everything I might need in Chicago packed.

I've always left the necessities here so that when I visit, I don't need to bring everything with me, and this time is no different. But I'm achingly aware that the next time I'm here, it won't be to visit Grams. I don't even know when it'll be or why I'll come.

This house is mine. Or at least, it will be once everything has gone through probate. But knowing that she won't be waiting for me...I shake my head, fighting the emotion that stings the back of my nose.

This time, when Kieran looks around the room, a smile spreads across his mouth. Inside, I might not feel ready to leave, but my suitcase is full.

"Ready?" he asks, holding his hand out for me.

"Sure," I say before grabbing my purse and walking toward him.

The instant my hand slips into his, warmth rushes up my arm and everything feels a little bit easier.

"You look worried," he says as his eyes dart around my face.

"I never know what to expect from you," I confess.

"Isn't that half the fun of it?"

My stomach flips.

Yeah, I guess it is.

While I'm the safe and predictable one of our duo, he's the wild one who likes to push my boundaries.

"I'll take your silence as a yes," he laughs as he tugs me out of the house and into his car.

He starts the engine before turning to me and placing a flat black box on my lap. "I got you something."

"Oh," I breathe, staring down at it as butterflies fill my belly.

I pull the lid off and stare at the contents.

"Uh..."

Reaching out, he pulls the black satin from the box.

"What is it?"

"Can you look out the window for me?"

Confused, I do as I'm told.

The instant the light goes out, understanding hits me.

"Kieran," I gasp as he ties the blindfold around my head.

"Don't want to spoil the surprise," he muses. "Now, sit back and relax."

With my heart racing, I attempt to do as he says while he drives us to wherever we're going.

Of all the things he's done to me over the last few days, cutting off my sight hasn't been one.

"Eyes on me, Luck."

I shudder as his words hit me. They're as clear in my mind as if he just spoke them.

"You okay over there?" he teases.

Shifting in my seat, I let out a sigh.

"Brilliant."

"You need to relax," he points out.

"Easier said than done when you can't see."

"I know exactly the thing," he offers. "Take your leggings off."

"W-what? No. There is no way in hell I'm—"

"Be a good girl, Luck. Take your leggings off for me and spread your thighs."

His words send a tsunami of heat straight to my clit, and I

squirm in my seat—something he doesn't miss, if his groan is anything to go by.

"People will see me."

"Maybe," he says without missing a beat. "But they'll only be jealous."

"Or we'll end up front page news again for a very different reason," I mutter.

He chuckles. "I'm willing to risk it."

"Kieran," I breathe.

I have no idea where we are. I'm so disorientated with my sight gone that I don't stand a chance of trying to figure it out.

"I'm waiting," he demands, his voice deep and unwavering.

Shit. He's serious.

With my heart racing and my hands trembling, I shove my insecurities down and try to drag up some courage.

"That's my good girl," he rasps as I sit up and tug my leggings over my ass.

I shudder as the cool air rushes over my heated skin, and it only gets worse when his fingers slide through me.

"Oh my god," I cry, still sensitive from this morning.

"Always so wet for me," he muses as his fingers sink lower and push inside me.

"S-Shouldn't you be focusing on not killing us?"

"I've got it under control. Trust me?"

"Apparently," I quip.

"Aw, you know I'll take good care of you, baby."

And that, I can't really argue with.

Embarrassingly, it only takes a few minutes for me to be coming all over his fingers.

I don't know how he did it so fast, but he's learned exactly what I need to get off. Sadly, he's also learned exactly when to pull back to keep me right on the edge as well.

"On the way back, you can return the favor," he says,

before pulling his hand away and leaving me sitting there in a puddle of my own desire.

I cringe, thinking about the mess I've left on the fabric.

"Oh my—"

He grasps my chin and drags me over the center console to kiss him.

I groan when his tongue drags against mine, allowing me to taste myself on him.

He sucked his fingers clean...

Desire pools between my thighs again as I imagine how he looked doing it.

"Wait," I cry into his kiss as reality hits. "You should be driving."

He chuckles with his lips still against mine.

"We parked a while ago, baby," he says softly.

"We'd better be somewhere quiet."

Pulling back, he drags his thumb over my bottom lip.

"Trust me," he whispers. "Now get dressed. We've got places to be."

"Can I—"

"No," he barks before I even get the words out about removing the blindfold.

I'm still pulling my leggings up when he opens his door, letting a rush of air flow in.

"Kieran," I hiss, but I doubt he hears me because a beat later, the door slams.

"Come on, beautiful," he says before taking my hand and pulling me from the car.

The trees rustle with the strength of the wind as the cold rain hits my face.

Unable to do anything but follow along, I put my head down and let him guide me, silently praying that no one can see me.

"Trust me."

Swallowing down my apprehension, I allow him to lead me

The sound of the rain cuts off, letting me know that we've entered a building, as does the scent of air freshener. It doesn't help me with where we are, but it does significantly increase the chances of someone seeing me.

"Kieran," I whisper-hiss.

"Not much farther," he assures me, his hand flexing on the small of my back.

We keep moving before he brings me to a stop. There's a whoosh and then we're moving.

We're in an elevator.

Blood rushes past my ears, my stomach a riot of nerves as I try to figure it out.

In only a minute or two, there is a ding, the doors open, and he guides me out.

My feet sink into a luxurious carpet, leading me to think we're in a hotel.

Why, though? We just left a perfectly good house.

"Stop a moment," he says before the familiar sound of a door opening hits my ears.

"Okay, almost there," he says, pushing me forward.

The scent changes. It's subtle, and most people probably wouldn't notice, but I do.

I guess that's what happens when you lose one of your senses.

"And stop there," he says, grabbing my hips and positioning me exactly where he wants me. "Now, I need you to do something for me, okay?"

I nod, too nervous to find my words.

"Count to twenty, and then you can remove your blindfold. Then, like the good girl you are, follow the instructions." He leans closer, the length of his body pressing against my back. "I'll make it worth your while."

32

EFFIE

I startle as a door closes behind me, but despite my need to open my eyes, I do as I'm told and continue counting.

Nine, ten, eleven, twelve...

What the hell is he doing?

I squeeze my eyes tighter, my hands twitching at my sides with my need to pull the blindfold off.

Everything is silent around me, the air sweet yet fresh.

I have a couple of ideas spinning around my head.

But why? That's what I can't figure out.

Fourteen, fifteen, sixteen...

My imagination begins to get the better of me.

Has he brought me somewhere kinky?

I'm sure places like that exist here. I've just...never had a reason to look into them.

My heart pounds harder and my body trembles as I count down the final numbers.

Eighteen, nineteen, twenty...

Blowing out a long breath, I try to steel myself for what I might find when I pull the blindfold off.

No sooner do I slip the satin fabric from my face, the light burns, and my eyes water. But despite my view being blurred, it doesn't stop me from gasping in shock.

I am in the most beautiful hotel room. And hanging before me on the four-poster bed is...the dress.

My heart jumps into my throat as I vividly remember the moment when Kieran stepped into my dressing room and helped me zip it up. The way he looked at me, and the way I burned for him.

If only I knew then what I know now...

My core clenches as I think about what could have happened.

I shake my head, a salacious smile playing on my lips.

What has he done to me?

In only a few days, all of my thoughts somehow lead back to sex. And not just sex. Sex with Kieran.

I've never really cared before. If I had an itch, I scratched it. But it never consumed my life.

I'm starting to think that it could become a problem.

Taking a step closer, I reach out and drag my knuckles down the smooth fabric of the dress.

"Kieran Callahan," I breathe, my chest tight and a messy ball of emotion clogging my throat.

There is a tag on the hanger, and when I turn it over, I find the words "wear me" in Kieran's writing.

I shake my head before I look at the bed and find a box.

"Open me."

With a smirk playing on my lips, I pull the lid from the black box and peer inside.

There's a beautiful pair of shoes. Ones that I always gaze at in the mall but would never buy myself. There is also a pretty lace pair of panties. And then there is another, smaller box.

I frown. It's too big for jewelry.

"Oh my god," I gasp when I get my first look at what lies inside.

There's another note.

"Wear me. I dare you."

Plucking the pink silicone toy from its box, I hold it up, studying it. Desire courses through my veins as I try to imagine what it'll feel like inside me.

Thankfully, he left the instructions with it—which I embarrassingly read to make sure I wear it right. I'm not exactly a sex toy expert.

With it still in my hand, I look up at the dress as butterflies flutter in my belly.

He wants me to dress so beautifully and yet...beneath the surface...

He'll be the only one who knows.

Everything south of my waist tightens and my temperature rises.

I'm still standing there when my cell pings in my purse.

I immediately pull it free, because I know it's him.

Kieran: You have one hour.

"Oh my god."

Picking everything up, I take it with me to what I'm hoping is a bathroom hiding behind the door on the other side of the room.

The moment I step inside, my chin drops.

The counter is covered in my things.

I spin around and look into the shower, finding my shampoo, conditioner, and favorite shower gel.

A laugh tumbles from me as I take in everything he's done.

My cell dings again.

Kieran: Fifty-five minutes.

I twist around, expecting to see him standing in the bedroom watching me. But he isn't.

He just knows you that well, a little voice says.

"Okay, okay," I say as if he's watching before placing everything on the side and stripping out of my clothes.

I shower, and then I do my hair and makeup. I keep it light and natural. I want to look like me, not some of the girls he spends time with.

Jealousy threatens to bubble up at that thought, but I swallow it down. There is no room for that tonight.

With a towel wrapped around me, I sit on the edge of the bed with the sex toy in my trembling hand.

I have never done anything like this before.

But I want to.

Sucking in a deep breath, I lie back and open the towel.

A gasp rips from my lips as I push the cool silicone inside myself and my core tightens around it.

"Kieran," I moan as I push it deeper. It moves easily. Considering I've been alone for almost an hour, I'm embarrassingly wet.

All probably part of his plan.

I sit up and gasp again as the part of the toy inside me hits a spot that threatens to make my eyes cross. The part on the outside presses against my clit.

This is a bad idea...

But that doesn't mean I lie back and pull it free.

No.

Instead, I get to my feet, wiggling my hips to test how it feels.

Closing my eyes, I take a moment to savor the feeling.

Tomorrow, everything is going to change.

I'm going to get in my car and follow Kieran back to my old life.

My heart aches, but it's time.

Refusing to linger on those thoughts, I grab the panties Kieran bought for me. After pulling them on, I reach for the dress and slide it up my body.

It's not until I have the zip halfway up that I remember why he was in the dressing room with me that day.

I laugh at my reflection in the mirror before letting my arms drop.

I'm about to give up and turn around when the bedroom door suddenly opens.

His eyes land on me and I stop breathing.

His chin drops as his gaze roams over me, his green eyes darkening with each second that passes.

"I forgot how fucking outstanding that dress looked on you."

A smile pulls up the corners of my lips as my skin tingles with awareness and my pussy clenches around the toy inside me.

"C-can you?" I ask before spinning around, giving him my back.

I shudder as he steps up to me and his warm breath washes over my neck and down my back.

"Oh god," I breathe.

The room is so silent that the sound of the zipper climbing is almost deafening. Although, the moment he leans closer and whispers in my ear, he is the only thing I can focus on.

"Have you been a good girl for me?" he asks as his hand skims down my side, over my hip, and then cups me between my thighs, over the dress.

"Kieran," I gasp as he presses against the toy, increasing the pressure on my clit and forcing it deeper inside me.

A groan rumbles deep in his throat as he teases me. But almost as soon as he's discovered the toy, he releases me and takes a huge step back.

"Shoes on, Luck," he commands.

I glance back over my shoulder and find him standing with his arms crossed and a stern look on his face.

"Uh...okay," I whisper before doing as I'm told.

As soon as I'm ready, he takes my hand and leads me across the bedroom toward the door.

The thought of having to spend the evening surrounded by other people when the only one I want to spend time with is him makes my steps falter, but he doesn't allow me to stop.

"I hope you're hungry," he says before pulling the door open.

But the hallway I was expecting to find on the other side isn't there.

"Are we...are we in a suite?" I stutter as we walk into a huge living room. Beyond the massive cream couches there's a dining table set for two in front of floor-to-ceiling windows that showcase the city Grams loved so much.

"Just me and you, baby," he says before leading me over to the table and pulling out my chair.

"W-why?" I ask.

"Why not?"

I watch as he pulls out the chair opposite, his eyes on me the whole time.

"It's our last night. I thought we should do something special."

"You know I don't need all this," I say, gesturing to the over-the-top hotel suite.

"Maybe not. But you deserve it."

I shake my head.

This is a man who claims he doesn't do romance.

This is—

"I've got something for you," he says, lifting a small black box above the table and holding it between us.

"I think you've already done enough. The dress, the shoes, the—"

"Toy?" he adds with a wiggle of his brows.

My cheeks burn red hot, and I wriggle on my chair.

"Feels good, doesn't it?"

I bite down on my bottom lip.

"It's okay, Luck. You can tell me how wet it's making you. How badly you need to come already."

"Jesus," I mutter.

"Open it," he urges, holding the box closer.

With a nod, I reach for it.

My heart jumps into my throat.

This one has to be jewelry.

The thought of him buying me a new ring flickers through my mind, but I quickly shut it down.

Tomorrow, the facade will be over.

Lifting the top, my breath catches when I find a pair of diamond-encrusted angel wings staring back at me.

My eyes burn with emotion.

"They open," Kieran says softly as I pull the necklace from its silk cushion.

"Oh my god," I gasp when I separate than, finding a photograph of both of us and Grams at one of his high school football games. "Kieran, this is—"

"I had to put myself in there too," he says. "Didn't want you to forget about me."

I sniffle, desperately trying not to ruin my makeup already. Something tells me he'll want the pleasure of doing that a little later.

"As if that's possible," I whisper, my voice cracked with emotion. "Thank you."

As I move to put it on, he's out of his seat and coming to help me.

"She'll always be with you, Effie. But now, she really is right here," he says, tapping the wings that lie beside my heart. "And so am I."

He's gone before I can blink, and I watch as he lowers himself back into his seat.

He's wearing a simple white shirt with the sleeves rolled up to the elbows and the first three buttons undone. It's understated but hot as hell. So are his black slacks that fit him like a second skin. They've been custom-made; there is no way a pair from a store would hug his ass and thighs the way they do.

"I ordered all your favorites," he informs me before a knock sounds and a man with a tray appears.

A basket of calamari is placed between us and my stomach growls.

"Wine?" he asks, gesturing to the ice bucket beside the table.

"Thank you," Kieran says, speaking for both of us.

The server fills our glasses before he disappears again.

"For someone who doesn't date, you're doing a pretty good job."

His smile grows. "I don't date because I don't want to, not because I can't. And...is this a date?" he asks, quirking a brow.

"Looks like it."

"A pretty dress. A fancy meal. Enough orgasms until you pass out. I guess it sounds like it too."

I laugh, although there isn't much humor in it. Just sadness laced with a powerful coating of desire.

Tomorrow, this is all going to be over. Is it bad that I'm already mourning the loss?

33

KIERAN

I barely taste our food. My full focus is on her.

I knew she'd hate going out tonight, that she'd prefer for it just to be the two of us. But I wanted to do something special. Something memorable.

Tomorrow, that's all this is going to be. A memory. And I want to make sure it's a good one.

She eats in silence, savoring every bite of her salmon fillet.

I'm pretty sure she thinks she's doing a good job of hiding how she's really feeling. But she's not.

Every minute or so, she squirms in her seat. And every time she does, my cock jerks.

I knew she'd follow orders and wear the toy I left for her. I didn't need to check earlier. But I had to. There was no way I'd be able to sit here now only assuming.

I smirk every time she shifts in her seat, desperately trying to get some relief. But it's not going to happen. In fact, it's only going to get worse.

I want her begging for me. So desperate she can barely remember her own name.

I want tonight to go down in history. I want her to compare every other man, every other night to this.

"Aren't you hungry?" Effie asks when she notices I've barely touched my meal.

It's unlike me. I usually devour everything within touching distance. But I'm feeling off-kilter tonight.

"Oh," I say, letting my eyes drop to her lips and then to her chest. Just like the day she tried it on, her tits look insane. The only difference is that tonight when she—and by she, I mean I—take it off, those beautiful tits are going to fall straight into my hands before I suck her rosy pink nipples into my mouth, driving her crazy. "Trust me, I'm starving." I lick my lips. "Just not for food."

Now I'm the one shifting in their seat as I tug at my slacks, trying to give my swelling cock a little more space.

An innocent smile curls at her lips. But I know better now. My best friend isn't as innocent as she makes out. Especially not after what she's let me do to her recently. I'm hoping tonight won't be any different.

"Kieran," she breathes.

"Damn, I love it when you say my name like that."

"I bet you say that to all the girls," she teases.

I bark a laugh, but it's lacking any actual amusement.

I'd rather gag most of the women I spend time with than be forced to listen to them fake moaning like it's going out of fashion.

Look, without sounding like an arrogant jerk, I know what I'm doing in bed. I'm confident that I could get any woman to orgasm. And I'm happy for them to do that in whatever way they like. What I don't need is the over-the-top screaming just to increase my ego. As Effie likes to tell me, it's already large enough.

"Funnily enough, I don't."

She rolls her eyes as if she doesn't believe me. But the truth of it is, the only person I ever want to hear moaning my name is her.

Needing a distraction from thoughts of things I can't have, I discreetly slide my cell from my pocket.

"I don't believe you," she mutters, stabbing a potato with her fork.

"I'd never lie to you, Effie."

Her eyes jump to mine, and for a second I hate myself for the comment. Although from the wrecked expression on her face, I think she hates it more.

"I know," she says sadly, aware that she's done just that recently before stuffing the potato into her mouth.

Glancing down at my screen briefly, I place my finger on the slider that controls her toy. I wait for her to swallow before I turn it up.

"Oh my god," she squeals, her eyes widening as her fists hit the tabletop, making everything on it rattle.

My smirk grows as she lifts from the chair.

"Shit. Kieran. That's—fuck."

I turn it off as fast as I turned it on, and she slumps back in her chair.

"You good?" I ask.

Her cheeks, neck, and chest are rosy, and her breathing is erratic.

Oh, tonight is going to be fun.

"That was...How did you—"

"App," I say, holding my cell up so she can see.

"Should have known."

My smile grows.

"Eat up, Effie. Something tells me you're going to need all the energy you can get."

"Would you like me to bring dessert?" our server says after collecting our plates.

"In twenty minutes. But can we have it on a cart?" I respond without looking at him. I can't. I can't look away from Effie.

About a minute before our server joined us, I'd turned her toy on.

She's now sitting across from me, trying to keep herself composed, which is getting harder and harder to do as I steadily increase the speed.

'Don't come,' I mouth, reminding her of the instruction I gave her only a minute or two ago.

She purses her lips and narrows her eyes, glaring pure death at me.

Her hands have vanished beneath the table. I can picture her clinging to the chair for dear life as she fights against her own body and her need for release.

The server takes his sweet ass time to clear our plates, and just before he finally leaves, Effie can't take it and lets out a whimper.

"Please," she cries the moment the hotel room door closes, leaving us alone once again.

Holding her eyes, I slow the vibration until it stops.

"I hate you," she seethes.

"No, you don't," I state as I push my chair back. "Because you know it'll be worth it. You know that when I do let you come, it'll be better than anything you've experienced before."

Stepping up beside her, I hold out my hand.

Her palm is sweaty as it slides against mine, and I smirk as I pull her to her feet.

She groans as the toy moves inside her.

Stepping closer, I let my lips graze her cheek before finding her ear. The length of my body presses against hers, and I can't help but smile as she leans against me, searching for what I can give her.

"Tell me, Lucky. How close were you to coming in front of a stranger just then?" I whisper.

She sucks in a sharp breath of air.

"Does that turn you on? The thought of someone seeing what I get to see?"

She whimpers, her hands coming up to rest on my chest.

"Does that embarrass you?" I ask, reaching down to tilt her chin up so she has no choice but to look at me. "There is nothing wrong with wanting an audience, Luck. In fact, it's hot. Really fucking hot."

Her lips part at my confirmation, but no words leave her mouth.

"It won't be happening though. Tonight, you're all mine. The only person that gets to watch you as you fall apart is me."

Her eyes close for a beat as she absorbs my words.

"Eyes on me," I command, making them spring back open again. "Come on," I say, taking a step back. "It's time for dessert."

Without instruction, she follows me to the bedroom, closing the door behind her.

But she doesn't go any farther. Instead, she just stands there, unsure of herself.

I hate it. I hate that she's second-guessing anything right now.

Her body is buzzing. She's desperate for it. But also, she's struggling to get out of her head.

It was predictable, and exactly why I did this tonight. I didn't want her at Grams' overthinking everything.

Tomorrow, we return home. And as hard as I know that's going to be for her, she's ready.

Tomorrow is also the day our engagement comes to an end.

My stomach twists so tightly, acid rushes up my throat at the thought.

But I remind myself that it's just like pulling off a band-aid. Once it's done, the pain will hit briefly, and then it'll be all over and we can continue as if it never happened.

It's the right thing to do. For both of us. Even if right now, it feels like the worst.

"Effie."

Her eyes lift from the floor, instantly locking on mine.

Her lips part and her chest rises and falls steadily.

"Are you okay?" I ask, closing the space between us and cupping her jaw in my hands.

She stares up at me with her big, beautiful blue eyes. She's wearing contacts tonight, and although I love her glasses, without them like this, it's like she's looking straight down into my soul. It's as incredible as it is terrifying.

She nods. "Yeah. Can you make me come now?"

I can't help but laugh.

"Not right now," I confess. "But soon. I need you to do something for me first."

She continues to hold my eyes, waiting for instructions like the good girl she is.

"I love this dress," I tell her, letting my hands run over her curves.

The second I grip her breasts and squeeze gently, her head falls back, a moan ripping from her lips.

"But I love what's hiding beneath it more."

Without warning, I grip her shoulders and spin her around. My fingers return to the zipper running down her back, but this time, I lower it.

Her breathing increases, letting me know that she's with me.

It's all I want for tonight. To let go of reality and everything we're going to face tomorrow and just enjoy.

Lifting my eyes, I find the mirror on the other side of the room that allows me to watch.

Once it's undone, I slide my fingers up her bare back, loving the way her entire body shivers at my touch before pushing the thin straps from her shoulders and letting the fabric cascade down her body.

Reaching out with my pointer finger, I drag it down her spine.

She arches, pushing her heavy breasts and peaked nipples out before wiggling her hips as I get to the only garment she's now wearing.

Tucking my thumbs into the sides, I slide the lace down her thighs, letting it pool at her feet.

"Beautiful," I breathe when I stand to full height again.

I keep her eyes held captive in mine, my hand locked on her waist, as I pull my cell from my pocket and turn her toy on again.

She jolts in surprise, and I drag her back against me, pressing my erection against her ass, letting her know what the sight of her like this does to me.

Sliding my hand up her body, I take the weight of her breast in my palm.

She moans, her head falling back against my shoulder, her eyes closing.

"Watch," I demand. "Look how beautiful and sexy you are."

Her breath catches as she follows orders and watches me tease her as the toy in her pussy reignites her lost release.

I kiss across her shoulder and up her neck, but my eyes never leave hers.

At least, not until she's right on the edge of coming.

Then I release her, turn the toy off, and force myself to take a step back.

Without looking over my shoulder, I keep going until my

legs hit the couch behind me, and only once I'm sitting do I give her another order.

"Hands and knees, Luck. I want to see you crawl to me before you suck my cock."

34

EFFIE

Heat rushes through me like a tsunami.

Those words shouldn't be so hot.

I swear, if any other man said them to me, I'd walk right over and kick him in the balls.

But Kieran...

What is it about him that makes my knees weak?

Spinning around, I stare at him sitting back on the couch with his legs spread wide and his arms resting along the back of the cushions.

To anyone else, he'd probably look relaxed. But if you look closer...

His green eyes are so dark they're almost black, his fists are curled tight, as if he's trying to stop himself from reaching for something—me—and the length of his hard cock is pressing against his slacks.

The sight of him makes my stomach flutter with desire.

His eyes drink me in, moving from my face to my chest, down to my pussy and then all the way to my feet before climbing back up.

When he finds my eyes again, one of his brows lifts impatiently.

With my heart racing in my chest and my hands trembling with anticipation, I drop to my knees.

His eyes widen at the sight of me, and it spurs me on.

His reaction only gets better as I lean forward and begin doing exactly what I was told.

Any hesitation is eradicated when a muscle in his neck begins to pulsate.

Fire burns through my veins as I close the distance between us.

His eyes hold mine for most of it, but then suddenly, he rips them away in favor of something behind me.

Confusion washes over me until the image of us in the mirror comes back to me.

Holy shit.

My mouth runs dry, and I fight to swallow as I close in on him.

"So fucking hot," he groans, his eyes coming back to mine.

I can't help but smile at him like a loon.

Pleasing him is becoming one of my favorite things to do.

"Now, get my dick out. I want to see how good you've gotten at sucking it."

All the air rushes from my lungs as I slide my palms up his thighs toward his waist.

My hands tremble, making it hard to undo the button and pull down the zipper, but despite my struggle, he doesn't help. Instead, he just watches me with heated eyes, patiently waiting for me to do as asked.

Finally, he lifts his hips, helping me out, so I can drag his slacks and boxers down his thighs.

The second his hard dick springs free, I lick my lips, more than ready to get a taste of him.

He's still got his arms resting back against the couch

cushion as I wrap my hand around him and lean forward, licking his tip like my favorite popsicle.

"Fuck," he barks, his hips jumping forward to take more. But I don't give it to him.

He isn't the only one who can be a tease.

I lick and suck around his crown, driving him wild.

His eyes alternate between watching my mouth and the view in the mirror behind me. I can only imagine what I must look like. He seems to be enjoying it though, and that's all that matters.

The toy in my pussy is a constant reminder of just how close he's got me to orgasm twice already this evening. I both love and hate the pressure of it.

"Lucky," he warns when I don't take him any deeper into my mouth.

Finally, he moves his arms, and my heart slams against my ribs, knowing that he's about to regain control.

I wonder if that's why I didn't give him more.

I wanted him to take it.

I want him to grab the back of my head and push his cock into my mouth exactly as he likes it.

A moan spills from my lips when his fingers thread into my hair, holding tightly and sending a shot of pain down my neck.

"Good girl," he groans, pushing all the way to the back of my throat.

Unlike the first time he did it, I don't gag.

It might have only been a few days, but that's all it's taken for me to relax and let him in. For me to take him just how he likes.

I can only imagine how well I'd be able to please him if we had another week...another month...a lifetime.

Closing my eyes, I curse myself for that thought.

Kieran and I might be a lot of things, especially after this weekend, but we're not endgame.

For a moment, I let myself grieve that thought.

Well, he only allows me a moment, because not a second later does the toy in my pussy begin vibrating again.

I release him as I cry out, but he's not having any of it, and he holds me in place as my eyes fly open.

"Eyes on me always," he rasps as he holds his cock as deep as I can take it.

My eyes sting, and my lungs burn.

"Breathe through your nose," he encourages.

I do the best I can, but shit...he's big.

When he finally pulls back, I suck in a deep breath of air, filling my lungs, knowing that he's going to dive straight back in.

And he does.

He uses me, fucking my face exactly as he likes, and I am fucking here for it.

The toy buzzes inside me while teasing my clit, bringing my lost release to the forefront again.

"Gonna come down your throat," he rasps in warning—not that I need it.

I know his tells and I am ready for it.

His dick swells even bigger, stretching my lips wider and filling my mouth to the max before he groans out his release.

His cum slides down my throat, and the buzzing stops, suddenly halting my own release.

"You're not coming on a toy, Luck," he states. "It'll either be on my tongue or my dick."

Oh fuck.

I sag against his thigh, exhausted despite the fact I haven't found my release yet.

No sooner has he slipped from my mouth then he stands, lifting me with him.

"On the bed. Arms up and legs spread."

I glance at the four-poster bed and see something I missed earlier.

There are ties on each corner.

Excitement spreads from my core, making my fingers and toes tingle.

I do as I'm told, and in only minutes, he has me secured.

He stands at the end deliciously naked, his cock already hard again from just looking at me like this, with his cell in his hand.

Despite watching him lift his finger to the screen, I startle the second the toy turns on.

"Kieran," I cry, my hips bucking off the bed as much as they can.

He doesn't do anything else; he just stands there watching me squirm as if I'm the most interesting thing he's ever seen.

"Please," I beg, tugging against my restraints as if I'll be able to slip free.

He smirks but doesn't move or say anything.

Suddenly, there is a bang from the other side of the door and my heart jumps into my throat.

"What was that?" I ask in a rush.

His smirk grows, and so does my confusion and panic.

There's another bang, and then everything goes silent.

My heart is racing so hard I can barely think straight, and it only gets worse when he turns the toy off, spins around and walks to the door.

I squeeze my eyes closed, terrified that someone is standing on the other side.

"Ah, it looks like our dessert is here," Kieran says, forcing my eyes to open.

A huge sigh of relief rips past my lips as I watch him wheel the cart into the room.

My eyes feast on the contents as images of where this is about to go fill my head.

"You ordered a chocolate fountain?" I ask in disbelief.

One side of his mouth kicks up as he reaches for a strawberry, holds it under the silky river of chocolate, and lifts it to his mouth.

"Like I said, I ordered your favorites," he says before opening his mouth wide and biting off the end of the strawberry.

I swear to God, watching him eat that innocent piece of fruit is the sexiest thing I've ever seen.

The way his full lips move, the pop of his jaw, the way his throat works as he swallows, all the while standing there buck naked with his hard cock jutting out before him.

Outstanding.

"Want some?" he asks, wheeling the cart beside the bed.

The sweet scent of the chocolate and the fresh fruit selection makes my mouth water, and I lick my lips in preparation.

"You know I do," I breathe.

He crawls onto the bed beside me, although not close enough to touch me, before grabbing another strawberry, coating it, and holding it above my mouth.

"Kieran," I hiss, lifting myself from the mattress.

I stick my tongue out just as a blob of chocolate drops. I catch it and moan as the sweetness explodes in my mouth.

"More," I beg, opening my mouth like a little bird who needs feeding.

With a smirk, he lowers the fruit, allowing me to bite the end.

He watches me with dark eyes before turning it to himself and eating the rest.

He allows me to eat three halves before he changes tack.

Stabbing a marshmallow, he drowns it in chocolate before moving it over. But this time, he doesn't come anywhere near my mouth. Instead, he coats both of my nipples with the warm liquid before dragging it down my stomach.

"Oh my god, please," I beg.

His eyes shoot up to mine. The promise within them is almost enough for me to come.

Holy shit.

He's not even touching me, and I'm riding a knife's edge.

"Oh my god," I cry out when he pulls the toy from inside me, leaving me empty, my muscles clenching around nothing.

The marshmallow continues lower, and my legs tremble as he covers my pussy in chocolate.

I buck and moan at the gentle brush of the candy against my clit.

But it's the promise of what's coming next that has me really desperate.

"Please," I beg shamelessly. "Kieran, I need—"

"I know what you need," he confirms, lifting the stick and stealing the marshmallow from the end. "Mmm, delicious."

His smirk is nothing but pure filth, and I love it.

"I need you to tell me, though."

"Lick me, please."

"Where?"

"Everywhere."

He shakes his head. "You're going to need to be more specific."

"My pussy, Kieran. I need you to lick my pussy." My plea is frantic, but I don't care.

I've never needed a man more in my life.

No. Not a man.

Him.

Kieran.

Finally, he moves, sitting himself between my spread thighs.

He continues to study me for a few seconds before he folds over me, placing his hands on the mattress on either side of my ribs and ducking his head to flick my nipple with the tip of his tongue.

I cry out, that simple move enough to send shockwaves through me.

His eyes hold mine as he cleans me up, licking all the chocolate from my breasts before he descends my body.

My breathing is erratic, and my body is burning by the time he presses his hands against my thighs and dives for my pussy.

I'm so far gone for him that only a few swipes of that talented tongue and I freefall into my first all-consuming release of the night.

And what a fucking night it is.

L ast night was...out-of-this-world amazing.
　　The things that man can do to my body...well...
they should be illegal, I swear.

I wake with my body aching in places I wasn't aware could ache, but nowhere hurts more than my heart.

Today is the day I leave St. Louis.

Today is the day that our fake engagement ends.

Today is the day real life returns.

Yesterday, there was a part of me that thought I was ready.

Right now, I realize that was a lie.

I'm nowhere close to being ready.

Squeezing my eyes closed tighter, I will myself to go back to sleep. To shut it all out and hope today never actually comes.

It's too late, though.

It's already here.

With a pained sigh, I admit defeat and turn over. Stretching my hand out, I search for Kieran, needing to extend our connection for just a few more moments.

Unsurprisingly, I come up empty.

The bed beside me is empty and cold. He hasn't been here for a while.

Reluctantly, I rip my eyes open and scan the room.

It's empty, although there are harsh reminders of what happened last night everywhere I look.

Our clothes are in piles on the carpet. The cart with the leftover dessert is haphazardly shoved from the bedside. Clutching the sheets to my chest, I sit up. The sight of the ties that bound me to the bed last night is the final straw, and I'm out of bed and running toward the bathroom faster than my legs want to move.

My knees hit the floor in front of the toilet a beat before I vomit.

"Fuck," I hiss once I'm confident I'm done and fall back on my ass.

The tiles beneath me might be warm, but they're not very forgiving, and I only allow myself a minute or two to wallow there before forcing myself back to my feet.

The last thing I need is for Kieran to find me in this state.

I've been a broken mess since he turned up here. All he's done is try to make everything better, more manageable. The last thing he needs today is for me to fall apart again.

He's excited to return home. To see his brothers and his friends.

After everything he's done for me, he deserves that. He deserves for me to be strong.

I brush my teeth, finger-combing my hair and wrangling it into a messy bun. We had a bath in the ginormous tub at some point last night, and not only did I pass out with wet hair, but I'm pretty sure he fucked me again beforehand.

God. Last night was a blur of touches, kisses, teases, and orgasms.

If he wanted to get me out of my head about what today

holds, then I can safely say that he achieved it. But the comedown is...intense.

I step out of the bathroom and swipe the shirt he was wearing last night from the floor. Wrapping it around myself, I do up a handful of buttons before stepping out into the living room.

I scan the big room, and my breath catches when I don't immediately see him.

My heart sinks into my stomach.

I didn't consider the fact he wouldn't be here on the other side of the door when I woke.

But I guess it's the right thing to do.

He's already putting space between us.

I need that.

I need to figure out a way to walk on my own two feet and restart my life.

Sure, he's always going to be there. His presence in my life has never been in question. But it's not going to be like this weekend, or even the last few weeks.

He has a life. A career.

Hell, so do I. Or at least, I did.

Hanging my head, I move toward the small kitchenette where I spot a coffee machine.

The easiest thing would be to order room service, but the thought of having to see someone puts me off.

My coffee is almost done when a door opening has me spinning around.

A breath I didn't know I was holding comes rushing from my lungs when my eyes land on a sweaty, exhausted-looking Kieran.

He walks through the living area in a pair of black shorts, a t-shirt that is soaked and stuck to his torso, and he has a towel wrapped around the back of his neck.

His hair is dripping with sweat and sticking up in all

directions, and he has a good few days' worth of stubble covering his sharp jaw.

My thighs clench as I vividly remember how it felt rubbing against my thighs last night as he repeatedly licked chocolate from my body.

"Hey," he says, smiling at the sight of me, but as I study him, it's immediately obvious that it doesn't meet his eyes. "I wasn't expecting you to be awake yet."

"No, I wasn't either," I mutter as I lift my mug to my lips and blow across the top.

"That's your first, then," he laughs, ignoring my morning grumpiness. He's more than used to that by now. "I'm going to shower, then I'll order breakfast."

I grimace, the thought of food making my stomach turn over again.

"Are you okay?" he asks, a frown marring his face.

"Too much champagne," I say. We went through two bottles last night.

Honestly, I'm not sure if he ordered the champagne for the drink or if he just wanted the ice...

I shiver at the memory of him teasing a cube over my heated skin.

It felt so damn good.

Especially on my—

Head out of the gutter, Effie.

It's over.

Done.

You're just friends again now.

"Give it half an hour. You'll be starving."

Lifting the edge of the towel, he wipes it over his hair before backing away.

"I won't be long," he says as I step around the kitchen counter, my eyes on the huge couch in the living room. He's almost at the bedroom when he speaks again.

I'm not expecting it, or the deepness of his voice, and it startles me.

"My shirt certainly looks better on you," he confesses.

"O-oh...um..."

"Enjoy your coffee," he says with a smirk before ducking into the bedroom and out of my sight.

"Fuck," I hiss as I lower my ass to the couch.

He's just Kieran, I remind myself. *Your best friend.*

Squeezing my eyes closed, I try to calm the riot of emotions inside me.

There's a part of me that is desperate to say, "fuck the rules," and follow him into the shower. But there's another part that just wants this morning over with.

I want to get in my car alone, put some Taylor Swift on, and try to get myself together, to find even just a little bit of the strength I'm going to need back in Chicago.

The sound of the shower running taunts me, but no matter how much I might want to join him, I know I can't.

The line has been drawn between us now.

Put it behind you, Effie.

You agreed to this.

Focus on the future, not the past.

I repeat that little mantra over and over as I sip my coffee, and the second Kieran emerges fresh from the shower, I jump from the couch and rush into the bedroom.

"What do you want for—"

I slam the door before he can finish the sentence.

Grabbing the small bag I found in the closet yesterday evening, I gather everything I need before locking myself in the bathroom.

After dumping everything on the counter, I turn the shower on before stumbling back.

I hit the wall as a sob rips from my throat.

I don't know how I'm supposed to do this.

Dropping my head into my hands, I fight like hell not to break down.

Not now.

Not here.

He'll see it on me the moment he looks at me.

Wait until you're back in your apartment in Chicago, and then you can shatter alone.

Sucking in a series of deep breaths, I try to regain control of my breathing, but it's shot to shit when he suddenly knocks on the door.

"Effie, are you okay?" he calls, making my heart jump into my throat.

Summoning as much strength as I can, I drop my hands and call out.

"Yeah."

"What would you like for breakfast?" I want to say his voice is deeper than usual, but I'm pretty sure I'm just trying to convince myself that he might be as affected by this as I am.

It's unlikely. Highly unlikely. Kieran has sex without emotions or connection almost every night of the week.

To him, the last few days have likely just been an extended one-night stand.

But it wasn't. He said it himself that it was different with you.

"I'm okay, thank you," I call back, hoping like hell he can't hear the anguish in my voice.

"Yeah, that's not happening, Effie," he warns, and damn it if his tone doesn't send goosebumps skittering across my skin.

"Just order me something. You know what I like," I snap back, a little harsher than I intended.

"Okay, yeah. Effie, are you..." His voice trails off, and I hold my breath as I wait to see if he's going to continue. "I'll tell them thirty minutes, okay?"

"Sure. Great. I'll be there," I say, wishing there was a way for me not to be.

The last thing I want to do is sit across the table from him like we did last night, pretending that everything is okay.

I can't see him, but something tells me that he lingers at the door.

Attempting to shake thoughts of him from my head, I unbutton his shirt and shrug it off.

I'm about to drop it to the floor when a waft of his scent hits me, and before I know what I'm doing, I lift the fabric to my face, inhaling a potent shot of him.

Just one last taste before I let him go.

With my foundations crumbling faster by the second, I let the shirt drop to the floor and spin away, stepping under the hot spray.

Not content with the warm water, I turn it up until it's scalding me.

I stand there for as long as I dare before getting out and wrapping a towel around both my body and my head.

I wash my face, take my contacts out, and replace them with my glasses before blow-drying my hair.

I'm stalling. I know that. Hell, Kieran probably knows that too, but I'm powerless to do anything else.

In the end, I waste so much time that Kieran has to call to tell me that the food is here.

With my stomach in knots and my heart in tatters, I walk out to discover a table full of food.

He glances up at me, his expression dropping at the sight.

He wants to fix things; I can see it in his eyes.

But there is nothing he can do now.

He's gone above and beyond best friend duties these past few weeks. I can't ask anything else of him.

"I couldn't decide," he lies. "So I ordered everything."

"So I see," I mutter as I lower myself to the chair.

"Coffee?" he asks, lifting the pot toward my mug.

"Yeah," I agree, watching as the dark liquid pours out.

I'm pretty sure it's the only thing I'm going to be able to stomach.

Proving that I was right about how he's coping, Kieran eats more than should be humanly possible as I sit there picking at a croissant.

"The gym was pretty insane," he says, filling the silence between us. "Empty too. I had a good session."

"That's good," I mumble, unable to find any enthusiasm.

He continues talking, but it doesn't make anything better.

"Are you done?" I finally ask, speaking for the first time in ages.

"Yeah," he says, resting back in his chair and placing his hands on his stomach.

"Then we should go. We've got a long drive ahead of us."

Pushing my chair back, I stand and walk toward the bedroom to collect my stuff.

"Y-yeah, okay," he agrees behind me.

One minute I'm praying to get out of that hotel room, and the next, my wish has come true and I'm back in Kieran's car.

The hotel he brought me to is the one with the fancy spa.

It's not really a surprise. I saw the Callahan branding on everything possible inside the room, but I didn't really give it much thought. But this time, as we walk through the foyer, there are people.

I can't help but cringe as I consider just how many witnessed me be guided in blindfolded yesterday.

I guess it doesn't matter. I'll never come here again.

Kieran might feel comfortable in fancy places like this, but it's not really my thing.

He opens the passenger door for me, continuing to be a gentleman, and after placing our bags in the trunk, he joins me.

"Are you sure you're okay?" he asks for the millionth time this morning.

I get it. I look and sound anything but okay, but what exactly does he want me to say?

"Just anxious about returning," I whisper, hoping it'll help pacify him.

"It'll be fine. Everyone is going to be so happy to see you."

I don't disagree. I'm sure they will. But I'm also not sure anyone has really missed me.

Jasmine, my assistant, who stepped up to take over my role in my absence has handled everything brilliantly. She might email and message me with questions, but I can't help but wonder if she's just trying to keep me in the loop more than anything else.

Do they even need me back?

It's not a question I need to be thinking about right now.

I love my job. I love my colleagues. But I've never really clicked with them. Hell, I've never really clicked with anyone but Kieran.

God, how sad is that?

I blow out a long breath and stare out the window as Kieran makes his way back to Grams' to collect all our stuff.

We're almost there when the sight of the passing houses no longer gives me the distraction I need.

Ripping my eyes from the window, I reach for my purse and pull my cell out.

As usual, my screen is full of notifications that I usually ignore. But there is one news story that catches my eye, and before I can think any better of it, I tap it.

Chiefs star confesses to fake engagement.

36

KIERAN

I notice the second everything changes.

Effie's body stiffens in the seat beside mine before she pulls her legs up and wraps her arms around them as if she's trying to hold herself together.

"W-what's wrong?" I ask, although deep down, I know.

I haven't told her what I've done because I knew it would bring too much into last night. It was already bittersweet as it was.

If she knew the news was going to break today, dragging everything that's happened—her mistakes—back to the surface again, then there was no way she'd have enjoyed it as much as she did.

And fuck, did she enjoy it.

Image after image of her from last night plays out in my mind like a movie.

Crawling to me, tied to the bed, begging and pleading with me to let her come.

It was everything I wanted it to be, and more.

Everything she needed.

I just wish I could have protected her from the backlash of her thoughtlessness.

I tried to soften it as best I could, but no matter which way Kat spun the story to the press, it was never going to look good. But I did what I could to protect Effie the best I could.

Last night, I could somewhat ignore it and live in our little bubble of bliss. But this morning... the instant I woke up, I knew it was looming. I hit the gym hard. Harder than I have in a long time. But I needed it. I needed the chance to outrun my demons. To try to get my head straight so that when I faced Effie, I was stable and in control.

I thought I'd managed it, but of course, the second I woke up this morning, everything came crashing down.

All I really wanted to do was lounge around in bed with her. Pull her warm, soft body into mine and snuggle close.

But I couldn't. That was over.

We'd set the rules, and I was keeping them.

Sure, the temptation to shatter them to smithereens was there, but where would it get us?

We couldn't continue. We couldn't be a couple.

I can't be the man that she deserves, and there is no point even trying.

I'd fuck it up. I'd hurt her.

If things were different...if my father got his way and I spent my days working for Callahan Enterprises, then yeah, maybe we could have turned our friendship into something more.

But as it is, with my career, I can't.

A bitter laugh explodes from Effie at my question as I pull into Grams' driveway. "Everything, Kieran. Everything is wrong."

She throws the door open and races from the car before I have a chance to form a response.

"Fuck," I bark, slamming my palm against the steering wheel. "Fuck."

I'm out of the car and chasing her into the house in a heartbeat.

"Effie," I call when I don't immediately find her in the living room. But another door slamming deeper in the house lets me know where she's gone.

My footsteps pound through the house as I close in on her bedroom.

"Effie?" I question softly as I knock on the door and push it open. "Ef—"

My breath catches when my eyes land on her and take in her expression.

Her features are tight, her eyes dark and full of tears.

"I'm sorry," I whisper, moving closer. "But we agreed. Today is—"

"I get it," she mutters under her breath. "This was all my fault. I lied. B-but—"

"But what?" I ask, my brows pinching.

"H-How c-could y-you?" she stutters.

I frown. "I...I don't know what—"

Suddenly, she marches toward me and thrusts her cell at me.

"Everyone hates me, Kieran," she cries.

Taking her cell, I scan over the news article she was reading.

Disbelief washes over me, and I slowly begin shaking my head.

"N-no, this...this isn't what I said."

"Well then, who did?"

Pain explodes in my chest as I stare down at Effie. Tears now streak down her cheeks, her bottom lip trembling as she wraps her arms around herself.

"I...I don't know."

"Keep reading. They're saying that the only reason I have a job at KC Foundation is because I've been blackmailing you."

"WHAT?" I roar. "I never said any of this, Effie. I swear."

A bitter, sad laugh spills from her as she turns her back to me and walks toward the window that showcases the backyard.

"It doesn't really matter, does it? It's what's been printed."

"Effie," I say, closing the space between us and wrapping my hand around her forearm.

"No," she snaps, tugging herself away from my touch. "Just go, Kieran."

"W-what?"

"Just go back to Chicago. It's your home. It's where you belong."

"No," I breathe, refusing to accept what she's saying. "No. It's your home, too. And we're going back today. Together." Okay, so not exactly together, because we both have cars to drive back, but... "Effie."

"I...I can't do this, Keiran. Us. This. Everything. I...I'm not ready. I'm not strong enough."

"But you are," I plead. "You're the strongest person I know. The best person I know."

"Then leave me to do what I need to do."

"But—"

She spins around and pins me with a look that's full of fire and pain.

Fuck.

All I've done is try to make this all easier for her. And yet, All I've done is made it worse.

"I'll stay, too," I offer.

"No," she states firmly. "You have commitments in Chicago. And to be honest, I think it's probably for the best that we have some time apart." Her nostrils flare as she sucks in a breath. "Thank you for everything you've done. And I really am sorry for causing all this. But I can't return. I just...I can't."

I stare at her, watching her body tremble with a mixture of anger, frustration, and pain.

"I can't leave you like this."

Sucking in a deep breath, she holds her head high and rolls her shoulders back.

"You have to. This...whatever this is...It's done, Kieran."

She turns her back on me, and it's all I can do to suck in my next breath.

Her shoulders shake as she silently cries, and I stand there completely useless.

My body screams at me to reach out and drag her in for a hug. But my head...that tells me to do as she said and walk away.

But how? How can I return to Chicago and leave her behind?

"Please, Kieran." Her plea is so quiet I almost miss it.

"Effie, I don't know if I can—"

"You can," she assures me. "You have people waiting for you. Just...message me when you get home so I know you're safe."

"What about you?"

She shrugs.

"I need more time."

"But you will come home?"

Silence follows my question and my fists curl, my nails digging into my palms in an attempt to stop myself from physically reacting.

I want to look in her eyes. I want to do whatever it takes to bring her with me.

But it would be the wrong thing to do.

She may be taking responsibility for landing us here, and

sure, our fake engagement is on her, but things between us...they're on me.

I was the one who came up with that idea.

It was a good fucking idea. But...

Fuck.

Lifting my hand, I rub at my chest.

Not knowing what else to do, I take a step back, putting some space between us.

It's not until I'm standing in the doorway that I speak again.

"Have I...have I broken us?"

Effie hangs her head. "No. I was broken long before you arrived in St. Louis."

"I refuse to accept that. You're perfect."

A laugh bursts out of her.

"Go out with the guys tonight. Blow off steam. Be...be Kieran Callahan."

"Fuck, Effie," I say, rubbing the back of my neck.

"I'll see you soon, okay?"

I take two more steps back, my heart pounding so hard in my chest I'm sure it's about to explode.

"I...I love you, Effie. Don't ever forget that."

And before I break down and refuse to do as she's asked, I take off. I'm almost at the end of the hallway when I hear her reply.

"I love you too, Kieran. Always."

I take one last look around Grams' house before snatching the bag I'd left in the living room before we went to the hotel yesterday, and I walk out with my head held high despite the fact I'm falling apart inside.

As soon as I close the car door behind me, a huge rush of air passes my lips, and I lean forward, resting my forehead against the wheel.

I suck in ragged breaths, hoping the pain in my chest will subside.

But it doesn't. If anything, it only gets worse.

I don't know how long I sit there for, but time doesn't matter. It doesn't change anything.

Nothing is going to change this.

Sitting up, I look at the house again as fond memories flicker through my mind. So many of my favorite times happened here with Effie, both as kids and in the last few weeks.

Pressing my hand to my chest, I rub the spot directly over my heart in the hope of soothing the ache.

But it does fuck all.

Something tells me that nothing will.

Movement inside the house catches my eye, and I stare through the window into the guest room—my room. She never comes to the window, but I know she's there watching me.

My skin tingles with awareness, but knowing that she's waiting for me to go, I take it as my cue.

Starting the engine, I put my car in to reverse and take off, leaving my best friend and my heart behind.

37

EFFIE

Kieran: Just got home. Are you okay?

Kieran: Effie?

Kieran: Please just let me know that you're okay.

Kieran: Please, Effie. I'm worried about you.

I blow out a ragged breath as I wipe my tears from my cheeks.

I haven't stopped crying since he walked out of the house.

For a moment there, I thought he was going to refuse.

There was a part of me that wanted him to. That fickle romantic part wanted him to pull me into his arms, kiss the top of my head, and tell me that he was never going to leave me.

But the sensible side of me knew that it was wrong.

Reading that article, all the awful comments that people had left at the bottom...it broke the final part of me that I was clinging to for dear life.

I'm going to be the most hated woman in Chicago. As far as they're concerned, I played their favorite player for nothing but my own gain.

It's so far from the truth, it's laughable. But there isn't much I can do about it now.

If the notifications that have been piling up on my cell are anything to go by, the story is everywhere.

I've ignored every single message but the ones I'm staring at through watery eyes.

It's been six hours since he left. I'd been waiting for the message to come through for over an hour, getting myself worked up with a million and one what-ifs.

Either he forgot, and the moment he got back to Chicago, he pushed me out of his mind, or he had a crash and he was stuck inside a wreck in the middle of nowhere and no one knows.

Of course, there was also the most sensible option, which was that he was just stuck in traffic somewhere.

When the message finally came through, my sobs returned with a vengeance.

He left.

He really listened to what I was saying and went home.

Pulling the covers up higher, I press my face into the pillow he slept on and breathe in his scent.

This isn't going to help me get over everything that's happened and let him go, but I figure that I'm allowed to wallow today at least.

Tomorrow, I'm going to get my shit together.

I'm going to get up early. I'm going to clean the house—clean house, clean mind—and then I'm going to reassess my life.

I hadn't considered not returning to Chicago until Kieran questioned whether I would. Now I'm wondering if it's really what I want.

Sure, my job, my apartment, and my life are there...but they don't have to be.

I could have a life anywhere.

I have money and zero attachments.

Kieran is my only person, and honestly, I don't know if we're ever going to be the same after the past few weeks.

Plus, he might live in Chicago, but it's not like he's there all that often, especially during the football season.

Brightness sears into my eyes, and I roll over, attempting to hide from it.

But no matter how long I lie there praying for darkness again, it never comes.

Instead, I'm left with nothing but the harsh light of day.

Prying my sore eyes open, I blink against the sunlight, cursing myself out for being so tragic last night that I couldn't even muster the energy to shut the curtains.

With a groan, I flip onto my back and stare up at the ceiling.

If I thought a bad night's sleep was going to make everything better, then I'd be sorely mistaken.

Everything hurts just as much as it did before, and it only gets worse when I glance at the empty spot beside me.

It might be standard to wake up alone with Kieran here, but I also know that I'm not going to find him baking in the kitchen, or coming in sweaty from a run.

Just like Grams, he's gone.

Refusing to plummet into a dark world of grief and sadness, I force myself to get out of bed.

After brushing my teeth and splashing my face with cold water in the hope it'll fix my red, puffy eyes, I make my way to the kitchen for coffee.

However, I stop myself before I turn on the machine.

New day.

New you.

New start.

Instead of immediately going for caffeine, I reach for a pouch of powdered greens that Kieran left here.

I make it just like I've seen him do before and then lift the bottle to my lips.

"Oh my god," I complain after swallowing the first mouthful. No wonder Tate complains about Kingston forcing this on her.

My nose wrinkles and my top lip peels back as I stare down at the potent liquid.

So gross.

But despite wanting to pour it straight down the drain, I pull on my big girl panties and swallow down the rest as fast as I can.

No pain, no gain, right?

"Ugh. Gross," I mutter, wiping my mouth with the back of my hand.

Feeling a little bit better about my attempt to improve my life, I continue to make my coffee.

That goes down a lot better, although it isn't enough to fix anything.

Ignoring my aching chest and my sore eyes, I grab a notebook and a pen and find a blank page.

A blank page.

A fresh start.

What do I want to do?

New chapter, I scrawl across the top of the page before grinding to a rapid halt.

I sit there for a long time trying to come up with some options, but I don't have anything.

Well, other than begging Kieran to come back. But that can't happen.

He's where he's supposed to be.

But what about me?

In the end, I give up with ideas for my new start and turn the page.

On side I write, *St. Louis,* and on the other, *Chicago.*

The pros and cons come a little easier, and thirty minutes later, I have lists in every column.

What I don't have, though, is a clear answer.

With nothing else to do, I make another coffee, grab my cell, and head outside, hoping that inspiration will strike in Grams' favorite place.

I've read articles before where people have sworn they've had messages from loved ones from the afterlife. Would it be wishful thinking for something from Grams? Some kind of clue as to what path my life should take from here on out?

My ass has barely hit the swing seat when my cell starts ringing.

I know who it is before I look down.

I didn't reply to the endless stream of messages he sent me since arriving home last night.

How could I? What was there to say?

Tears pool in my eyes at the sight of him on my screen.

It's a photograph I took of him after an epic win. His smile is so wide and his eyes are alight with excitement.

Usually, I love seeing it. But today, everything is different.

I sit there with my thumb hovering over the slider to answer, but I never swipe.

I can't.

The thought of hearing his voice again so soon sends a shot of fear through me.

I'll break down the second I hear it; I know I will.

In the end, the call drops, and I slump on the swing and let out a heavy sigh.

Everything is such a mess.

Unlocking my cell, I pull up a web browser and do a quick Google search, which I hope will help.

How to find yourself again.

38

EFFIE

Two weeks pass torturously slowly. Every day I wake up thinking that I'll feel more positive, that everything will hurt less, that I'll figure my shit out, but it never happens.

I keep adding to my pros and cons list, and I do actually have a few things on the *New Chapter* page, although admittedly, I'm not sure they're entirely realistic.

Moving to an exotic island and learning to train dolphins might be a little out there as far as ideas go.

Every single day, Kieran has been calling and messaging.

I still haven't answered a single one of his calls, although two days after he left, I did finally respond to his messages.

He was sounding more and more desperate, and I was genuinely feeling sorry for him.

Even though what we had that weekend was over, and even though I'm pretty sure he's broken my already shattered heart on some level, he's still my best friend.

Always will be.

"Oh shit," I gasp, tumbling to the ground inelegantly.

For the last week and a half, I've been working through a thirty-day yoga flow.

It was one of the things I read online to help with my self-discovery.

I'm not really an exercise kind of girl. Over the years, I have tried several different things, although mainly at-home classes, because I'm not a fan of making myself look like an unfit fool in front of an audience.

But I'm really enjoying yoga. It's given me something to look forward to daily, which is saying a lot right now.

It gives me time to breathe, to empty my mind, and to focus.

I haven't had that since the weekend with Kieran, but I can't help but feel like practicing yoga might be healthier than letting my best friend fuck me into oblivion.

Picking myself back up, I shake out my arms and legs before getting back into position.

While I might be enjoying this, I have a long way to go before I can consider myself any good at it.

And I'm certainly not doing it in front of anyone else. No one needs to see me bent in half with my ass in the air.

I work through the rest of the flow. It's a beginners' class, but even still, many of the poses are a challenge, especially for someone as uncoordinated and out of shape as me.

By the time I'm in the final pose, my body is covered in a sheen of sweat and my heart is pounding. It's a really good feeling. I'm starting to understand why Kieran is so obsessed with exercising. It's a buzz, and it's helping to build me up a little every day.

I'm nowhere near back to being my old self, if she even exists now, but I'm starting to see some improvement.

The online class ends, and the house falls silent.

I continue lying there, breathing steadily and letting my mind drift.

I think about my apartment back in Chicago and the life I lived there.

I have received numerous messages from people back home checking in on me.

I've replied to some, like Jasmine and Braxton.

Technically, Brax is Kieran's friend, but we get along well and I appreciate his concern. Either way, I've kept him at arm's length so nothing gets back to Kieran.

Eventually, the air conditioning gets the better of me. With goosebumps pricking my skin, I get to my feet. My muscles pull in ways I've never experienced before.

My legs tremble as I make my way toward the bathroom. My leggings and sports bra stick to me, making my fingers twitch to rip them off.

But as I'm passing my bedroom, my cell starts ringing.

I almost ignore it and continue to the shower, but something makes me turn toward it.

Convinced that it'll be Kieran's daily check-in that I never answer, I prepare myself to ignore it, but the moment I see my boss' name staring back at me, I freeze.

It's not the first time he's reached out. He sent his condolences when he heard the news about Grams, and he's checked in regularly since I've been gone.

He's a great guy, and I totally understand why Kieran and his brothers chose him to run the foundation. He's fantastic at his job, and he's a really lovely and supportive person.

But seeing his name causes a ball of dread in my stomach.

He told me to take all the time I needed, that Jasmine and my team would cover for me, that my job would be there when I was ready to return, but what if something happened and...

Before I can finish that thought, I swipe the screen and lift my cell to my ear.

"H-hello?" I croak.

I've barely left the house for two weeks, let alone used my voice, unless I'm talking to myself.

"Hi, Effie. How are you?"

The question is a formality, and I answer it as quickly as possible in the hope he gets to the point.

I may have been debating whether my life in Chicago was for me or not, but the thought of the decision being made for me, of Henry taking it away from me...that doesn't sit right.

My hand trembles as I wait for him to spit out the real reason he's calling me.

"I'm so sorry to call you out of the blue, and I fully understand that you're on sabbatical, but—"

Oh my god. Oh my god.

My heart races and my palms begin to sweat.

Please don't take this decision out of my hands.

"Jasmine has been involved in an accident." It's awful, and I hate myself for it, but I sag in relief, dropping to the end of my bed. "She's going to be okay, but she's currently in intensive care and will be out of action for some time."

"Oh my god, that's awful," I say, finally finding my voice.

"I know I have no right to ask this, and you are totally within your right not to even respond, but were you planning on coming back anytime soon? Because—"

"Yes."

39

KIERAN

The office door crashes back against the wall, causing the person sitting behind the desk to bolt to her feet.

The second she sees me standing in the doorway, she relaxes, although only marginally.

"Kieran, I—"

I've ignored her numerous calls since the news broke yesterday morning.

I didn't want to have this conversation over the phone; I wanted to look our publicist in the eyes when she explained why she'd thrown Effie under the bus. Exactly what I demanded she didn't do.

"Why the fuck did you do that?" I demand, my voice hard and unwavering.

"I didn't," she argues, pushing her chair back and walking around her desk as if that'll help pacify me.

Anger burns through me, radiating off me in waves. As she gets closer, she must read it, because her confident strides falter.

Clenching and unclenching my fists, I try to stop them from trembling quite so violently.

"If you didn't do it, then who did?"

Her mouth opens and closes like a fish, but she doesn't manage to get the words out.

"I told you the truth in confidence," I shout, the disbelief I felt yesterday morning after Effie showed me the article—the lies—Kat released.

I was already feeling weird knowing that my filthy weekend with Effie was over, that when she woke up, we'd return to normal. I didn't need to be hit with this as well.

"And then the next thing I know, I'm reading everything I told you not to say online."

"I know, I know. And I've dealt with—"

"What good is that now? The damage has already been done."

Kat sucks in a deep breath.

"Kieran, I know you're upset—"

"Upset?" I echo. "I specifically told you to protect her."

"I can assure you it will not happen again."

"How did it happen this time? Jesus, Kat, I thought you were better than this."

"Our intern overheard our conversation."

My eyes widen at her confession.

"Your intern?" I say in disbelief.

"She's been dealt with."

"Fired?" I ask, because there is no way anyone who is willing to sell us out so easily should ever be able to step inside this stadium.

"Yes."

I shake my head, still struggling to stabilize my emotions.

"Good. I will not let anyone out there believe that Effie is a bad person."

"It'll blow over. You know it will."

Irritation ripples through me. Kat might be our publicist

and understand the world we live in, but she'll never fully appreciate what it's like to be at this end of the stories, to have the public turn on you for fake news.

She's right. "It will blow over, but that isn't the point. It should never have happened in the first place."

"I agree, and I can only apologize."

Shaking my head, I spin on my heels and storm out of the office and then soon after the building.

The stadium is my home, but right now, it's the last place I want to be.

"Go on, run. Run. That's it. TOUCHDOWN," I scream excitedly as I watch one of the boys at the summer camp we're helping out at this week slam the ball over the line.

His teammates pile on top of him as the ref blows for the end of the game, cementing their win.

Spending time at summer camps is one of my favorite things to do.

Being back in Chicago in time for the first camps to start up has been a lifesaver.

It's been two weeks since I did what Effie wanted and walked away, leaving her and St. Louis behind me.

They've been the worst two weeks of my life.

I thought it was bad after I fucked up our chance of going all the way last season. But that had nothing on this.

I swear, it would have been easier to leave a limb behind in St. Louis than Effie. Okay, so that might be a slight exaggeration, but fuck.

A huge part of me is missing, and I have no idea what to do about it.

Nothing fills the hole.

It was hard when she first left to look after Grams. I missed her so badly.

But at least then I had a piece of her. If I called her, she'd answer.

If I'd had a bad day, I'd be able to hear her voice and it would make it a little better.

I haven't lost her. She's still there.

For a few days, all I could think was that I'd done the wrong thing.

She didn't respond to anything, and I was constantly thirty seconds away from grabbing my keys and driving back.

I knew I shouldn't; I knew deep down that I did the right thing. But fuck, I wanted to.

I wanted to see if she was okay. I wanted to pull her into my arms. I wanted to kiss her, damn it.

"Good game, Coach," Brax says, clapping me on the shoulder. A little harder than necessary, if I'm being honest. "Shame the best team didn't win."

"Pfft. That's a lie and you know it."

Today was our first day with these rugrats, and it's been a pretty good one.

It's the first time since I returned that I've been able to switch off even slightly.

We'll drop in and out over the next few weeks to see how they progress with their normal coaches.

Being a part of these young players' lives is such a privilege. It's why I started the foundation.

Over the summer, we'll spend time at a whole host of different camps across the state, making memories and hopefully inspiring the future of the NFL.

"Whatever," he says as both teams turn our way.

I always love the first day. The kids have such stars in their eyes.

I know that people say our egos are already huge, but seeing those little eyes with so much awe and admiration makes me feel like I'm king of the world.

I also love how their relationship with us changes as they get to know us.

Right now, we're their heroes and completely untouchable, but by the time our camp comes to an end, they realize we're just normal people like them. And while we may be their coaches, we almost always part as friends. They are excited to embark on their next season, and we're ready to watch their progress and see where they end up.

The group stands before us with red faces and heaving chests, ready for their post-game speech.

"You all did some fantastic work out there. Coach Rogers and I were really impressed with your starting point, and we can't wait to see the skills you learn over the next few weeks.

"We've both written some feedback for each of you, which highlights your strengths and weaknesses. Things we think you should focus on during the next few weeks."

They all nod, eager to read what we have to say.

"All of you need to clean up, get some food, and get an early night. You thought today was hard? It's only going to get harder. But I promise you something," I say, making a point to look each of them in the eye. "It's going to be so worth it.

"How many of you want to be in our position in ten years' time?"

A round of "yes, sirs" sounds out and a smile pulls at my lips. Unlike most I have given out over the last two weeks, this one is genuine.

"Hard work and determination. I can't promise you that the road to the NFL will be easy or painless. At times, it'll be the opposite, but when you make it, it'll be better than you're imagining, I promise you that.

"Now, go and hit the showers. Your coaches will provide you with our feedback later."

It takes a few seconds for them to take off, but once the first one moves the others follow.

We chat with their camp coaches for a few minutes before Brax and I head out.

I've been working with these coaches for years, and they're all fantastic teachers and guardians for our future players.

The camps we provide are everything aspiring players could possibly want. We've designed them with the help of both players and coaches who have experienced everything professional football can offer.

Our camp is full on. We put both boys and girls through rigorous training. But only those who show real possibility manage to secure a place. And eighty percent of our players are from underprivileged backgrounds. The kind of kids who have an abundance of potential but whose parents can't afford the kind of training they need.

I'm so fucking proud of this program. It's hands down the best thing I've done with my life so far.

Sure, playing pro is fucking insane, and I thank my lucky stars every time I step out on the field. But this...I get so much enjoyment and fulfillment from being a part of this. A part of the future.

I'm building a legacy. Not just for me and my name, not for the Chiefs, or any of my teammates specifically, but for the families of the kids who just ran off to shower. We're building their legacy, and that means everything to me.

"You hungry?" Brax asks when we get to his car.

I didn't have plans of letting him drive me here this morning, but he turned up at my apartment and stood his ground.

Apparently, he's concerned about me and thought I'd appreciate not having to drive. I'm pretty sure he thought that as soon as I began driving south, I probably wouldn't stop until I hit St. Louis. There is a very good chance that he was right, too.

I'm not sure whether I'm grateful or not.

I smirk. "Yeah, man. I'm hungry."

"Perfect. I know just the place."

Leaving him to whatever he's planning, I take full advantage of my passenger princess role and pull my cell from my pocket.

As always, a little hope bubbles up that she might have messaged.

She has been a little better recently, allowing me to think that everything is going to be okay.

But still, our friendship is nowhere close to what it was.

The weight of that being my fault presses heavily on my shoulders.

I never should have suggested we temporarily take things to the next level.

It doesn't matter if my intentions regarding getting her out of her own head worked or not. Not if this is the outcome.

The fear that she might not come back to Chicago is real.

I don't know of anywhere else she would go. But she's got money; the world is her oyster.

My stomach knots as regret trickles through my veins.

If it weren't for me, she'd be back here now, living her life.

You'd also be unaware just how fucking amazing she is.

No. I already knew that.

I blow out a heavy breath and close my eyes for a beat.

It's not until Brax speaks that I remember he's sitting right next to me, witnessing my turmoil.

"She'll come back," he says confidently.

"How do you know that? Has she told you something she hasn't told me?"

He glances over, and I see the answer in his eyes.

309

"You know she hasn't. I just don't think she'll be happy ending up anywhere you aren't."

"I hope so."

We have a while until the new season starts, but I'm not sure how I'd survive it without my lucky charm in the stands, cheering me on.

"Trust her. She just needs time." He's said this exact thing over and over again, but if anything, I'm struggling to believe it more now.

As the weeks go on, it's going to get easier and easier for her to forget what she has here. There will be more and more reasons not to return.

At some point, I might not be enough.

"What is this place?" I ask when he pulls into a parking lot.

"Burgers. I found it when I was down here last summer."

"Amazing," I say, although I don't really mean it.

I've been keeping up with my routine of exercise and healthy eating these past two weeks, but I swear nothing tastes like it used to.

Everything in my life has turned grey and bland.

Without Effie, there is no color.

I follow Brax inside, both of us tugging the caps of our hats down in an attempt to hide.

Usually, I don't mind getting spotted and signing a few autographs, especially for kids, but right now isn't one of those times.

Thankfully, the young server is oblivious, and she guides us to a secluded table as requested.

"Wanna hit the gym tomorrow before heading out here?" Brax asks, trying to keep my mind and body active.

"Sure," I mutter absently as I stare at the menu.

He wants to say more, I can sense it from him without even looking up, but he refrains.

I fucking hate that I've turned into one of those guys you have to walk on eggshells around, but I can't help it.

Pulling my cell free again, I tap out a message.

Kieran: Have you had a good day?

40

EFFIE

I'm a nervous wreck by the time I pull up into the secure underground garage of my apartment building.

Leaving St. Louis, or more specifically, Grams' house, was as hard as I thought it was going to be.

The place and everything inside might be mine now, but there was a part of me that felt like I was abandoning Grams.

It's silly, I know that. But I guess that's the thing about emotions and grief. They're not reasonable or predictable.

Different things hit you out of nowhere. Some make you laugh, but many make you cry, and many make you feel empty like something is missing.

I said I was looking for a sign, and after hanging up the phone with Henry, I felt like universe had sent me one.

I felt awful for Jasmine, of course, I did. But I can't help but wonder how long it would have taken me to admit to myself that I needed to return. I could spend weeks, months, even years trying to convince myself that there might be something else out there for me.

Truth is, Kieran was right. Chicago is my home. It has been for years.

And no matter what happens between us after that wild weekend—as I like to call it—he is still my person.

I'm not expecting our relationship to return to what it was before. I'm not sure that's possible. But I'm confident that it's not all over. Or at least, I hope so.

Then why haven't you told him that you're back?

I shake that little thought of reason from my head and pull into the space I haven't parked in for a very long time.

It's been four days since I answered Henry's call and agreed to return.

But while I think he was secretly hoping that I'd jump straight in my car and head back, I wasn't so keen.

I knew I needed a little more time, so I agreed to ease myself in with a few days of remote work. I told him that I'd return to the office Monday.

At the time, it was a week away. This weekend, let alone Monday, still seemed like a million miles away. But as it always is, I feel like I blinked and it's here.

I kill the engine, slump back, and close my eyes.

The drive was good, but I'm exhausted.

My eyes hurt after focusing in a way I haven't for a long time, and my body aches. Probably from the positions I've been twisting it up into recently.

"Move or you'll be here all night," I tell myself in the hope a pep talk will perk me up a little.

My car is loaded with so much more stuff than I left with. I have two suitcases and bags of I don't know what really.

I grabbed a few of Grams' belongings that I wanted for my apartment, but the rest of it is just random stuff I've collected over the past few weeks. Like my new yoga mat.

Grabbing one suitcase and a couple of bags with the essentials in them, I make my way toward the elevator.

The very moment I step into the entryway, the scent of

home washes over me. It's so familiar. It's almost like I've never been away.

Pressing the call button, I wait for the elevator as I catalogue all the things that have happened since I was here.

In some ways, it's like time has stood still and I've done nothing, but in others, it feels like everything has happened and that I'm now standing here as a different person.

I ride to the top of the building in a daze.

I'll be honest, when I first let Kieran convince me to get this place, I felt like a bit of a sell-out.

I have always tried to be the opposite of my parents. Done everything I can to show them that my life doesn't revolve around money like theirs does. But despite everything I stood for, I fell in love with this apartment the instant I stepped inside.

I didn't even know we were looking at it. Kieran instructed his realtor, and she brought us here. It was the fourth place I looked at, and the moment I stepped over the threshold, it had a totally different feel from all the others. It felt like mine. Everywhere I looked, I could picture myself.

I tried to fight it because I did not need a penthouse apartment with views overlooking the city. But Kieran was adamant that I deserved it, and he told me that if I didn't sign the agreement, he would do it for me. That absolutely wasn't happening, so I signed, and I guess the rest is history.

The elevator dings, welcoming me home, and after sucking in a deep breath, I hold my head up and walk out.

There are four apartments up here. One belongs to a young couple, another is an older single man, and the fourth, I have no idea. None of us have ever seen them. But then, we don't ever really see each other.

As I turn the corner to my front door, I can't help but smile at the sight of my two palms alive and thriving.

Releasing my bags, I dig out my key and finally let myself back into my home.

The minute I walk in, the scent of cleaning products hits me, and as I look around, I find that everything is perfect.

My housekeeper is amazing.

Locking myself in, I abandon my things in the hallway and walk through my open living area and straight toward the floor-to-ceiling windows that showcase my home city beyond.

But there is only one building in the distance that steals my attention.

The Chiefs Stadium.

Tingles run down my spine as I think about one specific player whose life is in that stadium.

Guilt twists me up inside that he doesn't know I'm here.

The first thing I should have done when I agreed was to tell him. But fear stopped me.

I knew that he'd be here waiting for me.

He'd probably have takeout from our favorite Thai place and a bottle of champagne to celebrate my return.

But as much as I might want that, I'm not sure if I'm ready to face him.

How can I look him in the eyes again after what we did together?

He's explored every inch of my body. He's been inside me.

I know how he tastes, and the other way around.

I cringe heavily just thinking about it.

Those are things you shouldn't experience with your best friend.

Or at least, you shouldn't if you want to continue your friendship.

My cell burns a hole in my pocket, but I don't pull it out.

I tell myself that I'll reach out over the weekend. That I'll have tonight here to get myself settled back in, and that I'll be ready to face him once I've had a good night's sleep.

I'm lying to myself. I know I am.

But what else is there to do?

Ripping my eyes from the stadium, I collect my luggage and tug it toward my bedroom.

Flipping open my suitcase, I grab my toiletries and a clean pair of pajamas and take it all to the bathroom, and I fill the tub.

Pouring a generous amount of bubble bath into the running water, I watch as the white foam multiplies. My muscles ache to sink into the too-hot water, but before I do, I head back to the kitchen and pour myself a large glass of wine.

Thanks to the new routine I forced myself into, I'm awake early, and to my surprise, I'm alert and ready to go.

Of course, it would be easy to roll over and wallow, but I told myself that my days doing that are long over.

I'm back home, and it's time to restart my life.

I get up and get dressed into my yoga pants and sports bra. I drink my greens, which I actually don't hate as much as I used to, and then I locate my TV remote and find the YouTube channel I'm following for the next tutorial.

With my mat in place, I get to work as the sun lights up the city beyond.

I loved doing this in Grams' living room, but there is something even more magical about having this view.

I focus on my breathing and try to find my Zen. Or at least, I think that's what I'm supposed to be doing. I'm still a beginner.

After an hour, and more positions that I never knew existed, I lie on the floor with my muscles like jelly and my heart racing.

I never thought I'd like this feeling, but it's energizing in a way I never expected.

Eventually, my stomach growling forces me to get up, and after a quick look through my cupboards, I decide that staying in isn't an option.

Sure, I could order in, but that's not going to help drag me back to reality.

So instead, I grab a zip-up hoodie, my cell and keys, and I head out.

I have every intention of going to our local deli for one of their famous breakfast bagels and then back home.

I didn't realize I'd missed it quite as much as I do, but now that I'm here, it hits me hard.

I find a bench to enjoy my bagel and coffee. I had every intention of going straight back to my apartment, but with the sun warming my face, I find myself doing the opposite.

I feel stronger than I have in a long time, or at least, my body does. Inside, I'm still a complete mess, but I think being here helps.

Without paying much attention to where I'm going, I just walk, taking in the sights that I haven't seen for months.

After being in Grams' small town, I have a new appreciation for how big and busy everything is here.

It reminds me of when I was first sent here for boarding school and we'd come into the city for field trips.

I might have traveled with my parents, but we never really went on city trips, and I wasn't ever taken on business trips with them. I was either left at home with whatever nanny they'd decided was suitable at that time, or I was with Grams.

I'd seen plenty on the TV and in movies, but there really was nothing like the real thing.

Chicago felt like home right from the very beginning. And as much as I dreaded coming back, that same feeling of belonging is surging through my veins right now.

Before I know it, I'm standing in front of a very familiar building.

Letting my eyes roll up the huge panes of glass that cover every side, I finally get to the top. To the home of the KC Foundation.

Without stopping to think, I pull my keys from my pocket and walk toward the entrance.

My fob lets me in immediately, and I'm soon walking through the swanky reception area and to the elevators.

Again, I tap my fob, and just like I've never been away, it instantly takes me to my floor.

Seeing as it's Saturday, the offices are deserted. It's an eerie sight, but one that I embrace.

I walk through the large room that's full of everyone's desks until I get to the management offices at the very end.

A smile spreads across my face as I step up to my door.

My name is still there.

I stare at it for a moment before pushing my door open and stepping inside.

It's just like returning home last night.

Everything is exactly as I remember it.

I wasn't aware whether Jasmine had moved in, in my absence, but looking at it right now, it's obvious she hasn't.

Knowing that Henry kept it for me makes my chest swell.

He knew I'd come back, and he wasn't lying when he said my job would be here no matter how long it took.

Rubbing at the spot over my chest, I walk farther inside and take it all in.

Sitting in the center of my desk, right in front of my chair is a pad of paper.

WELCOME HOME, EFFIE.
WE'VE MISSED YOU.

41

EFFIE

After getting sucked into work, it's long after lunch by the time I emerge from the building to the bright, blinding sunlight.

I take off toward home with the good intentions of showering and then mustering up some courage to speak to Kieran.

Just the thought of hearing his voice again sends a rush of nerves through me. I have no idea how I'm going to face him.

I stop at the store and buy myself some essentials and dinner, and just as I'm walking out, a flier on the neighborhood noticeboard catches my eye.

Adult dance classes for skills of all ages at a local dance company.

Shaking the crazy thought away, I keep walking.

I've got yoga now. Once work starts again on Monday, I'm not going to have time for anything else.

Thankfully, the walk back to my apartment is short, and I ride the elevator up with my arms loaded full of bags, more than ready to switch off for the day.

You still have to call Kieran, a little voice says.

Ignoring it, I begin putting my groceries away, but before I know it, I'm rearranging my cupboards. I know I'm only putting off the inevitable, and no matter how long it takes me, the same conversation will still be waiting.

He's told me numerous times since he left that he wasn't the one to give the media the story. He's assured me that despite having told the publicist the truth, it was an intern who sold the story they'd agreed to cover up.

To begin with, I was angry and hurt. I guess, a part of me still is, and maybe always will be. But now that a little time has passed, I can see that all that really came out is the truth. Sure, there was no mention of Grams or my reasoning, which might have made me seem a little less unhinged. But ultimately, I did lie. I did make up a fake engagement with my best friend for my own benefit.

I may not have spent a lot of time online recently, but the few times I have logged in, I've cringed hard whenever a new article about it has appeared.

It was a stupid and naive thing to do.

Maybe it would have been okay if my best friend wasn't a name that everyone knew. Maybe I could have gotten away without being America's most-hated woman for a few days.

Of course, it's mostly blown over now.

I guess, in the end, it hasn't hurt his reputation. Things like this never hurt the one the nation loves; it's always the nobody that ends up with scathing messages and death threats.

Thankfully, while I may have received my fair share of the former, I haven't seen the latter.

I'd like to think that if I had, I wouldn't have taken it seriously, or to heart, but it's hard to say how I'll feel about anything these days.

Things that usually wouldn't affect me are suddenly making me cry. I saw an advertisement raising money for sick animals the other day, and I bawled like a baby.

Once I can no longer organize anything else in my kitchen, I drag myself through to the bathroom to shower and quickly find myself decluttering my bathroom cabinet of all the liquids and potions I've bought over the years and never used.

Hours have passed by the time I finally make it back to my kitchen and embark on cooking dinner.

I may not have called Kieran, but my apartment is very tidy. I've fully unpacked, and I've sorted out my closet with very strict rules about getting rid of things. There is a huge bag sitting in the hallway ready to go to Goodwill.

I just wish the saying "tidy house, tidy mind" was right.

There is nothing tidy about the shit in my head these days.

After making myself dinner, I curl into my favorite seat on the couch. It allows me the best view of the stadium. It's sad, I know, but if I'm here and I know Kieran is there training or whatever, then I feel closer to him.

You're too dependent, a little voice says.

Closing my eyes, I suck in a deep breath.

I've never considered my closeness with Kieran to be anything other than a good friendship before.

But everything is different now. I'm overanalyzing everything. Especially the way he made me feel that weekend...

Dragging my hair away from my face, I twist it up into a messy bun before grabbing my cell.

I open the stream of messages that have come in from him throughout the day.

> Kieran: Happy Saturday! Do you have much planned?

> Kieran: What's the weather like with you?

Kieran: I'm spending the morning in the gym, then out with Kingston and Kian later.

I glance at the time.

He'll be with them now.

My stomach knots at the thought of interrupting his time with his brothers.

Nope.

I'll just call tomorrow when he's not busy.

Forgetting about the one thing I was going to do today, I open up Instagram instead.

It's a risk, one which I've regretted every single time I've done it over the past couple of weeks, but still, I torture myself with it.

My notifications are off the charts, but I only open the ones from people I know. Which, embarrassingly, is limited to Kieran, Brax, Tate, Lori, and a couple of girls from work. My circle is ridiculously small.

That's probably a part of my problem with Kieran.

I don't have any other friends. No real ones.

They're either connected to him, or I work with them. But even still, we're not exactly close.

If I had something outside of him, maybe all of this wouldn't seem so bad.

Hell, maybe if I had a girlfriend to dissect it all with, it would be easier to understand.

Maybes aren't going to solve any of this, though. I'm not suddenly going to find women who are happy to listen to all of my woes and help me navigate a way through it.

A laugh spills from my lips at a video Brax shared of a dog being a goofball.

I don't know if it's a coincidence, or he's seen that I'm online and begins typing, but he does.

> **BraxtonWhitlock28:** Hey, how's it going?

> **EffieCampbell:** It's...going. Things are getting better every day.

> **BraxtonWhitlock28:** You'll get there.

> **BraxtonWhitlock28:** Any news on your return?

My heart slams against my ribs, and my cell trembles in my hands.

I don't want to point-blank lie to anyone. But I also don't want to tell the truth either.

> **EffieCampbell:** How's camp been this week?

I hate myself for completely changing the subject on him, but I don't know what else to do.

> **BraxtonWhitlock28:** It's been great. Kieran is in his element.

A smile pulls at my lips. Of course, the football season is his favorite part of the year, but being able to drop into the summer camps that the KC Foundation works hard to run, and meet the future NFL stars, is a huge deal for him.

And it should be. The KC Foundation is his baby. He's the one who wanted to give back and help underprivileged families allow their kids to follow their dreams.

Of course, to a point, it's my baby too.

We came up with the idea together, and along with Kingston and Kian, we turned a dream into a reality.

In only a few short years, we've accomplished so much and helped so many aspiring players get one step closer to achieving their dreams.

Kieran is proud, and rightly so. He's helping to mold the future of the sport he loves, and that's huge.

> EffieCampbell: I always love watching him with the kids. It makes him really happy.

> BraxtonWhitlock28: You know you're welcome any time. He'd love to have you there.

My breathing falters. It would be so easy to turn up and surprise him.

But that's even more panic-inducing than picking up the phone and talking to him.

Brax and I message a few more times before he lets me know that he's heading out, and my cell falls quiet.

Jumping over to my feed, I begin scrolling, but I come to a stop when I see another advertisement for the dance classes.

I read the post, which gives much more information than the flier. Before I know what I'm doing, I've opened up a web browser and I'm searching the dance company to find out more.

They have adult classes on Monday and Thursday evenings covering all kinds of dance. But it's the ballroom and Latin classes that spark my curiosity.

Grams and Gramps used to go to weekly dance classes. She inspired me from an early age, and once upon a time, I knew everything from the Cha-Cha to the Waltz.

I even taught some to a reluctant Kieran. Memories of dancing with him in the bandstand not so long ago come back to me. My nose itches as I battle with my emotions.

That was before anything happened between us, but it was building. I might have been doing my best to ignore it, but I'd never been as aware of the way his body pressed against mine as I was that night.

I let out a sigh, my eyes lifting to the windows and then up to the sky.

Grams would love it.

With a smile playing on my lips, I sign myself up for both classes.

Maybe this is the start of finding myself a life outside of Kieran and work.

Who knows, maybe I'll find a friend. Or maybe even a boyfriend.

My brows pinch.

No, not a boyfriend.

Before I know it, my alarm is going off first thing Monday morning, so I can do yoga before going to the office for the first time with my coworkers in months.

Today my return to Chicago will no longer be a secret.

Nerves flutter violently in my stomach.

Right now, as far as I'm aware, only Henry knows that I'm back. But the second I step into the KC Foundation offices, all that will change.

Everyone knows the Foundation is Kieran's. The gossip mill will be rife.

I should have called him yesterday.

I got close. I had his contact open in front of me.

But...I couldn't hit that button.

I'm a coward.

I hate that he's going to find out from someone else. He'll hate me for it too.

Is this really what we've become?

I force my heavy, sleeping limbs into my yoga gear before making my morning greens and unrolling my mat.

The sun is only just rising above the buildings, casting the whole city in a beautiful orange hue.

Sucking in a deep breath, I raise my arms above my head and let everything go.

This is my time. Nothing in the world matters but me right now.

42

KIERAN

"And how are you feeling for the upcoming season after the way the last one ended?"

I stare at the woman interviewing me.

It's meant to be about the summer camps, but as always, they manage to spin things around.

Forcing a smile on my face, I tell her what she expects to hear, what Kat will expect me to say—not that I owe her anything right now.

"I'm excited. We achieved so much last season, and with that, plus some fresh blood on our roster, I think we're going to have a fantastic season."

"There have been rumors about some big signings this year. Are you able to shed any light on that?"

I smirk. She knows full well I can't. Assuming I knew, of course.

I haven't exactly been fully focused on everything in the last few months.

"All I can say is that we have an exciting season ahead of us. We're all relaxing and recuperating, ready to hit it hard once training camp starts."

"And of course, we have the Chiefs Summer Ball approaching," she says excitedly.

"Of course," I agree. Our annual fundraiser marks the end of the off-season and celebrates a summer full of successful camps.

Usually, I look forward to our events. They're always a good night, and I always have a very beautiful woman—or two—on my arm.

This year, though, despite it still being a few weeks away, I can't think of anything worse.

There's only one woman I can picture attending the ball with me, and she barely responds to a message right now.

"Any clue to who your lucky lady will be this year?"

She leans forward in her seat and looks at me from beneath her lashes.

It's not the first time she's attempted to flirt with me.

I get it. She's hot, and I do have a bit of a reputation.

But not today. And certainly not with her.

She might as well be a guy, for all the interest my body shows in her.

It's been that way since I first laid a finger on Effie.

No other woman exists.

"No," I state, and thankfully, for the first time this afternoon, she takes my cue and winds up the interview.

I'm not usually so ill-tempered during these things, but my patience is getting shorter and shorter these days.

As fast as I can, I make my way out of the building, putting any thoughts of the interview and her blatant come-on behind me.

The sun burns my eyes and I take my cap off before twisting it around and putting it back on, lowering the bill so I can hide.

Crossing the road, I walk into the coffee shop and order myself a drink and something to eat.

My legs bounce the entire time I sit in the back corner.

I'm restless, and I don't know how to stop it.

I spent almost three hours in the gym this morning, pushing myself until my limbs were trembling and I was covered in sweat.

But it wasn't enough.

Nothing is.

Pulling my cell from my pocket, I hit call on Effie's number as I leave the coffee shop and walk down the street toward my car.

"Hi, you've reached Effie Campbell. Sorry, I can't take your call right now. Please leave a message and I'll get back to you as soon as possible."

It doesn't matter how many times I hear that same message; it still sends goosebumps racing over my skin.

I miss her.

I really fucking miss her.

Unable to go home and do nothing, I head toward somewhere that'll help take my mind off things. Or at least, I hope it will.

"Good afternoon, Kieran," Melissa, Kingston's assistant, says with a smile the moment I step foot on the top floor of the Callahan Enterprises building.

"Hey. Are they being nice to you today?"

"When aren't we nice?" a deep voice growls from behind me.

"Like, every single day," I tease as I spin around to face my eldest brother.

He smirks at me. "Sucks to be the youngest, huh?" he mocks. "I'm heading out. Kian and Lori are in his office. Just… make sure you knock. I've seen more of that man's ass than I ever should recently."

"Kingston," Melissa groans.

"What? They should not be enjoying work *that* much."

"Because you and Tate are any better?" I counter.

"We are professional."

"My ass," I scoff. I know for a fact that his desk has seen just as much action as I'm sure Kian's has.

"How's Effie?" he asks with genuine concern.

I shrug. "Okay, I think."

"Still won't answer her phone?"

I shake my head.

"Just give her time."

"I am. I just need—"

"I hate to break it to you, but this isn't about you. It's about her."

"I know. I know," I confess, feeling like a selfish asshole.

She's lost a hell of a lot more than I have recently. I should be respecting her need for space. I mean, I am. But I'm not entirely dealing with it all that well.

"It'll all work out," he promises with a supportive shoulder squeeze before he lets Melissa know when to expect him back and disappears into the elevator.

"He's right, you know," Melissa says softly, confirming that she's fully aware of everything happening in my life right now.

Of course, a lot of it has been public knowledge recently. But something tells me she's aware of almost as much as my brothers are.

"Yeah," I agree, rubbing the back of my neck.

The problem is though, they all mean that Effie will heal enough to speak to me again. They all think that the only thing I'm worried about is my friendship with her.

That is a huge concern of mine, but it's more than that. It's bigger than that.

It has been since the very first moment I kissed her.

She sparked something inside me. Something I don't need or want or have time for.

But despite all those things, it's there and it's growing.

What's the saying? Distance makes the heart grow fonder.

Fuck. I need her.

Melissa smiles softly at me.

"If you need anything—"

"Thank you, Melissa," I say sincerely before taking off toward Kian's office.

"Kingston is right," she calls after a couple of seconds. "Make sure you knock."

I chuckle, more than aware of what kind of business my brothers get up to inside their offices.

Lifting my hand, I rap my knuckles on the door.

The windows have been tinted, not allowing me to see inside, and the last thing I need right now is to see a couple getting hot and heavy while I'm getting absolutely fucking nothing.

"Well, well, well, look what the cat dragged in," Kian says when I poke my head inside.

Thankfully, he's sitting behind his desk pretending to be king of the world, while Lori sits opposite him with a notebook and pen in hand.

"Kieran," she says softly, before abandoning everything on Kian's desk and coming over to hug me. "How are you?"

"Good."

"Liar." Kian snorts.

"Whatever," I say, releasing his girl and moving toward one of his fancy couches.

They share a look that instantly has my hackles rising.

"What?" I bark.

"Do you know what?" Kian says, pushing his chair back. "We should call it a day and go for a drink."

Okay, now I really am concerned.

Kian Callahan never actively chooses to go out day drinking over work.

"What's going on?"

They share another look.

"Stop that. Speak with actual words."

Fuck me, couples are annoying.

"Nothing is wrong. It's just been a long day and—"

"It's three in the afternoon," I point out, interrupting Lori.

"Kieran, you look like a fucking mess. We're going for a drink," Kian states, pulling big brother rank.

My mouth opens to argue, but I quickly discover that I don't have anything to say.

I may not have risked glancing in a mirror for a few hours, but I have a very good idea of how I look.

My fingers have run through my hair one too many times already today, and I know my eyes are dark from lack of sleep.

No matter what I do, every time I fall asleep, she's there, and I wake up thinking it's real and searching for her.

It's fucking pathetic, and it needs to stop.

I'm supposed to be doing exactly what I told that reporter this morning.

I should be relaxing and getting ready for the upcoming season.

I need to be ready. I need to be in peak condition before the rigorous schedule hits.

"Don't you have work to do?" I finally mutter, knowing I'm not going to get out of this. Once Kian has made up his mind about something, it happens.

"Nothing that can't wait a few hours," Lori says softly before she disappears down the hallway, leaving me alone with my brother.

"She's really got you tied up in knots, huh?"

"W-what?" I stutter, pretending not to know what he's talking about.

With a smirk playing on his lips, he shakes his head.

"Pretend all you want, but I've been there. I know exactly what you're going through right now."

I narrow my eyes at him, my jaw popping.

"As if. No one ever wanted to be your friend," I quip before spinning on my heels, ready to march toward whichever bar he has in mind.

Maybe a couple of glasses of scotch will help settle me.

"Missing your best friend barely scratches the surface of what you're going through right now," Kian says, making my steps falter. "You're in denial. That's cool. But eventually, you'll figure it out. So will she."

"I don't know what you're talking about," I shoot over my shoulder.

All he does is chuckle.

Asshole.

"Ready?" Lori asks, stepping out from behind her desk with her jacket on and purse over her shoulder.

"Does he have to come?" I ask, thumbing over my shoulder to indicate Kian.

"Sadly," she laughs.

"I heard that," Kian snaps.

"You were meant to."

Thankfully, I'm no longer the focus of their conversation as we make our way to a bar a few blocks over.

Lori and I find a seat while Kian goes to the bar to order.

"How are you really doing?" Lori asks, her voice serious all of a sudden.

Why did I think coming to see them would take my mind off all of this?

"I'm fine," I state, as if she'll believe me this time.

She tries digging a little deeper, but she doesn't get very far before Kian arrives with drinks.

My scotch glass doesn't even hit the table. I take it from his hand, lift it to my lips, and swallow it down in one go.

"Should I get you another?" Kian quips.

"That would be fantastic," I say, smiling up at him.

He rolls his eyes but spins around to order another without complaint.

The side of my face burns with Lori's attention.

"How are your brothers?" I ask, changing the subject.

Both of them recently finished high school and are planning their move to South Carolina for college.

Wilder is a kickass football player who I suspect is going to go far. He did well securing a place with the Trinity Royal Titans. They're a fantastic team. Their head coach is a hardass who will push him in all the best ways.

"Yeah, they're good. Wilder is...well, Wilder. He's ready to embark on college life. Hendrix is a little more skeptical."

"He'll be fine once he gets there."

"That's what I keep saying. I know it's not as easy for him academically, but he'll find his place. Plus, he has Noelle by his side."

"They together yet?" I ask, happy to focus on them. Hendrix is totally in love with Noelle, and the feeling is most definitely reciprocated. Not that either of them will do anything about it.

"Nope. Still fighting the inevitable. Just like two other people I know," she says, quirking a brow at me.

"Whatever," I mutter as Kian returns—with two drinks for me this time.

"Just promise me you won't drive home," he says before sliding them in front of me.

"You got it, Dad," I mock.

The scotch helps. I relax more than I have in a few days, and finally, my knees stop bouncing.

It doesn't stop me from checking my cell every ten minutes to see if she's messaged me.

But as usual, it remains silent. Well, silent from her, at least.

When I got back to Chicago, I turned most of my notifications off.

Every time my watch buzzed, my heart would jump into my throat thinking it was her.

Now, I only have messages and calls with notifications, which has slowed it down somewhat. I still can't get rid of the little bit of hope that it'll be her making the first move.

Kian is busy telling me a story about why Kenzie, one of our little sisters, was suspended from school again when my cell buzzes.

I already know it won't be from her, but I'm powerless to check.

Kian continues talking, something about Kenzie pranking some other kid and embarrassing him in front of the entire class, but his voice fades to nothing.

And it disappears completely when I read the message that just came through from a friend in the IT department at the KC Foundation.

Effie is back.

43

EFFIE

I get changed in the office bathroom as I chastise myself for signing up for the dance class tonight.

I knew my first day back would be a lot, but I completely underestimated just how exhausting.

From almost the instant I stepped off the elevator, someone has wanted to talk to me, mostly just to check in and give me their condolences in person. While I appreciate my team's concern, I really didn't need to keep repeating that I was, in fact, okay.

Henry had called a team meeting first thing where everyone got me up to speed with everything, and then he left us to it.

I was hoping that coming back remotely last week would mean I could hit the ground running. And to a point, I have, but there was still a lot to take on.

My team has secured some incredible funding for the foundation in my absence, and Jasmine has done a fantastic job stepping into my shoes, but there is a lot to catch up with.

My head was spinning by the time everyone started leaving for the day, but I think it's in a good way. It still is hours later.

Being able to focus on work has meant the grief and pain I had been drowning in have been pushed a little further back. Not forgotten, I'm not sure I'll ever lose it completely, but it hasn't been the most prevalent feeling today. If I'm being honest, being overwhelmed takes center stage there.

All I really want to do is go home, order takeout, and curl up on the couch.

But I refuse to allow myself to do that.

So, with sore, tired eyes, I get changed before heading toward the studio where tonight's dance class is being held.

I haven't attended a class of any kind for years, and as I step through the doors to find huge photographs of beautiful, talented dancers lining the entrance hall, I start to second-guess myself.

This isn't a local community dance class designed to get inactive people moving. This is a real dance company.

I don't think I've ever felt more out of place in my life.

With my legs frozen, my eyes move from image to image. Every type of dance is on show, but it's the couple locked together mid step that really steals my attention.

Grams wanted to be a dancer. She used to tell me about her dreams of being a professional. It never happened for her. She met my gramps and then soon after discovered she was pregnant with my dad.

She was never bitter about the way her life went. The opposite, in fact. She loved my grandfather will all her heart. My father too, for all the good it did.

But she never stopped dancing.

Knowing that she's looking down at me with a smile, I raise my chin and continue forward.

"Good evening," a lady says, suddenly appearing from down a hallway. "Are you here for the ballroom class?" She slips behind the small reception desk and wakes up her computer.

"I-I am," I stutter, my voice giving away my hesitation. "I'm sorry, I'm a little nervous."

Lifting her eyes from the screen, she gives me an encouraging smile.

"You have nothing to worry about. Maria is a fabulous teacher, and the group is wonderful. This place will be like home in no time."

"Thank you," I say, feeling a little better.

"Can I take your name?" she asks, and I move closer.

After she's checked me in and we've had a polite chat about my previous dancing experience, she directs me down the hallway to studio two.

My heart races and my hands tremble as I draw closer to the door I need.

Behind me, I hear some others enter and chat with the receptionist, but I don't look back. If I do, there's every chance I'll walk straight back out the door and never return.

You're taking control of your life. Doing things for you.

Keep moving forward.

So I do, and only a few seconds later, I push the door open.

A lady in a leotard and floaty skirt stands in front of a wall of mirrors, looking down at her cell. But the moment I step inside the room, she looks up and smiles at me.

"Hi. Welcome. Come in, come in."

I do as I'm told and scan the rest of the room. There are a couple of other people around the edges, getting themselves ready, and I immediately panic that I don't have shoes like them.

I should have done more research before turning up here like this.

My hand lifts to the necklace Kieran gave me and I fiddle nervously with it as she moves closer.

"I'm Maria. You must be Effie?" she guesses.

Great, I'm the only new person. That's not going to help me blend in.

"Y-yes." I glance around again, watching a couple warm up. "I'm not sure I'm ready for this."

"Nonsense. Everyone is ready to dance," she says with a wide smile.

I'm hit with a memory of Grams so hard, it almost knocks me to the floor.

Emotion crawls up my throat and my nose itches.

No. Do not break down here.

"Another wise woman once told me the exact same thing," I confess, my voice cracked and my eyes filling with tears.

"Well then, two of us can't possibly be wrong."

A sad laugh erupts.

"I don't have shoes or—"

"Stop worrying. I don't expect you to be an expert on day one."

"Thank yo—"

"Effie?" a deep voice asks.

Twisting around, I find someone I was not expecting to see here.

"B-Brax?" I stutter, unable to believe my eyes as the giant of a man walks toward me.

He's wearing a white athletic top that clings to his wide frame and every one of his muscles, a slim-fit pair of sweats, and...dance shoes.

What the hell?

"W-What are you doing here?" I blurt, kicking myself as I hear my own words.

He laughs.

"You dance?"

Oh my god, Effie. Shut up.

"Yeah," he agrees. "It's great for balance and coordination.

My mom got me into it years ago," he tacks on when I just stare at him dumbfounded.

Of course, I know that players often take dance classes. It's not all that unusual. I just wasn't expecting...

"I'm actually glad you're here. My usual partner has sprained her ankle."

I shake my head, still staring up at him in disbelief.

"Will you," he asks, holding his hand out, "dance with me?"

I don't move or do anything for long seconds.

"I might be really bad," I blurt.

"As might I." He winks, and I begin to relax. "Come on," he says, gesturing me over to where he's abandoned his bag.

I lower my purse and rucksack beside his duffel bag before he talks me through a warm-up.

"When did you get back?" he asks, finally addressing the elephant in the room.

Guilt hits me, and his expression falters.

"He doesn't know. Does he?" He doesn't need a verbal response; he can read it on my face. "Shit, Effie. This is—"

"I know, Brax. Every day, I've wanted to tell him. But...but things between us—"

"I know what happened," he tells me.

I'm not sure if I'm relieved he knows or not.

I close my eyes, trying to process my thoughts, but before I get a chance to figure out what to say, our teacher begins the class.

"I think we need to go for a drink after this, don't you?" Brax says firmly.

I nod, although I'm not really sure I want to.

He's going to tell Kieran no matter what I say.

His loyalties will be with his teammate. As they should be.

Hell, he should tell Kieran.

I barely hear our teacher as she begins the class, and it's not until Brax turns toward me, takes one of my hands in his, and wraps the other around my waist that I come back to myself.

I stare up at him, confused, but then the music starts and he begins to move.

"Waltz," he whispers. "Do you know the Waltz?"

I nod, but it's already obvious I do, because I fall into step with him as our teacher talks us through the step pattern.

Squeezing my eyes closed, I'm immediately a child again.

"That's it, Effie. You're such a beautiful dancer."

Gramps' hand tightens on mine as he guides my body, and Grams talks me through the steps.

I stumble, getting my left and right mixed up, but after a few minutes, I get into a rhythm.

"That's it. Slow, slow, quick, quick, slow."

I forget where I am and lose myself in the music, the movement, the memory. So when Brax speaks again, I startle.

"You're a beautiful dancer."

Dragging my eyes open, I stare up into his.

"My grams taught me when I was a child," I say proudly.

"She did a good job. My grandmother and my mother were both avid dancers. I could dance long before I could throw a ball."

"I guess that explains the fancy footwork on the field," I tease.

"It sure helps."

Over the next hour, we perfect our Waltz before moving onto a Foxtrot.

By the time Maria brings the class to a close, my heart is racing and the hair that has escaped my ponytail is sticking to the light sheen of sweat on my neck. I feel amazing, and I can't wipe the smile off my face.

"Effie, you were fantastic," Maria says, coming over to check in on me.

"It was my partner."

She chuckles. "Of course, that helps. But you were fantastic on your own. Good rhythm and form."

"Thank you."

"Will we be seeing you again?" she inquires.

"Definitely. I've booked for Thursday."

"Fantastic. Enjoy the rest of your night."

She moves to another couple as Brax removes his shoes and pulls his sneakers on.

"Shall we go and get that drink?" he asks as he throws his bag over his shoulder.

Together, we walk out, the conversation flowing easily between us.

I feel like a completely different person from the nervous, overthinking woman who stepped into this building an hour ago.

We've barely stepped outside when Brax's cell begins ringing.

He digs it out of his pocket and curses when he sees who it is.

"I'm really sorry, I'm going to have take a rain check."

"Okay, sure."

He stares at his still-ringing phone before looking back up at me.

"Talk to Kieran, okay? I won't say anything until you do."

A breath I didn't realize I was holding comes rushing out of me.

"Okay. Thank you."

The call rings off and he lowers his hand to his side.

"In return, don't mention I was here with you. This is the only place I've managed to keep my attendance under wraps. I don't need hordes of women turning up to be my next partner."

"Of course. Your secret is safe with me."

"See you Thursday?" he asks before his cell begins ringing again.

"Thursday," I agree before he takes off across the parking lot toward his car.

I'm still smiling and swaying my hips as I walk toward my front door.

Dancing really is good for the soul.

I'm not convinced the advertisement for that dance class wasn't a sign from above.

Thanks, Grams.

I unlock my door, intending to order takeout and then have a quick shower.

My apartment is dark as I step inside, and I don't bother turning the hallway light on. It's not until I get to the living room that I flip a switch, and the second I do, a scream rips from my throat.

44

KIERAN

I t was still light when I let myself into Effie's apartment. My heart was racing and my hands were trembling.

Trying to contain the anger and frustration that was threatening to explode was almost too much.

I didn't want to believe the message I received. But he had no reason to lie to me.

The instant I walked in here, I knew.

I could sense her presence. And then, just to confirm it, I walked into her bedroom.

It was tidy, her bed was made, but it was obvious that she'd been living here.

She's had a housekeeper looking after the place. All the other times I've been here when she was in St. Louis, everything was perfect. Almost like walking into a show home.

After confirming what I already knew, I lowered my ass to the armchair that faces the front door and waited.

I figured that if she was at work, she wouldn't be too late.

Effie is a creature of habit. In the past, unless she was on a

344

tight deadline, she would always leave at the same time and take the same route home.

She's not a partier or even one to go for drinks after work, so I doubted she'd be doing that on her first day back.

So, when she didn't return around the time I expected, I started to get suspicious.

She's here. I know she is.

But where?

The sun sets behind me as I remain in the chair, waiting.

I'm not leaving until I've seen her. Until I've looked her in the eyes.

But as the hours pass, my need to pull her into my arms and tell her that I'm sorry for everything that's happened gets engulfed by rage.

I want to know why she's been lying to me.

I need to know why she hasn't told me she's back.

But more than anything, I need my best friend back.

These few weeks have been awful. With the pain of losing Grams, and then Effie too...

I shake my head.

I'm angry, but that won't stop me from getting on my knees and begging to have her back in my life.

Dramatic? Maybe.

But I don't care.

I need her.

I'm starting to believe she's never going to appear, and my irritation rises further.

Thoughts of her being back in town for ages and not telling me float around my head.

She's barely been talking to me. I was happy to believe that she was in St. Louis while ignoring me. But was she right under my nose all this time?

Before long, I'm sitting in the dark, aware that I'm probably going to scare the shit out of her when she does finally let herself in.

But I can't find it in me to care.

I've almost given up hope when I hear a key slide into the lock.

My heart jumps into my throat.

All this time, all I've wanted is to see her, to talk to her, to be able to look into her eyes and know that she's not drowning like she was in St. Louis.

The fact she's here should tell me that she's finding a way to get on with her life, but I still need to see it with my own eyes.

Each of her light footsteps rocks through me like gunshots. But nothing compares to the moment she finally flips the light on.

Her eyes widen with fear the exact moment she finds someone in her apartment a beat before she lets out a blood-curdling scream.

But I don't focus on her fear. I can't. Not when I'm fueled by nothing but fury.

I surge to my feet and march closer to her, leaving the couch between us. "Where the fuck have you been?" I bark.

"What the fuck, Kieran?" she squeals, her right hand covering her chest, where her heart is most likely trying to beat out of it.

As she tries to catch her breath, I let my eyes run down her body.

She's wearing a zip-up hoodie and leggings. Her hair has been pulled back into a ponytail, although most of it has escaped and is curling around the sides of her face and neck, and her cheeks are flushed.

"Where have you been?" I repeat, needing an answer.

"Fuck you," she spits. My eyebrows shoot skyward in shock.

Effie has never spoken to me like that before.

"Excuse me?" I seethe, watching as she takes off toward the kitchen.

She remains silent as she yanks the refrigerator open and pulls out a bottle of water.

She twists the top with more force than necessary, and I can't help but wonder if she's picturing doing it to my head.

She takes a drink, and my eyes automatically drop to her throat as she swallows.

My mouth waters, and I lick across my bottom lip, remembering how sweet that skin tastes.

But any good memories of our time together are thwarted when she slams the bottle down so hard on the counter it sloshes out of the top.

Her eyes narrow on mine as anger radiates from her.

Welcome to my world, sweetheart.

"You do not get to let yourself into my home and then stand there and make demands like I owe you something."

"You do fucking owe me something. You owe me the truth," I bellow.

She huffs in disbelief.

"What truth, Kieran?"

"That you're back. Did you not think I'd want to know the second you drove into Chicago?"

Her shoulders slump a little. As much as I'm glad to see her back down, I fucking hate it in equal measures.

I need this.

I need the fire, the shouting, the screaming.

I need to know that she cares too.

"Do you think I didn't want to?" she confesses. "Do you think it wasn't the first thing I wanted to do when I found out I needed to come back? Do you think I haven't stared at your contact every single day, trying to summon up the courage to talk to you? To hear your voice?"

Some of my anger dissipates at her words and the wrought expression on her face. "W-what?"

"Henry called me last week. Jasmine was in an accident."

I stare at her blankly.

Why didn't I know this?

"I drove back on Friday. I've been here all weekend. Is that what you wanted to know? That I've been lying to you for a week? That I've been here for four days without telling you?"

The longer I stare at her, the more my anger ebbs away, and what she just told me settles in my head.

"You were scared to call me?" I ask, hating that I've done anything to make her feel that way.

I want to be her safe place. Always.

"Things are fucked up, Kieran. Everything is fucked up."

"Only if we let it be," I say, my voice softening.

A bitter laugh spills from her lips.

"We broke everything, Kieran. What we were before...it's gone. We can never go back to that. Not since we—"

She sucks in a sharp breath, cutting herself off as a huge wave of fear washes through me.

I can't lose her. I just can't.

"Fucked?" I offer.

Effie shakes her head, dropping her face into her hands.

"I'm not doing this right now, Kieran. I don't have the energy."

"Fine. Then don't. Go and do whatever it was you were planning. I'm ordering food; I'm starving."

"What?" She balks. "That wasn't an invitation to stay."

My teeth grind, that fire reigniting inside me at how easily she can cast me aside.

I thought I meant more to her than that.

Is she right, have we fucked all this up?

Pain shoots through me, my stomach twisting with anxiety.

"If you want me to leave, why don't you tell me to my face?"

She stares at me, her eyes wide and her nostrils flaring.

It takes her a few seconds to find the strength, but to my surprise, she does.

"I want you to leave."

Her voice comes out strong and unwavering.

It hits me like a truck, and I can't help but take a step back.

Disbelief coats every inch of me. There's no way she can't read it on my face.

I'm too shocked to be able to smother my reaction.

"Effie?"

"I'm not fucking around, Kieran. I can't do this. It's been a long day, and—" She pauses to breathe. "Do you know what? I don't owe you an explanation. Just...not now."

"So, when?"

"I don't know."

The worst part about those three words is that she means them.

"But—"

"There is no but. I might be back, but that doesn't mean I'm ready to deal with everything. I'm confused, Kieran. Everything we did...Everything that happened..."

"It was just a bit of fun," I offer, clutching at straws as panic hits me. "Just because I've licked your pussy, it doesn't mean we can't be—"

"Stop," she says, holding her palms up. "Just stop. When I'm ready to talk, I'll call you."

"No, you won't."

"Maybe, maybe not. But that's my prerogative."

"Yeah," I mutter sadly. "I guess it is."

Our eyes hold as our chests heave.

We're both as angry as each other at this whole situation.

Despite wanting to hash it out and figure out a way forward, it's never going to happen like this.

She's right.

I need to leave. Even if it feels like ripping my own heart out while doing so.

"This isn't over," I warn before taking a step back, letting her know that I'm conceding.

Her lips kick up, but the smile she gives me is anything but happy.

"It might have to be."

With that final kick to the balls, I spin on my heels and march toward her front door. But my need to have the last word gets the better of me, and just before the door closes behind me, I call, "It'll never be over with us, Effie. Ever."

"What the fuck are you doing, man?" a familiar voice asks.

The question hurts. It's the same one I demanded of Effie when she got back to her apartment tonight.

"Leave me alone," I slur.

"Not happening. Bill called us to come and drag your ass out of here. The bar closed an hour ago."

I try to focus on the two looming figures standing before me, only they don't seem to be standing still. They're... swaying.

"More," I mutter, reaching for my empty glass, but instead of picking it up and lifting it to my lips in the hope there's scotch, I knock it to the floor. It shatters at my feet.

I stare down at the broken pieces. It's a good representation of my life right now.

I let my team down, and I let my best friend down.

What am I going to fuck up next?

"Come on, man."

Hands grab my arms and before I know what's happening, I'm being hauled from the stool I was slumped on.

"Thanks for the call, Bill," Jamie Franks calls. He's our tight end. A fucking good one, too.

Together, he and Brax escort me out of the bar.

"Get the fuck off me," I bark, fighting to get away from them the second we get outside. "I don't need your fucking help."

"Of course you don't," Jamie mocks. "Do you even know which direction your apartment is?"

I scoff. Of course I fucking do.

"Get him in the car," Brax demands before I'm shoved forward.

I trip on the curb and fall into the car.

Probably not my finest hour, but there's a high chance that I'll have forgotten about it by morning.

All I can hope is that no one is filming me.

The drive home is a blur, but I'm very aware when I'm hauled out of the car.

"Evening, Gavin," I slur as we pass the doorman of my building.

"Jesus. What happened?" he asks as I'm dragged toward the elevators.

"Partied a little too hard," Brax says, as aware as Gavin is that this isn't normal behavior for me.

Sure, I drink. But I know my limits. I never lose control.

Or at least, I didn't until tonight.

Until she told me to leave.

45

EFFIE

Kieran's final words echo through the air long after the door slams behind him.

A sob threatens to erupt, but I fight it.

He has my key. He could change his mind and come back any moment, and the last thing I want is for him to find me breaking.

I stand by everything I just said to him.

All of it was true.

But that doesn't mean it didn't hurt.

I don't think I've ever stood up to him like that before.

Well, aside from when I told him to leave me in St. Louis.

Things really have changed.

Once I'm confident that he's gone, I run to the front door, still battling my raging emotions as I put the safety chain across to stop him from walking back in.

As soon as it's in place, my legs carry me to the bathroom without conscious thought.

I turn the shower on and then strip down to nothing.

It's not until I'm standing under the stream of water that I finally break down.

Powerful sobs rock through my body as I cry into my hands.

Unable to hold myself up, my back collides with the cold tiles, and I slide down the wall until my ass hits the floor.

For the longest time, I sit there sobbing for everything I've lost.

When I eventually lift my head, my eyes are sore and my throat is rough.

Climbing to my feet, I make a half-assed attempt to clean myself before wrapping my body and hair in towels and shuffling toward my bedroom.

Without bothering to remove the towels, I crawl into bed, numb everywhere apart from my heart. That feels like it's been in a war and is bleeding out.

M y eyes don't want to open the next morning when my alarm starts blaring.

Blindly, I reach out and turn it off.

But as much as I want to go back to sleep, guilt keeps me from drifting off.

I made myself a promise when I passed the city limit for Chicago, and I don't want to break that already.

I remain where I am until my alarm goes off again, and this time, I force myself to sit up and swing my legs over the edge of the bed.

I startle when my feet hit the towel I fell asleep in before looking over my shoulder for the other one.

Reaching up, I touch my hair and cringe.

I can only imagine how I look.

After pulling on a clean pair of yoga pants and a sports bra, I force myself to stand in front of the sink to brush my teeth.

"Jesus Christ," I gasp as I take in my reflection.

I don't stand a chance of covering all this up before I'm due at the office.

That won't stop me from giving it a damn good go, though.

By the time I've completed my new morning routine and find myself back in the shower, I feel marginally better.

I focus on what I need to do today, on the meetings I have, and the phone calls I need to make. It's easier to think about that than it is to replay everything that happened from the moment I stepped into my apartment last night.

With more makeup on than I'd usually wear to work, I grab my purse and head out, already knowing that today is going to be a nightmare.

Thankfully, not being close with my colleagues meant that I didn't get much more than a few concerned stares during our morning team meeting. I kept it as short as I could, allowing me to retreat to my office a little under an hour after the meeting started.

I had loads more I needed to talk to my team about. There was so much I needed to be caught up on, but I didn't have the bandwidth.

There's always tomorrow.

Dropping into my chair, I wake my computer up and begin sifting through the seemingly endless number of emails that need my attention.

I get through three when my cell dings with a message.

Telling myself to ignore it, I open the next email and begin to read.

But my cell goes off again.

After reading the same line four times and not taking in a single word of it, I reach for my cell.

Deep down, I know it isn't Kieran.

I hurt him last night when I sent him away.

It isn't going to be a repeat of when he left St. Louis. He isn't going to call and message me daily. He isn't going to beg me to talk to him.

Instead, he's going to punish me by severing all contact.

Knowing someone so well is as much a blessing as it is a curse.

> Brax: So, Kieran knows you're back then.

> Brax: Would I be right to assume you didn't get a chance to explain?

"Fucking hell," I groan.

He continues to type as I try to figure out what to say.

> Brax: Shall we move that drink to tonight? I can pick you up from work. Dinner, maybe?

I should say no. Going out with Kieran's friend would be wrong.

But...isn't he my friend, too?

And he's willing to listen. I really need someone to do that right now.

Kieran is usually my sounding board.

Him or Grams.

I swallow the messy ball of emotion that threatens to clog my throat.

I haven't had that for weeks, and I need to get all this off my chest. I need the weight to lift.

Without overthinking the consequences, I allow myself to have a friend.

> Effie: Dinner sounds great. I'll be finished at six. Can we have tacos?

> Brax: Whatever you'd like.

I hesitate before sending my next message, but in the end, my concern over my best friend gets the better of me.

> Effie: Is he okay?

> Brax: No. But you already knew that, didn't you?

"Shit," I hiss.

The rest of my day passes slowly. Even my colleagues seem to notice my mood and begin to look at me differently, Even Henry asks if I need to go home during our afternoon meeting.

I assure him that I'm fine, but I don't think he believes a word of it. But thankfully, he returns to discussing our targets for the next two quarters.

Every year, we reach more future football stars, and that means our funding needs to increase.

When we originally started, we received donations from players and a handful of businesses connected to Callahan Enterprises. We're so far from that now, it's incredible but also terrifying.

The kind of figures I'm trying to secure blow my mind. But it's worth it.

By the time the clock ticks around to six my stomach is growling, reminding me that the pastry I grabbed from the coffee shop downstairs on my way in this morning was nowhere near enough.

Nerves flutter in my stomach as I ride the elevator to the ground floor. Brax is waiting for me; I had a message five minutes ago.

I know how Kieran will react to this when he finds out. And I'm confident that somehow, he will. But what does he expect me to do? Hide under a rock and live my life without anyone but him?

Loneliness dances beneath my skin and forces me forward.

As the doors open, I find Brax leaning against one of the thick pillars that litter the reception of our building.

A few people are looking his way. I can understand why. Even without knowing who he is, he has a presence. And of course, it doesn't help that he's taller and broader than any other man in this building.

"Ah, Miss Campbell. Your chariot awaits."

"You're such a goof," I laugh.

"That's what all the girls say. I think it might be why I'm perpetually single." His voice holds a mocking tone, but I'm not entirely sure he's joking.

I have heard plenty of stories that he isn't missing out on female attention. Kieran is more than happy to share some of his wilder nights with friends, but as far as I know, Brax has never had a girlfriend.

I'd always assumed it was for the same reasons Kieran chooses to continue to play the field.

"Girls love a funny guy," I argue as he gestures for me to go ahead.

"I'm sure they do," he mutters behind me as I say goodbye to the security guard on shift.

My steps slow as I take in the car parked right in front of the building in the designated taxi lane. Trust a football player to have the arrogance to ignore the rules.

"Someone has been throwing their cash around like it's a football," I tease.

"Treated myself," he says as he steps up to the red Maserati and opens the door for me.

The amount of attention he'd garnered inside is nothing compared to the number of eyes that are on him—on us— now.

Unease trickles through my veins.

Someone is going to take a picture of us together, and it'll be online before my ass hits the passenger seat.

"Thank you," I say with a smile. It's the first genuine one I've given anyone all day.

"Still in the mood for Mexican?" he asks once he joins me and brings the beast of an engine to life.

"Yes," I state, my stomach growling all over again as I think about the tacos I've been craving all day.

"Any preference on place or are you happy for me to choose?"

"Nope, wherever you want to go."

As Brax speeds out into traffic, I sit back in his ridiculously comfortable passenger seat and watch the world go by.

He aimlessly chats about his day for a while, allowing me to lose myself in thoughts that aren't my own for a few minutes.

But it all comes crashing down when he tests the waters and mentions Kieran.

"Brax," I warn, the pain last night caused rushing to the surface again.

"Understood," he says with a laugh that makes my brows pinch. "You need tequila before we dive into that."

"Maybe not even then," I mutter under my breath.

Before long, we've left the city rush hour traffic behind and we're heading down the freeway.

A little concern nags at me that he's taking me as far away as possible so we're not spotted.

Is he really that worried about being seen with me?

But then I remember the show of helping me into his car outside the office, and I stop myself.

"Here we go," Brax finally announces as he signals and pulls toward a building that is obviously a Mexican restaurant. It looks like it's been plucked straight out of Mexico with cacti surrounding the building and a huge sombrero on the roof.

"Best tacos in the state," Brax announces proudly.

"Then how come I've never heard of it before?"

"Also the state's best-kept secret."

No sooner have we stepped through the door than we're greeted by a guy with a heavy accent and the friendliest smile I've ever seen.

We're guided to a quiet table, and after Brax takes it upon himself to order our drinks, we're left with the menus.

"Bit presumptuous, don't you think?"

He smirks at me from across the table, and I can't help but smile back.

Brax is a good guy. Hot, too. But for some reason, when he turns his entire focus on me, I don't get butterflies. My heart doesn't race and my blood doesn't turn to lava.

I'd begun to think it was all in my head. That after Kieran left St. Louis, I'd made up this infatuation with him.

But then I found him in my apartment last night, and once the fear had subsided, the desire returned.

It never used to be the case. I used to look at him and see him in the way I do Brax. But something changed.

Probably about the time he kissed you.

Or maybe when he tied you to the bed and made you—

I slam those thoughts down. They're not needed or useful.

"Trust me. A margarita from here will fix you right up."

"Trying to get me drunk, Mr. Whitlock?"

"Absolutely not. Carrying Kieran's ass home last night was more than enough."

My brow wrinkles as a server appears with two shots of tequila, a soda for Brax, and a huge margarita for me.

"You had to carry him home? Why? From where?" I ask once we're left alone again.

Brax pushes a shot toward me.

"Drink. Take the edge off. Then, I'll tell you."

Hesitantly, I lift the glass.

I'm not a huge fan of shots, but what have I got to lose?

Together we lift them to our lips and swallow.

"Oh my god," I complain as the alcohol burns down my throat. "So?" I demand.

"You need to start. I need to know what happened before I was called to rescue his ass."

46

KIERAN

It's safe to say that I've never experienced a hangover like I had this morning. Or more specifically, this afternoon, by the time I finally woke up.

I've been drinking since I was...thirteen, but I've always been good at knowing my limits. Plus, football has always been my main focus. Partying and getting drunk always came second to that. Can't necessarily say the same about girls. But everyone has to have a vice, right?

But as much as I want to blame the alcohol for all the pain, I know it's not completely responsible.

Today has been hell.

Everything has been hell since that morning I woke up knowing that Effie was no longer mine.

I slump lower on my couch as I continue feeling sorry for myself.

I'm too far gone to even care at this point.

I don't mope. Generally, I'm not a sad person. The weeks that followed losing the playoff game don't count; that was an anomaly.

Usually, I'm good at picking myself back up and getting on with shit.

But right now, getting on with my life is the last thing I want to do.

I hate that I can't find anything within me to push myself forward, but it's gone.

Everything has gone.

All the feelings I was smothering in St. Louis when Grams died so I could be there for Effie have risen to the surface, along with the frustration and anger over her hiding the fact she was home is dragging me under.

I don't know how long I've been sitting here staring at nothing. I don't even have the TV on. My apartment is completely silent. There is nothing but my irritating thoughts and regrets to keep me company.

Over and over, I keep replaying last night in my head.

I should have handled it differently. I think I was aware of that at the time, but I was fueled by anger.

I'd be lying if I said there wasn't a little bit of relief in there too. But it wasn't enough to calm my temper.

I've been so fucking worried about her, and for four days, she'd been right here under my nose.

Fuck.

Even now, almost twenty-four hours on from finding out the truth, my hands still tremble with rage.

She lied to me.

Okay, so it was a lie by omission. But that doesn't stop it from hurting.

What if I'd gotten bored of waiting for her and decided to drive to St. Louis?

A million and one what-ifs flicker through my head, none of them helpful and all of them building my irritation.

I should move. I should force myself into my gym to burn off some steam, but I can't make myself do it.

So instead, I remain exactly where I have been for hours now.

I haven't even bothered to eat.

A bitter laugh spills from my lips.

Is this what it's like? To have your world ripped to shreds by a girl?

It's funny, because never in a million years did I think that Effie would be the one to do it.

For years, I've trusted her with my heart...with my everything.

I truly thought she was one person I could always rely on.

I never even considered there could be an end for us. That I might have to be forced to live a life without her.

Pain shoots through me.

That can't happen. It just can't. We have to get through this.

By the time my buzzer for my apartment goes off, I'm a mess.

I really need to hit something. The healthiest option would be a treadmill, but I don't think it'll have the effect I'm hoping for.

It's been years since I was in a physical fight. These days, it's not worth losing my starting position on the team for, but fuck if I don't want to go at it with someone right now.

If I called Kian, he'd probably be up for it. It was always the two of us that ended up settling an argument with our fists, with Kingston on the sidelines watching, having probably started the whole thing, and then smirking as the two of us got hauled away by our dad.

I might have always hated being the little one, but I loved my brothers something fierce. I still do.

They're my rocks. Just like Effie.

My teeth grind.

There isn't a part of my life that she's not involved in.

I have no idea how I'm meant to eradicate her.

I don't fucking want to eradicate her.

But what the fuck am I supposed to do now?

Twice...she's told me to leave twice now. Is there any coming back from that?

Does she hate me because of the article?

Does she regret our weekend together so much that she can barely look at me now?

Funny how two people can see things so differently.

That weekend was hands down the best weekend of my life.

For the first time in...well, ever, I was able to be myself. Authentically myself.

Effie didn't look at me like I was weird when I showed her what I liked, the things I wanted to do to her. She didn't expect anything from me. She embraced everything; she trusted me to look after her. And she was so fucking beautiful and addictive at the same time.

And yet...it seems that it might have been one of her worst weekends.

Lost in my depressing thoughts, I forget that my buzzer went off until it rings again, the irritating sound cutting through the silence I've been drowning in.

"FUCK OFF," I bellow.

It's pointless. No one can hear me. I live in the penthouse, just like Effie. But mine is the entire top floor of the building with balconies on three sides.

It's my haven. Or at least it was until some motherfucker interrupted my peace.

But despite my lack of response, they clearly don't want to give up because it buzzes again.

Sucking in a deep breath, I finally push myself from the couch and stomp over like a petulant child who doesn't want to do what he's told.

"What?" I snap as I jam my finger against the button. I cringe. Gavin, our long-suffering doorman, deserves better than my shitty attitude.

I'm relieved when a different voice answers.

"Now, now. That's no way to respond to one of the guys who stopped you from sleeping on a dirty bar floor last night."

My mouth opens and closes, but no words come out.

"Let me the fuck up, Callahan. I've got food."

My stomach growls on cue.

"What food?" I enquire, making him laugh.

"Knew that would get you. Tacos."

Fuck.

"What are the chances of you sending the food up alone?"

"None. Now let me the fuck up."

"I hate you," I seethe.

"Fine by me, asshole."

Unable to deny the tacos, especially if he got them from the Mexican place he's taken me to a couple of times, I reluctantly allow Brax access before unlocking my front door.

I'm in the kitchen opening a beer when he marches through my apartment like he owns the place with a knowing smirk playing on his lips and a brown paper bag tucked under his arm.

Drinking more alcohol is the last thing my body needs right now, but for once, I don't care about what I'm putting inside it or about being in peak condition. It's not mid-season. I can have a few days where I say fuck it and give into temptation while I wallow in self-pity.

"Ah, I see you woke up this morning and decided to make better choices."

"Fuck off, Whitlock. I want the tacos, not the attitude."

"Well, unlucky for you, you get both."

The second he lowers the bag to the counter, I snatch it and drag it closer.

Immediately, I rip it open and reach inside for a container.

Inside lie two delicious tacos, and for the first time today, I'm able to think about something other than Effie and last night.

In seconds, I have one out of the container and in my mouth.

I groan in delight before devouring it as if I haven't eaten in weeks.

"Jesus," Brax mutters as he takes a seat at my island and watches me in horror. "You're a hell of a lot messier than my date tonight."

I glance at the clock.

"If you're here at nine o'clock after a date, I'd say you have bigger issues than how politely she eats."

"Maybe she's a good girl."

"Then what the fuck is she doing with you?" I counter.

He smiles at me but doesn't say anything else.

"I was coming to see how you were doing, but I can see that from the state of you."

"If I want your opinion on my life, I'll ask for it."

"Wow, you really are full of rainbows and sunshine tonight, huh?"

"Fuck off."

"Uh...nah. I think I'm okay here for a bit."

I glare at him, both annoyed as hell and relieved that he's turned up to check on me.

I don't know if I said anything to clue him into why he had to carry me out of a bar last night, but from the knowing look in his eyes, I'd say that he's more than aware.

"So..."

"You're an asshole," I scoff, reaching for the other taco.

"Takes one to know one. Now, start talking."

"Nothing to say."

He raises a brow.

"She'd been back for four days, Brax. Four fucking days and she didn't tell me. And then when I confronted her about it, she told me to leave."

"Oh shit, no wonder you're pissed. No one tells the mighty Kieran Callahan what to do."

"Are you trying to help or just make shit worse?" I bark.

"You need to pull your head out of your ass and talk to her like a normal person."

I stare blankly at him.

"What?" he asks, reaching for the second beer that's sitting on the island between us.

"It's Effie, bro. You need to talk to her. Listen to her. She's hurting."

My brows shoot up.

"And how do you know that?" I snap.

"She just lost her grandmother, Kieran. She's grieving and probably not thinking straight."

An argument sits on the tip of my tongue, but I swallow it down.

Brax might be a bit of a joker, but he knows more about grief than I do. I hate that he does, but there isn't much I can do about that.

Letting out a sigh, I stare down at the container, wishing there was another taco.

"Everything is such a mess," I finally confess.

"Maybe so, but it's not unfixable."

"She lied about us being engaged, and—"

"Then you allowed the world—and her—to believe it was true for longer than you should have."

I shake my head before grabbing a napkin and wiping my mouth.

"I shouldn't have fucked her," I blurt.

"Maybe," he muses helpfully.

"What is that supposed to mean?"

"What if you were meant to fuck her? What if you should still be fucking her?"

My breath catches in my throat.

Do I want to fuck Effie again? Hell yes.

She was...she was incredible.

Do I think she'll ever give me a chance? Not for a single second.

Knowing that hurts. Really fucking hurts.

"We had an agreement. Four days only and then we forget it."

"And have you spoken to her about that?"

"No, she sent me back here after discovering that Kat fucked us over. And she's ignored me ever since." I huff. "You already know this shit," I point out.

"I know, but I'm not entirely sure you know it all."

Lifting my beer bottle, I down what's left before throwing it in the trash and reaching for another.

"The fuck are you talking about?" I bark, far from understanding his cryptic bullshit.

"You want her," he states simply.

"I don't. I'm not interested in a relationship. I want my best friend back."

"That might be what you think you want, but I suspect you're lying to yourself."

"And I suspect that you're in interfering asshole, but what are we going to do about it?"

47

EFFIE

The rest of the week passes in a blur of meetings and conference calls. I'm chasing my tail having been away for so long, and I don't like it.

I used to be on top of everything, know everyone and how they were helping KC Foundation. But right now, I feel like I'm swimming upstream and getting absolutely nowhere.

Jasmine has done a great job, there's no doubt about that. But without her, it's hard to figure everything out.

I haven't been to see her yet; I'm not sure I'm ready to visit a hospital. I know that Grams was only ever in one for appointments, she was lucky really, but still, it's going to bring it all back.

I tell myself that she's got her family and friends around her, and that she doesn't need to be reminded of work, or the fact I've been dragged off sabbatical because she's in the hospital.

Shaking my head, I refuse to focus on those thoughts. They're not helpful.

I'm trying really hard to fight through all the hardship.

Like the fact that all I want to do is pick up the phone and call the two most important people in my life.

But I can't.

Neither will answer.

For very different reasons, of course, but it's the same outcome.

I curl my legs beneath me as I lower my ass to the couch and stare out at the sunset with a mug of hot chocolate in my hands.

Chicago really is a beautiful city. Just like the day I returned, I feel like I've come home. There is just one massive thing missing.

Since I sent Kieran away, I haven't heard a single thing from him.

His daily messages have stopped, adding to the grief I'm already battling.

I know that I'm the one who sent him away. This is my fault. But it doesn't make it hurt any less.

The only thing that makes me forget is dancing.

I'm so glad I took a chance on that class.

And Thursday was even better. I wasn't blindsided by my new partner; I wasn't scared of putting myself out there and trying something new. I was able to just embrace it.

Now, I can't wait until Monday night. Something tells me that those two hours of my week are going to be my favorite.

I glance at the clock. Seven p.m. on a Saturday night.

It's not unusual for me to be home at this time. I'm not exactly a party animal. Kieran is the social butterfly of our friendship, especially in the off-season. He manages to find a party or an event to attend almost every night of the week. It's how he picks up women—not that he has to try very hard.

My chest constricts and my stomach knots at the thought of him with someone else. It's stupid. He's probably been hooking up with supermodels and tying them to his bed since he first arrived back here.

He told you he didn't do that with others, a little voice says, but I bat it away.

Just because he said it, doesn't have to make it true.

He was on a mission to get me out of my head and make me happy. Who the hell knows how much of what he said was true?

For all I know, I was the worst lay of his life, and while I'm here regretting agreeing to our little deal because it's fucked everything up, he's regretting ever touching me because of how awful it was.

That's not true and you know it.

"Fuck's sake," I mutter, chastising myself for getting lost in these kinds of thoughts.

Continuing to ignore the docuseries I selected to watch on the TV, I grab my cell and open Instagram.

The first picture that appears hits me like a bat to the chest.

Kieran is standing between his brothers with a killer smile on his face.

I glance at when it was posted.

An hour ago.

All the air rushes from my lungs as my eyes return to his.

Just like the two older Callahan men, his eyes sparkle with life and excitement.

All three of them are in tuxedoes, heading out for some fancy event.

Emotion crawls up my throat until my nose itches and my eyes burn.

I may not have often gone to an event with Kieran, but I always knew where he was going or what he was doing.

But tonight, I had no idea.

He looks so good. So...normal. And I'm here on the verge of tears over a freaking photograph.

Noticing that there are several photographs, I swipe through them in my quest to learn more.

To my relief, I don't find any women. Just more suited men. When I hit the final image, I discover what's happening.

They're having a poker night.

They don't happen all that often, maybe once or twice a year, but Kieran's dad and a few associates organize them. And because the older generation are chauvinistic assholes, they're always men only.

The servers who provide them with drinks and snacks, however, are a very different story.

Jealousy stirs deep within me.

Kieran has fucked them in the past. I doubt tonight will be any different.

Unable to stop myself, I click on his name, seeing as Kian has helpfully tagged him in the photograph, and find myself on Kieran's profile for the first time since I left St. Louis.

It doesn't matter that he hasn't posted anything new; I scroll through like I've never seen it before.

My chest aches as I experience just a snapshot of his life.

As per my request, there are hardly any images or references to me on his account.

As much as I love him and am proud of the life he's created for himself, I don't want to be in the limelight. Something I really should have thought more about before telling Grams what I did.

I hover hesitantly over the symbol that will take me to his tagged posts. I already know the content that has been posted about me over the past few weeks, and it's not good.

Liar.

Game player.

Betrayer.

Deceiver.

Unloyal.

Snake.

I've read it all. Every single toxic thing that journalists and the public combined said about me after the team's publicist "accidentally" allowed part of the truth about our engagement to be released.

Kieran assured me it was an accident. That an intern sold what she thought would make the best story.

It's plausible, sure. Kat, the team's publicist, has never done something so underhanded before. She usually has the players and the team's backs.

I hope it's the truth. But really, it doesn't matter. The story came out, and I very quickly became enemy number one amongst Kieran Callahan fans.

Not a place I ever thought I'd find myself. And certainly not a place I'd wish to be.

Reading it all again is the last thing I want to do, but I can't stop myself.

Some of the posts have new comments, and each one cuts through my heart like a knife.

All of their words are lies. I never set out to play or hurt Kieran. I never wanted anything from him. Even the comments explaining how I was clearly hoping that by creating a fake engagement he'd realize he was madly in love with me and go through with it are a million years from the truth.

Kieran isn't in love with me. I don't have any wild fantasies of us running into the sunset together and living happily ever after.

I'm not aware that my cheeks are wet from crying until my buzzer rings through the apartment, dragging my attention from my cell.

A familiar mixture of grief, anger, disbelief, and frustration courses through my veins.

Swiping at my cheeks with the backs of my hands, I drop my cell to the couch and pad toward the front door to find out who it is.

My first thought is Brax. He's been such a good friend this week. Honestly, I'm not sure I'd have survived without him.

He's given me an outlet to talk. A safe space to just be me. It's not quite like being with Kieran, but right now, it's the closest I'm going to get.

Sucking in a deep breath in the hope I can hide my distress, I press the button and say hello.

"Hi, Effie. It's Tate and Lori. Sorry to drop in unannounced, but are you free for a couple of guests?"

I glance down at myself and cringe.

Tatum and Lorelei are two of the city's most beautiful women. I highly doubt they're currently dressed in leggings, which may or may not have a hole at the crotch, and an old college sweater that has seen better days.

"O-oh, hey," I say, unable to ignore them. "I'm not really dressed for visitors." I cringe at myself.

"We're not here for your outfit, Effie. We're here for you."

My heart slams against my ribs. Their words are a welcome reminder that while I might feel lonely, I'm not actually alone.

Feeling awful that I haven't reached out to them, I press the button that will allow them entry to my building and the top floor.

"See you in a few, girl," Lori sings before the line goes silent.

I stand there nervously for a few seconds, wondering if I should prioritize getting changed or tidying up.

In the end, I opt for a quick tidy.

If they're as perceptive as I think they are, they'll take one look in my eyes and know that I'm barely holding it together. My choice of clothing won't matter.

I'm dumping a couple of abandoned mugs and glasses in my sink when voices fill my apartment.

With one last little pep talk, I go to greet them.

"Effie, it's so good to see you," Lori says, immediately pulling me into her arms and squeezing tight.

Tears burn red hot behind my eyes, but I force them to stay down.

Just as we part, a small noise erupts from behind her.

"Oh my gosh, look at you," I breathe, taking in the changes to Prince since I last saw him. "Those cheeks."

A wide smile pulls at my lips as Tate happily passes him to me.

"Oh, you are getting so big and so handsome," I tell Prince as he smiles back at me. "How are you doing?"

With him safely in my arms, I walk him around my apartment, letting him look at everything.

My skin prickles at Tate and Lori's attention, although not in a bad way, as I continue baby-talking to Prince.

Everything is fine until I point out the Chiefs Stadium in the distance and tell him that it's where Uncle Kieran plays all his games.

My voice cracks on his name, and there's no way they don't hear it.

"We brought ingredients for cocktails," Lori announces, and when I spin around, I find her unloading a bag of alcohol onto my kitchen counter. "Thought you might need it. Cosmos all around?"

"You got it," Tate says as she walks around the couch with a bag of her own, although something tells me there isn't alcohol in that one.

Ten minutes later, the three of us have freshly made cosmos, and Prince is happily playing on his interactive mat on the floor.

I met Tate when I was a teenager. Kieran brought me to a

Callahan Enterprises event, and she was also there with her brother. We've always gotten on well, but we've never been close. And Lori? Well, she's awesome.

They both are. They both have the confidence I wish I could possess. Hell, they've managed to claim themselves two of the most eligible bachelors in Chicago.

The fact they're with the two older Callahan brothers does give us something in common. But still, the relationships they have with Kingston and Kian are very different from the one I have with Kieran.

"So," Tate begins, making my heart race. "How are you?"

My lips part, ready to lie to them, when Lori jumps in.

"And we want the truth, Effie. No bullshit."

My words fade away, and embarrassingly, tears take their place.

48

KIERAN

"Finally," Mom breathes as soon as I step into her kitchen.

A wide smile spreads across her lips, and she walks toward me with her apron covering her designer dress.

She lives for our Sunday family meals.

Things haven't always been easy for our family.

I was too young to remember when our parents separated and the details of that split, but Kingston wasn't. He blamed and punished our mom for years for her infidelity.

I don't want to say that I don't care, because I do. Of course I do. But what happened in our parents' relationship all those years ago is impossible to know. We don't know how either of them felt or why they made the decisions they did.

Mom hurt Dad badly, but I refuse to believe he was innocent in the whole thing.

All that matters to me is that everyone is happy now.

Neil, our stepfather, is fantastic. He treats Mom well and is a great dad to our half-sisters.

I embrace Mom, taking a moment to absorb her love and support.

Am I still annoyed about her over-the-top reaction when she discovered my fake engagement? Yeah, a little. But time has given me a little perspective, and I know she was just excited.

Kingston's wedding to Tatum was...controversial.

I understand why he didn't invite her. She does, too. But I don't think he was aware of just how much it hurt her.

When Kian and Lori got together, she was excited because she knew Kian would invite her. They're so much closer. But that hasn't happened yet. They're keeping their plans under wraps at the moment.

And then the news broke about me and Effie, and her excitement just bubbled over.

I get it. She wants each of us to find our happily ever after. She's nothing if not an old romantic.

Much like Grams, Mom has had these wild ideas for years that Effie is the woman for me. I'm pretty sure every time I mention her she holds her breath in case I'm about to tell her what she wants to hear. Obviously, it's never happened.

After a long embrace, she pulls back and stares up at me.

All three of us tower over her, forcing her to crane her neck to meet our eyes.

"Oh, Kieran," she sighs, a sad expression on her face. "What are you doing?"

I frown, confused by her words.

"Have you spoken to her?"

Those words only make my frown deepen.

"Can we not do this?" I ask as I pull the refrigerator open.

I'm going to need one of Neil's beers if she's insisting on having this conversation.

"Kieran, you're not happy."

Oh, Jesus.

"If you were, I'd let it go. But I can see in your eyes that you're struggling."

"It's been a tough few months," I explain.

Even if things were good with me and Effie, it would still be true. Losing Grams was hard. I smothered my own grief in order to look after Effie and support her through hers. But I'd be lying if I said I wasn't still suffering with her loss.

Abandoning her cooking duties, she grabs a glass of wine and takes a seat beside me.

"Talk to me, sweetie," she says softly, reaching for my hand and squeezing encouragingly.

"There's nothing to talk about."

She raises a brow, not believing a word of it.

"Mom," I complain.

"Oh, Kieran. I know things are complicated, and I don't expect you to give me all the details, but you and Effie...you're too good together to throw it all away."

"We're just friends," I argue.

Even saying the words hurts.

Losing her would always hurt. She's been such a huge part of my life. But right now, it feels like a whole lot more than losing a friend.

"You two have never just been friends, Kieran. You've just been waiting for the right time."

"There won't be a right time. Effie deserves so much more than anything I could offer her."

Mom's lip purse with irritation. "That's bullshit."

My eyes widen in surprise. Mom hardly ever swears.

"Mom."

Her shoulders widen. "No, I'm serious, Kieran. There isn't anything that Effie wants that you can't give her. She just wants you."

"What?" I shake my head, unable to believe what she's saying. "No, she doesn't."

Mom chuckles to herself. "Kieran, I love you, but you're clueless. That girl has been in love with you for years. And in case you haven't figured it out yet, the feeling is most definitely mutual."

I stare at her, blinking, unable to find any words to respond.

Thankfully, there's a commotion at the front door, and not two seconds later, Kingston, Tate, Prince, Kian, and Lori join us in the kitchen.

Mom hops up to greet everyone and leaves me with her words spinning around my head.

The rest of the day is a blur. Everyone talks to me, but no words really go in. Makenzie and Matilda are...well, as hyperactive as any teenage girls. They're exhausting, Kenzie especially. I swear that kid never stops talking, ever. Tilly is a little calmer, more pensive.

By the time we're saying our goodbyes, I'm more than ready to lock myself in my quiet apartment.

As per usual, King and Tate are the first to leave. He may be embracing family life a little more these days, but things are still strained. He's trying, though, and that's more than can be said for how things were before he married Tate. She's a good influence on him.

Kenzie begs for Kian to stay longer, as she always does. She idolizes our big brother and has him on a pedestal, so high I'm amazed she can see him up there.

I'll admit that I'm a little jealous.

Sure, I get plenty of attention. But most of it is surface level.

Other than my family, the only person who looks at me like I'm something special, something more than just a football player, is Effie.

That thought hits me hard in the chest.

I miss her.

I miss her so fucking much.

Mom tries talking to me again, but I let most of it go over my head.

She doesn't know what our relationship is really like. She has no idea what it's been like the past few weeks.

I drive home on autopilot, wishing things were different, wishing I could go to her place and spend the evening talking and laughing like old times.

And without realizing it, that's exactly where I end up.

Idling on the side of the road, outside her apartment building, staring up at her windows.

As I sit there, rain begins hitting the windshield.

It gets harder and harder, cutting off my already terrible view of her apartment.

She's right up there, or at least, I assume she is.

So close, and yet so far.

I need her.

"Fuck it," I say to myself, pushing my door open before I can think better of it.

I'm soaked before I get even halfway across the street. It should be enough to make me turn back, but it's not.

I need to see her.

I need to be near her.

Pulling my keys from my pocket, I let myself into her building just like I did the other night.

My heart is in my throat as I ride the elevator to the top floor of the building, and when I lift my hand to push the key into her lock, my hand is trembling.

I should have learned from last time.

She doesn't want me here.

I should listen to that and respect her wishes. But I'm a selfish asshole, and my need for her is too strong.

Her apartment is silent as I slip inside and quietly close the door behind me.

My heart pounds, but the need rushing through my veins is too strong to ignore.

The large clock in her living room tells me that it's a little after seven as I move through her apartment.

She's here; I know she is.

There are signs everywhere. Her keys are sitting on the cabinet in the hallway. There are dirty dishes in the kitchen, an abandoned book on the couch. Her scent fills the air, and so does her presence.

As I close in on the bedroom, I hear something.

Running water.

My heart lurches, and my cock jerks.

As I move closer, her soft voice hits my ears.

She's singing, but there's no music.

Pressing my palm against the ajar door, I push it open.

Steam fills the room, cutting off some of my vision. But not enough to stop me from seeing her.

She's lying in her bathtub surrounded by bubbles, and she's got AirPods in.

Her head is resting back and her eyes are closed.

My head screams for me to leave. I've seen her; I can back away now and go home knowing that she's okay.

But I can't move.

I'm rooted to the spot.

Effie continues singing, and my heart continues to race, my need for her getting stronger and stronger.

My hands begin to tremble, before it spreads through the rest of my body.

Unfiltered, potent need.

Unable to turn back, I shove the door wider, letting it crash into the wall, and I step into the bathroom to announce my presence.

49

EFFIE

A shadow falls over me, and my heart jumps into my throat as fear floods though my veins.

My lips part, ready to scream as my eyes pop open.

But before I can register what—or who—is standing over me, a large, hot hand covers my mouth, cutting off any noise I was about to make.

"Be a good girl, Luck."

The panic surging through my body stops me from recognizing the words. But my body knows.

My muscles relax, aware that I'm not in any immediate danger. Well, my body might not be. My heart is another matter entirely.

I stare at him with wide eyes, silently begging for him to explain himself.

"Look at you," he muses, letting his gaze shift from mine in favor of my body.

He probably can't see much, considering the amount of bubble bath I poured into the water, but it doesn't seem to matter.

His eyes darken with desire, and he drags his bottom lip between his teeth.

Despite knowing better, a steady throb starts up between my thighs.

I miss you.

When his attention hits my closed legs, he swallows thickly.

"Spread your thighs," he demands.

The rational voice in my head screams at me not to do it.

But my body is on an entirely different page, and without instruction from my brain, my legs fall open.

Kieran swallows again, making the tendons in his throat pull and ripple.

My eyes drop lower, and I frown when I find his clothes soaking and sticking to his hard body.

My mouth waters as I burn up, my blood rushing like lava through my veins.

"Fuck," he rasps before our eyes collide again.

I'm so lost in his heated gaze that I don't notice him reach out.

My entire body flinches when his palm lands on my breast. And when he pinches my nipple, I thrash so hard that water sloshes over the edge of the tub.

It if hits him, he doesn't react.

Instead, he continues teasing me.

My nostrils flare as I fight to drag in the air I need.

Every squeeze or pinch of my nipple sends a potent shot of desire straight to my clit.

He builds me higher and higher, reminding me just how in tune he is with my body.

I'm trembling with my need for more, with my need for release, but all he does is stare down at me.

I should be screaming at him to leave. But I can't. I'm frozen.

His eyes are blazing, but his expression is blank.

Even if I wasn't racing toward an intense release, I don't think I'd be able to read his thoughts.

With his hand still clamped around my mouth, his other sinks into the water.

I gasp before screaming into his palm when his fingertips graze my clit.

"That's it, Luck," he encourages, his voice raspy, as he pushes his hand deeper, his fingers finding my entrance.

I whimper, my hips bucking as he pushes inside.

"Ride my hand. Show me what a dirty girl you really are."

His words...

Fuck. His fucking words.

"Yeah, you've missed it, haven't you? You've missed being my whore."

His thumb presses against my clit as his fingers curl inside me, finding my G-spot.

Oh my god.

"That's it, Luck. Show me how beautiful you are when you come."

Unable to do anything but what he requests, I fall over the edge, my body convulsing and sending water splashing in all directions as I cry out into his palm.

It goes on and on, letting both of us know just how long it's been since I got off, and he watches every second of it.

Finally, he stands and releases my mouth, allowing me to suck in greedy lungfuls of air.

I stare up at him in disbelief.

He's here.

He just barged into my apartment, into my bathroom, and—

"W-what are you do—"

"Get out," he barks, his fists clenching and unclenching at his sides as if he's struggling to control himself.

"What?"

"Get the fuck out of the tub, Effie."

Without questioning him, I wrap my hands around the edge and haul myself out as Kieran marches from the room.

"Kieran, what are you—"

I'm about to grab a towel when he marches back in.

He makes the most of my parted lips and stuffs some fabric into my mouth before covering the bottom half of my face with his hand again.

"Be a good girl," he says before spinning me around and walking me out of the bathroom and then my bedroom.

Water runs down my body, leaving wet footprints behind us.

The cool air of my apartment makes my skin prick with goosebumps, and the moment the floor-to-ceiling windows that showcase the city beyond come into view, a full-body shudder works through me.

Kieran doesn't stop moving me forward, and before I know what's happening, I'm standing right in front of the windows.

My nipples harden and the ache between my legs gets more and more intense.

For a few seconds, I stare out at the world beyond my apartment, but then my eyes refocus, and I find our reflection.

My breath catches as another wave of desire rolls through me.

Kieran isn't looking outside; his eyes are locked on me.

My heart rate picks up, my temperature soaring.

His free hand grips my hip tighter before he suddenly slides it up my body, cupping my heavy breasts.

"How many men are looking at you right now?" I suck in a sharp breath. "How many of them want you?"

I moan, my hips rolling of their own accord.

"Oh no," he warns before kicking my legs wider. "You don't get yourself off. That pleasure is all mine. And every single motherfucker out there is going to learn something very important."

His hot breath rushes down my neck and over my chest, making me shudder.

"You're mine, Effie. Your pleasure, your body, your everything. Mine."

I sag back against him and gasp. His clothes are wet and cold.

"Hands on the window," he demands, pushing me forward. "Ass out."

I do as I'm told.

"Find them. Scan the windows for anyone that's watching."

And I do. My eyes scan the buildings before me, searching for anyone who might be looking out.

My heart pounds so hard it makes my head spin. The thought of being watched is terrifying. But also...I'm not sure I've ever been this turned on, this wet.

I'm not at his mercy in the same way I was at Grams'. I'm not bound or tied to anything. But that doesn't matter.

Right now, I have no control.

Kieran holds all the power.

It's exactly as it should be.

He moves behind me, but his hand remains locked on my face, keeping whatever he stuffed into my mouth in place.

Instead, I wait, sucking in deep, hungry breaths through my nose.

"You're going to let them watch you come."

Oh my god.

Suddenly, he's back. His crotch hits my ass, and his hand slides down my stomach.

Every muscle south of my waist clenches in anticipation.

I cry out when his fingers connect with my clit, my hips jumping forward.

"Such a good whore for me," he muses as he works me. "Your pussy loves an audience. You're so wet right now, Luck. So desperate for everyone to watch you get fucked."

The fabric in my mouth muffles my pathetic, needy whimper.

He works me until I'm on the cusp of my second orgasm, but he doesn't let me fall. Instead, he edges me right there in front of the city of Chicago.

My skin is covered in a sheen of sweat, my muscles are quivering, and my pussy is desperate for a release. But he won't give it to me.

I lose count of how many times he lets my release fade before the familiar sound of a zipper being opened hits my ears.

"Oh, you really want my dick, don't you?"

I nod eagerly, or at least as much as I can, with him holding me captive. I'm too far gone at this point to even try to deny it.

He fucks me hard and fast with his fingers before suddenly pulling them free.

I look up just in time to see him plunge them into his mouth to lick them clean.

His eyes hold mine, and I swear, my orgasm gets a little closer just from watching him.

"Ass out," he demands, and the second I do as I'm told, I'm rewarded with the head of his dick dragging through my folds.

My pussy clenches with my need to feel him inside me.

I try to beg, but nothing but muffled whimpers can be heard.

And then, he's there. Gently pushing against me. Teasing me with what I want.

His free hand wraps around my hips, and I get another second to suck in a breath before his hips punch forward, and he fills me in one quick thrust.

I cry out into my gag, my head falling forward as my body fights to stay upright.

"Watch them," he growls behind me, giving me little choice but to look out again.

I can't see anyone, but it doesn't matter.

My skin prickles like I have a million eyes on me as Kieran sets a punishing pace behind me.

My sweaty palms slide against the glass as I happily take everything he's got for me.

"Fuck. Yes. Look at you getting fucked. Dirty whore. You're a dirty whore, Luck."

His grip on my hip is so tight, I do not doubt that I'll have bruises tomorrow.

Tomorrow.

I have a fleeting thought about what all this means and what tomorrow will bring, but it's cut short when Kieran notices that I've closed my eyes.

"Watch, or I'll stop."

Instantly, my eyelids open, and I find him staring at me in our reflection.

Despite locking down his emotions earlier, right now, there is a riot of different things going on behind his eyes.

My chest tightens, and my heart aches. But he doesn't give me time to really focus in on them.

Effortlessly, he pushes me forward, and I shriek when my chest hits the cold glass.

Wrapping his hand around my thigh, he lifts my foot from the floor and spreads me wide open.

"Now they can see who you belong to," he rasps quietly in my ear. "Mine. Luck. You. Are. Mine."

I whimper and mewl as he fucks me. Every drag of his cock gets me closer to my release.

I'm balancing right on the cusp of it when he slides his hand to my pussy and pinches my clit.

I don't just fall off the cliff; I fucking fly.

The world around me ceases to exist as I finally ride out the orgasm he denied me for so long.

I've barely come down from my high when he pulls out of me.

I cry out at the loss, not ready to lose him again so soon.

But I soon discover it's not over.

He twists me around to face him before picking me up and pressing me back against the window.

As soon as he has me in position, he pushes back inside me.

With one hand gripping my ass to hold me in place, the other wraps around my throat.

My eyes widen with the pressure he applies, but I don't fight him.

Why should I? I trust him implicitly.

He doesn't say another word.

Instead, his eyes hold mine as he fucks me.

What I see in those dark green depths terrifies me.

I want this. I want what we had back at Grams' so badly.

But at the same time, I'm petrified of fucking everything up for good.

Right now, we still have this.

But whatever this is, isn't enough.

It's not even close, and I'm too scared to admit that I want more.

Because I know that it's not something Kieran is willing to give.

Even to me.

50

EFFIE

I t was a pair of my panties.

That's what Kieran stuffed in my mouth to stop me from talking as he fucked me.

He kept me pinned against the window, staring into my eyes until I came around his dick again. And only when I had, did he let himself go.

The groan he let out as he spilled inside me still echoes around my apartment all these hours later.

It was so erotic. So hot.

But as perfect as that moment was, it wasn't meant to last.

He left me there naked in front of the window.

I watched as he took a step back and tucked himself away.

He ran his eyes over my naked body with a mixture of heat, disappointment and anger in his dark gaze.

And then he took two steps back.

I wanted to beg him to stay. To tell him we could go back to how things were that weekend.

But my fear stopped me.

It might be good for four days, a week, maybe even a month.

But then what?

I wouldn't survive if he dropped me for someone else.

With my gag still in place stopping me from saying a single word, I had little choice but to watch as he walked away from me again.

This time was worse because I didn't tell him to go.

He wanted to go.

He'd gotten what he came for and he left me in a used heap on the floor.

I don't know how long I stayed there for, silently hoping he'd realize his mistake and come back.

But he didn't. So in the end, I climbed onto my weak, shaky legs and returned to my bathroom.

I climbed back into the tub and sat in that cold water until my teeth were chattering, running the events of the evening over and over in my head.

I should have done something to stop him.

But I never have had the strength to say no to Kieran.

My tears splashed into the water as I purged the frustration and sadness his visit left me with.

How hard would it have been for him to carry me to my bed and crawl in with me instead?

At some point, with shivers racking my body and regrets eating me up, I managed to dry myself off and slip between the covers. There was nothing comforting about the warmth though.

Rolling onto my back, I stare up at my ceiling.

I should have gotten up almost an hour ago to do my yoga, but I haven't been able to find the strength or inclination to do it.

So instead, I continue to lie here, replaying last night over and over.

I'm only punishing myself, but I can't help it.

He probably went home having scratched his itch and forgot all about it.

Makes me wonder why he came to me and didn't call on one of his usual hookups.

Maybe he thought I'd be less work.

I cringe.

That can't be right. I've seen how shameless and desperate the women he usually spends time with can be.

He had no idea how I'd react to him turning up.

Maybe that was the point. Maybe it was a test.

I drive myself crazy, thinking up a million different reasons why last night happened. None of them make me feel any better about it.

What happened is obvious.

He played me. And I let him.

I wonder how it makes him feel to know he has that much control over me.

I told him to leave only a week ago, but yet, he can turn up and get exactly what he wants.

Fuck. I'm pathetic.

And...I really need to change my locks.

I really can't risk that happening again.

Kieran Callahan is going to break me.

No, he's going to shatter me to smithereens. And I can't let that happen. Not when I've worked so hard.

Finally, I throw the covers back and get to my feet with a new strength fueling me.

Or at least I do until my thighs pull and my pussy aches in a way that reminds me all too vividly about the events of the night before.

I can't let him do this.

He can't infiltrate every inch of my life.

He makes me want him in a way I've never wanted anyone before.

It's not fair.

I refuse to be the kind of woman who mopes around because a man doesn't want her.

Kieran and I have managed for years without me losing my mind over him.

I can go back to that...can't I?

Shutting down my thoughts about the man who may or may not still be my best friend, I set out to get ready for work.

By the time I leave my apartment, my hair has been styled to perfection, and my makeup is flawless. On the outside, I look like I'm coping. But on the inside, I'm about to fall apart at any moment.

I don't look at my cell all the way to the office. I tell myself to stay strong because I'll either have nothing from him, which will hurt, or I'll have a message...and something tells me that will be the most painful of all.

Seeing his face, his words...I'm not sure I can deal with that right now.

But despite telling myself all this, I can't stop myself from reaching into my purse and pulling it out.

I hold my breath as I wake it up and stare down at my notifications.

I have quite a few, but as I scroll through them, my heart sinks when I discover that not a single one is from him.

A pained sigh passes my lips, and I stuff it back into my purse and try to put everything about Kieran Callahan to the back of my mind.

It works for two hours before I find myself face-to-face with the man I'm trying my hardest to forget.

I'm sitting in our monthly management meeting, trying to keep up with everything, frantically scribbling into my notebook when the office door opens, and a deep, familiar voice fills the room.

My entire body freezes, and I have to fight to keep my eyes on the paper before me.

I can't look up and see him. If I do, I have no doubt that I'll embarrass myself in front of my colleagues.

I already wonder what they see now when they look at me. Can they tell that I'm as broken as I feel?

"Kieran, it's good to see you," Henry sings.

Not only is Henry our CEO, but he's a huge Chiefs fan and gets stars in his eyes every time Kieran steps inside the office.

Usually, I find it endearing to watch the man who's always in control lose grip on everything in the presence of one of his favorite players, but not today.

Today, I just need to survive his presence.

It's not unheard of for Kieran or one of his brothers to attend, seeing as they're all on the board of directors. But it didn't occur to me that today might be the day that Kieran decided to continue messing with my head and my body.

It would have been too easy to send Kingston or Kian.

Sucking in a deep breath, I try to school my features.

Of course, everyone knows we're friends, and I'm sure they're all more than aware of the recent scandal involving our fake engagement. But thankfully, everyone here is too professional to mention it. Although, I'm sure the gossip was rife when it first hit the press.

My skin tingles with awareness, letting me know where Kieran's attention is long before my eyes find him.

But despite knowing, my breath still catches in my throat.

Just like last night, his expression is blank, not allowing anyone to get a read on him.

"Do you mind?" Kieran says after a beat of silence, gesturing to an empty seat.

"No, of course not. You're always welcome. We're just discussing plans for next year."

"Fantastic," Kieran says with a wide smile.

The sight of it would be enough to knock me on my ass if I weren't already sitting down.

The second he lowers himself into the chair, I look down again, although not before I notice the attention of Alison, our fundraising manager opposite me.

"You okay?" she mouths.

I smile politely and nod once before returning to my notes.

I like Alison; she's fantastic at her job and a really lovely person. But just like everyone else I work with, we're nothing more than colleagues.

The meeting continues, and everyone discusses the fresh ideas that are thrown around, but while they're all passionate about our future endeavors, I barely hear a word.

Kieran might have put himself at the other end of the table, but that doesn't mean I don't feel his heated stare every time he turns it on me.

By the time Henry brings the meeting to a close, my need to get out of the room and breathe in some fresh air is out of control.

"Excuse me," I say, squeezing past a couple of the guys who've decided to stop and have a conversation right in front of the exit.

Blood rushes past my ears as I slip out of the room and make a beeline for the bathroom. It might not provide me with the fresh air I need, but at least I'll have a few moments alone.

The instant I'm inside, I lock myself in a cubicle and just take a breath.

My heart is racing and my hands are shaking.

This is his foundation. He has every right to be here.

But he isn't here for any kind of update on how things are going. He's here for me.

He fucked me up last night and walked away.

The only reason he's here is to see how much damage he's caused.

And like fuck am I going to let him see the truth.

It might already be too late for that, a little voice points out.

As much as I might think I acted indifferently in that meeting, Alison noticed I was out of sorts with his arrival. And if she noticed, then there's no way that Kieran didn't.

Eventually, I make use of the facilities and step out of my hiding place to wash my hands and freshen up.

With a new coat of gloss on my lips and my hair smoothed over, I hold my head high and walk out of the room.

Best case scenario, Kieran has already left, probably feeling smug that he forced me to flee the meeting room and hide in the bathroom. Worst case, he's still here talking to everyone just to taunt me.

Trying to focus on what I need to do this afternoon, I push thoughts of his whereabouts from my mind and head to my office.

The second I step inside, I discover just how naive I was only moments ago.

Kieran hasn't left, and he isn't making small talk with any staff.

He's standing in the middle of my office looking like a GQ model.

The scent of his cologne hits me before I'm even inside my space.

Everything in me screams to run, but I can't.

So instead, I channel what little strength I have left and lift my eyes from the wooden floor, focusing on him.

"I have a lot of work to do," I explain in the hope it's enough to send him on his way.

He certainly didn't feel the need to hang around and discuss things last night.

"I'm sure it can wait ten minutes," he says, pushing from my desk and taking a step toward me.

I sidestep around him, needing to put something between us.

He glances at the desk that separates us with a smirk.

"Effie," he starts, his smile growing.

"No, Kieran. You don't get to come here, give me that smile, and expect everything to be okay."

His expression falters.

Oh my god...he really did think that.

"I don't have time to talk about this now," I say, dismissing him.

"Have you had a lunch break yet?"

I haven't, but like hell am I telling him that.

"Yes, and I have a lot to do. If you want to talk, then—"

"I'll meet you when you're done?"

I shake my head, and before I can think better of it, words that I instantly regret spill from my lips.

"I've got a date."

51

KIERAN

Her statement hits me like an eighteen-wheeler.

"I've got a date."

They're not words I hear from my best friend.

She doesn't date.

Okay, that's a lie. She has dated in the past, but after a few disasters, she declared that she was out of the game and if there were a man out there for her, he'd have to find her.

She was done searching for Mr. Right.

And I guess I just kinda accepted that that was still the case.

Never did I think that she'd change her mind.

I guess losing loved ones and grief does weird things to people.

But then another thought hits me.

Was it me?

Did I do this?

"A...a date? Like... a date with a man?"

Her nostrils flare in irritation.

"Yes, Kieran. I haven't suddenly become a lesbian."

Images of last night flicker through my head.

No, she certainly has not. She wanted my dick too much to have turned to the other side.

"Who with?" I demand, my fists curling at my sides as I try to process this new information.

I fucked her last night.

I made her mine last night. I literally whispered it in her fucking ear.

At what point was she going to tell me that she's dating someone?

When she gushed all over my fingers, or when I pushed her up against the window and made her come on my dick?

Heat surges through me, desire and anger colliding in one toxic mix that's going to land me in trouble.

Walk away, a little voice screams.

Walk away before you say something you don't mean.

"No one you know," she says dismissively as she wakes her computer up and turns toward it as if I don't deserve any of her time or attention.

Fury explodes and I step closer to her desk.

"Please can we do this another time? I've got calls to make."

"Does he know?" I blurt, pressing my palms to her desk and leaning closer.

Her sweet scent hits me and my mouth waters as I remember how incredible she looked last night, naked and at my mercy.

"Know what?" she asks impatiently.

Leaning over her desk, I drop the tone of my voice and rasp, "That you're my dirty whore."

She's on her feet in a heartbeat, her chair shooting out behind her and colliding with her bookcase.

"We're done here," she fumes. But while her eyes are narrowed and her lips pursed in anger, her eyes soften.

"Oh, Luck. We've barely started."

"Kieran," she warns as I stalk around her desk. "No. No,"

she snaps as she twists around to stop me trapping her in the corner.

It hits me right in the dick.

"Does he know?" I demand, my voice a little harsher this time.

She glares at me, and her fire lights something inside me.

"Does he know that I let the entire city watch as I fucked you like the dirty whore you are last night?"

She shrieks as I surge closer and slam my palms down on the desk on either side of her hips.

"Kieran," she warns, but there isn't any strength behind it.

I stare her dead in the eyes, our breaths mingling.

"Tell me you didn't want it," I taunt. "Tell me that you didn't enjoy every second of last night."

She bites down on the inside of her lip.

I smirk.

"You want it again, don't you?"

"No, Kieran. We can't."

I move closer and press my knee in the small gap between hers, giving her little choice but to spread her legs.

"Says who?"

"Me. We've already fucked things up. We can't keep—"

Her words are cut off with a gasp as I reach for her throat and tip her head back so she can hold my eyes as I step closer.

"We can do whatever the fuck we want, Luck. And right now, you want me."

She tries to shake her head and deny it, but my grip is too tight.

"I know you. I know you better than anyone else on this fucking planet, and right now, your panties are soaked. All you can think about is how it felt when I pushed you up against your windows last night and fucked you. You keep clenching your pussy, wishing you could feel me inside you again.

"Who do you belong to, Effie?"

Her eyes widen and she purses her lips, refusing to answer me.

"Tell me. Whose whore are you?"

"Yours," she cries.

Her pulse thunders beneath my fingers, telling me how much she loves it.

Being with her last night taught me something.

Showed me exactly what I was missing. And I don't just mean sex.

I mean her. Everything about her.

I don't just want her in my life.

I don't just need her as my friend.

I am fucking desperate for every single part of her.

It's scary. Really fucking scary.

It's everything I always said I didn't want. But right now, with her right in front of me, none of that matters.

Not having her in my life is more terrifying than attempting to navigate whatever this thing is between us.

Her lips part as if she's going to try to deny what we both know is true, but I don't give her a chance to say a word.

Instead, I push my hand under her skirt and drag my fingers up the soft skin of her inner thigh before rubbing her through the lace of her panties.

My smirk grows when I discover that I was right.

She's soaked.

Leaning forward, I brush my nose against hers.

It takes every ounce of self-control I possess not to kiss her, especially when she leans in for it.

"Mine," I tell her before tugging her panties to the side and dragging my fingers through her folds, coating myself in her juices.

Her hips jump from the desk and she cries out, forgetting where she is.

"That's it, Luck. Let everyone in this office know who owns you."

Her lips slam shut and her eyes widen as reality slams into her.

"Kieran, we can't—"

"Oh, but we can," I counter, pushing my fingers lower and sinking them inside her.

Her muscles ripple around me, welcoming me home as she falls back onto her palms, giving me better access.

"Fuck, yeah," I groan as I take in the sight of her before me. "Spread your legs wider."

She does so without hesitation. Even when she hates me, she trusts me.

That realization slams into me, making it hard to breathe.

I stare down at her pussy, watching as my fingers disappear inside her.

"So fucking perfect," I muse before looking up and finding her eyes. "And so fucking mine."

"Kieran." My name is nothing more than a plea on her lips as I curl my fingers and find her G-spot.

"Cancel your date, Effie," I demand as I work her closer and closer to her release.

"Fuck you," she gasps, making my brows shoot up.

"That can certainly be arranged. Against the windows again so the entire office can see?" I ask.

Fear washes across her face.

"N-no."

I chuckle.

I might have taken her in front of her window last night, and she might think it was a risk. But I know better. I'd never let anyone else see her like that. She's mine, and mine only.

"Cancel your date," I repeat as she's riding the edge of her release.

"No, no," she chants.

403

"Don't make me do it for you."

I brush her clit with my thumb and she flies off the edge.

A cry falls from her a beat before she remembers she needs to be quiet and slams her lips shut.

Slipping my hand around the back of her neck, I help hold her up as she loses control.

"That's it, Luck. Why would you want to be with anyone else when you could have this?"

She glares at me as her body comes down from its high.

"Fuck, you look good spread out on your desk for me."

I push my fingers inside her again, making her entire body shudder with aftershocks before I lift them to my mouth.

She watches with heated eyes as I suck them clean.

"I-I need to get back to work."

"After you've canceled your date," I state as I step back, allowing her to sort herself out.

"I'm not—" Her words are cut off as I push my hand into my jeans and rearrange myself.

My dick is painfully hard. My need to take her is all-consuming.

But I won't.

Not yet.

"You will. You want to go out to dinner tonight? I'll take you."

"No, Kieran," she huffs, quickly losing patience with me as she smooths her skirt down.

Our gazes hold, our silent battle of wills continuing.

"Fine," I finally concede, although, I'm not happy about it. "You go out on this date tonight. But I guarantee that the whole time, you'll be thinking about me."

"Jesus. Arrogant much?"

I shrug. "Why not? We both know that he'll never be what you need. That he'll never give you what you want."

Her jaw ticks as if she's holding back her response.

"You don't know anything about what I want," she mutters quietly.

We both know she's lying.

"Call me when you're done tonight. I'll show you how you should really end a date."

With that promise ringing in the air, I march from her office, slamming her door behind me.

My heart is still racing, jealousy surging through my veins when I get to my car and shut myself in.

"FUCK," I roar, slamming my palm down on the steering wheel.

I don't know what I expected to happen when I turned up here earlier.

I saw the meeting in my diary and I couldn't ignore it.

My heart pounds harder as I picture some asshole taking her out tonight, sitting across from her at a restaurant, trying to steal a kiss—or more—when he drops her off at home.

My fists curl, a fresh wave of anger racing through me.

Who the fuck takes a girl out on a Monday night, anyway?

Fucking asshole.

Minutes pass as I sit there, trying to calm my racing heart.

My head screams to go back upstairs, demand she cancel and refuse to leave until she does. Another part of me wants to stick around and wait so I can follow her.

But deep down, I know both are wrong.

In the end, I force myself to start the engine, and I finally back out of the space and head toward the stadium. There is only one thing I can do when I'm feeling like this.

I need pain, and a lot of it.

52

EFFIE

I nearly did it. I nearly did what he said.

More than once, I picked up my cell and almost cancelled on Brax.

But then I remembered that it wasn't actually a date.

I'd lied again.

As planned, I worked late. But I was on tenterhooks the entire time, wondering if Kieran was going to come bursting back through the door to finish off what we started earlier.

"You're mine."

"You're my dirty whore."

A shudder works its way through me as I hear his words as vividly as if he just whispered them in my ear.

He makes out like he's being serious when he says things like that.

But he can't be.

Kieran doesn't do serious. He doesn't do relationships.

All he's ever wanted is a bit of fun to distract him from real life for an hour or two.

It's just sex talk.

Words that are said in the heat of the moment.

We had a fun weekend together. That was all it was.

Until last night...

What even was last night?

It had been nothing but radio silence from him since I sent him away, and then he turns up and does that?

And then again today...

I drop my head into my heads and groan loudly.

It does little to fix the mess in my head.

We need to talk. That's what needs to happen.

We need to lay everything out on the table and figure out what we're both really thinking.

The thought is terrifying. What if it is all in my head? What if it all is nothing more than a bit of fun for him?

I'm not sure I'll survive hearing those words.

As much as I'm trying not to want more, I can't help myself.

I spend my nights dreaming about what it was like being with him, and my days wishing he was still in my life.

I miss him more than I thought possible.

My body moves on autopilot as I get ready for our dance class.

I've been so excited to attend again, but now, all I feel is dread.

I never should have told Kieran I had a date.

What if he's downstairs waiting for me?

Waiting for my date?

Not only have I lied to him, but I've potentially implicated one of his best friends.

Before I reach for my purse to head out, I grab my cell.

> Effie: I screwed up. I told Kieran I have a date tonight.

> Brax: Is that your way of asking me out?

A laugh erupts from my throat.

> Effie: No, it's me warning you that he might do something stupid.

Brax: What's new there?

Brax: I can handle Kieran.

I sigh, irritated that he's not taking this seriously.

> Effie: He didn't take it well.

Brax: I wouldn't have expected him to.

I hesitate, unsure how to respond.

Brax: You're not doing anything wrong. Hold your head high and put on your dancing shoes. See you soon.

"Fuck," I hiss.

My hopes for him giving me a reason to cancel were futile.

Deep down, I knew they would be, but still.

Stuffing the last of my things into my bag, I throw it over my shoulder before grabbing my purse and heading out.

The whole way to the parking lot, I'm looking over my shoulder.

I wouldn't put it past Kieran to follow me.

But as I make my way across town, I don't see any evidence that I'm being tailed. Not that I have any experience with such things.

By the time I park outside the studio, I'm confident that I'm alone, and with a new sense of excitement for tonight, I head inside.

Unlike last Monday, I walk through the building with my head held high, like I belong.

It's nice.

The lady at the reception desk welcomes me back, and I walk toward the class with the warm fuzzies from being remembered.

No sooner do I step inside, Brax turns to look at me with a wide smile on his face.

Nerves rush through me, and without instruction, my head twists around to look behind me.

You're not doing anything wrong.

You're not dating him.

Attending this class together wasn't even planned.

"Hey," Brax says, coming over to rescue me from the doorway.

"Hey," I whisper nervously.

"He's really got under your skin, huh?" he asks.

My cheeks blaze bright red, knowing just how true his words are.

I duck my head in a pathetic attempt to hide it, but Brax is too observant.

He chuckles.

"Can we not?" I beg as I lower my bag beside his and unzip my hoodie, ready to start.

"You two are a fucking nightmare," he mutters.

"Hey," I complain.

"It's true. You're like two teenagers who are too scared to ask each other to prom."

I glare at him. "This situation is a little more serious than that."

"Maybe. Maybe not."

"What is that supposed to mean?" I demand before he falls silent.

"We're so different. He's..." I wave my hand around as if it explains my thought process. "And I'm..."

"None of that matters," Brax says softly. "What matters is how you feel."

I sigh.

"You love him."

"Well, yeah. He's my best friend."

"Let me rephrase," he says with a teasing eye roll. "You're *in love* with him."

"Okay, everyone. Shall we get started?" I barely hear our teacher as she begins the class. And it's not until Brax grabs my hand that I become aware I should be doing something.

He pulls me into position, and we begin with our Foxtrot.

It's fast and energetic, and thankfully, it helps to drag me from my own head.

Am I in love with Kieran?

Brax smiles down at me as if he hasn't just thrown my world into chaos as he leads our dance.

Releasing a heavy breath, I finally allow myself to let go of everything happening outside this room and just enjoy the moment.

B y the time I walked out of the studio, leaving Brax behind on the phone again, I felt lighter.

I don't know if it was the exercise or just an hour with a friend, but the weight that was pressing down on my shoulders as I entered the building had lifted.

I was more than grateful.

As I walked to my car, I placed an order at one of my favorite takeout places, and after picking that up just over ten minutes later, I locked myself in my apartment, poured a glass of wine, and enjoyed my meal.

Of course, thoughts of Kieran are never far from my mind. Especially when I look up and find my smeared handprints on my windows.

My stomach knots and heat shoots straight to my clit as I picture us standing there last night.

It's so vivid.

My small body trembling and desperate as he held me exactly where he wanted me. As he used me exactly as he wanted to.

Desire sits heavy between my thighs as I keep my eyes trained on the exact spot we were in last night.

I'm so lost in my memories that I startle when my cell buzzes next to me.

I give myself a moment to calm down before I reach for it. But the minute I glance at the screen, it all comes crashing back again.

The shock of seeing his name on my screen means I open the message before my brain kicks in.

Kieran: How is your date going?

"Shit," I hiss, aware that he'll have seen that I've read it.

I didn't have any intention of continuing with the lie about tonight, but reading a message so quickly when I should be enjoying the company of another man really says it all.

Kieran: You lied to me again, didn't you?

My heart slams against my ribs as I try to figure out how to respond.

I did. I lied to him. But I had my reasons.

Fear. Fear was my reason.

Before I get a chance to think of anything, he starts typing again.

Kieran: I think we need to talk, don't you?

His question doesn't calm my racing heart.

I agree, we do need to talk.

But what if I'm not ready to hear what he has to say?

What if I'm too scared to say the things I want to say?

> Effie: Yes.

Kieran: Wow, your date must have really worn you out if that's all you can say.

> Effie: I wasn't expecting to hear from you. You surprised me.

Kieran: You love it when I do that *smirky emoji*

> Effie: Do you have any window cleaner?

Kieran: Why?

Kieran: Oh...send me a picture.

Lifting my cell, I open the camera and zoom in a little.

Heat surges through my veins in a way I'm sure it would if I were sending him a dirty picture. I mean, I am sending him a dirty picture...of my windows.

I can't help but laugh at how different I am from all the other women he's been with. I've seen some of the pictures they send him, and I can honestly say that not a single one of them has been a window.

Before I talk myself out of it, I hit send and wait.

Kieran: Why didn't I set up a camera? Do you think one of your neighbors filmed it?

Panic fills me, and I'm on my feet and at the window before I know it.

My eyes scan the buildings before me as my heart pounds and my hands tremble.

They could have all watched me get fucked against a window.

They may have all enjoyed it...

But as I scan the windows, I realize that I don't see anyone.

> Kieran: I'd fucking love to watch that. Would be the best porno I've ever seen.

Effie: Stop, please.

> Kieran: That's not what you were saying last night...

> Kieran: Or this afternoon...

> Kieran: How is your desk? Did you manage to clean up the wet patch?

Effie: You are so gross.

> Kieran: I wasn't the one who made the mess...

> Kieran: My fingers still smell like you, though. Makes me hard every time I sniff them.

"Holy shit," I breathe, my thighs clenching.

> Kieran: I'm not doing anything about it though. The next time I come, it's going to be inside you.

Fuck. He's good.

> Keiran: Where do you want it?

> Kieran: Mouth?

> Kieran: Pussy?

> Kieran: Ass?

Effie: This wasn't what I meant when I agreed that we should talk.

> Kieran: All three? I knew my girl would be up for the challenge.

I squirm, the pulsating between my thighs increasing before I spin around to sit back on the couch; only, my legs take me in a very different direction. I need a distraction before Kieran has me doing things I'll regret.

Like video calling him...

> Effie: You're a nightmare.

> Effie: When are you free?

> Kieran: Right fucking now. Where do you want me?

> Effie: After work tomorrow?

Talking in person is dangerous. The last few times we've been in the same room, we've either ended up shouting at each other or fucking. But I figure if I book us a table somewhere, we're safe.

> Kieran: I'm out of town tomorrow and Wednesday. Thursday?

> Effie: I'm busy Thursday.

> Kieran: Another date?

> Effie: Something like that. Friday?

> Kieran: You got it.

> Effie: Okay. I'll book something and let you know.

> Kieran: Perfect. Now back to me coming inside you...

> Effie: We're not talking about that.

I shake my head as I put my cell on the counter and begin removing my makeup.

> Kieran: I'm sorry I left without a word last night.

My eyes widen as his apology crashes over me.

> Kieran: But I need you to know that it was one of the hottest nights of my life.

Fuck. "Me too."

> Effie: And you've had a lot of hot nights...

> Kieran: None of them stand up to the time I've spent with you.

"Oh my god."

I stare at myself in the mirror, trying to see exactly what he sees.

Without my makeup, my eyes don't look as big or as bright, and the freckles I've always hated over my nose are obvious. My lips aren't thin, but if you compare them to the perfectly filled ones of the models and actresses he usually spends time with, they don't stand up. My skin is clear, probably one of my best features. My hair has been scraped back for dancing, but it's long with a slight curl. It's not shining and platinum, though. It's...a kind of dirty blonde that I'm sure many women wouldn't put up with.

Sure, I've always been a little envious of the women he spends time with; they're all incredibly beautiful. But I've never compared myself like this before.

I've always been Kieran's best friend. I didn't need to compare to them.

I was never going to be the one he was going to take home.

But now...now he's saying things like that to me and...I don't know what to think.

> Kieran: Stop freaking out.

> Effie: I'm not. I'm in the middle of something.

> Kieran: Oh?

> Effie: We'll talk Friday. I hope camp goes well.

Putting my cell on "do not disturb," I strip out of my athletic clothes and slip into the shower, the things he's said to me tonight spinning around my head.

"None of them stand up to the time I've spent with you."

If he doesn't mean that, it's going to crush me.

53

EFFIE

Kieran gives me whiplash.

One moment it's radio silence, and the next, I get messages almost every hour of the day.

I don't know what changed, but something certainly has.

His anger seems to have gone. Instead, he's just...horny.

Was I disappointed when he didn't let himself into my apartment on Monday night and have his way with me?

Yes, okay? Yes.

The whole time I was in the shower, I kept looking over my shoulder.

After I climbed into bed, every noise I heard, I thought it was him.

I wanted it to be him.

I wanted a repeat of the night before, damn it.

Every night since has been the same.

Despite knowing that he's out of town, I still hold out hope.

Kieran is known to be hot-headed, and the way our messages have been going...yeah, I wouldn't be surprised if he blew off camp and turned up at my door.

He's still holding firm on the promise that the next time he gets off is going to be with me. I even think he's being serious.

I mean, the photo he sent me last night leads me to believe him.

He was hard. Really fucking hard.

Just looking at his full frontal shot with his tight abs, V lines, and erection had my core clenching.

I've always missed him when he's been away, but never like this.

My body is craving his. And as tempted as I've been to take the edge off myself, I've been a good girl.

He told me back in Grams' house that he owned my pleasure. He told me how he's the one who decides when and where I orgasm.

Am I torturing myself by keeping to that promise? Abso-fucking-lutely.

Am I going to break it? Only if he tells me to.

But as much as we're both suffering. I've refused to do anything further.

He's brought up the idea of phone sex numerous times in the last two days, but I've turned it down.

A photo of him is one thing, but before anything else happens, we need to have that chat.

I need to know where his head is at. Hell, I need to firmly figure out where mine is, too.

As much as I like to think this could be the beginning of us coming back together, there is also the fear that it could still rip us apart.

He was meant to be heading back today, but he decided to stay another night. The group of kids he's been working with this week has stolen his heart, by the sounds of it, and he wants to see their game in the morning.

As much as I'd hoped he might surprise me with a late-night visit when he got back into town, it's clearly not going to happen.

Stop thinking with your pussy and start using your head.

A delirious laugh erupts as I pull into the parking lot outside the dance studio again.

I thought Kieran was good at edging before, but this week is really testing my patience.

I arrive early. I'm not surprised.

I had a couple of appointments this afternoon to ensure I'm ready for the weekend. I don't want to be presumptuous, but I think big things are going to happen...

After abandoning my bag and slipping on my new dance shoes, I pull my cell from my purse.

> Kieran: Is it tomorrow night yet?

> Effie: I can't wait to talk...

> Kieran: Me too. It's gonna be a hot and steamy...talk...

Heat rises, turning my cheeks red.

I've booked a table at my favorite Italian. It's quiet and intimate, but I'm hoping it's busy enough that anything other than talking will be out of the question.

That's not to say that I'm hoping the rest of our night will be as subdued...

Assuming we're on the same page with where we go from here, of course.

Butterflies flutter in my stomach.

Sure, I thought about what it might be like over the years. But it was never a serious thought, just a silly teenage girl musing over things that'll never happen.

> Effie: Be good.

Kieran: Never. The only one here who needs to follow orders is you.

Those butterflies return, but they're lower this time.

I don't hear the door open, or anyone enter, but I do sense the shadow that falls over me.

"There can only be one man who makes you smile like that," Brax teases.

Putting my cell to sleep, I try to smother my grin, but the moment I meet his eyes, it spreads even wider.

"So, things are going well?" he guesses.

Kieran hasn't been the only one I've been messaging this week. Brax is aware that we've reconnected, although I haven't dived into the dirty details. Those are between the two of us.

"Things are...developing."

Brax raises a brow. "I see."

Shoving my cell into my purse, I push to my feet, for all the good it does. I still have to crane my neck to look Brax in the eyes.

Being barely five feet, I'm more than used to it, especially after having Kieran in my life for almost as long as I can remember.

I've always liked being small, but I've never loved it as much as when Kieran throws me around like I'm nothing more than a ragdoll. I love being at his mercy.

As we catch up, or should I say, as Brax probes me for information, the others fill the room along with our teacher, and all too soon, she's inviting us to join her and start the class.

We run through our waltz before our teacher leads us through the steps for a tango.

It's a seductive dance, and Brax and I spend the whole time giggling like school kids.

By the time we're done, my cheeks ache from laughing so

hard. Doing this class was the best decision I've made in a very long time.

Every time I dance, I feel Grams smiling down at me.

But that's not the only reason. She might no longer be here, but I know she more than approves of the decision I've made to see where this thing goes with Kieran.

It's what she always wanted.

I might be scared, but what if it's worth it?

What if we don't ruin everything between us? What if it only makes it better?

"Drink?" Brax asks as we step out of the building and into the warm summer evening air.

The sun is beginning to set, ducking behind the tall buildings surrounding us.

"I could be persuaded by a cocktail or two."

"You really are in a good mood," he teases.

"You know, for the first time in a really long time, I actually feel like things are looking up."

"I'm glad. You deserve it," he says, glancing over at me with a smile. "I got a lift here. You good to drive?"

"Nope," I say, digging into my purse for my key. "But you can. Show me your game, number twenty-eight."

He doesn't drive as far as last time, but the restaurant he takes me to is just as incredible.

We're seated in a window that looks out over the city. The view just adds to the vibe in the modern tapas restaurant.

Between us, there is a whole range of dishes that we've been working our way through for the last thirty minutes. I didn't stop for lunch, seeing as I was going to disappear early, and after an hour of dancing and laughing, I was famished.

421

Brax teases me for more details about Kieran, but I hold my tongue. Until the two of us have properly talked, the rest of the world—including him—is going to have to wait.

We've already had too much exposure in the media.

I've tried to forget about all of that when making my decision about where we go next. Those articles, or more so the comments that came with them, are a huge part of my fear where a relationship with Kieran is concerned.

By the time I've finished my third cocktail of the night, my laughter comes even easier and the room around me is a little fuzzy.

"I think it's time to call it a night," Brax laughs before requesting the check.

I'm buzzing as we leave the restaurant and make our way down the street to my car.

"My lady," he teases as he opens my passenger door for me.

"Why, thank you." Reaching up on my toes, I give him a chaste kiss on the cheek before inelegantly falling onto the seat.

He's shaking his head as he shuts me in.

Exhaustion hits me as we make our way to my apartment building.

"You can borrow my car if you want," I offer. "I can get an Uber to work tomorrow."

"It's cool. I'll call one now," he says, pulling his cell from his pocket after killing my engine. "Twenty minutes."

"You're not standing on the street for twenty minutes. You might get abducted by a ravaged group of female fans."

He smirks. "Here's hoping. Something tells me that my date tonight isn't going to put out."

"Aw, poor little Braxton missing out on all the action," I tease as I lead him toward the elevator.

When he doesn't respond, I turn around a little too fast to look at him.

"Whoa," I cry, reaching for the wall for support.

"I think you're more of a two-cocktail kind of girl," he mocks.

I chuckle. "We've been so focused on my potential love life, we haven't even touched on yours," I say, feeling guilty for not paying him more attention.

"That's because I don't have one," he points out.

"What? But you're a Chief; you must have at least three girls on your roster."

He laughs again but doesn't confirm or deny my statement.

The minute we're inside my apartment, Brax marches to the kitchen and grabs me a bottle of water from the refrigerator.

"Drink," he demands. "You'll thank me tomorrow."

"Thank you," I say as I take it from him.

Looking up, my eyes meet his, and out of nowhere they start burning while a lump crawls up my throat.

"What? What's wrong?" he asks, his eyes wide with fear.

I shake my head in an attempt to level myself out.

"Nothing. I'm just...I'm really grateful for your friendship these past few weeks. I need you to know how much I appreciate you."

He smiles softly, his body shifting as if he's uncomfortable with the compliment.

It's weird seeing arrogant and cocky football players being unsure of themselves. It also makes me feel incredibly lucky to be close enough to be able to see it every now and then.

"It's nothing," he says, rubbing the back of his neck.

His phone dings, announcing the arrival of his Uber, and he takes a step back.

"I should go, let you catch up with Kieran." He waggles his

eyebrows telling me exactly what he thinks we're going to be doing.

My cheeks heat. While I'll stand firm on the phone sex, I can't say our upcoming exchange will be entirely innocent.

"Thanks for tonight. It was fun."

"It was. See you Monday?"

"Monday," I promise, already excited for our next lesson.

I hesitate as I close the door behind him, wondering if Kieran was lying about returning tomorrow.

Tingles erupt at the thought of him surprising me.

I'm wearing a sappy smile as I walk through my apartment and to my bathroom to shower and get ready for bed.

It's not until I crawl between the covers that I finally wake up my cell and see what's waiting for me.

I haven't turned my social media notifications back on, and to be honest, I prefer it that way.

After the news articles about me and Kieran broke, it was crazy. I never want to experience that again.

Now, I open my socials when I'm ready, not because I'm being bombarded.

A wide grin spreads across my lips when I find a whole stream of messages from Kieran.

I still haven't confessed to what I was doing tonight, and despite him not really mentioning it, I know it's driving him crazy.

Kieran: Is it my turn for your attention now?

Effie: I guess that depends on what you have in mind.

Kieran: Seeing as I've been waiting hours to hear from you? All kinds of things...

Effie: Kinky Kieran...

Kieran: You have no fucking idea.

54

KIERAN

All week, all I've wanted to do is jump in my car and drive back to the city to her.

Whenever I'm away, I miss her. But this is different.

Now, I really know what I'm missing.

My dick aches just like it has done all week, but as much as I want to wrap my hand around it and find a release, I don't. Instead, I ignore it as I shower, readying for my last morning with this group of kids before I head home to my girl.

My girl...

Fuck. I really hope that's true by the time the sun sets tonight.

It's terrifying, and every time I think about it, anxiety knots my insides, but it's right.

I know it is.

Effie Campbell was made for me. I refuse to let fear ruin this for us anymore than we already have.

She wants to talk first, and as frustrating as that is, I can't help but agree.

I need to tell her what I want.

I need to tell her all the thoughts that have been in my head recently, and not just the dirty ones.

I need to go out on a limb and hope like hell she's on the same page.

If she's not...

No. I refuse to even consider that as an option.

My watch buzzes and I glance down, but I don't pay any attention to the email that just came through; all I see is the time. How many hours I've got until I can see her.

With a groan, I finish off my shower, my dick taunting me the entire time.

"Soon," I mutter. "Real fucking soon."

I arrive at the camp staff room early. It's hardly a surprise, seeing as I was awake long before dawn. Early starts are normal for me, but add the anticipation for tonight and it was almost impossible to relax.

I make myself a coffee before sinking into one of the couches.

Pulling my cell free, I ignore all my notifications and open my messages.

My conversation with Effie opens immediately, and I scan through the conversation we had last night, my blood heating with the suggestions I made for what I want to do to her tonight.

> Kieran: Good morning beautiful. I hope you got a good night's sleep...

> Effie: Hey handsome. Can't say I did. Someone filled my head with all these dirty thoughts and I tossed and turned all night.

> Kieran: You really shouldn't be conversing with such men.

> Effie: It's too late. I've been corrupted.

> Kieran: Dirty whore.

I smirk as I imagine her sitting at her desk, already squirming in her seat.

Spreading my legs wider to give my semi a little more space, I glance at the door. The temptation to leave already is almost too much to ignore.

If I did, I'd be with her by lunch.

I could surprise her in her office again, but this time, I'd crawl under her desk and eat her out as she continued with her day.

I groan, attempting and failing to stop my dick from reacting to the vivid image in my head.

I've got a fucking problem, and only fucking my girl is going to fix it.

> Kieran: Can't fucking wait to see you.

> Effie: Table is booked for six-thirty.

A laugh tumbles from my lips.

So naive, my little lucky charm.

So fucking naive.

> Effie: I've got a meeting. Have fun this morning, and drive safe x

> Kieran: I'll drive slow and safe if you ride me hard and fast later…

A laugh bursts out of me when she replies with three angel emojis. Innocent and angelic, my ass. She's right; I've well and truly corrupted her.

"Everything okay?" Jamie asks when he joins me.

After Brax bailed on this trip, Jamie agreed to come and attempt to impart some knowledge to the future generation.

He might be a grumpy motherfucker most days, but he's fantastic with the kids. And they all love him. He doesn't usually let anyone near him—most of the team included—and even at a young age, I think the kids realize what a privilege it is to get to know him.

"Everything is great, man," I say, unable to contain the wide smile that spreads across my face.

"Fuck. You look entirely too happy," he muses as he stalks toward the coffee machine.

"What's there not to be happy about? It's Friday, the sun is shining, we're about to go and play ball with some of the most talented kids in the country and—"

"You're getting laid tonight?" he finishes for me.

Have I talked a little too much about my plans with Effie this evening? Quite possibly.

"Here's hoping. What about you? Nailed down any plans?"

While I might be able to say that Jamie is one of my closest friends, I don't entirely know him all that well. He doesn't wear his heart on his sleeve like Brax. And he very much keeps his personal life to himself.

"Nah, probably just have a quiet one at home."

"Wild," I tease.

He shrugs, not giving a fuck what I think. I admire that about him. He's unashamedly himself. He doesn't do anything he doesn't want to do, and he sticks to his guns.

I might still be early in my NFL career, but already it's obvious that quite a few players could learn a thing or two from guys like Jamie.

Having used all the words he wanted to this morning, he drops onto the couch opposite me and focuses on his cell.

Getting the hint, I go back to mine.

I reply to my brothers and my mom, who have all messaged me, before diving into my inbox.

Effie would have a coronary if she were to see the number sitting on top of the app.

I reply to my agent, and I'm busy reading through something from Henry at KC Foundation when Jamie suddenly announces that we need to move out.

Abandoning the email, I jump to my feet and follow him to the field. The sooner we get this game done, the sooner I can be heading back to Chicago to my girl.

Thankfully, the second the whistle blows to begin the final game of the week, time seems to speed up.

I guess I shouldn't be surprised. Football is my second-best distraction in life. Effie, or more specifically, sex with Effie is in the number one position.

Jamie and I bark orders from the sidelines as the teams we've been training this week go head-to-head in their final battle.

Both of our quarterbacks call some epic plays as we stand there watching like proud fathers.

As much as I want to continue watching them play, I'm ready for the final whistle to blow. These kids are all heading home this afternoon. I really hope they're proud of everything they've achieved during their time here. If they can take it with them and implement even one thing into their teams at home, then it'll have been worth it.

The second the game is over, my team—the winners—set their sights on me and run at full speed.

I make a show of trying to outrun them, but ultimately, I allow them to wrestle me to the ground before they pile on top of me.

Once we've finished celebrating, the entire camp turns their attention on me, including the coaches, and I have little choice but to stand up and say something.

I know these camps are my babies, but they wouldn't be possible if it weren't for all the people standing around me.

They deserve so much more credit than me for all the work they do to make them happen.

I had a dream, just like the kids before me do, and I didn't stop until I achieved it. Hell, I'm still trying to achieve everything.

While the players of the future may look at Jamie and me and think we've got everything, we're both striving for more. That's the thing about being a professional athlete. Nothing is ever good enough. We always want to achieve more, to be better.

By the time I say goodbye to the staff and once again thank them for everything they do, Jamie and I grab our bags and head for his car.

The moment my ass hits his passenger seat, I pull my cell out and shoot Effie a message.

> Kieran: I'm coming for you, Luck…

My message is delivered, but it doesn't show as read.

Irrationally annoyed that I'm not her main focus right now, I drop my cell into my lap and stare out as Jamie follows the GPS to take us home.

We chat away about camp and football news we've heard recently, but we don't dive into anything too deep or personal. Jamie never does. It makes me curious as fuck to know who he really is, but apparently, we're not close enough for me to have that privilege.

This life can suck you dry if you put too much out for everyone to take. But we're not the public or even the press; it's okay to open up to teammates. After all, we fucking get it.

We're about an hour out when I unlock my cell again and go back to the email I abandoned earlier. It's nothing very exciting, and after reading through the plans for Q1 of next year, I go through a load of others that are awaiting my attention.

When I get bored, I open up Instagram. I figure I can get a bit of an Effie fix before I get to see her in person. She doesn't post much on her page, but there is enough to get me through.

Only, I don't get to her page; I don't even get a chance to look at my notifications, because the first picture that comes up on my feed has me blinking in disbelief.

No.

Ripping my eyes from the image, I read the caption.

Our teams aren't the only ones trading players in the off-season.

Fury races through my veins as I look up again.

Effie never told me what she was doing last night. She teased me about going on a date, but I took it as a joke.

I thought she was taunting me.

I didn't think she was serious and was going to be out in public, kissing my teammate.

55

EFFIE

Honestly, the person who thought it was a good idea to hold a meeting this afternoon needs to be shot.

No one wanted to be there. I caught every single person around the table glancing at a clock more than once. All of us were too busy mentally preparing for the night and weekend ahead of us.

It's comical really. I've never been that person.

Sure, I always look forward to my evenings and weekends —who doesn't? But I've never had plans so important or exciting that I've wanted to change the clock just to get out early.

The last two hours of the day feel like a week, but finally, the meeting is brought to a close, and no sooner have I fled the meeting room than my computer is shut down and my purse is over my shoulder. I am out of there.

Anything I haven't done can definitely wait until Monday.

My hands are trembling and butterflies are rioting in my stomach as I drive home. I barely even remember the journey; I am on total autopilot as I mentally plan what I am going to do the minute I walk into my apartment.

Kieran is on his way home. He messaged a couple of hours ago to say that they were on the road. For all I know, he could already be back at his apartment by now, also getting ready for tonight.

My foot taps on the floor as the elevator rises through the building, and the second I'm inside, I begin undressing.

I shed clothes as I move toward my bedroom, and by the time I get to the bathroom, only my underwear remains.

That soon hits the floor, and I step into the shower before I've let it warm up.

I shriek when the cold water hits me, but I don't shy away.

Seeing as I've already been waxed from head to toe, I don't need to waste time shaving anything. Instead, I wash and deep condition my hair in the hope it does what I want it to, and I scrub every inch of myself clean.

I've been on a handful of dates over the years, but none of them have made me feel like this.

I'm buzzing with excitement and anticipation.

No one would guess that I'm going out with a man I've known almost all my life. They'd probably think I'm going on a first date with a stranger because of how nervous and giddy I am.

But I guess that's the power of Kieran Callahan.

I let out a sigh as I rinse the conditioner from my hair.

Is this it?

Is tonight the beginning of something I didn't even know I needed in my life until recently?

It's funny how things can change so quickly.

One minute I was happy being his best friend, and then the next...

I shake my head in disbelief, my cheeks heating as I think about just how much time I've spent fantasizing about his body —his dick—recently.

433

I've never been truly infatuated with a guy in my life. Until now, it seems.

Wrapping myself in a towel, I wring my hair out before standing in front of the mirror, ready to make myself look my best.

Those butterflies go wild all over again as I think about what tonight might hold.

I apply my makeup before drying and curling my hair. For once, it behaves itself, and I'm happy with the soft waves that hang over my shoulders.

Happy with my appearance, I pad toward my wardrobe and pull out a box. Inside hides the most expensive and sexiest underwear I've ever owned.

Not only are they sexy as hell, but they're also red and black.

Chiefs' colors.

Reaching for the garments, I fasten the garter belt around my waist before pulling the stockings up my legs. They're so thin and delicate, I don't know how I don't destroy them as I slide them on.

The panties—if you can call the scrap of fabric panties—are next, and then I reach for the bra.

I tried it on in the store the other afternoon, but I still gasp when I step in front of my full-length mirror.

"Holy shit."

My tits look fantastic, and when I twist around, I must admit that my ass looks pretty good too.

This was definitely a good choice. Kieran is going to lose his mind when he undresses me later.

Happy with the outcome, I spin back to my closet to grab my dress.

It's a classic little black dress that fits me like a second skin.

It isn't something I would have chosen before. But then, I

wasn't going on a date with the Chicago Chiefs star running back before.

The temptation to go with a safe option when I was shopping was strong, but then I remembered Kieran's reaction when we were dress shopping in St. Louis and I decided to think outside the box.

I really hope it pays off.

Gently, I remove it from the hanger, and I'm pulling the zipper down ready to step into it when there's a loud bang from my living room.

My heart jumps into my throat, and without thinking about it, I race out to see what it was.

"Oh my god," I gasp when I find Kieran storming through my apartment. For a couple of blissful seconds, I assume that he couldn't wait to see me any longer.

But then, everything comes crashing down.

His eyes drop down my body, taking in my barely-there outfit. But instead of driving him wild with desire, all it does is fuel his anger.

"Kieran, what—"

"Where is he?" he demands, his voice hard and determined.

My brows pinch with confusion.

"W-where is who?" I echo, but he's not listening to me. Instead, he's already barged past me. "Kieran, what the fuck are you doing?" I shout, chasing after him.

He blows through my apartment like a storm, throwing doors open and searching every inch.

"Kieran?"

When he's finished, he marches up to me. His body is rigid, his chest heaving, and his nostrils flared. He stares down at me like he hates me.

My initial instinct is to wrap my arms around myself and

cower, but then I remember that I haven't done anything wrong, and I stand tall. Or at least as tall as my small body will allow.

"I trusted you," he seethes quietly.

My frown deepens.

"What are you talking about?"

"Have you ever told me the truth? Have you just been lying to me all our lives? Do I even know you?"

Each question strikes me like a baseball bat to the chest.

"W-what?" I stutter, too shocked by his questions, by his anger to be able to form a coherent answer.

He shakes his head. His eyes run over me again, but it's like he doesn't even see me.

"When were you going to tell me that you're fucking Brax?"

My chin drops in shock.

"Brax? I'm not fucking Brax," I shriek.

"When you told me you had a date last night, I thought you were fucking joking."

"I-I was."

He sinks his hand into his pocket and brings his cell out with a flourish before unlocking it.

"Then what the fuck is this?"

He holds it up for me to see, and my stomach sinks into my feet.

It's a photograph of me kissing Brax on the cheek last night. The image captures so much more intimacy than there really was.

It was a friendly, chaste kiss.

A laugh bubbles up, and I can't stop it from spilling free.

I didn't think it was possible, but Kieran's expression hardens further.

My lips part to tell him everything, but my words are quickly swallowed when he beats me to it.

"Just because I called you a whore, it didn't mean you needed to turn into one."

His words are like a knife through my heart.

I stand there staring at him in disbelief as hurt rushes through my veins like a tsunami.

"How long has it been going on?"

"It's not. Nothing is—"

"Is that why you didn't tell me that you came back? Did you come back for him?"

My mouth opens and closes like a fish, but the words are stuck.

His accusations are ridiculous.

"Kieran, I would never—"

"Fuck. This is my fault, isn't it?"

His constant changes of direction give me whiplash.

"I asked him to check in on you. You weren't responding to me after I left and...FUCK," he bellows, sinking his fingers into his hair and tugging until I'm sure he's about to pull it out.

"Kieran, stop, please."

This time, he's the one to laugh, but there is no joy in it, only pain.

"I was going to tell you that I've fallen in love with you tonight. I was going to tell you that the only reason I've never wanted anyone else is because I was waiting for you. I was going to tell you that you were it for me."

He shakes his head as tears fall from my lashes. Finally, I allow my arms to fold around my ribs as if they'll help to keep me together as a mixture of red-hot fury and utter disbelief battle within me.

"Kieran," I whimper.

He glares at me. There is none of the love he mentioned previously. There is nothing but hurt and hate.

"No, I'm done, Effie. I'm so fucking done with all this bullshit. You want Brax? Fucking have him."

437

Before I can respond, he's gone, storming through my apartment.

"Kieran, stop, please," I beg, but it doesn't help.

The front door slams behind him, and my knees buckle.

"KIERAN," I sob. But it's too late.

He's gone.

56

KIERAN

I scream the second I step out of her building. The few people that are on the street look over in fear before rushing away. Probably the wisest decision they've made all day.

Unable to stand still, I take off toward my abandoned car, but I don't stop when I get to it. I can't. I need to move. I need to burn off some of this anger.

I drag my hand down my face.

Some of the things I said were a low blow, I know that.

They were mean and unfair.

But it's too late now. I've said them.

The damage is done.

Just like it was when she got caught with Brax.

Pain slices through my chest again as I think about those images.

I didn't react in the car with Jamie when I found them. Well, not outwardly. Inside, I was a fucking mess.

And it really didn't help when we got stuck on the freeway because of an accident.

Everything inside me, all the reasons I never wanted to get

involved with a woman, all the bullshit I've ever seen my teammates go through over the years bubbled up inside me until I could barely contain it.

The second he dropped me off, I was sprinting to my apartment for my keys so I could go and confront her.

I didn't give myself even a second to try and think rationally. I was too far gone.

The damage had been done. The pain had been caused.

All I could think about was telling her that I knew.

As I pace back and forth, the anger barely lessens.

Watching her stand up for herself should have been hot.

She doesn't do it very often.

It should probably also have been a sign that I needed to tone it down.

But I couldn't. I was fueled by nothing but anger and bitter disappointment.

How could she do that to me?

All the air rushes from my lungs.

I'd convinced myself that she wanted the same thing as me. All week, I've told myself that we're on the same page.

How fucking stupid was I?

This is exactly why I don't do serious. It comes with too much drama and heartache.

When I'm confident I can drive without plowing my car straight into the nearest building, I pull the door open and take a step to get in. But before I do, I look back at the main entrance.

If she weren't guilty, wouldn't she have run after me? Pleaded her innocence?

My eyes roll up the building to her penthouse windows, but I don't stand a chance of seeing anything from down here.

With my heart feeling like it's lost a fight with a meat tenderizer, I finally drop into my car and take off.

I swear, I leave the final whole pieces of it behind.

I realized a few things this week. Not only am I in love with Effie, but I'm pretty sure I have been for a very, very long time.

She's always been the one. The first person I've wanted to tell when things go well, the person I want to confide in when shit goes wrong. No matter what happens, she's the one I want next to me.

And then when things escalated in St. Louis, I didn't realize how much I enjoyed falling asleep with her and then waking up the next day with her in my arms.

I certainly knew how much I missed it when I got back here without her.

My apartment doesn't feel like home anymore. My bed is lonely.

Everything is fucking lonely.

Even when I've been with my brothers, my teammates, something is missing.

I thought this was going to be our time. That we could start over together.

My mom and Grams have been pointing us in the right direction for years. We just couldn't see it.

Well, now I can.

I can see it clear as fucking day, and one of my best friends has ruined it for me.

I always suspected there could be more between them, but I'd convinced myself that it was just in my head.

How fucking wrong I was.

She just told you that nothing is going on, a little voice whispers in my head, but I dismiss it.

I don't need a reason or answers right now.

I just need action.

I pull up at the stadium only minutes later and swing my car in next to Brax's.

As soon as I step out, I crack my knuckles.

Fuck, I need this.

I don't pay attention to who else is here.

After letting myself into the building, I make a beeline to the gym.

Everyone is under the impression that all we do is party and go on vacation during the off-season, but that couldn't be further from the truth for most of us. It's Friday night, and I guarantee that there will be more than a few guys here working out.

I walk down the red and black hallways that have always meant so much to me.

As a little boy, all I dreamed of was playing for the Chiefs. They've always been my team.

The day I got drafted from college was the best fucking day of my life.

I've worked my ass off every day since to prove myself worthy of this team. Worthy of my position.

My palms slam on the double doors, swinging them wide open and announcing my arrival to anyone who isn't lost in their own little world.

Easton Brooks, our quarterback, is the only one who looks up from the weights bench.

"Callahan?" he questions, a deep V forming between his brows as he studies me.

But it's not him I came here for.

Ripping my eyes away from him, I scan the rest of the equipment, searching for the asshole who's ruined everything for me.

I find him on a treadmill, his AirPods in and totally unaware that anyone else has entered the gym.

I storm forward, uncaring about everyone else in here witnessing what's about to go down.

The very moment I'm in reaching distance, I twist my fingers in the back of his sweat-damp shirt and drag him backward off the machine.

His legs go in different directions and he scrambles to stay upright while trying to work out what the fuck is happening.

Shoving him to the floor, I loom over him, giving him just a second to predict what's coming next.

"Kieran, what the—"

"You fucking asshole. How long?" I bellow. "How long have you been fucking her?"

Before he has a chance to get a word out, I drag him to his feet and throw my fist into his face.

The second it connects, pain radiates from my knuckles and up my arm. But instead of lessening my anger, it feeds it.

No sooner have I pulled my arm back, I get ready to go again.

It doesn't matter that he's back on the floor, that he's at a disadvantage. I'm blind to everything but what he's taken from me.

The one thing in my life I care about more than anything. I lunge forward to take another swing, but a large pair of hands grip my upper arms and drag me back.

"That's enough," Easton barks as two other guys rush toward Brax to help him up.

"I'm fine," he mutters, shaking them off and dabbing his cut brow with his hand. Then, he looks up at me. But there isn't anger or irritation in his eyes like there should be. Instead, there's understanding and compassion, and I hate him even more because of it.

"How could you?" I bark, refusing to fully acknowledge what his expression is telling me.

I don't want to believe anything but what those photos showed, the story they told.

"Bro, you're a fucking idiot."

"That's not gonna help," one of the guys beside him mutters.

"It doesn't matter," Brax says, lifting his shirt and wiping

443

sweat and blood from his face. "Motherfucker will believe what he wants to believe."

I surge forward in the hope Easton has loosened his grip, but I'm bitterly disappointed.

"I know what I saw," I seethe.

"Yeah? And I know the truth." I sneer at him. "We'll talk," he states before swiping his towel from the machine. "But not like this. Go home, Kieran."

Without another word, and without looking back, he marches from the gym.

It takes long seconds before Easton finally lets me shrug out of his grip.

"The fuck, Callahan?" he demands once he's stepped in front of me.

"Fuck off," I grunt, not willing to get into it with him.

His lips flatten and his nostrils flare.

"You do not get to come in here throwing punches and think you can walk out again like nothing happened," he warns.

Easton is a fucking killer quarterback and a fantastic captain.

I respect the fuck out of him both on and off the field, but right now, I barely have any respect for myself, let alone anyone else.

"You need to start talking."

"I don't need to do anything," I shoot back, my anger kicking up a notch again.

As soon as I step into his space, he lifts his hands and shoves me hard in the chest.

"Back the fuck down," he warns.

"Come on, man," Jamie says, having appeared at some point during our standoff.

"Fine," I huff, aware that I sound like a petulant toddler, before I turn my back on them and storm away.

57

EFFIE

The first time my cell rings, I don't bother looking at it. I already know it won't be Kieran.

Not that I'd actually want to talk to him if he did call me.

Right now, I'd happily never speak to him again.

I sit curled up on my couch with my legs pulled up to my chest and my arms wrapped around them.

My eyes are puffy and sore from crying, and my heart feels like it's been ripped out of my chest and stomped on, but despite the hurt, the anger still simmers beneath the surface.

How dare he talk to me like that?

But then another memory slams into me.

"I was going to tell you that I've fallen in love with you tonight."

Another sob erupts as I remember his words so vividly.

He was going to tell me exactly what I wanted to tell him.

Any excitement or fear I was feeling over the changes in our relationship have vanished. There is nothing but agony in its wake.

How could he think I was dating Brax?

I thought he knew me better than that.

If I wanted Brax, I could have done something about it a long time ago.

Just like you could have with Kieran, a little voice pipes up.

When my cell begins ringing for a second time, I reach out and turn it over to see who it is.

My breath catches when I find Brax's smiling face filling my screen.

The tears I thought I'd run out of fill my eyes all over again.

All he's been is a good friend.

Sure, we might have been captured looking more intimate that we actually were last night. But that's just the media. Kieran knows all too well how they can spin things to suit them and their story.

I blow out a long, slow breath.

Brax knows that we should be out on our big date right now.

If he's ringing, it's because he knows something has gone wrong.

My stomach knots.

Did Kieran go to him first? Or was it his next stop after here?

"Shit," I hiss when the call rings off.

Brax is a good person. A really good person.

If he knows, then he won't let it go. Not until he's confident I'm okay.

It takes two minutes for him to try again. And this time, I lift my cell up. My thumb hovers over the screen to connect the call.

I really don't want to talk to anyone. The instant he hears my voice, he'll know just how bad it is.

Aware that if I don't respond, he'll probably turn up at my

door demanding answers, I reluctantly accept the call and put it on speaker. I don't have the energy to hold it up.

"Hey," I croak.

"Effie, I'm so fucking sorry."

A sad laugh falls from my lips.

"None of this is your fault. You don't owe anyone an apology."

"I should have been more careful. I should have been keeping you away from the media and—"

"Brax, stop. None of it matters."

A heavy sigh fills the line.

"No, I guess you're right." Silence falls for a few seconds. "How bad was it?" Brax finally asks.

I cringe.

"You know what Kieran is like," I say in an attempt to play it down.

Over the years, I've learned just how hot-headed my best friend can be. But usually, I'm the one talking him down instead of on the wrong end of his temper.

Or at least, not until recently.

"What did he say to you?"

I shake my head, fresh tears burning my eyes again.

"It doesn't matter. He was angry, said some stuff I'm sure he's already regretting. I assume you've seen him?"

"Yeah."

"And..." I prompt.

"And same as you. Not sure he's regretting it all that much, though."

I let my head fall back and close my eyes.

My life used to be so simple and quiet.

What happened?

Kieran happened.

"Do you need company?" Brax offers.

"Not sure that's a good idea."

"Effie." He sighs. "I'm your friend. We both know there is nothing going on. As you said earlier, we haven't done anything wrong."

"I'm okay. Promise." It's a lie, and we both know it. I might have stood a chance at convincing him if my voice didn't crack, but that's not what just happened.

"Effie."

"Seriously. I'm just going to have an early night. Things might look brighter in the morning."

"I hate this," Brax says quietly.

"I know. Me too. But there isn't a lot we can do about it. I'll speak to you soon, okay?"

"Okay. Effie?" he says quickly before I kill the call. "Everything will work out."

"Of course. Night, Brax."

I cut the call and sink back into the couch.

Everything hurts. Every single inch of me.

At some point, I managed to drag my ass to bed last night. But that doesn't mean I got any sleep.

All night, I tossed and turned, replaying the events of the evening over and over in my head.

It was meant to be so incredible.

We were going to have good food, a few drinks, and then...

The sun might have risen on a new day, but nothing feels better.

If anything, it all feels worse with every hour that has passed.

The pain, the anger, the disbelief only grows.

How could he think those things of me?

He was mad, I get that. But shit.

He was cruel.

I hope he's regretting it. But there's a part of me that wonders if he does.

Was last night the final straw? Did it just remind him of why he doesn't do relationships? Not that what we had could be described as one. If anything, it was a car crash.

A fucking disaster.

You never should have let him kiss you in Grams' kitchen.

We knew taking things to the next level was a risk. But I never thought we'd end up here.

Hurting.

My head pounds as I push myself out of bed. I didn't drink a sip of alcohol last night, but I feel hungover.

I pad through to my bathroom to freshen up before grabbing a hoodie from my closet and heading to the kitchen for coffee.

With a bit of luck, it'll help bring me back to life.

Despite the sun already being high in the sky, illuminating the city in a beautiful warm glow, I don't really see it.

Everything is gray and muted.

I start the coffee machine and jump up on the counter as I wait for it.

Was coming back here a huge mistake?

Maybe I should start over.

I never figured out how that would look. My notebook still sits mostly empty. But maybe it was the best option.

I don't move from the counter. Instead, I sit there with the cold from the granite top working through my body.

It's not until I've made my second cup that I finally hop down. After locating my notebook of ideas that I'd left to fester in my suitcase, I curl back up on the couch and stare down at the page.

I can't help but laugh.

The ideas I wrote down are ridiculous.

Flipping the page, I find my pros and cons list for coming back or staying in St. Louis.

I scan down the list.

Right now, St. Louis is tempting.

A nice quiet and empty house. No pressure of work. No hustle and bustle of the city.

No Kieran...

Even with all of this up in the air, could I really live anywhere without him?

No matter what happens between us, he'll forever be my person.

Lifting my hand to wipe a tear away, I stare out at the stadium.

This place will forever be his home. And that means, it needs to be mine.

I can't leave him.

No matter how vile the words are he says to me. No matter how hard things get or how badly my heart hurts.

I just can't do it.

The sound of my buzzer rips through the air and I startle.

My heart jumps into my throat, and for hopeful seconds, I think he's come back.

Placing my empty mug on the coffee table, I race toward the console at the front door that will allow me to hear his voice.

My hand trembles as I press the button.

"Hello?" I say in a rush, desperate to hear his voice.

Please, please be him.

"Morning," a deep voice sings, and while it might be familiar, it isn't the one I really want.

A pained breath escapes as I take a step back, my shoulders sagging in disappointment.

"Effie?" he questions when I don't respond. "Shit. You thought it was Kieran, didn't you?"

"N-no," I lie. "Come on up."

I'm vaguely aware that I should probably refuse and send him away.

It's probably stupid to think that Kieran might be watching, trying to confirm what he already thinks he knows, but I can't help but be suspicious.

It doesn't stop me from hitting the button that will allow Brax entry to the building, though.

I leave the door open for him and walk into the kitchen to wash my mug and restart the coffee machine.

"No need for that," he says after his heavy footsteps move through my apartment. "I brought coffee and pastry."

A smile pulls at my lips before I spin around and look at him.

"Oh my god," I cry. "Brax, what the hell?"

Racing over, I stretch up on my toes to get a better look at his swollen eye.

"Tell me he didn't," I beg.

Brax shrugs one shoulder. "It's nothing. Barely even hurts."

"Bullshit," I snap. "Your eye hardly opens."

"Okay, fine, it's a little tender. You should see him, though."

My breath catches at the insinuation that they've been physically fighting.

I can't remember the last time Kieran got into a physical altercation, but it has been known to happen in the past. Brax, though, doesn't scream brawler.

I have, however, been known to be wrong in the past.

Concern for Kieran rushes through me, and I reach for Brax's hands as he places the takeout tray and paper bag on the counter.

I breathe a sigh of relief when I don't find any evidence of him hitting anyone.

"I'm joking. Kieran is fine."

Irritation rolls through me that Brax has been dragged into this bullshit and ended up hurt.

"You should have hit him. He deserves it," I mutter.

No, I don't really want them fighting. But I can't help the small, violent part of me that wants Kieran to be hurting just as much as I am right now.

"He's an asshole. I won't deny that." Brax laughs. "Have you spoken to him?"

I shake my head. "Nope. And I have no intention of doing so for quite a while."

"Go on then," he says after passing me my coffee and bag of pastries. "Tell me everything."

58

KIERAN

Since the moment I got back here on Friday night, I haven't stepped foot outside my apartment.

I've ignored anyone who's come to the door. My cell died sometime on Saturday morning, and it's remained the same way ever since.

I don't want to see anyone. I don't want to listen to anyone. And I certainly don't want to discover anything that's been posted on social media.

If there are more photos of them together, I don't know how I'm going to react.

I want to say that time has given me perspective, and I guess, it has a little. But mostly, I'm still angry.

I know we weren't technically together, and that Effie was free to go out with anyone she wanted. But Brax? My teammate? There are a million other men in this city she could have chosen.

I push myself harder on the bike.

Other than failing to sleep, and drink, hitting the gym is the only thing I've done all weekend.

My muscles are screaming at me to stop. But I can't.

Working out is the only thing I can do to stop my mind from running at a million miles a minute.

I need the relief.

Seeing as I've run out of food, I've been forced to order in. I don't want to face even a delivery guy, but I don't have much choice in the matter.

It's due any minute, and I have every intention of pushing myself until the buzzer rings.

The more miles I do, the higher the chance that I might get some sleep tonight.

Every time I lie in bed and close my eyes, the only thing I can see is them. Together. Her lips on his skin.

The image is haunting me. And my own imagination is kind enough to summon up pretty vivid pictures of where it could have gone next.

Them in her apartment...rolling around in her bed...

Would he treat her like glass, or would he give her what she really craves?

The buzzer rings, dragging me back to reality with a bump.

No sooner have my feet hit the floor than my knees buckle and I go crashing to the ground, the side of my head bouncing off the treadmill beside me.

"Fuck," I grunt, lifting my hand to rub my temple.

I groan in irritation when blood covers my skin.

Fucking brilliant.

By the time I get to the door, it's trickling down the side of my face.

Impatiently, I jab my finger against the button to let the delivery guy up before going to get a paper towel.

"Just leave it on the side," I shout when I hear movement at my front door.

The door slams closed, and I breathe a sigh of relief that I'm alone once more.

Happy that I'm not at risk of bleeding out, I throw the towel in the trash and spin around to collect my dinner.

As I look up, my heart jumps into my throat and my breath catches.

"You motherfucker," I sneer.

Brax shrugs. "You know as well as I do that sometimes, you've just got to play dirty."

"I've been ignoring you for a reason," I mutter, before reaching out and snatching my food from his hand.

I march to the kitchen and pull the containers out while he watches me.

"You can leave now you've made your delivery."

"Not a fucking chance. We need to talk." He frowns. "You're bleeding."

"How is my best friend? I assume you've spent all weekend fucking her." The words are bitter as they leave my lips, but I can't hold them back.

"You're a fucking asshole," he states before pulling out one of my kitchen stools. And as if that isn't bad enough, he then reaches out and steals one of my spring rolls.

"Haven't you taken enough?" I bark.

"I haven't taken fuck all, and you know it. And yeah, as it happens, I have seen Effie this weekend. She's a fucking mess, in case you were wondering."

I shake my head.

"Oh, can I—"

"Fuck off," I bark, slapping his hand away when he reaches for more of my food.

"Touchy," he mutters.

"I really fucking hope your eye hurts."

"Even if it did, I wouldn't give you the satisfaction of telling the truth."

"I'm not in the mood for this."

"Well, that sucks for you, because this is happening."

"Wonderful," I breathe before pushing a forkful of egg-fried rice into my mouth.

"Kieran, you're a fucking idiot. Do you really think me and Effie have been fucking around behind your back?"

I keep eating, refusing to give him an answer.

"She fucking loves you, man. You," he repeats, just to make sure I heard him. "Even if she was out dating someone, they'd never measure up to you."

I shake my head, refusing to hear it.

"You two are as bad as each other. Both of you need to put your stubbornness and fears aside and just fucking go for it."

We fall silent and he watches me eat, thankfully not attempting to steal anything else.

Finally, I lower my fork and stare him dead in the eyes.

"You're really not fucking her?"

The motherfucker laughs. Right in my fucking face.

"No, Kieran. I'm not fucking Effie. I've never fucked Effie, nor will I ever. She's your girl."

"She looked like yours the other night."

"It's just the fucking media. We went out for dinner after... after work, and she had a couple of cocktails. We were just joking around.

"She was so fucking excited to see you. She was giddy with it. You were all she could talk about."

My heart slams against my ribs as I absorb what he's saying.

All the things I said to her Friday night come back to me, and I want to punch myself in the face.

I was a jerk. No, I was worse than that.

Fuck.

She really doesn't deserve a fuck-up like me.

"I'm sorry," I blurt, making Brax's brows shoot up.

"I appreciate it, bro. But I'm not the one who needs to hear that."

"She'll never forgive me for Friday night."

"She probably shouldn't. But I think you might be pleasantly surprised."

———

Brax stayed for an hour berating me for my life choices.

He'd probably tell you that he was being a good friend—a better one than I deserved—and steering me in the right direction.

But it's safe to say that by the time he left, I was feeling pretty shitty about myself.

Deep down, maybe I did know that it was all media bullshit.

But sitting in Jamie's car, obsessing over every inch of those photographs, did something to me. It fed into every single one of my insecurities, my fears, and they took hold.

It might have taken me a lot of years to come to my senses, but I love Effie. I'm pretty sure I always have, and I know that I always will.

But the thought of us getting together, finally exploring this other side to our relationship that is so fucking awesome, only to lose it down the line...it would kill me.

Being friends is safe. Sure, we can have our disagreements and bicker about stupid things, but we'd never fall out to a point where we'd part ways.

As a couple, it could happen.

Hell, it does happen.

Across the country, thousands of couples split every single day. They tear their worlds in two and divide everything they've built together.

I refuse to be in that position with Effie.

But what if that didn't happen?

What if we could find a way to be the best friends that we've always been and more?

Is it possible? Or will we be putting ourselves on a journey to destruction?

Driving back into Chicago, I let that fear take over.

In her apartment, I allowed it to fuel me and the words spilling from my lips.

I regret every single one of them.

She'd have every right never to forgive me.

But I'm going to try my hardest to get her to.

I've just finished showering when my buzzer rings again.

My heart immediately jumps into my throat.

Could it be her?

It's wishful thinking, I know.

I race toward the front door and turn the camera on. I'm not being blindsided by my visitor this time.

The second the screen comes to life, a laugh breaks free.

"Hello, Uncle Kieran. Can we come up?"

It might be Kingston's voice that hits my ears, but all I can see on the screen is Prince.

"You can. Not sure about your daddy, though."

"Bad luck, Bro. Guess you're waiting out here," Kian says with a laugh.

Unable to turn down my cute nephew, I let them in and open my door.

In only a few short minutes, they're stepping inside.

"Aw, who's the cutest little boy in the world?" I sing, immediately diving for Prince, who's smiling up at me from his pushchair. "Isn't it a little late for a walk?"

"He won't sleep," King complains.

When I look up, I see the evidence of that fact written all over his face.

"We sent Lori and Tate for an evening session at the spa," Kian explains.

"And how is that going?" I muse, unable to contain my smirk as I bounce Prince on my hip.

"Wonderful," Kingston grumps.

"It's been pretty fun...for me. First, Prince pissed all over his dad. Then he refused point blank to eat his pureed avocado and instead sprayed it in his dad's face. And now, he won't sleep. I've never seen Kingston so close to losing his shit. Ever."

My smirk grows as I picture all of this happening.

"You're trying to feed your kid pureed avocado?" I ask, although it's no surprise really.

"He loves it when Tatum gives it to him."

"She probably laces it with something that tastes good," Kian says before I have a chance.

"Did Effie do that?" Kingston says, suddenly changing the subject as he nods toward the cut on my temple.

"Very funny," I mutter, although I refrain from telling them the truth. It would probably be less mortifying to admit that Effie was responsible. "You want beers?"

"Why else do you think we're here?" Kian says, getting comfortable on my couch.

"Assholes."

"Hey, language," Kingston complains.

"Dude, he's a baby."

"Yeah, and when his first word is asshole, I'll know who to blame."

Rolling my eyes, I place Prince in Kian's lap as I pass him in favor of the kitchen.

My apartment is the opposite of baby-proof, and every time he's here, I freak out that he's going hurt himself and it'll be all my fault.

After handing out beers, I grab my boy back and sit with him on the floor.

Kingston passes me his bag, and I grab a few toys to entertain him with.

My skin prickles with both of my older brothers' attention on me.

Questions are coming. It's just a matter of how long they make me wait.

"Have you spoken to Effie?" Kingston eventually asks.

"Not since Friday night, no. Why?"

"Do you really think we're that stupid?" Kian asks, sitting forward and resting his elbows on his knees, concern filling his eyes.

59

EFFIE

I don't call in sick to work unless I can't drag my ass out of bed.

But this morning, I was really tempted to.

Returning to the world after my weekend of solitude and heartbreak was terrifying.

Putting it off wasn't going to get me anywhere, though. So, I forced myself to do my morning yoga flow in the hope it would give me some motivation, before getting ready for work.

Everyone in the office greeted me as if everything was normal. As if my world hadn't completely imploded over the past few weeks.

I go through the motions of dealing with emails, returning phone calls and attending meetings.

Physically, I'm present. Mentally, I'm fucked.

Throughout the day, I get messages from Brax, Tate, and Lori checking in on me. I reply because it would be rude not to, but I don't tell them the truth. Instead, I lie and say that I'm coping, that work is a welcome distraction.

It's not.

I'm not sure anything would be a good enough distraction from the pain in my chest.

All I wanted to do was make Grams happy in her final weeks.

It was one simple lie that I didn't think would change anything.

But look at me now.

I've lost everything.

My hand lifts to my necklace, and a sob bubbles up my throat.

Squeezing my eyes closed, I fight to keep my tears at bay.

Blowing out a shaky breath, I focus on the email I was writing.

I only manage a few more sentences before the phone on my desk rings.

"Good afternoon, Effie. I have someone down at reception for you."

My brows pinch in confusion.

I don't have any external meetings today.

"O-oh, um..."

"Lunch date, apparently," the receptionist says cryptically.

My heart lurches.

My head knows that it won't be Kieran, but my heart...that battered thing needs a little more convincing.

"I'll be right down," I confirm.

My heart is in my throat as I descend through the building.

Despite meeting him later for our dance class, I figure that I'm probably about to find Brax waiting for me.

But as I spill from the elevator and turn toward the reception desks, my breath catches in surprise.

Kieran's mom stands there with an empathetic smile playing on her lips.

The emotion I was battling with upstairs returns full force.

Seeing it, Elizabeth rushes forward, wraps her arm around my shoulder, and ushers me out of the building.

In only seconds, she has me in the back of a town car, hidden away from the world.

"Oh, sweetie," she whispers, pulling me into her arms. "I'm so sorry I didn't get here sooner."

Her warm embrace is the final straw, and I completely fall apart.

With Grams gone, and my own mother cold and distant—even when she is trying—Elizabeth is the closest thing I have to a mom.

I didn't realize how much I needed one until this moment.

Uncaring about the mess my makeup is making on her designer dress, she holds me against her, her hand gently rubbing up and down my back.

"I'm so sorry, sweetheart," she muses. "It's okay."

I don't know how much time passes, but when I finally suck in a shaky breath and sit back, I discover that we're no longer outside work, but instead, the car is sitting in front of The Broadway.

It's been a long time since I've spent any time in the luxury Callahan spa hotel.

"I-I need to get back to work," I stutter, my voice rough from crying.

"I've sorted everything with Henry, don't worry."

Her driver holds the back door open for us, and with her hand locked in mine, she gently tugs me out of the car.

I keep my head down, not wanting anyone to see what a mess I am.

Thankfully, we don't stop at reception. We don't even have to wait for the elevator.

As we step out on the lower floor, I find the spa completely empty.

Memories of the morning Kieran took me to the new spa in St. Louis come back to me.

He was trying so hard to do something nice for me, and all I wanted to do was get back to Grams.

I didn't appreciate what he'd done for me at all.

"W-what's going on?"

"My eldest son owed me a favor," she explains, before leading me toward the ladies' changing rooms.

The moment the door opens, laughter hits my ears.

My initial reaction is to cringe, but then familiarity trickles through me and I relax.

"Oh shit," Tate exclaims the second she sees me, and before I know what's happening, I find myself as the filling in a Tate and Lori sandwich.

"Aw, I have the world's best daughters-in-law," Elizabeth muses.

No one points out that Tate is her only official one. Lori is close; she and Kian are engaged.

But me...right now, I couldn't be further from joining their family.

"What's going on?" I ask once I've been released, despite the fact I can guess.

"We made King close up shop for the afternoon," Tate says with a smirk.

Lori holds her arms out wide and spins around with a smile on her face.

"This place is all ours for four hours."

"Seriously? He allowed that to happen?"

"It's amazing the power that my best friend has over that man," Lori teases. "There is nothing he wouldn't do for her."

"The fewer details about how she's managed to achieve that, the better," Elizabeth laughs.

"Now, now," Tate teases. "We know you possess the skills as well."

Elizabeth blushes. "Back in the day, maybe."

"Are we going to stand around in here talking all afternoon, or are we hitting the spa?" Lori asks.

She and Tate are already in fluffy white robes, and Elizabeth is busy getting ready.

"I don't have—"

"You're cute," Tate says before thrusting a tote bag at me.

"Thank you," I whisper, my emotions beginning to get the better of me again.

Thankfully, when I pull the swimsuit from the bag, I find that it's a little more appropriate than the one Kieran selected for me.

That very first morning when his eyes ran down the length of my body was probably the start of everything going wrong.

I'd never seen that kind of heat directed at me before.

It threw me for a loop. Although, I can't use his reaction as an excuse for why I didn't tell him the truth while we were in that jacuzzi.

I should have done it.

How differently would all of this have gone if I'd told him the truth?

As much as I like to think it would have changed things, something tells me we would have always ended up here.

The media may never have gotten involved, and I may not have hurt him like I did. But I think we were always meant to have that weekend together.

Maybe without all the drama, we'd have been able to put it behind us and continue with our friendship...

Or you'd both have been in a better place to embark on your romantic relationship.

I let out a heavy sigh.

"We'll leave you to get ready," Elizabeth says, now also dressed in her robe.

"If you're not out in ten, we'll come and get you," Tate warns softly before the three of them disappear.

I stand there for a few seconds with the swimsuit clutched in my hands and my head spinning out of control.

Numbly, I strip out of my work clothes and pull on the swimsuit. Just like I knew it would, it fits like a second skin, and despite looking demure in my hands, it's actually quite sexy.

I pull my robe on, and I'm about to put my purse into a locker when I feel my cell vibrate.

Pulling it out, I find a photo memory on the screen.

My heart aches as I stare at mine and Kieran's smiling faces from four years ago.

We both look so young, so happy.

We were carefree college students with our whole lives ahead of us.

He surprised me with a trip to Mexico, and we had the best time.

Just the two of us hanging out. We spent the entire trip laughing.

Sadness rushes through me.

Before I can stop myself, I have our conversation up on my screen.

There hasn't been a message since he told me he was heading home on Friday.

But I'm about to change that.

> Effie: I'm sorry. I love you, and I'm sorry x

I stand there staring, waiting for it to be delivered, and maybe even read.

But it never happens.

Refusing to regret reaching out, I stuff my cell back into my purse and secure it in the locker.

As I walk out to join the others, my head spins with all the reasons it may not have been delivered.

"There she is," Lori sings from the jacuzzi. All three of them have glasses of bubbles in their hands and wide smiles on their faces.

Shrugging off my robe, I climb into the jacuzzi and reach for the fourth glass.

"Best idea we've had in a long time," Tate sighs before sipping her drink.

The next four hours pass in a blur of heart-to-heart, laughter, champagne, and relaxation.

All three of them obviously want details about what's happened with Kieran, but they didn't linger on the subject. Instead, they distracted me with tales of the other Callahan brothers, of Prince, of work, and everything in between.

It's amazing. And the perfect reminder that while I might be feeling lonely after losing Grams and all this shit with me and Keiran, I'm not actually alone.

I have three formidable females who are willing to shut down an entire spa to help me relax.

I have a friend who is willing to take a punch in the face for me.

And a best friend who...may have lost his title.

The whole time we're laughing and enjoying ourselves, the message I sent to Kieran still lingers in my mind.

Has he read it now? Has he responded? Or have I been blocked and it'll never be seen?

That final thought is like a kick in the chest.

Surely, he won't have blocked me over this?

He just needs time.

As much as I'm looking forward to my dance class, I'm nowhere near ready to leave when Elizabeth points out that our time is nearly up.

These few hours of escape have been everything I didn't

know I needed. I feel lighter. Of course, my heart still feels like it's been through a blender, but there is a little positivity seeping back in.

Thoughts of not belonging here have vanished, and my motivation is returning.

Despite telling myself that I'll wait until I'm alone to check my cell, it's the first thing I do the second I open my locker.

Hope builds within me.

But it all comes shattering down again when I discover that I don't have a reply. And when I open the message thread and see that it's been read, all the good work that had happened in the spa vanishes.

After saying goodbye to Tate and Lori, Elizabeth delivers me back to the office so I can collect my things and my car.

She hasn't asked what happened since stepping into the changing room, but it's obvious that something has.

Instead, she gives me a hug, tells me to call her if I need anything, and lets me climb out.

I'm on autopilot as I return to my office, tidy up my desk, then go and change again.

If I'd had any warning about our spa trip then I could have taken my dance clothes with me. I guess that would have ruined the element of surprise.

The drive to the studio is a disaster. The entire city seems to be gridlocked, and by the time I pull up in the parking lot, I'm frustrated and tense.

So much for the spa.

I park beside Brax's fancy Maserati and rush toward the building.

I wave at the receptionist to let her know I'm here before crashing through the doors with only a minute to spare.

Brax is in his usual spot on the other side of the room, lacing his shoes, but despite the noise I made entering, he doesn't turn to look.

I race over, pulling my dance shoes out of my bag as I go, and once I'm beside him, I toe my sneakers off.

"Sorry. The traffic was a nightmare," I explain.

I glance over, but he doesn't respond. He also doesn't lower his hood or acknowledge my arrival in any way.

"Brax?" I question, my brows knitted together.

It takes another second for him to move, but when he does finally turn, it's like the world has been pulled from beneath me.

"Y-you're not—"

"Okay, are we ready to get started?" Maria says, her soft yet commanding voice filling the studio.

He holds his hand out, but I'm frozen.

"May I have this dance, Luck?"

60

EFFIE

I continue to stare up into Kieran's green eyes as my heart pounds and my entire body trembles.

He's here.

He's standing right in front of me, asking me to dance.

How?

Why?

Where is Brax?

"Effie?" he whispers when I don't do anything.

My mouth opens and closes, but no words come out.

I'm speechless.

Dumbfounded.

I never in a million years thought he'd be here.

I sense someone step up beside me, but I can't look over. My eyes are locked on Kieran's.

He's nervous. It's not something I see often, but it's there.

He has no idea how I'm going to react, and the longer I just stand here completely useless, the more he's beginning to freak out.

"Are you two ready to show me some moves?" Maria asks as if nothing unusual is happening here.

I manage to nod in agreement, and a second later, my hand slips into Kieran's huge paw.

Wrapping his arm around my waist, he presses his other palm against my lower back before tugging me closer.

I gasp as our bodies collide, then as if he does this every day of the week, he leads.

How?

I continue to stare up at him in disbelief as my feet move in time with his.

"W-what is happening?" I whisper, finally finding my voice.

His eyes search mine before they drop to my lips for a beat.

"I'm sorry," he responds, his deep voice giving away the emotions he's battling. "I'm sorry, and—" He sucks in a deep breath. "I love you, too."

My message.

He's replying to my message.

A breath rushes out of me, and I just about manage to catch the sob that wants to follow it.

His grip on my body tightens before he releases me, spinning me out and then drawing me back in.

I know Grams taught him to dance before. But she didn't teach him this.

I shake my head in disbelief as our hips come together again.

"H-How...How are you doing this?"

He ducks lower so his forehead presses against mine. "I told you, Effie. I'd do anything for you."

Tears burn my eyes.

"Y-you're really here?" I ask, still unable to fully process what is happening.

"Don't mind me crashing your date, do you?"

A laugh tumbles from my lips.

"It's never been a date, Kieran. Brax and I—"

"I know," he assures me. "I know everything."

"Including these dance moves, apparently."

His smirk grows, and damn it if it doesn't make him even hotter.

"Fantastic. You two are natural together," Maria praises.

"Yeah," Kieran muses without breaking eye contact with me. "We are."

Oh my god.

The song comes to an end and Maria immediately instructs us to go straight into our new tango.

My lips twitch with a smile. Learning a waltz is very different from a tango.

"What the hell?" I laugh when Kieran releases me and takes two steps back, ready to start.

Completely dumbfounded, I stand there as the beat drops and he stalks back toward me, spins me around, and presses his front to my back.

Heat from his huge, hard body surges through mine, lighting me up from the inside out.

Lifting my arm in the air, I shudder as he drags his palm down my skin, making goosebumps erupt across my body.

"How have you done this?" I breathe as his knuckles skim over the side of my breast, something Brax never did. My nipples pucker and pressure begins to build in my lower stomach.

The tango might be erotic and seductive, but Brax was always a total gentleman.

Kieran, however...

Spinning in his arms, I gaze up at him as I wrap my leg around his, rubbing myself against him.

His nostrils flare and he sucks in a sharp breath.

He's hard.

Desire shoots through me, leaving heat pooling between my thighs.

Kieran's hot hand burns against my lower back, taunting me with everything he's capable of before he dips me.

Blood rushes to my head as I flip it back, but that isn't the most shocking thing because...

"We're alone," I whisper once he's righted me again and my gaze finds his.

Kieran's eyes blaze with heat. But there is more than just that, there's an apology, a promise. Everything I've craved.

"Is that right?" he muses, pressing our bodies closer.

"You planned all this?"

"Maybe."

I shake my head. "You learned the tango for me."

"Trust me, this right now is no hardship."

I don't know where Maria and the others have gone, but I don't care.

Ducking lower, he brings his lips within touching distance of mine, making my heart beat even harder.

"I'm sorry for all the things I said. I was angry and hurting and—"

"I'm sorry for not telling you everything. But I promise you, nothing ever happened between—"

"I know. Can you forgive me?"

"Kieran," I breathe. "I'll always forgive you."

"Good, because I'll fuck up. I know I will. I won't mean to, but—"

"So will I. I'll probably be needy, and get jealous, and I'll—"

"You've got nothing to get jealous over, baby. You're the only woman I see. It's been that way for quite some time now."

"Argh," I cry when he suddenly moves, spinning me around him. "You're really good at this."

"Who do you think Brax's first partner was?"

473

I still for a moment when he positions me in front of him.

I blink at our reflection in the floor-to-ceiling mirrors before us.

My cheeks are flushed, my chest is heaving, and my eyes are sparkling with happiness and desire. And that's only made worse when Kieran drags his hands up my sides.

Brax always stopped on my ribs, but Kieran...he goes all the way.

A filthy moan rips from my lips as he squeezes my breasts, forcing my head to fall back against him.

"Y-you're kidding, right?"

He gives me a megawatt smile.

"Yeah, Luck. I am. Fuck, you're hot."

With his eyes still locked on mine in the mirror, his lips descend on my shoulder.

His kiss is electric.

Heat floods through my veins as his lips trail up my neck and then to my ear.

"I can't believe you danced with my best friend like this," he rasps, squeezing my breasts again. A moan rumbles in my throat, and I rub my ass against him, causing him to hiss as if he's in pain.

"I thought I was your best friend," I complain.

"Not anymore. You're my girl. And one day, Effie Campbell...one day, you're going to be my wife."

Before I have a chance to say anything, he spins me back around and frames my face with his hands.

"Will you be mine?" he asks.

"Yes. Yes, yes, yes."

His lips crash against mine and his hands slip back, his fingers threading through my hair, holding me in place as his tongue invades my mouth.

Desire flows through me as I kiss him back just as eagerly, my hands sliding up his hard chest.

Like teenagers, we make out in the middle of the room as if we've got all the time in the world.

Our hands roam as we lose ourselves in each other.

"Missed you," he whispers between kisses. "Hate my life without you."

"Same," I agree.

"I lied before," he confesses, making me pull back to look at him with my heart in my throat. "When I told my mom that I wasn't in love with you. I was, I always have been, I just... hadn't figured it out yet."

An emotional sob erupts before I jump into his arms.

He catches me easily, and I wrap my legs around his waist.

Both of us gasp as I rub against his erection.

"We need to get out of here before I do something I shouldn't."

"Okay," I breathe, more than ready to take this tango to the next step.

"Would have been fucking hot in front of those mirrors though," Kieran says as he lowers my feet back to the floor.

I glance over my shoulder and see myself on my knees before him with his dick in my mouth.

"Effie?" he asks when I don't respond.

"Y-yeah," I muse. "Hot."

His attention burns the side of my face, and when I rip my gaze from the mirror, I find him staring at me with a smirk playing on his lips.

"Whatever you're thinking about, I want it."

"You don't even kn—"

"Don't need to. The only thing I do know is that I'm going to make every single one of your filthy fantasies come true."

After changing into his sneakers, he throws his bag over his shoulder and waits for me to do the same.

"What happens next?" I ask, pausing before turning to leave.

"We're meant to be having a date to talk," he reminds me.

Biting down on my bottom lip, I let my eyes trail down the length of him.

He's wearing a black hoodie and grey sweatpants.

And those sweatpants—or more specifically, what's hiding beneath them—are not in any fit shape to walk into a restaurant.

"I think we've done enough talking," I decide. "Takeout at my place?"

"I thought you'd never ask."

Taking my hand in his, he leads me out of the dance studio. I don't know what time it is, or how much of the lesson is technically left, but I don't care.

"What about Brax's car?" I ask as we walk up to it.

"He'll take it home. He's in that coffee shop over there, just in case this all went very wrong."

My eyes shoot to the coffee shop in question, and right there in the window is the man I thought I was meeting for our dance class.

"He's a good guy," I muse, lifting my hand to wave at him.

"Yeah. He is. Even if he has been manhandling my girl."

"It's dance. It's art."

"Mmm. If you say so."

When we get to my car, he pulls the passenger door open for me before jogging around to the driver's side and dropping into the seat.

"Buckle up. You're in for a wild ride."

"Oh my god," I squeal as he wheelspins out of the parking lot.

"Don't say I didn't warn you."

I swear, the drive back to my apartment has never taken so long. The air between us is thick with desire.

No sooner has he parked and killed the engine than he's at my door and throwing me over his shoulder.

"Kieran."

"Can't wait any longer, Luck," he says as he jogs toward the elevator.

"Ow, shit," I complain when he spanks my ass.

"Get used to it. You've got a number of things you need punishing for."

I slam my lips shut as the elevator doors open.

He presses the button for the top floor before dragging me from his shoulder and slamming me against the back wall.

"You've been a bad girl, Luck. A really bad fucking girl."

My core aches at his words.

"Do you know what bad girls get?" he asks.

His dark, desire-filled eyes bore down into mine and his jaw ticks with impatience.

"Orgasms?" I tease.

"Punished, Effie. They get punished."

61

KIERAN

"Faster," I complain when Effie fumbles with her keys.

Every muscle in my body is pulled tight with need.

How I made it all the way back here without pulling over and fucking her on the hood of her car, I don't know.

Reaching for my crotch, I tug at the fabric before squeezing my dick.

"Okay, okay," Effie says a beat before the door swings wide open.

The moment I'm over the threshold, I kick the door closed and drop our bags to the floor.

For three seconds, the only sound that can be heard is our heavy breathing.

But then, Effie turns to me, and everything changes.

"Kieran," she gasps as I lift her from her feet, wrap her legs around my waist, and press her back against the wall.

My lips find hers and I plunge my tongue past her lips, my hands roaming over her body.

I need every inch of her right now.

Our kiss is wild, dirty, and desperate, and I'm here for every second of it.

"Oh my god," she moans as I drag my lips across her jaw and down her throat. "Yes, yes."

"Need you," I groan.

It's been far too long since I've had her taste on my tongue, since I've pushed inside her hot body.

"Please," she whimpers as I curl my fingers around the hem of her tank and peel it up her body.

It falls to the floor, and I immediately reach for her sports bra.

I need her naked more than I need my next breath.

"Beautiful. So fucking beautiful."

I find her lips again as I battle with the tight fabric.

"The fuck is this about?" I bark when I fail at ridding it from her body.

She giggles, and the sound of it makes my dick jerk.

Why haven't we been doing this for years?

"Let me," she says before crossing her arms over her front and peeling the fabric from her body with ease.

"Bett—fuck," she cries when I lift her higher and suck one of her nipples into my mouth.

"Perfect," I mumble around her.

"Oh god," she cries as her head falls back against the wall.

I switch to the other side, sucking and nibbling on her sensitive skin.

"Please, Kieran. More. More," she begs, reaching out to pull my hoodie from my body.

"You're perfect," I state before claiming her lips again and tugging her from the wall.

Forgetting about my hoodie, she wraps her arms around my shoulders and holds on as I carry her through her apartment.

Her lips move down my throat, and I scan the room, taking in all my options.

The couch, the coffee table, the kitchen island, the windows again.

Fuck, that was hot.

But while I might want to take her on every available surface of her home, this time, I opt for something a little more normal.

As soon as we're in her bedroom, I throw her onto the bed and watch her bounce.

Mine.

She is all fucking mine.

"Kieran?" she questions when I don't immediately follow her.

She pauses in the middle of the bed and pushes up on her elbows.

She's wearing only her yoga pants and sneakers. Her chest is heaving, and her breasts already have hickies and bite marks covering them. I can only imagine how she'll look when we're finished.

My cock jerks as I think about her with my marks all over her.

"What are you waiting for?"

Lifting my hand, I comb my fingers through my hair.

"Nothing. Just taking a moment to appreciate how fucking awesome you are."

"Okay, but could you do that maybe while your head is between my thighs?"

A laugh erupts from my throat.

"See," I say as I stalk closer. "Perfect."

She watches intently as I drag her sneakers off, tug her socks from her feet, and then tuck my fingers around the waistband of her yoga pants and panties.

She trembles as I drag them down her legs and abandon them on the floor.

"Fuck," I groan, standing back to full height. "Spread your legs for me. Show me what's mine."

Slowly, she pulls her knees up, sliding her feet along the sheets.

She's teasing me, but I love it.

Make me wait.

Make me want it even more.

My fists clench as my heart pounds harder and precum soaks my boxers.

My eyes jump to hers, and I find a smirk playing on her lips.

"Bad, bad girl," I muse before dragging my eyes back down her body.

Slowly, painfully fucking slowly, she parts her legs.

My mouth waters and my hand lifts to rub at my jaw.

"Fuck, yeah," I groan.

She's waxed and so fucking pretty.

"Kieran, please."

The sound of her needy whimper drags me from my head, and I reach behind me to pull my hoodie from my body.

It hits the floor, and my sweats, boxers and sneakers go next.

"Hands and knees, Luck."

Without missing a beat, she does as she's told. Grabbing her hips, I drag her back so her knees are on the edge of the mattress.

"Been dreaming about this pussy, about you being my good girl."

"Yes," she moans as I palm her ass.

"But I need to deal with you being bad first."

Pulling my hand back, I spank her ass.

She cries out, her entire body jolting forward.

I stare down at the glowing red print, my chest expanding with pride and possessiveness.

"Count," I demand before doing it again.

"Two," she cries.

"Those are for not telling me that you came back," I explain.

"Three. Four."

"For making me think you had a date."

"Five."

Her fists twist in the sheets as she rocks her ass back, silently begging for more.

Rubbing the bright red print, I drop to my knees behind her, my eyes zeroing in on her pussy.

"Fuck, Luck. You're dripping down your thighs."

She whimpers.

"Words. Give me words."

"Please."

"Please what?" I ask as I grab her ass and spread her open.

"Please, make me come."

I blow a stream of air across her sensitive skin, making her whimper like a needy whore again.

"Head on the bed, ass in the air," I demand before dragging my tongue up the length of her pussy.

Her cries are muffled by the sheets as her body trembles violently.

"Louder. I want to hear every single cry, moan, and plea that passes through those pretty lips."

She shifts, and I suck on her.

"Kieran."

My dick jerks as her taste floods my mouth again. It's so hard it hurts. It takes every ounce of restraint I possess not to just fuck her into oblivion.

That's going to happen. I just need to get her nice and ready first.

I groan as I eat her, letting the vibrations push her closer to her release.

It's tempting to edge her, but I'm too fucking desperate to sink inside her.

It's been too fucking long.

There is going to be so much time for that later.

"You're going to come all over my face, and then I'm going to make you do it again all over my dick," I promise her. "But that's only going to be the beginning. I really hope you don't have any important meetings tomorrow."

I dive for her again before she can respond. I suck her clit and push two fingers deep inside her, working her to her first release of the night.

She cries out my name as her pussy drags my fingers deeper.

Pulling back, I wipe my face with the back of my hand before standing to my full height and spanking her again.

I'll never get bored of seeing my handprint glowing on her ass.

Her body is limp and pliant as I flip her over, and when I find her eyes, they're dark and sated.

"Oh baby, you needed that, didn't you?"

She nods as her eyes drop down my body to where I'm slowly stroking my dick.

She swallows thickly, spreading her thighs wide in invitation.

"Not as much as I need that."

I smile, shaking my head in disbelief.

I made a decision in the middle of last night when I couldn't sleep. And I'm pretty sure it's going to turn out to be the best one I've made in my entire life.

I need Effie.

I need her in my life, no matter what.

As soon as the sun was up, so was I.

I was standing outside Brax's building before he rolled out of bed, demanding his help.

Did I think it was going to lead to me spending the day learning to waltz and tango with my teammate? Nope. But do I regret it? Hell no.

Putting myself out there after how I reacted on Friday was a risk, but anything that involves Effie is a risk worth taking.

She's everything.

My everything.

Crawling onto the bed, I slide my hand down her thigh, up her torso, and to her throat.

My fingers flex against her soft skin, testing the waters.

"Fuck me, Kieran. Make me yours."

"Jesus." This woman is going to be the death of me.

As much as I want to take her hard and fast, make her scream until she's hoarse, right now, we need to do something else.

Slipping my hand around the side of her neck, I lower myself over her and find her lips.

We've got the rest of our lives to fuck in every which way that exists. But we're only going to have one first time making love.

"I love you," I say, staring her dead in the eyes. If there is any doubt in her mind, I want to eradicate it right here, right now.

"I love you too."

Dropping my forehead to hers, I drag the head of my cock through her folds before finding her entrance.

"This is it, Effie. From here on out, everything is me and you," I promise.

Tears fill her eyes. "Me and you."

Both of us gasp as I push inside her.

She's always felt insane. So tight, and wet, and perfect. But this time, it's even better.

There is nothing between us.

No lies, or smothered feelings.

"Kieran," she whimpers as I push deeper.

"You feel it too, don't you?"

She nods as a tear escapes, trickling over her temple and soaking into her hair.

Stealing her lips, I kiss her as slowly and as gently as I fuck her.

I've never felt anything like it.

No matter how deep I get, it's not enough. And I fear it never will be.

A lifetime with my lucky charm won't be enough.

We move together, clinging to each other, kissing and whispering promises of forever for the longest time.

But despite wanting it to last forever, our bodies defy us.

"Kieran," Effie whimpers, her body trembling with her need for release.

"I've got you, Luck. I'll always have you."

Pressing two fingers against her clit, I give her the extra push she needs to fall over the edge.

My name is nothing but a plea on her lips as she falls into a powerful release.

"Oh my god," she gasps as wave after wave of pleasure rushes through her.

And because she's a good girl who knows the rules, she keeps her eyes on me the whole time, allowing me to see the tears that spill over.

"Beautiful," I praise as I continue to hold her gaze and let her drag my own orgasm out of me.

62

EFFIE

Kieran wraps me in his arms, and with his cock still inside me, we lie together in the middle of my bed for the longest time.

Eventually, my heart rate returns to normal, and the aftershocks from those two powerful releases ebb away.

With my face nuzzled against his chest, I breathe him in.

Tonight has been...a lot.

Seeing him standing there in my dance class was unexpected. But for him then to pull me into his body and bust out all the moves...

How? Just how?

"Brax spent all day teaching me."

His voice startles me, and I sit up so I can look at him.

"W-what?" I stutter.

"You asked how I knew all the moves," he states, making me frown.

I was not aware I asked that question out loud.

My cheeks burn bright red, and he smiles softly when he sees it.

"Brax taught me."

I shake my head.

"I'm sorry, you spent all day learning how to tango with Brax?"

A laugh bubbles up. I try to fight it, I really do.

"I'm glad you find that amusing," he deadpans.

"Please can you do it again so I can watch?"

His fingers descend to my ribs and he tickles me. I shriek as he rolls me onto my back, his cock slipping from me.

"Kieran, please," I half cry, half laugh. "Stop."

He rolls onto his back, taking me with him and sitting me across his lap.

The instant my pussy connects with his dick, I grind down on him.

His nostrils flare and his throat works on a smile.

"You sure missed my dick, huh?" he muses, watching me shamelessly pleasure myself on him.

"Like you wouldn't believe."

"Did you get yourself off without me, Luck?"

I bite down on my bottom lip coyly.

"Effie?" His voice is deep and gravelly. It hits me right in the clit.

"You own my pleasure," I finally say, repeating the words he told me at Grams'. "I only come when you let me."

Pride covers his face.

"How has it taken me this long to discover how perfect you are?"

I shrug one shoulder as I reach down and hold him up.

"You gonna fuck me?" he asks, watching my every move.

"Yeah," I state. "Yeah, I am."

I sink down on him and cry out.

Will I ever get enough of this? Of him?

I really hope not.

"Hey," I say, walking into my kitchen to find Kieran standing in nothing but a pair of tight boxer briefs, chugging water.

The way his throat works as he swallows makes things flutter that should really be worn out by now.

He let me have control when I was on top earlier for about five minutes.

Then he sat up, held my hands behind my back with one of his, and topped me from the bottom.

He just can't help himself. And honestly, I wouldn't want it any other way.

Being at Kieran Callahan's mercy is my favorite place to be.

"Hey," he repeats as his eyes run down the length of me.

I'm wearing one of his Chicago Chiefs t-shirts. It swamps me and hangs almost to my knees, but I love it. The fabric is worn and so soft, and most importantly, it has his number on it.

"You should always have my number on you. It's hot," he muses as he abandons his glass and moves closer.

"How are you feeling?"

I smile up at him, loving the way he takes care of me.

After our first round in bed, he lifted me up and carried me to the bathroom. He set me on the counter and allowed me to watch as he filled the bathtub. After lowering me into the soothing water, he disappeared for a few minutes before returning with a bottle of water and some cookies. Add the fact that he was still gloriously naked, and it was the best bath I've ever taken.

"Amazing. Hungry."

My confession makes his entire face light up.

He spent so much time in St. Louis trying to get me to eat. Thankfully, in the weeks that have passed, my appetite has come back. I'm pretty sure the yoga and dance classes have been helping with that.

"What would you like?" he asks, closing the space between us.

The second he's in touching distance, he wraps his hand around the back of my neck and pulls me in for a kiss.

I sigh with contentment as his lips graze across my jaw and down my neck.

Touching him, kissing, everything...it's so right. So natural.

"You," I laugh.

He groans in appreciation.

"After you've eaten, you can spend all night enjoying me."

He glances up, his eyes dancing with excitement.

"Thai?"

His thumb drags across my bottom lip, and he stares at me like he'll never get enough.

I know the feeling.

"If that's what you want."

After kissing me until my legs are trembling and the only thing I can think about is sinking to my knees and feasting on him, he sends me to the couch with a gentle tap on my ass.

My cheeks blaze as I think about him spanking me earlier.

I loved it.

"Sore, Luck?" he asks when I not-very-discreetly reach back and rub my ass cheek.

Glancing over my shoulder, I give him what I hope is a seductive smile. "In the best kind of way."

Tingles run down my spine as I saunter to the couch. He's watching my every move.

Once I'm seated, I look back, and my heart tumbles in my chest.

He's got the happiest smile playing on his lips.

I know because I can feel the same one on mine.

He makes quick work of ordering our dinner before pulling a bottle of wine from my refrigerator and grabbing two glasses.

After pouring us both a large glass, he settles beside me.

The apartment is in silence and the lights of the city—and the stadium—twinkle before us.

I take a sip of my wine, feeling more relaxed and happier than I have been in a long time.

Of course, we've both got a lot of things to work through, but I'm confident that we'll figure it out.

We just need to start working together.

The last few weeks have been a blip. Both of us were scared and unable to process the changes and what we really wanted.

"You know, this is far less scary than I expected," Kieran confesses. "I thought a proper relationship would feel like pressure. But right now, I feel like the weight of the world has been lifted from my shoulders."

I sigh, smiling up at him.

"Don't get too ahead of yourself; it's only been a couple of hours."

"That doesn't matter. It's you, Effie. You always make everything better."

"You do too."

"This is it now. You're never going to get rid of me."

"Thank God," I laugh. "I learned recently that I don't do very well without you."

"I'm sorry. I—"

"Stop," I beg, pressing my fingers to his lips. "We've both apologized. We're moving on now. Looking forward to the future."

He nods before capturing my fingers and sucking them into his mouth.

I clench my thighs together, and somehow, he notices the slight movement. His eyes darken.

"Dirty whore," he muses the moment he releases me.

"Your dirty whore," I correct.

He steals my glass back before dragging me beneath him on

the couch and kissing me senseless. He doesn't let me up for air until my buzzer goes off, announcing the arrival of dinner.

I walk into the office the next morning with a smile on my face and a bounce in my step that I don't think I've ever had before.

I've barely had any sleep, but it doesn't matter.

My adrenaline is pumping, and I'm ready for what the day holds.

Last night and this morning were just amazing.

It was everything we had for those few days in St. Louis and more.

This time, there is no deadline.

No rush to fit as much in as possible before time runs out.

Now, we have forever.

Reaching up, I run my fingers over the angel wings of my necklace, my smile growing.

Grams did this.

If it weren't for her being ill, for the lie I told to make her happy, none of this might have happened.

I'd still be perpetually single, and Kieran would be...

Yeah, the less time I spend thinking about that, the better.

My cell buzzes as I step into my office.

Pulling it free, a laugh tumbles from my lips.

> Kieran: I miss you already.

He insisted on driving me to work this morning. He has no plans today, so he could have easily stayed in bed, or on the couch watching shit on TV, but he didn't. He wanted to be the best boyfriend he could be and drive me to work.

My heart flutters.

491

Kieran Callahan is my boyfriend.

> Effie: I miss you too x

Kieran starts typing immediately, but before his message comes through, I get another.

> Brax: How did it go?

> Effie: You are in so much trouble…

> Brax: I wouldn't expect anything else. But any specific reason?

> Effie: You tangoed with my boyfriend!!!

> Brax: 🙄🙄🙄

> Effie: You recorded it, right? I need to see it.

> Brax: Sorry, that was for me and Kieran to experience alone.

> Brax: I probably shouldn't say this but…your boy has moves. Those hips.

"Oh my god," I laugh as I drop into my chair.

> Effie: Do you have a little crush I need to know about?

> Brax: Hell no. Just pointing out what a lucky girl you must be 😌

I sigh as I think about all the hip action I've experienced recently.

> Effie: I am a very lucky girl.

> Brax: I'm buzzing for both of you. Do I need to find another dance partner now, though?

> Effie: Of course not. Kieran will be there on Thursday night for you…

Brax: 😐

I burst out laughing again as I picture the two of them spinning around the studio. Which one would take the lead…

> Effie: I'll be there Thursday. But Kieran wanted me to tell you that if you touch me like he did during the tango, you won't see another season…

Brax: I can handle Kieran Callahan.

> Effie: No more fighting.

Brax: Yes, Mom.

Still laughing, I place my cell on my desk and wake my computer up.

Thoughts of how miserable I was here yesterday flicker through my mind. It's amazing how fast things can change.

My cell buzzes again, and the moment I see Kieran's name, I remember that he was typing.

Kieran: I'm not very good with words, actions are more my thing, but I need you to know how serious I am about this. About us. You're my everything, and always will be. Endgame, baby.

My smile is ridiculous as I read his words.

> Effie: I've never been more serious about anything in my life. You're mine, Kieran Callahan. Warn those jersey chasers, because I will throw hands if anyone dares go near you.

Kieran: Damn, I think I need to see that.

> Effie: Behave.

Kieran: Never.

Effie: You're distracting me.

Kieran: My number one goal in life always.

Kieran: I'm hard thinking about what you did this morning.

A wave of heat flows through me.

Effie: Cold shower before hitting the gym then?

Kieran: Won't help. I just need you.

Effie: Later.

Kieran: It's too long 😞

Effie: I'll remind you of that when you're at an away game.

Kieran: No need. You'll be coming with me.

All the air rushes out of my lungs.

Effie: Kieran...

Kieran: Not being without you ever again.

A knock on my door forces me to stop replying, and as soon as I call out, Henry pokes his head inside.

He gives me a double take, and I can only assume it's because of the smile on my face.

"Do you have a few minutes?"

"Of course."

Effie: Gotta go. See you later. Love you x

63

KIERAN

Despite being busy all day, it's fucking dragged.

I was still sitting out the front of the KC Foundation office when I pulled my cell out to message her.

The elevator doors had barely closed on her, and I already missed her.

As much as I love being back here, I'm mourning our time in St. Louis where it was just us with no other commitments or distractions.

Before sending her a message, I opened the ones I'd received from Brax both last night and this morning.

> Brax: Smug motherfucker

> Brax: Do don't anything I wouldn't do.

> Brax: Are you still alive?

> Brax: Kieran, you need to let her go to work…

>> Kieran: You're a funny motherfucker. Heading to the gym. See you soon.

> Brax: Surprised you have the energy for that.

When I eventually pull out of the space I shouldn't have been parked in, I've got a huge smile on my face, and just like I told Effie in my message, my boner is tenting my sweats.

Fuck.

How the hell am I meant to get rid of that when my head is full of her?

The drive to the stadium is short, and after having a few firm words with myself, I'm able to climb out of the car without giving anyone an eyeful.

"Ah, there he is," Brax says loudly as I walk into the gym.

He turns all eyes on me, letting everyone see the sappy smile that I know is playing on my lips. I can't fucking help it.

Brax walks over and gives me a guy hug, his fist slamming against my back.

"I'm so fucking happy and relieved for you, man."

"What's going on?" Easton asks, stepping up to us with a curious look on his face.

"Kieran and Effie, that's what's going on," Brax explains for me.

"Oh, shit. Really?" he asks, his eyes wide.

"Yeah," I confess, rubbing the back of my neck.

"That's awesome, man. So, is the next engagement announcement going to be legit?"

"Yep," I state confidently.

"Oh my god, you're already planning it," Brax says as a few others come over to join us.

"Might be," I say nonchalantly.

"Congrats, man," Jamie says with what almost looks like a smile on his face. "I hope it works out for you."

I nod at him, and he retreats again to the weights bench.

"I can't believe after everything you've said about relationships and being tied down that you're about to dive in headfirst," Easton points out.

He's not wrong. Watching other teammates with wives and

girlfriends is terrifying. The thought of being one of them is equally scary. But knowing that it's Effie who's going to be by my side makes it so much easier to picture.

She knows me better than anyone. She knows my job, my schedule, and everything that's expected of me. She's always aware of what the media is capable of.

Unease twists in my gut.

There have been some brutal things said about her online since the news broke about our fake engagement and then the "truth" that followed.

I can only imagine what this next chapter of our lives is going to cause.

But I'll protect her with everything I have.

Once the guys have had their fill of gossip, we get to work.

Preseason is still a while away, but they're all as eager to have an even stronger season as I am.

We made the playoffs last year. But this year...with Effie by my side, we're going to go all the way. I can feel it.

I spend the morning at the gym before Brax, Easton, Jamie and I hit up a local coffee shop for lunch. We get more than a few stares when we walk in together, something that some of us embrace better than others.

I then head back to talk to Kat about the new development in my life and my desire for any talk about my girlfriend to be squashed before heading home.

My steps falter as I step into my apartment.

I love it here. I always have. But suddenly, everything feels wrong.

This place is no longer my home.

Before I can think too much about it, I stalk through to my bedroom, drag a suitcase from my closet, and begin filling it.

My apartment might be bigger, but it's not where I want us to be.

As soon as I have everything I think I'm going to need, I

head back to Effie's apartment. I don't have any regrets; although, I am a little anxious.

I know we're on the same page with where we want our relationship to go, but we didn't specifically talk about plans for moving in together.

I spend the afternoon unpacking. Thankfully, I've spent almost as much time in Effie's apartment as I have on my own, so I find homes for everything without much effort.

By the time the end of Effie's workday rolls around, I won't lie, I'm a little nervous.

What if she's had a reality check during the day and decided that being with me will be too much for her?

Did I come on too heavy?

I told her that she's coming to all my games, and I've just moved myself into her apartment.

Refusing to second-guess my actions and focus on how right everything feels when we're together, I focus on her, on the future, on everything I want to experience with her.

I pull back up outside the building with ten minutes to spare and head inside.

My heart crashes against my ribs as the elevator takes me toward her floor.

As I step out and walk through the office, all eyes turn my way.

It's not unusual, but I feel it more than normal.

They'll have all read the articles about us in the media, no doubt.

The sight of her name on her door brings a smile to my lips, although I can't help feeling like it's wrong.

Effie Callahan would look so much better.

I knock once and then step inside.

It's empty, and my heart drops.

Taking a seat at her desk, I spread my thighs and rest my head back as I wait.

My knee bounces as my nerves build again.

She's still here; her purse is under her desk.

It only takes a few minutes before there's movement outside her office and her soft voice floats through to me.

My fists clench, and I force my leg to still.

"Okay, great. See you tomorrow," she says before pushing her door handle down and letting herself inside.

She doesn't see me for a few seconds, too lost in her own thoughts, but then she looks up.

"Oh my god, Kieran," she gasps as her notebook flutters to the ground.

"Is it my turn now?" I ask simply.

"Y-yeah," she stutters, bending down to collect everything she dropped.

"Don't do that," I warn, watching her with her ass in the air. "Unless you want to get fucked over your desk."

She stands and shoots a heated look over her shoulder.

"Oh, you do."

"Kieran," she warns, trying to cover up her thoughts.

"You're right. Maybe another time," I force out. "I've got plans."

"Oh?" she asks.

"Yep. Grab your things. Let's go."

She studies me for a beat, and I wonder if she can see my apprehension.

If she can, she doesn't say anything.

"Okay," she agrees before closing down her computer and grabbing her purse.

With her hand locked in mine, I drag her out of the office, uncaring about anyone seeing us.

I'd shout it from the rooftops if I could.

After holding the passenger door for her, I jog around the driver's side of my car.

"Where are we—" I cut off her question with my lips the minute my ass hits the seat.

My hand wraps around the side of her neck, and my tongue sweeps into her mouth.

She kisses me back just as eagerly, and it settles some of the unease I've been battling all afternoon.

She still wants this.

The beep of a horn behind us finally puts an end to our kiss.

"So, you missed me?" Effie guesses with a laugh.

"Like you wouldn't believe," I state as I start the engine and pull away.

"What are we doing?"

"Open the glove box," I demand.

She glances over at me as I pull up to a stop sign.

"Okay," she whispers as she leans forward, doing as she's told.

Her gasp lets me know that she's found it.

"Put it on."

Hesitantly, she pulls the blindfold out and holds it in front of her for a few seconds.

"Effie?" I question when she doesn't immediately follow orders.

But then, her hands move and she slips it over her head.

"Good girl."

Reaching over, I place my hand on her thigh, needing some kind of connection with her as I drive us to our next destination.

Effie

My breathing is erratic and my heart is racing.

I trust Kieran with my life, but he's blindsided me with this.

I was expecting him to maybe take me for dinner before going home and continuing what we started this morning.

I squirm in my seat. All I've done all day is clock watch. And I swear that every hour has been slower than the last.

I knew he was picking me up, and all I wanted was to slip my hand into his and leave for the night.

"You okay there, Luck?" His teasing tone washes over me.

"Wonderful."

"Have you been thinking about me today?"

"Would you believe me if I said no?"

"From the way you're rubbing your thighs together, I'd say no. Tell me what you've been picturing?"

"E-everything," I stutter, my mouth running dry and my cheeks heating.

"Like..." he prompts.

"You fucking me." It won't be enough, but I'm just as willing to tease him as he is me.

A warning growl is all I get in response.

"I thought about what you'd do to me when we get home."

"Better."

"I pictured you demanding I get on my knees the second we step inside my apartment."

"Your apartment?" he questions.

I frown. In all my fantasies, we're never at his place.

"Yeah."

"Go on."

So I do. I tell him about him fucking me over the sofa, eating me out in front of the windows again, and then all the other places we could make use of as we make our way to the bathroom to clean up before starting all over again.

I have never been this brazen before. But Kieran makes me brave. Knowing that he's opened himself up to me with what he likes has given me the strength to do the same.

I know his secret and I'll treasure it forever. Just like I know he will with all of mine.

The car comes to a stop, and he kills the engine.

"The last time you brought me somewhere blindfolded, it was the beginning of the end," I say. The words and the memories of our stay at The Cove make my heart ache. It was so bittersweet.

"We're having a do-over. This time, it's just the beginning."

"Okay," I muse as he opens the door, allowing a rush of hot air to flow over me.

My skin prickles with goosebumps as I wait for him to get me.

In seconds, I'm on my feet and being guided somewhere with his arm around my shoulder.

Birds sing above us, and there are the unmistakable sounds of rush hour in the city.

I wrack my brain for where he might have brought me but come up short.

It could be anywhere.

In only a minute, we move inside a building. But there are no clues as to where.

After the doors close behind us, it's silent, and other than the faint smell of cleaning products, there is nothing else to go on.

"Come on, nearly there. "

We walk for a few more minutes and pass through a number of doors before fresh air hits me again.

I frown.

Surely, he hasn't walked me through a building only to bring me back out again?

We continue moving, and after a few steps, the ground beneath me changes. It gets softer.

Understanding dawns, and I can't keep the smile off my face.

We walk for another minute before he brings me to a stop.

My hands tremble as he spins me toward him and cups my face in his hands.

"What are you doing, Kieran?" I whisper.

His fingers press against my lips, stopping me from saying anything else.

Slowly, his hands lift and he slips the blindfold from my face.

I blink against the bright sunlight and discover that my prediction was right.

We're standing right in the middle of the Chiefs field.

"Effie, a few weeks ago, you wore a ring that made Grams the happiest woman in the world. It made all her dreams come true, and I want to do exactly the same for you.

"Some might say this is fast, but honestly, it's not. I'm pretty sure I've been falling deeper and deeper in love with you for years. I just needed a little help to figure it out."

"Kieran," I whimper as tears blur my vision of him.

He quirks a brow, reminding me that I shouldn't be talking.

"Seeing that ring on your finger did things to me. It annoyed me because it wasn't anywhere near good enough for you. It frustrated me because I wasn't the one who put it there. And it terrified me because it made me realize that one day, someone would put one there, and I couldn't stand the thought of it not being me."

Suddenly, he sinks to one knee right there in the middle of the stadium and pulls a small black box from his pocket.

"I thought my dream had come true the first day I ran out onto this field with your birth date stamped on my front and back."

I squeeze my eyes closed for a second, fighting the tears.

Kieran Callahan chose number eleven for his jersey because it's my birthday.

A sob erupts, and I rip my eyes open, staring down at him as he opens the box.

But I don't see the jewelry; all I see is him.

"But it didn't. It turns out my dream has always been you.

"Effie Campbell, my lucky charm, will you be my wife?"

An emotional laugh falls from my lips.

This is crazy.

We made up last night. It's ridiculously fast.

But then, I think about what he just said, and he's right.

We've been building toward this for over a decade now.

I nod, unable to speak through the lump in my throat.

Kieran's brows lift, silently demanding that I use my words.

"Yes, Kieran. Yes."

He's off the ground in a heartbeat, his arms around me and his lips on mine.

Wrapping my arms around his shoulder, I stretch up on my toes and kiss him back.

Time stands still, and we lose ourselves in the moment.

"I love you, Luck. I love you so much." His voice is barely a whisper and cracked with emotion. When I pull back and look into his eyes, I find that they're flooded with unshed tears. The sight completely undoes me.

"Shit," he suddenly gasps. "The ring."

I laugh when he releases me to pick it up off the ground.

"Oh my god, Kieran," I breathe when I finally see the size of it.

"This is the kind of engagement ring you deserve, Effie. I

can't believe Grams thought I'd ever buy you that tiny diamond."

"It's beautiful," I whisper as he slides the huge platinum brilliant-cut diamond onto my ring finger.

"No, you're beautiful," he breathes before claiming my lips again. "There's one other thing," he says when he pulls back and rests his brow against mine.

"Oh?" I pant, barely able to catch my breath.

"I've moved into your apartment."

I laugh, although I'm not really surprised.

When Kieran Callahan wants something, he does everything he can to get it.

Including me.

EPILOGUE

Effie

My stomach tumbles so violently, I'm pretty sure I'm going to vomit.

It's been almost two months since our moment in the middle of the Chiefs stadium, and just like he confessed, Kieran had in fact moved himself into my apartment.

After leaving the field, he drove us both straight back home. He apologized for not taking me out for a fancy dinner to celebrate, but I didn't need it. I had no desire to be around anyone but him.

All I have ever needed is him, and I was more than happy to go home and order takeout.

To be honest, it's pretty much how we've spent every night since then.

We've managed to keep our engagement under wraps so far. Obviously, our closest friends and Kieran's family know. But thanks to Kat, who had everything to prove after her last fuck-up, we've managed to keep it from leaking to the press.

I didn't think it was possible, but somehow, she's done it.

It's been incredible. Everything has been perfect and so easy.

He's been spending his days either at camps, doing interviews and appearances, or working out in preparation for the upcoming season. And I've been working and dancing. Unlike Brax feared, he didn't need to get a new partner. That doesn't mean that Kieran and I don't still tango every now and then. We've discovered it's better for everyone if we do that in private, though.

But tonight, everything is going to change.

It's the KC Foundation's annual summer ball.

I attend every year, but usually, I'm single and Kieran has a beautiful supermodel on his arm.

Jealousy drips through my veins at the thought of another woman touching my man.

Mine.

And after tonight, everyone is going to know that.

It's our first public event as a couple.

Tonight, we're attending together, and we're announcing our official engagement.

Thoughts of what's going to be posted, or more so, the comments that are going to follow make me feel nauseous again.

As if they know that I'm on the verge of freaking out, there's a knock at the door.

Rushing over, I open it and allow Elizabeth, Tate, and Lori to step inside.

"Oh my word, Effie," Elizabeth gushes. "You look so beautiful."

"Thanks," I say awkwardly.

I might be better at accepting compliments from Kieran now, but everyone else is a different story.

"He's going to lose his mind when he sees you," Tate adds.

Kieran is currently with Brax and a few of the guys getting photographs taken.

They should be heading our way any moment.

We're all meeting in the bar before heading to the event.

I run my trembling hand down my Chiefs-red dress. It fits my body like a second skin and is cut low down the front, showing off a healthy bit of cleavage. It's tight to my knees and then flares out, and the sequins that cover it sparkle in the light. It's the kind of dress the old me would have refused to wear. But Kieran has made me brave in all kinds of ways. Plus, his reaction to it will be so worth it.

"I hope so," I whisper out of Elizabeth's earshot.

Lori chuckles.

"You look nervous, sweetie," Elizabeth says.

"It's all going to be okay," Tate assures me. "Kieran won't allow it any other way."

"I know," I breathe. And I do. But it's still scary.

Stepping forward, Lori pulls a bottle of champagne from behind her back. "Liquid courage?" she says before glancing around for glasses.

"Here," Tate says, having found some in the kitchenette of our suite at The Broadway.

In seconds, we all have a glass of bubbles in our hands.

"To Kieran and Effie," Elizabeth says, and Tate and Lori follow.

My cheeks blaze, but I appreciate their support and friendships in ways I'll never be able to express.

"I haven't eaten enough to drink this," I confess.

"It'll help with the paparazzi," Tate says encouragingly.

The benefit of being a no one at previous events has meant I've been able to slip in the back.

I usually stand at the windows and watch the commotion as Kieran arrives.

He always eats up the attention and makes the most of every photo opportunity.

My stomach twists.

Tonight, I'm going to be the one beside him attempting to do the same thing.

"Another," Lori says before emptying what's left of the bottle into my glass.

It's another ten minutes before my cell buzzes on the counter with a message from Kieran to let me know that they're almost here.

"Let's get this show on the road then," Tate announces before finishing her glass.

She and Kingston have a sitter for Prince, and she's planning on making the most of their night together.

Finishing my second glass, I check my reflection and attempt to stuff down my nerves.

It'll be better when he's standing beside me.

With my clutch under my arm, I follow the others from our suite and step inside the elevator.

Kingston, Kian, and Neil are in the bar, waiting for us.

The minute we enter, the three of them look up and find their women. I swear, the looks in their eyes is something else.

The amount of love and respect they have for their partners is awe-inspiring.

I'm so lost watching them all that I miss the man walking through the hotel entrance and making a beeline for me.

However, the second he steps up behind me and his warm breath rushes over my skin, my entire body comes alive.

"You look fucking insane, Luck," he groans in my ear, sending goosebumps skating across my skin.

Spinning around, I stare up at him.

"Wow," he muses, his eyes holding mine for a beat before dropping lower.

My body heats, my skin tingling wherever his gaze meets.

"You look..."

As he fights to find words, I take a moment to appreciate him.

Kieran can wear anything—or nothing—and look beyond hot. But Kieran in a tux...a low ache starts up between my thighs.

Any thoughts of what the night will hold or the gossip that's going to follow our announcement have vanished.

The only thing that matters right now is the man standing before me.

"Fuck, Luck," he groans, dragging his hand down his face. "You look insane. Do we have time to go upstairs and—"

"No," a deep voice barks, and when I look over my shoulder, I find both Kieran's brothers giving him a warning glare.

"As if you can say anything. When I visited your office, you were knee-deep in—" Lori slaps her hand over Kieran's mouth as Elizabeth's eyes widen.

"Enough of that, little brother," Kian teases.

"Are we ready to go?" Kingston asks.

Kieran's eyes come back to me.

He's excited about this event. He is about anything the KC Foundation does to raise more funds for our kids. But right now, I can't help but wonder if he's secretly planning to ditch it in favor of spending the night in our hotel room.

Fine by me.

"Grab your girl," Tate instructs. "The cars are waiting."

Kieran takes my hand, and together we follow the others out.

There are two limos out the front of the building.

One for them, and another for us.

Riding separately seems ridiculous, but seeing as this is our big night, Kieran wanted to make a point.

My stomach tumbles and my steps falter.

"Effie?" he whispers, concern laced through his voice.

Letting my eyes roll up his chest, I find his gaze.

"I'm okay. I've got you. I'll always be okay."

He sucks in a deep breath at my words before gently tugging me toward the car.

My nerves only get worse as we make our way through the city.

Thoughts about how badly this could go fill my mind.

Everyone is going to hate me.

No one is going to accept it's real this time.

"Hey," Kieran says, gently taking my face in his. "The only people's opinions that matter are mine and yours."

I suck in a deep breath as his dark green eyes search mine.

"Me and you, yeah?"

I nod, and he raises a brow.

"Me and you," I force out.

"Everyone is going to love you. And wearing that dress, I've no doubt that every man is going to want you."

His grip on me tightens a fraction as he battles with a little dose of jealousy.

"But I'm yours," I confirm.

"Fuck yes, you are."

The car pulls to a stop, and when I glance out of the blacked-out windows, all I can see is people.

"Oh my god."

"Effie, you are the strongest most incredible woman I know. Get out there, smile for the camera, and let the world know who you belong to."

His little pep talk helps a little bit, but even if it didn't, it's too late. The back door is pulled wide open, the commotion from the crowd gets louder, and my chance of getting out of this diminishes.

Not that I really want to. I want to stand beside Kieran during everything, but my fear is getting the better of me.

"We've got this," Kieran promises me as he climbs out of the back of the car. The screams of the crowd and flashes from the cameras go wild, and my stomach twists painfully.

But then he is right there, standing in the doorway and holding his hand out for me.

"I've got you, Effie. Always," he promises.

And without thinking about it, I slide my palm against his and allow him to pull me from the car.

There's a moment where the noise level drops. I don't know if it's shock or his fans' hatred of me, but it only lasts a heartbeat.

The screams and shouts come so loud and fast, I don't stand a chance at hearing what they're actually saying as my blood rushes past my ears.

Pinned against Kieran's side, I follow his lead, smiling for the cameras that flash all around us.

My heart drops into my stomach when he releases me, but then, he's in front of me with my left hand in his.

Oh god, he's going to do it. The world is going to hate me.

His lips press against my ring finger, and I stare up at him in awe as he holds my hand up for the world to see.

"My girl. My lucky charm, and soon, my wife."

I can't tell if he shouts it or whispers it just for me. It doesn't matter, because when his lips descend on mine, he's the only person in the world.

"I love you, Effie, and so will they," he promises between kisses.

Just as our kiss ends, someone in the crowd bellows, "About fucking time," and both of us burst out laughing.

"See, even they were waiting for us to get our shit together."

With my hand locked in his, I follow Kieran as he says hello to some fans, signs some autographs, and to my amazement, thanks those standing closest to us for their congratulations and well wishes.

By the time we step inside the building, my heart is so full I'm sure it's about to burst.

"That's it; it's official now. The world knows you're going to be Mrs. Effie Callahan," Kieran states as he backs me up into a corner and gazes down at me with heat burning in his eyes.

"I can't wait," I breathe.

Want more Kieran and Effie? Sign up to my newsletter for an extended epilogue!

Get your copy here.

Psst... have you been wondering about Brax and Kieran's dance lesson? You can read this deleted scene, and more, over in my Happily Ever After Book Club on Patreon.

Become a member now.

TRACY LORRAINE

BROKEN SAINT
SNEAK PEEK

Colton

From our very first play, we fucking owned it. We played like a well-oiled machine of savages. The Bulls didn't stand a chance, and every time Sawyer's eyes locked on mine, he stoked the determination burning bright within me.

We had their defense running circles around themselves as we scored over and over. It was fucking majestic, and exactly what I needed to remind myself of what I was doing with my life.

As the fans roar in the excitement in the stands around us, I close my eyes for a beat, feeling the steady thrum of my heart in every inch of my body.

Last play of the game and the chance to put the final nail in the Bulls' coffin.

We line up, the adrenaline of the win already coursing through our veins.

Luca calls the play as I glare Sawyer dead in the eyes, promising him a world of pain for the dirty tackle I can see him planning.

I shake my head, warning him against it before the whistle blows and we spring into action.

Luca fakes a throw in Kane's direction. The Bulls' defense follows it—well, all but Sawyer. His attention is still locked on me as Luca passes off the ball and I take off running.

My catch is flawless, and I tuck it under my arm as Sawyer attempts to take me down. But I've already got him, and we both know it.

The roar of the crowd rises to astronomical levels as I make the touchdown—but in only seconds, it becomes a blur as my teammates dive on me in celebration.

"Fucking yes," Luca screams in my face, bumping our helmets together as he holds the sides of my neck.

The last few seconds count down on the Jumbotron before the Saints' fans lose their shit once again over our epic win.

With Kane and Luca on either side of me, I'm turned toward the crowd, or more specifically the seats where Letty and Peyton sit for every single game we play.

They're both dressed in their boys' jerseys, jumping up and down, screaming in celebration. Even Kyan is beaming, his little chubby cheeks red with excitement as if he knows his dad is a fucking legend, in more ways than one.

But it's not my teammates' wives or cute little Kyan who catches my attention.

It's the woman standing right in the middle of them.

Wearing. My. Fucking. Number.

As if she can feel my attention, her gaze finds mine.

It's been years since I laid eyes on her. But the second our gazes meet, my dark to her honey, it's like no time has passed.

That tether I'd thought I'd finally managed to sever pulls between us. It's just like I remember. No. It's worse than that. It's stronger. More powerful.

And as I stand there locked in her stare while everyone

around me celebrates our win, there's only one thought in my head.

I'm fucked.

Totally fucking fucked.

I'm jostled to the side before Kane leans in closer.

"Surprise, Rogers. Looks like your night just got even better."

Broken Saint is now live and available with kindle unlimited. Download your copy now

ABOUT THE AUTHOR

Tracy Lorraine is a *USA Today* and *Wall Street Journal* bestselling new adult and contemporary romance author. Tracy has recently turned thirty and lives in a cute Cotswold village in England with her husband, baby girl and lovable but slightly crazy dog. Having always been a bookaholic with her head stuck in her Kindle, Tracy decided to try her hand at a story idea she dreamt up and hasn't looked back since.

Be the first to find out about new releases and offers. Sign up to my newsletter here.

If you want to know what I'm up to and see teasers and snippets of what I'm working on, then you need to be in my Facebook group. Join Tracy's Angels here.
Keep up to date with Tracy's books at
www.tracylorraine.com

www.ingramcontent.com/pod-product-compliance
Lightning Source LLC
Chambersburg PA
CBHW031729180726
48283CB00005B/1439